Dear Reader,

Last month I asked if you'd like to see more humour, romantic suspense or linked books on our list. Well this month I can offer you all three!

I'm thrilled to bring you the final part of Liz Fielding's critically acclaimed and very popular Beaumont Brides trilogy. But, if we're lucky, maybe Melanie's story won't be the end after all . . .

Two stories which can be classified as suspense, but which are very different in style and plot, are offered by Laura Bradley and Jill Sheldon. These authors have won plaudits from critics and readers alike for their earlier *Scarlet* novels.

And finally, those of you who've asked for more books by Natalie Fox will, we're sure, enjoy reading our exciting new author, Talia Lyon, who brings a delightfully humorous flavour to her story of three gals, three guys and the holiday of a lifetime.

As always, I hope you enjoy the books I've chosen for you this month. Let me have your comments and suggestions, won't you and I'll do all I can to bring you more of the kind of books *you* want to read.

Till next month,

Sally Cooper

SALLY COOPER,
Editor-in-Chief – *Scarlet*

LIZ FIELDING

WILD FIRE

(Part 3 of The Beaumont Brides)

Enquiries to:
Robinson Publishing Ltd
7 Kensington Church Court
London W8 4SP

First published in the UK by Scarlet, 1997

A copy of the British Library Cataloguing in
Publication data is available from the British Library

ISBN 1-85487-977-4

Printed and bound in the EC

10 9 8 7 6 5 4 3 2 1

WILDFIRE: Sheet lightning without audible thunder; a combination of highly inflammable substances, difficult to extinguish

CHAPTER 1

'With this ring I thee wed, with my body I thee worship, and with all my worldly goods I thee endow . . .'

A sigh rippled through the congregation as Edward Beaumont placed a ring on the finger of Diana Archer and made her his wife. He had been alone for a long time, ever since the death of his first wife, the beautiful and talented actress Elaine French, and everyone who knew him was delighted with this September love that had come to him so unexpectedly.

Only Melanie, his youngest daughter, balled her hands into tight little fists and blinked back a tear. Why couldn't she be happy for them? Diana was the kindest, loveliest of women, even if her daughter took some swallowing.

She looked around her. Her older sisters – her half-sisters, she adjusted the relationship mentally, although they had taken her so fully to their hearts that distancing herself from them in this way seemed another betrayal – were clearly delighted by this turn of events. But then they had seen Edward suffering at the hands of their mother. Maybe that was the problem. On the other side of the world she had witnessed her own mother's loneliness, her suffering. That was the gulf that set them apart today.

Her mother had never had any of this: the old church decked out in spring flowers, the solemn vows, the expensive reception that would follow it. Not that Juliet would have bothered about the rich trappings of ceremony – a simple register office wedding would have been enough – but her mother had been denied any public acknowledgement of Edward's passionate love for her. She had lived out her life with only her daughter to remind her of a love so great that she had sacrificed everything for it. And she had died before Edward had discovered what she had done and been able to put things right. If she had lived, this might have been her day . . .

Melanie caught her lower lip between her teeth and made an effort to concentrate on the service. But as she looked up she caught Heather Archer's gaze fixed upon her from the other side of the church and saw the shocking reflection of her own thoughts in the younger girl's face. Maybe she was remembering the other ghost at the feast, her own beloved father.

Melanie, the smooth skin between her dark eyes momentarily creased in the slightest of frowns, continued to regard the other girl, this new member of a family that seemed to be growing almost daily, first with the birth of Fizz's daughter, then Claudia's marriage to Mac. Now Edward was taking a new wife. There seemed to have been nothing but celebrations in the last year. But Heather, his new stepdaughter, eighteen years old and dressed like a black scarecrow in her student uniform of Oxfam cast-offs that would have looked more appropriate at a funeral than a wedding, wasn't celebrating.

The only difference between the two of them, Mel decided, was that Heather didn't care who knew it.

If she didn't make an effort to suppress the tears stinging at her eyelids, everyone would know how she was feeling too. Not that there was anything wrong with tears. Both Fizz and Claudia were dabbing at their eyes with delicate lace-edged handkerchiefs. Tears at a wedding were to be expected, almost mandatory, but they were supposed to be tears of happiness. Irritated with herself, reminding herself that she had been acting professionally since she was ten years old, she assumed a serene smile. But the need to lever a smile to her lips on what should have been the happiest of days forced her to come to a decision that she had been putting off.

It was more than a year since she had come to England. It had been a momentous year, a wonderful year. She had found a family she had never known existed, they had taken her to their hearts and she had wallowed in the kind of family life that she had never experienced before. But when she had added Beaumont to her name, Melanie Brett had somehow got just a little bit lost.

Luke should have understood. Her mother's

younger brother, he was surely sharing just a little of her feelings today? Except that he was now a part of the extended Beaumont family. Married to Fizz and with a darling baby daughter to take up every moment, he was distracted by his own happiness and she couldn't deny him that. Maybe if she had had a love of her own she would have been less wrapped up in the past. But for weeks the past had been tugging at her sleeve, calling her back, and it was, Melanie decided, time to take a look back, remind herself who she was. Before she forgot.

After Edward and Diana had left the reception, she sought out Luke to tell him what she intended to do.

'You're taking a year off?' he repeated, in all too obvious disbelief. 'Are you mad?'

'I've been working practically non-stop since I was ten years old, Luke. I'm not complaining, I nagged Mum to let me do it, I was the envy of all my friends and I loved every moment of it, but I'm entitled to a holiday. So I'm adding up all the holidays I've missed out on over the last ten years and I figure a year off is about right.'

'Can you take a year off in your business? Aren't you afraid that when you come back everyone will have forgotten you?'

'I'm prepared to take that risk.'

He still looked doubtful. 'You'll be bored to death in ten minutes.'

Melanie stifled her irritation. Luke didn't *mean* to be patronizing; it was just that he'd been a surrogate

4

father to her for so long that he couldn't quite come to terms with the fact that she was an adult.

'I won't be bored. And if I am I'll get a job. Something ordinary. I've never done anything ordinary.'

'I think you'll find that "ordinary" is over-rated.' Luke, still regarding her with concern, was distracted by his wife waving frantically from the other side of the room. 'Fizz wants to get back to the baby, Mel. Can we talk about this later?'

'There's nothing to talk about, Luke. I'm not asking your permission here, or asking you to hold my hand. I'm just letting you know my plans so that you won't worry. Will you say goodbye to everyone for me?'

Melanie watched Luke struggle to keep his silence, knowing that he wanted to tell her that nothing would ever stop him from worrying about his sister's little girl. Instead he said, somewhat gruffly, 'We'll miss you, Mel.' Then he bent and kissed her cheek. 'Keep in touch. If you need anything – '

'I'll send you a postcard.'

Her agent was less sanguine. 'You can't leave London now, Mel.' Trudy Morgan tapped a script lying on the desk in front of her. 'This,' she said, 'could have been written for you.'

'Really?' Mel was standing at the window staring down into the street where a mime artist had attracted a small crowd. He was working them with great skill, drawing them into his routine, making them laugh at him and at themselves. 'Then I'm sorry. But I meant it when I said I won't be available for a while.'

'Read it, Mel. You'll love it. And you're perfect for the part.'

Mel shrugged. She had no intention of taking a part in a sitcom but she knew Trudy meant well so she picked up the script, glanced at the character outlines. 'Don't tell me,' she said, pulling a face. 'I get to play the dizzy blonde, right?'

'The part could have been written for you.'

'Could it? I'm blonde,' she agreed. 'So is any other actress with access to a bottle of peroxide – '

'Maybe. But not everyone can play sweet and dizzy as convincingly as you, darling.'

Melanie knew her agent meant that as a compliment, and that was part of the problem. 'I'm sure this is a gift,' she said, replacing the script on the desk, 'but I've been playing a dizzy blonde since I was ten years old, Trudy. Pre-pubescent cute, boy-mad adolescent, teenager in the throes of calf love and then true romance and a wedding so beautiful that it made the fans weep in the streets. I'm twenty-one in a few weeks, Trudy. I'm sick of playing the sweet girl next door.'

'Ah.'

'Ah? What does that mean?'

'Nothing.' She took back the script and put it away in a drawer. 'I'll give you a call when the National are auditioning for Ophelia, shall I?'

Mel could usually tell when she was being teased but this time she wasn't quite certain. 'Does the

6

National audition leading roles?' she asked, her own tongue firmly in her cheek.

Trudy didn't laugh. 'You might get lucky.'

'I see.'

'I don't think you do.' Her agent, Mel realized with a shock, was angry. 'You may have been a soap queen in Australia since you were knee-high to a dung beetle, Melanie. And there was a time when every schoolgirl in Britain rushed home after school to watch the series too, so your name is well-known in Britain to a mainly young, mainly female audience.' She placed her hands on the desk and leaned towards Mel. 'That's good. That I can sell. That's your value to a producer. You have to capitalize on that.'

'What about *Private Lives*?'

'An *ingénue* role in a play directed by your father, launched on money put up by your uncle and starring your sister. And correct me if I'm wrong, but I seem to remember you were playing a dumb blonde in that too.'

'It was a box office success,' Mel protested. 'It made money hand over fist.'

'Well, Luke Devlin has the Midas touch, even when he's indulging his niece. And all that tear-wrenching publicity when Edward Beaumont told the world that you were his love-child didn't exactly harm the box-office. As a dizzy blonde you're bankable, Mel, but you haven't got the track record for anything tougher. And this is a tough business. No one can afford to take the risk that you'll fall flat on your face.'

7

'Taken to its ultimate conclusion, that suggests I'll still be playing the same role when I'm fifty.'

'You'd never be out of work.'

'Frankly, I'd rather quit now.'

Trudy did not back down. 'Well, maybe you should think about that, Melanie. That way I won't be wasting my time chasing parts that you think you're too good for.' She eased back slightly, tilting her head in a gentle query. 'Or maybe you can persuade Uncle Luke to underwrite your career,' she suggested, with calculated cruelty. 'I warn you, he'll find Shakespeare a lot more expensive than a popular four-hander.'

'I notice you haven't suggested I appeal to my father?'

'Your father has been in the business a long time. He's got more sense.'

'He was keen to do *The Three Sisters* with Fizz and Claudia.'

'It would have had a certain curiosity value,' Trudy admitted, 'although it has been done before.'

'I see.' Mel's heart was beating with almost painful slowness. 'Tell me, Trudy, are you trying to tell me that I'm at my personal zenith? That this is as far as I'm ever likely to go?'

'Who can tell?' She waved her hand dismissively as Mel began to protest. 'You don't lack talent, darling, or you wouldn't be in my office, no matter who your father is. But we have a problem with the public perception of you. You're light, you're fun. But would *you* pay good money to go and see yourself as Lady Macbeth?'

8

That didn't even merit a response. She was far too young for the part and they both knew it. 'No, but it might be fun to try Portia. Or what about Nora?' she said, in a moment of inspiration. Ibsen's childlike heroine made her point exactly.

Trudy's reaction was less than flattering. 'Are you serious? That's a role for an accomplished actress – '

'I know, darling,' she said, putting on a grand dame voice. 'Someone terribly distinguished . . .' Then she shrugged. 'And years too old for the part. They used to say the same thing about Juliet.'

'Melanie – '

'And you have to agree that on the surface Nora is just about the dizziest creature in the theatrical canon.'

'Yes, but – '

'Yes, *but*, Trudy. It's all just an act. I know. And I know exactly how it's done. I do it myself every time I step on stage or in front of a television camera.'

Trudy was stunned. 'You're telling me that you're prepared to turn down a sitcom by writers with a track record for success, a role that could turn you into a household name, for a *dream*?'

'Why not?' Everything she'd said was true. And if it made Trudy think twice about her career she was quite prepared to let her believe it. 'We all need dreams, Trudy. They might as well be big ones.'

'And if you fell flat on your face?'

'I would have tried.'

For a moment the older woman was lost for words, then she busied herself about her desk, straightening papers, pins. 'Yes, well, dreams come expensive. Your problem, my girl, is that you don't have to work to eat. I do.' This time the dismissive gesture had a finality about it. 'I can't afford to waste my time on dreams. Call me when you've come to your senses.'

'That's the whole point, Trudy. I have come to my senses.'

'What's sensible about taking a year off when you're being offered work? Save your holiday for the time when the phone doesn't ring.'

'This is more than a holiday. I've missed out on a lot of ordinary life.'

'Ordinary life?' Trudy snorted. 'All you'll do is lotus-eat on some Aussie beach and listen to your friends tell you how wonderful you are while they eat your prawns and drink another crate of beers.'

'You really think I'm that shallow?'

'I think that's about as close to ordinary life as you're ever likely to come. Ask Claudia what it takes to become a real success, Mel. Your sister sweated her socks off to get where she is but she has no illusions; she knows that the theatre is a looking-glass world where it takes all the running you can do to stay in the same place. If you want to actually get somewhere you have to work at least twice as hard as that.'

'I'm not running away from hard work. I'm refusing to repeat myself endlessly until I start to believe that's all I can do.'

'Really? Well, you're in the fortunate position of

10

being able to take that line. You've been working for ten years and your clever uncle has invested all the money you've earned, so you can afford to be picky. Perhaps that's your real problem. You've never had to struggle or call on any deep reserves of strength to see you through months, years even without a decent part. You're like an oyster without the grit, Mel, a soft-centred chocolate, a little treat that slides down without any effort. Maybe you should go away and grow up a bit. But you won't do it lying on a beach contemplating your navel.'

Mel had been holding her feelings in check for weeks, trying not to show her unhappiness because she knew she was being unfair to her family. She knew her feelings were unreasonable. It had been her mother's decision to stay away from Edward and he'd suffered every bit as much as she had. But that didn't make them any less real, and Trudy's scathing attack was the final straw.

'You think not knowing who your father is until you're nineteen years old is easy? You think working on a soap opera day in and day out and still getting good school grades is easy?' She placed her hands flat on the desk and looked her agent straight in the face. 'You think sitting and watching your mother die is easy? You've seen me this year with my father and Claudia and Fizz, playing happy families at first nights and weddings and christenings. But don't think you know me, because you don't.' She straightened, gathered her jacket and bag and paused in the doorway just long enough to say, 'Don't call me,

11

Trudy. When I'm ready to start playing at make-believe again I'll call you.'

As the door slammed behind her, Trudy Morgan stared for a moment and then gave a hoot of laughter. She would never have believed Melanie had it in her. Still chuckling, she crossed to the window. Would the girl still be travelling on a head of steam by the time she reached the square, or would she have had time to calm down?

Steaming. Seeing through a red mist, positively vibrating with rage, her heart alone would have made redundant the entire timpani section of an orchestra. Melanie's whole body was focused on her one purpose: to catch the first available flight to Sydney where *she* was the home-town girl made good that the crowds turned out for, and not just another Beaumont. And a second-class, inferior sort of Beaumont at that. She didn't even see the white-faced mime artist do a classic double-take. Nor did she hear the ripple of laughter from his audience.

Swept along on a tide of blistering rage, she was carried by her angry momentum through the heavy glass door of the travel agent's office with such speed that the man approaching it from the other side was forced to step back sharply to escape an abrupt and painful rearrangement of his profile. And still she was oblivious to her surroundings until, on a reflex honed by an acute sense of self-preservation, the man grabbed her shoulders to prevent her from cannoning into him.

'Hey, there, slow down.' The abrupt jolt almost stunned her, so deep had she been in her fury, so intent in her purpose. Melanie had never been so angry, had no idea that it was possible to feel that way, and she raised her hand to her forehead, dazed by the suddenness with which she had been wrenched out of her temper. 'Are you all right?'

All right? Of all the stupid . . . of course she wasn't *all right* . . . Then she took a deep, shuddering breath. It wasn't this man's fault. It wasn't anyone's fault . . . it would have been so much simpler if it were.

'I'm sorry,' she began. 'I'm afraid I wasn't looking . . .' And then she *was* looking. Straight up into a pair of steel-grey eyes that were regarding her with more than a touch of impatience. His voice too, she realized, had been more irritated than concerned. And with awareness came the realization that his hands were still clamped to her shoulders. The man clearly thought that if he didn't hold on to her she might collapse at his feet. And his expression left her in no doubt that he didn't want the bother of picking her up again. About par for the day, in fact. She took a short breath and very firmly stepped back. 'I'm sorry,' she repeated.

And then one of the girls who worked in the office was at his side. 'Is everything all right, Mr Wolfe?' she asked. 'Are you hurt?'

His eyes never left Melanie's face and she gave another little gasp as something seemed to heat in them, something intense, something, she thought, almost desperate. Then, whatever it was was obliterated and his eyes were as cold as steel. 'I'm fine. I can't say the same for this young woman.' He stared at her for a moment longer, then he eased his shoulders in a movement so slight that it could scarcely to be classed as a shrug. 'You'd better slow down before you hurt yourself. Or someone else,' he said. Then he nodded briefly to the girl at Melanie's side. 'I'll call back for the tickets in about twenty minutes.'

Melanie shivered slightly, but couldn't have said whether it was the suddenness with which he had jolted her from her temper or the strange impact of the man's eyes that made her feel as if she had been touched by a force of nature. A damped-down, hidden force. Like a volcano.

'If you'd like to come and sit down, one of our assistants will help you.'

Melanie had quite forgotten the girl at her elbow, but now as she looked round the office she discovered herself to be the single point on which every gaze was fixed.

'What? Oh, no. No. It's all right.' She was already backing out of the office as fast as her slightly shaky legs would carry her. 'I think I'd better . . . that is, I need to think . . .' She stopped, took a steadying breath. 'I'll come back later.' Maybe. The girl's concern was palpable and Melanie did her best to produce a reassuring smile. 'I think I need a few minutes to gather my thoughts. I'll go and have some coffee.'

'Would you like to take some brochures with you?'

'Oh, no. Thanks. I know where I'm going.'

Or did she? Because despite what she had told

Trudy, she *was* rushing straight back to Oz and the comfort of old friends, going back not forward. But as the adrenalin rush evaporated from her system she certainly felt an urgent need to sit down somewhere quiet to try and make sense of what she was doing.

Sense was not going out of its way to co-operate. This time, as she crossed the square to a wine bar, travelling at considerably less than the speed of light, she saw the exquisite double-take with which the mime artist swivelled the attention of his audience towards her. Her momentum faltered slightly, but she kept on walking.

Before she had gone more than a few yards there was a tap on her shoulder. She swung round, determined to tell the man to find someone else to pick on, but there was no one there. A tap on her other shoulder and still no one. The crowd were laughing quite openly now, but she wasn't in the mood to play straight man to a clown. She took a deep breath and for a moment she remained perfectly still before turning to ask him, very politely, to leave her alone. But when she came face to face with him, he was standing with his hand over his heart, every line of his body exquisitely portraying the bashful little man in love with a beautiful girl. In spite of everything, she smiled.

That was a mistake. Encouraged, he immediately responded by producing an outrageous daisy from thin air, presenting it to her with a ground-scraping bow.

* * *

Three floors above the square, Trudy shook her head. The boy was superb. Graceful, funny, pathetic in turn as he wooed Melanie with his art. She was still smiling as she turned back to her desk and pressed the intercom on her desk. 'Get me Claudia Beaumont, will you, Lisa?'

A few moments later the telephone rang. 'Trudy?' Claudia's voice floated seductively from the receiver. 'How did it go?'

'Not well. She wouldn't even discuss the sitcom. I'm afraid it's going to take more than that to keep her in England.'

'Damn. Luke was certain that a new challenge would keep her here. Any ideas?'

'Not one. Unless you know of anyone smitten enough with the child to underwrite her in *A Doll's House.*'

'You're kidding.'

'I wish I was.' Claudia let out a long slow whistle. 'Precisely. I gave her rather a hard time, I'm afraid.'

'Poor Melanie.'

'She doesn't need your sympathy, darling, she gave me an equally rough ride, and if she was poor there wouldn't be a problem, she wouldn't be able to turn this down. I'm really worried about her going back to Australia. They adore her there and they'd give anything to get her to stay. They'll spoil her rotten, tell her how wonderful she is and before you know it she'll be back in the soaps. Can't Luke do something?'

'What for heaven's sake? She's twenty-one in a few

16

weeks' time. If she wants to take a year off and disappear – ' Claudia stopped.

'It seems out of character. She's a family girl, and she's been very protected. When I think of the way you behaved at her age – '

Claudia pulled a face at the telephone. 'You think there's something more than a holiday behind this?'

'Maybe. But she's worked hard for years in television,' Trudy pointed out. 'It could be that she's just lost the taste for it. What does Edward think?'

'He doesn't know. He'd already left on his honeymoon – but I know it'll break his heart if she drifts away.'

'Will it? He's got a new wife to keep him happy. And a new stepdaughter.'

'Heather? Puh-lease!' Claudia paused. 'Oh, dear God. You don't think that's behind this sudden need to get away? I would have said that Melanie didn't have a jealous bone in her body – '

'And I would agree with you. But on reflection it is possible that it's the new Mrs Beaumont who's brought on this attack of the sulks. The papers have made a great deal of fuss about the wedding . . . how Edward has finally got over the death of the precious Elaine.'

'Oh, don't. It's been a nightmare. If people only knew . . .'

'Well, they don't. They don't know that Edward loathed Elaine, that she made his life a living hell, and they don't know that he loved Melanie's mother. It

17

must have hurt. Happy ever after would have seen her mother in Diana's place.'

'But her mother is – '

'Dead?' Trudy paused. 'Forgotten?' she enquired, not very kindly.

'Of course not! Surely she can't think . . .? Oh, Trudy, what on earth can we do?'

'Nothing. Or at least nothing that isn't weeks too late. Isn't there a man around to distract her?'

'A man?' Claudia cocked an errant brow at the telephone. 'Don't let the thought-police hear you suggesting something so politically incorrect.'

'This is an emergency, Claudia. It's the best I can come with at a moment's notice.'

'Well, Andy Gilbert is still carrying a torch – '

'Good grief, Claudia, I said a *man*. Someone capable of driving every other thought out of her head. If he hasn't managed to do that by now he's not going to be any use to us . . . What this situation needs is a midnight lover . . .'

'A midnight lover?'

'The kind of man that dreams are made of, darling. Good grief, Claudia, surely I don't have to spell it out to you? You married one.'

Claudia laughed softly. 'If she finds someone like Mac you might never get her back, Trudy.'

'I'll take that risk.'

'Then I'll put my mind to it, although I have to warn you, men in that category are rarer than hen's teeth. I'm sure Dad could sort this out in a moment if he were here.'

'How long are the honeymooners planning to be away?'

'Who knows? Luke and Mac chartered them a yacht in the West Indies as a joint wedding present. Neither of them has any commitments to rush back for so they've decided to take their time, go where they like, do as they please.'

'Some people have all the luck. Claudia – you've worked with Mel. How good is she? Really?'

Claudia laughed. 'You're her agent, Trudy. Why are you asking me?'

'Because I want to know.'

There was small silence and then Claudia said, 'Melanie is better than anybody will ever give her credit for, Trudy, better than she probably realizes herself. The trouble is, she makes it look so easy that people assume she's not working at it, that she's just being herself.'

Trudy grimaced. 'That,' she said, 'explains a lot.'

Melanie laughed. She knew how it was done but the sponge flower compressed in the clown's palm expanded so swiftly that it seemed to appear from nowhere. But she still wasn't going to be sucked into his act for the amusement of the crowd. She declined the flower with a quick shake of the head and stepped around him. The crowd, with one voice went, 'Ahhhh . . .'

It was almost irresistible. Almost. But as she turned away he was there again. He was not tall. She was five feet seven in her thickest woolly socks and this man barely topped her, yet he was holding the crowd that had gathered to watch him in the palm of his hand with the power of his presence. The leotard moulded to his body displayed beautifully sculpted muscles and beneath the white make-up, the mournful painted-on expression, his bones were finely modelled. He would attract attention even when he wasn't performing.

And whether she liked it or not he had already made her part of his performance, the kind of mime perfected by Charlie Chaplin, the bashful little man falling in love with the beautiful, unattainable girl. Despite herself, she was drawn in, until when finally he presented her with the absurd flower once more, she laughed and took it, allowing him to kiss her hand.

She was still laughing as she finally walked away, her temper having evaporated as quickly as it had boiled up in the warmth and charm of his performance. He was well worth the ten pound note she'd dropped in his hat.

Then, as she crossed the piazza to a small wine bar, she felt another tap on her shoulder. She wasn't playing again! 'What do you want?' she asked, as she turned to face him. He shook his head, holding out her ten pound note, presenting it to her with a formal little bow.

Did he think it was a mistake? 'No, no,' she said, slightly embarrassed. 'Keep it. Please.'

He went through an exquisite routine: his heart was hers, he could not take her money.

They were beginning to attract attention. 'Don't be silly. You earned it. You were wonderful.'

He feigned modesty. She didn't believe it but laughed out loud at his nonsense and, apparently encouraged by this, he elaborately but silently invited her to join him for a drink.

'Well, that's an original pick-up line.'

'But did it work?' he asked, finally breaking out of character. 'What do you say?'

Jack Wolfe, a few floors above Trudy Morgan, in the penthouse suite, was also more interested in what was happening in the square than the protests of his younger brother.

'Come on, Jack, be fair. The way you boss me about, anyone would think you were my father.'

'I might as well be.' Jack Wolfe bit down hard, turning abruptly from the performance below him. 'Who else do you turn to when your rent needs paying? Or when you need funds for a rugby tour? Or when –?'

'That's just it, Jack,' Tom rushed in, not in the least abashed by this catalogue of his ingratitude. 'I've got a ticket for the rugby international at Murrayfield this weekend. They're like gold dust – '

'And undoubtedly as expensive. I'm sorry, Tom. I have no doubt that the England team will miss your support to a man and I wouldn't ask you to do this for me if it wasn't important, but I'm needed in Chicago – ' Tom opened his mouth to argue, but Jack had had enough '– and someone has to be in my apartment when the workmen come to fit the windows.'

'Why the hell do they have to do it this weekend?'

'Because they didn't do it properly the first time. If it's any comfort, I don't suppose they are any happier about it than you.'

'Oh, Jack, *bad-tempered* workmen . . . Can't Caroline sort it out? You're seeing her this evening, aren't you?'

'I've had to cancel that too. So you're not the only one who's suffering – '

'She gave you a hard time too, did she? I don't suppose she's used to being stood up.'

'And since I'd rather not encourage Caro's nesting instincts, I'm afraid for the purpose of this exercise, you are it, Tom. Accept your fate gracefully.'

Tom reserved all the grace at his command for the rugby field. For the glacial beauty his brother chose to squire about town he had nothing but undisguised contempt. 'Nesting instincts?' He snorted. 'You've got to be kidding. That woman has all the home-making instincts of the cuckoo.'

'I sincerely hope so,' his brother replied, with a wintry smile. 'Her lack of domesticity is one of Caro's most endearing qualities. But women have a way of disguising their true feelings and I am not prepared to take the risk.'

'Why?'

'Why am I not prepared to take the risk?' Jack asked, an edge to his voice.

But Tom was feeling reckless. 'If you like. I mean,

why on earth do you hang around with women like her? Aren't you afraid of getting frostbite? God, she's so thin I'd be afraid she'd break if I turned over in bed too quickly – '

'Fortunately, that is something that you will never have to worry about.'

'You can't punish yourself forever, Jack.'

'Punish myself?' The edge sharpened and Tom flushed. There was an unbreachable boundary about his brother, an inviolate area of his life that no one was allowed to mention. Tom had been too young at the time to really understand what had happened to his brother when Lisette died, but as he grew older he could see that blanking it off was a mistake. And that avoiding emotional involvement with women like Caroline Hickey, who were all appearance and no heart, would in the end destroy him. But knowing it and telling him were two different things.

'I'm sorry. I shouldn't have said that.'

Jack accepted his apology with a dismissive gesture and turned back to the window. The mime artist was trying to draw a girl into his act, the girl from the travel agent's who had been in such a state. She didn't want to play, he could see by her body language that she just wanted to get away, but as she turned to tell the clown to leave her alone he must have done something to make her smile.

It was a smile that lit up the square, a smile that seemed to underline his own emotional sterility, the terrible emptiness at his core that made it impossible to reach out and offer himself . . .

Just for a second, in the doorway of that travel agent's, he had had a glimpse of how it could have been as every instinct had urged him to take the girl into his arms and hold her, offer her simple human comfort. Except that people were never simple; if she had been a company in trouble he would have leapt in there, done everything he could to help without thinking twice. That would have been easy.

But people expected so much more, demanded so much more. He had failed once and he hadn't been able to handle it. The responsibility for another person's life was too much. So he had chosen to ignore the need he had recognized in a young woman's face and walked away from the risk.

The clown was doing a lot better. And now the act was finished he was following her, talking to her, taking her into the wine bar. It must be easier for a clown, Jack thought, with a white-painted face to hide behind.

'But what happened, Jack . . . it's a long time ago,' Tom persisted as he walked away from the window.

'You'll need a key,' Jack said, as if he hadn't spoken. He took one from his pocket and held it out. For a moment Tom looked as if he would baulk, then, with a shrug of resignation, he gave in and took it. 'Oh, and Tom – '

'I know. No parties.' He sighed.

Recognizing that his brother had finally accepted the inevitable, Jack Wolfe's expression softened a little. 'It's not that bad.'

'Yes, it is. You haven't even got a television.'

'You can listen to the match on the radio,' he pointed out, suddenly tired of pandering to a spoilt boy's complaints. 'And should you find time hanging heavy you could always try revising for your exams.'

CHAPTER 2

Melanie laughed at the clown's cheek. Then, as the slight Aussie twang in his voice rang a chord in her memory, she asked, 'Do I know you?'

'I cannot tell a lie. Our paths have crossed before.' And he bowed low from the waist. 'Richard Latham, actor *manqué*, at your service.'

'Richard?' She could scarcely believe it. It had been quite five years since they had both been in the same soap opera. They had both been little more than children and it was doubtful if she would have recognized the man, even without the white make-up. 'This is amazing! How long have you been in London? I suppose you saw me coming out of Trudy Morgan's office?' she prompted.

'A glass of wine?' Richard asked. 'Or shall we save time and order a bottle?'

'Neither. A cappuccino, please, Marco.' Richard looked disappointed. 'I'm afraid it goes straight to my head, but don't let me stop you.'

'No, there's no fun in drinking alone. Make that two cappuccinos, Marco,' he said, then turned back to Mel. 'Actually I saw you arrive at Trudy's,' he said, finally answering her question. 'I was waiting for you to come out.'

'But I might not have stopped to watch you.'

'You didn't,' he pointed out. 'I made you stop.' Then he shrugged. 'I have to admit it took two attempts. You didn't even notice me the first time. You seemed a bit upset.'

'Just in a hurry.' Richard was charming, and under the white make-up he was undoubtedly still as attractive as he had been when they worked together. But she had no overwhelming desire to confide in him. 'What are you doing performing in the street, Richard? I thought you'd left show business and gone to work for your father.'

'I did. But the company was taken over last year by one of those international conglomerates and the Latham family became surplus to requirements. Dad made things easy for them by having a heart attack. I was harder to get rid of, but in the end I had no choice.'

'I'm sorry, Richard.' Sorry too for the bitterness in his voice. 'How is your father now?'

'Relaxing. Pretending very hard that sitting in the garden is all he ever wanted to do with his life. That's not for me.'

'What is?'

'I've a few things to settle before I make any major decisions. What about you? Are the offers pouring in after your West End début?'

Melanie pulled a rueful face. 'My agent has a

27

sitcom lined up for me. She thinks it's exactly what I need right now. I don't.'

'But you'll do it.'

'Will I?'

'Of course. You're too nice, too sweet to seriously upset anyone by saying no.'

Slightly irritated by his patronizing attitude, she forgot her unwillingness to confide in him. 'I already have.'

'Then she'll leave it for a few days, let you work up a head of guilt and then she'll ask you again. You just won't be able to turn her down. Not twice.'

'Don't be ridiculous.'

'Ridiculous? Me? Think back just five minutes, Mel. You wanted to tell me to go to hell out there, but you couldn't bring yourself to. Come on, admit it.'

He was inviting her to laugh at herself and she did, although she didn't find it all that funny. 'Maybe you're right. Maybe I should cultivate a bit of attitude, stop trying to please everyone.' Maybe she should take a leaf out of Heather's book.

'When pigs fly. Tell me about this sitcom. What's wrong with it?'

'Nothing. I just don't want to do it.'

'Oh, hoity-toity!'

Melanie laughed. 'You see? I can be a bad girl when I want to be.'

'No, darling, not bad. You're one of the fabulous Beaumonts now. You're just showing a little artistic temperament. I'm sure Trudy knows you'll come through for her.'

28

'Not this time. And I do mean it. I'd rather do what you're doing.' He raised one painted brow dramatically and she laughed. 'What do you say, Richard? Do you need a partner. We made a pretty good team out there.'

'Sure, you're welcome to come and join in any time. But don't expect a cut. Not everyone is as generous as you. This doesn't even pay the rent.'

'Really? What does?'

'I'm working as a cleaner at nights in an office block. That one.' He pointed to the elegant Georgian façade of the offices across the square.

'Trudy's office?'

'She only has a suite on the first floor,' he said. 'A very nice suite, I grant you.'

'Oh, come on, Richard, you're having me on.'

'Not at all.' He fished a card out of the leather purse on his belt and handed it to her.

She glanced at it. 'Busy Bees Cleaning Services? You're kidding?'

'Maybe you should try it for a week or two. It would made that sitcom suddenly seem very desirable.'

'You could do better than that, Richard,' she said.

'Could I?'

'You were talented . . . you *are* talented . . .'

'So I should go back to the soaps? Good enough for me, but not for you, eh?'

Bitter about that too, then? 'I didn't mean that. There's nothing wrong with a good soap opera. And it's a lot easier than scrubbing floors.'

He said nothing for a moment, then he laughed. 'I'm sorry. I shouldn't take my ill-fortune out on you. And cleaning isn't that bad, really.'

'Isn't it?'

'There are worse jobs. You've lived a sheltered life, Mel. Maybe you should try it out here in the real world before you make any snap judgements.'

It was a sentiment that echoed her own thoughts and yet she didn't like the way it sounded coming from Richard. 'You make me sound terribly boring.'

'Not boring. You're a nice girl, Mel. Everyone likes you. But you're untouched. You've been protected from the first moment you stepped on to the television set; your mother saw to that. The producer was terrified of her, you know.'

'Yes, well, my mother had first-hand experience of what could happen to a girl in the big bad world of entertainment.'

'You mean she made you pay for her mistake.'

'She was just looking out for me, Richard.'

'She overprotected you. Sweet is great until you're about seventeen, Mel. After that you need to grow up a bit.' He sat back and regarded her thoughtfully. 'You could make a start by losing your virginity.'

Good God, did it show? Or was Richard simply guessing? She wasn't going to make the mistake of denying it; that way he would know for sure.

'Is that an offer?' she enquired, all her fabled sweetness on show.

'No, darling. If it had been going to happen for us it would have been on the set in the television studios

30

when you *were* sweet sixteen.' He grinned. 'That big sofa – '

'I get the picture,' she said, hurriedly. The sofa was infamous. 'Were you afraid of my mother, too?'

'I don't believe in making waves for the sake of it, not when there were so many other girls ready and willing. And now I'm afraid you've gone beyond that kind of careless lust, Melanie.'

'You mean I've passed my sell-by date?'

Richard grinned. 'It's never too late, sweetheart. But once you've reached twenty the whole thing becomes more important. When you've waited so long for Mr Right, he has to be perfect.'

'Oh, come on. I'm not that naïve. Prince Charming doesn't exist.'

'Precisely. That is your difficulty.'

'This is fascinating stuff.' Melanie propped her elbows on the table and rested her chin on her hands. 'So, Doctor, what do you recommend?'

'Well, you could go to a party, have a few drinks and fall under the first man who makes a move on you. Get it over with.'

'That doesn't sound very attractive.'

'You'd be surprised, but no, I can't see you doing that. What you really need is to be seduced by some dangerously attractive man, someone older, someone utterly unsuitable – '

'Do you mean married?' she enquired, with dangerous calm.

'No. Married is messy . . . you've only got to look at what happened to your mother . . .' He saw her

31

face and stopped. 'I'm sorry. I won't mention her again, all right?' Then he sat back. 'But this is supposed to be a learning experience, not a lifetime commitment. It wouldn't do to get cosy and settled down, not the first time.'

'Why not?'

He shrugged. 'Everyone needs their heart broken once, Mel. While they're still young enough to get over it.'

'It sounds painful.'

'It is. But if you've never felt it, how are you ever going to act it?'

She gave him a thoughtful look. 'Maybe I'll find someone while I'm on holiday.'

'Holiday romances don't count,' he said, dismissively. 'No one takes them seriously.'

'But you said temporary – '

'I said someone who'll break your heart.' And for no good reason she remembered the man she had nearly knocked down in the travel agent's. 'You've thought of someone,' Richard said. 'Come on, who is it?'

'No one.' She could see that he wasn't convinced, so she tried harder. 'But if I can't have a holiday romance I don't think I'll go on holiday after all. Maybe I should take a job instead. Where no one knows me. Tell me, Richard,' she enquired teasingly, 'just how dangerous is it wearing a pinny and scrubbing out dirty sinks?'

'For your information, I wear an overall and wield a bloody great vacuum cleaner.'

32

'It sounds like hell.'

'It's cheaper than going to the gym for a workout. And the women I work with are a great bunch.'

'Oh, *really*? So that's the attraction. They all think you're their personal Chippendale, do they? Tell me, are there any big sofas in this office block of yours?'

'A few,' he admitted. 'And you'd be surprised how many men work late at the office . . .'

'Oh? And how dangerous are they?'

He pulled a face. 'There are one or two I could think of who'd fit the bill,' he said thoughtfully. 'Why don't you try it?'

'You make it sound so appealing. Thanks, but I think I'll give it a miss.'

He sat back and looked at her through narrowed eyes. 'You haven't got the guts, huh? You'd rather make Trudy's day . . .'

'Oh, puh–lease, Richard. It's nothing to do with guts. How can I take a job when I can't even cross the road without being recognized?'

'If that's all that's stopping you, invent an *alter ego*. In a mousy wig, no make-up and unflattering clothes no one would look at you twice. If you don't believe it, try it, see if Marco waves you to the best table ahead of the queue then.' He glanced at the clock. 'Hey, I have to get back on the square. There are people out there just dying to find a good home for the foreign coins that they've been slipped in their change.' He grinned. 'Do stop by again soon.'

'To boost your takings? Just watch out, Richard, it might be my *alter ego* who comes calling.'

33

For a moment he considered her, then shook his head. 'I don't think so.'

When he'd gone, Mel ordered another coffee and looked out at the travel office across the square. Somehow the idea of the long haul to the other side of the world seemed less attractive than it had done. Less a holiday than an escape plan. But if she stayed, what would she do? Get a job? Something ordinary? She remembered her bold words when Luke had said she'd be bored in ten minutes. Just what would she do if she went to Oz? Look back, or take a step back?'

Her fingers encountered a coin in her pocket and she took it out and stared at it. Heads the warmth and friendliness of Australia? A guaranteed welcome. Or tails Richard's challenge? She hesitated. The whole idea was ridiculous, yet her heart was beating faster at the very thought, and now long had it been since her heart had beat with excitement? Since she'd first stepped on a West End stage? That had been nearly a year ago. Too long. Without stopping to consider the consequences, she tossed the coin up high into the air.

She watched it rise, twisting over and over. It seemed to hang in the air for a moment and then it began to fall. As she followed it back down her concentration was distracted by the figure of a man across the square, the man she had almost cannoned into in her anger half an hour ago. He was standing in the doorway of the travel agent, tapping a long white envelope against his thumbnail, watching Richard as he began his performance.

She remembered his cool grey eyes, the way her skin had tingled, the fine down on her arms rising as he had stared down at her. A feeling of –

She jumped as the coin she had tossed clattered to the floor beside her. Slowly she turned away from the window and picked it up without looking at it. She was all grown up, wasn't she? She didn't need a coin to make her decisions for her. She had already chosen. It was time for the sweet and virginal Miss Melanie Beaumont to throw caution to the wind and start taking some risks.

Then she shivered as if a goose had walked over her grave. And her head jerked up as she had a premonition that somehow, without quite knowing it, she had already stepped into the abyss. But the doorway of the travel shop was empty. The man with the airline ticket had gone.

Melanie took one last disbelieving look at her reflection in the hall mirror and stepped out of her apartment. There was no one about, for which she was profoundly grateful.

But her relief came a split second too soon. She had just closed the door behind her when she was confronted by the porter bringing up the mail. Unable to retreat without appearing foolish, she simply stood there . . . smiling and *feeling* very foolish indeed.

But the porter was not smiling back. 'Who are you?' he asked, sharply. With a slight shock Melanie realized that he had not recognized her and quite suddenly devilment warred with conscience. The man was clearly concerned to discover how this young women had bypassed the door security system and she knew she ought to put his mind at rest. Yet the temptation to try out her disguise, see how long she would be able to sustain it, was too strong. 'How did you get up here?' he demanded.

Despite her years spent in Oz her English mother had managed to keep Melanie's accent in check. But that didn't mean she couldn't do a mean Sheila given the chance. 'I took the lift, mate,' she said. 'Any objections?'

'Plenty. What's your business?'

'I wanted to talk to Melanie Beaumont.'

'So do a lot of people, but you can't just walk in off the street and knock at her door.'

'No?' *She should be chewing gum, she thought.* 'Who's stopping me?'

'I am. Beat it.'

Mel shrugged defensively and, with a very good stab at careless indifference, pushed herself away from the door. 'Well, she's not in anyway.'

'If you'll leave your card I'll be sure to tell her you called,' he said sarcastically, following her all the way to the front door to ensure that it was firmly fastened behind her.

That was when Mel turned to him and gave him her best smile and with her well-rounded English vowels back in place said, 'You're doing a really good job, George. Keep it up.'

She'd never actually seen someone's mouth drop open before. But George did a fair impression of a goldfish before he managed, 'Miss Beaumont? Is that really you?'

'You will let me in when I come home, won't you?' she said, grinning broadly.

'I would never have known you.' He peered at her more closely. 'I mean, now I know, I can see it's you.' He shook his head. 'Playing a joke on someone, are you?'

'Something like that. Don't tell anyone, will you?'

'No. No, of course not.'

It had worked! And it had taken so little to change her appearance. A short mousy brown wig over her own long fair hair and some heavy eye make-up that completely overwhelmed all her other features after a thick pale matt foundation had effectively flattened out the natural shadows of her face, disguising her bone-structure. And choosing clothes had been fun. The temptation had been to go for something hideously over-the-top. Instead she had modelled herself on Heather in a huge baggy black T-shirt which almost hid the microscopic skirt she was wearing. Her long tanned legs were blanketed in thick black tights and a pair of Doc Martens completed the transformation.

Grinning to herself, she headed for the Underground. She had invented a role for herself and she needed to stay in character. And her character wasn't the kind of girl who hailed black cabs at the drop of a hat. But she wondered if Richard would be as easy to fool as George. If he took a second look he might easily spot the make-up techniques she had used.

Richard was going through a simple routine when she sauntered across the square. Watching him, she could see that he was looking for someone to draw in as a foil for his performance. His eyes flicked over her as she joined the crowd, but did not linger. Too challenging, too aggressive in Heather's awkward, angular stance.

As he turned away she began to smile. Too soon. She saw the moment when he realized who she was. He was twenty feet away from her, but she still saw the little jolt of recognition that for a split-second disturbed the perfect line of his performance. When he spun back to face her he was perfectly under control, but as he advanced towards her she laughed and shook her head. She had no intention of becoming part of his act on a permanent basis and before he could reach her she had turned away and was walking across to the wine bar.

He was right about that too. Marco glanced at her sharply, not at all his usual, welcoming self. It was difficult to maintain that hard, aggressive look when all her natural instincts were urging her to smile at the man, but she managed it and after a moment he shrugged and waved her grudgingly to a table in a dark corner. She didn't have to wait long for Richard to join her.

'Nice one, Mel,' he said, as he slid in beside her at the banquette.

'How did you know?'

'You smiled a fraction too soon. You'll have to learn to hide that dimple if you want to fool anyone who knows you.'

'I've done pretty well so far. The hall porter where I live tried to throw me out when he spotted me outside my flat. Marco was not his usual smiling self. And you didn't rush to offer me one of your giant daisies.'

'True.' He ordered a coffee. 'So,' he said, turning back to her, 'does this herald a new Melanie Beaumont, or are you just kidding around?'

'Just kidding?'

'Having a lark. Giving your friends a bit of a shock. Is it just a joke? Or are you serious, going to go the whole hog? Are you going to get a job and try life out there in the big wide world?'

'Get a job? What as?'

'I'm working,' he pointed out.

'Yes, but . . .' He raised his dramatic brows. 'You can't really expect – '

'I don't expect anything, Melanie. You're the one who's having problems with your image.'

'I'm not having problems.'

'Of course not. You don't know what a problem is. And why should you bother to find out?' He stood up. 'Look, I have to get back to work, but if you're going to be around for a while there's a local actors' workshop that I go to. They're putting on a new play tomorrow night.' He shrugged. 'Maybe you could try out that outfit on them.'

'Maybe I will. Maybe I'll try something even more outrageous.'

'You won't fool me a second time. Meet me here at seven if you decide to come.'

'Well, gee, thanks, Richard,' she murmured to his departing back. That had to be about the least gracious invitation she'd ever received. And he hadn't offered to pay for the coffee either, she noticed.

Well, what had she expected? Had she gone to all that trouble simply so that Richard Latham would tell her what a clever girl she was for fooling everyone with her disguise? Good heavens, that had been easy. She flipped open her shoulder bag to pay for the coffee, anxious to be away.

Inside the little pocket at the back was the coin she had tossed. She had chosen risk without even looking and now it seemed to mock her. And she refused to be mocked.

Richard was right. It was all very well dressing up and fooling one's friends, but that was just like one of those stupid television programmes. All you had to do was smile and say 'Got you!' and it was over. And so what?

Busy Bees was situated in a building just one step up from a garage, in a street that could only be described as uninviting. Melanie, standing on the pavement outside, had a sudden failure of confidence. What on earth was she doing there? She didn't want a job. She just wanted to prove to Richard that she was capable of getting one.

Yet having taken so much trouble with her appearance, her clothes, her story, it seemed crazy to turn round and walk away. Instead she took a deep breath, pushed open the door to the office and, having abandoned her Australian accent in case it caused awkward queries about work permits, asked the woman sitting behind a desk if they had any vacancies.

'What can you do?'

'Cleaning?' she suggested, with just a touch of irony.

Janet Graham, the dour Scotswoman who ran the place, sighed. 'Cleaning. Of course. And have you any experience?'

Melanie considered that an odd question. Didn't everyone? Her mother had certainly made a point of ensuring she knew one end of a vacuum cleaner from another and the proper way to clean a sink. She suspected it had been her way of keeping her daughter's feet firmly on the ground. 'Of course I've experience, I'm a woman,' she replied, as if that was sufficient.

The look she received for her pains was searching. Flippancy, it said, was not appreciated. 'I meant professional experience. You don't look like a cleaner.'

'Don't I?' She didn't know that cleaners had a special look. She should have studied for the part. 'I'll put some rollers in my hair and tie it up with a scarf if that will help,' Mel offered, deciding that since she was obviously not going to get a job she might as well have some fun developing her character.

'That won't be necessary. If we take you on we

41

supply a uniform. With a cap,' she added, giving Mel's hair a glance of disapproval. She'd decided to cut the wig into a slightly spiky style.

'What's your name?'

'Devlin. Melanie Devlin.' Well, it was the name she had been born with. The name still on her passport. The name that would cause her the least amount of trouble.

'And have you any references?'

'Not for cleaning.'

'Somehow, Miss Devlin, that doesn't surprise me.' But she picked up a card from the desk in front of her and tapped it thoughtfully against her thumb. 'Could you do a job straight away?'

'Now?' Suddenly it wasn't quite so funny. Either flippancy was the stock-in-trade of cleaners, or Janet Graham was desperate. Pushed to decide, Mel would have come down on the side of desperate.

'It's an emergency post-party clean-up that's just come in,' she said, immediately confirming Melanie's judgement of the situation. 'If you do a good job, I'll think about taking you on.'

A post-party clean-up? Melanie's stomach quelled at the thought of what might be expected. What on earth was she thinking of? She could be lying on a beach right now . . . Yet she felt something close to excitement too. Until now her life had been oddly sheltered for an actress and this felt, if not exactly dangerous, certainly different enough to make her stomach flutter with something very like stage-fright. And it would show Richard Latham . . .

'No problem,' she said, taking the card with the job details. She could buy a pair of rubber gloves on the way.

The address to which Melanie had been directed was on the top floor of a converted warehouse overlooking the Thames not far from Tower Bridge. Expensive, large, and the furnishings suggested an austerity of taste that she might have approved of, but, since most of them were buried beneath the detritus of what must have been a long-sustained and well-attended party, it was difficult to tell.

'Yes? What is it?'

Melanie considered the young man who had opened the door, his eyes bloodshot, his demeanour suggesting the kind of hangover that required a long period of undisturbed silence in a darkened room.

'Mr Wolfe?' she enquired politely, although there was no doubt that she had come to the right address. Wolfe? She'd heard that name somewhere recently.

'Yes. Look, if you've come to complain about the noise . . .' he put his hand to his head '. . . the party's over.'

'I can see that, and I haven't come to complain. I am Miss Devlin,' she introduced herself crisply. Then she took a deep breath. 'I'm a . . . Busy Bee.' *Somewhere, deep down inside, she considered what she had just said. And she couldn't believe it. If Richard could see her now, he'd probably die laughing.*

'A what?' Then, 'Good grief, are you the cleaner? I thought you'd be older.' Pained by the sound of his own voice, the young man evidently decided he

43

didn't care how old she was. Instead he returned his
hand to his head.

'Does it matter? You sent for help and you certainly look as if you need it.'

'Yes, well, you'd better come in and make a start,'
he said, returning to an agonized whisper. 'Jack will
be home in a couple of hours.'

'Jack?'

'My brother. This is his place. He insisted I stay
here while he was away but he'll kill me if he finds it
in this state.'

'From the look of you he'd be doing you a favour.'
She looked around at the mess. 'What happened?'

'A few college friends dropped round.' He winced,
waved him arm vaguely at the disarray. 'Look, just do
your best, will you? I'm going back to bed.'

'Bed?' Losing sight of the fact that she was supposed to be a humble cleaner, Mel turned on the
hapless young man. 'You're not going to bed. You
made this mess and if you want it cleaned up in a
couple of hours, you're going to have to send for
reinforcements, or give me a hand. Frankly I don't
think even the Seventh Cavalry could arrive in time
to save you.'

'What?'

'Never mind. Come along, Mr – ' She paused,
unable seriously to envisage calling this young fool
'Mr' all afternoon. 'What's your first name?' she
asked.

He leaned towards her confidentially. 'I'll tell you
mine if you tell me yours.' And then he giggled.

44

'Oh, God,' she sighed.

'No, not God. Tom. Your turn.'

'Melanie,' she said.

'Menalie . . . Milenie . . .' He gathered himself and launched himself into the word. '*Melanie*. Nice name.'

'I'm glad you like it. And now we've got that out of the way, you'd better come with me.'

'Have a heart, Melanie – ' But she had taken him firmly by the wrist and was already wading through the bottles littering the floor in her quest for the ingredients to make a swift, if brutal hangover cure that was famous at the television studios where the soap opera she starred in had been filmed. Since she had always been stone-cold sober she had become a dab hand at making it for everyone else. It was scarcely any wonder that Richard thought she was boringly sweet and virginal. She was beginning to think he was right.

First she propped her unhappy employer against the central island in the kitchen. 'Stay there,' she commanded, using much the same tone she would use on a badly behaved puppy, then she began to assemble the gruesome cocoction in a glass. With one last twist of the pepper mill she turned back to the suffering young man. 'Drink this,' she commanded.

'You're joking?' One look at her face warned him that she wasn't doing any such thing and he shifted his bloodshot eyes to the mixture she was offering him. 'What is it?' he asked, taking the glass and sniffing at it suspiciously.

'It's not as bad as it looks,' she lied without shame. 'Just take a deep breath and swallow it down in one go.'

The effect was immediate and a few seconds later he shuddered, turned pale and ran. Mel, meantime, began flinging bottles, half-eaten pizzas and take-away curry cartons into a plastic sack without the least consideration for her employer's aching head. Her sympathy was entirely with his brother. By the time Tom had returned from the bathroom, still pale, but shocked out of his stupor, she was beginning to cut a swathe through the debris.

'Go and dump these while I start on the glasses,' she ordered, indicating the full sacks, then, as she spotted another pile of take-away cartons, she stopped him. 'Wait. Pass me those, will you?' she said.

He groaned; nevertheless he turned to obey, but his hands, still unsteady, fumbled and the cartons wobbled and slipped. 'Oh, heck.'

Mel's carefully chosen outfit might not have been the height of fashion, but it had been clean. Splattered from neck to hem in curry sauce, 'heck' was not the first word that sprang to her mind, and the smell rose to overwhelm her. And she didn't feel in the least bit sweet. 'Find me something to wear,' she said, and without stopping to consider the effect of her actions on an impressionable young man, she stripped off the T-shirt and skirt before it soaked through to her underwear, then bent to unlace her boots so that she could divest herself of the black tights which had taken the worst of the spill.

Tom hadn't moved. Her outer garments might have been hideous; her underwear, lace-edged oyster satin, was anything but. 'A T-shirt, an old pair of jeans?' she suggested quickly, realizing rather too late that she might have been a little precipitate in divesting herself of her clothes.

'Right.' He swallowed. 'Er – can I say that you're a great improvement on any Mrs Mop I've met before?' He was definitely on the mend.

Melanie hid her satisfaction at this indication of recovery, putting her hands on her hips and glaring at him. 'And you're an authority on the subject, I suppose.' He blushed painfully and she realized, with a sudden rush of sympathy, that he was younger than she'd first thought. Nineteen or twenty, perhaps. No more. 'Maybe I'm not everyone's idea of Mrs Mop,' she allowed, a little more kindly, 'but I'm not working in my underwear.'

'Gosh, no,' he repeated. Definitely younger than he looked. 'A T-shirt. I'll find one.'

'And some jeans.'

'Jeans.' He backed out of the kitchen, presumably in order to keep her satin-clad figure in sight for as long as possible, and she finally favoured him with an encouraging smile that displayed her dimple to its best effect. 'Oh, my . . .' he mumbled.

Realizing that the dimple might have been a mistake, Melanie made a strategic withdrawal to luxurious cloakroom near the front door and accepted his offering of clothing, with belated modesty, through the door.

The jeans, soft from much use, were a mile too long and she had to roll them up over her ankles. The T-shirt had seen better days too and came down to her knees. Scarcely flattering.

Melanie gave her wig a tug to make sure it was still firmly in place and then regarded her reflection with disfavour, wondering what Trudy would make of her transformation from soap queen to Cinderella. Personally, Melanie had always considered that Cinderella was a bit of a wimp. Stopping at home to do the cleaning while everyone else had the fun was not, in her opinion, a proper role model for the modern girl. Still, if she was ever induced to play Cinderella, she'd be able to give real authority to the part. And, giving the jeans one final hitch up, she returned to the fray.

She looked around her and took a deep breath. She'd transformed her own appearance comprehensively, and it was to be hoped she could do an equally dramatic job of transforming the flat or young Tom was going to be in trouble when his brother came home. She'd never had a big brother, but Luke had come close and it didn't require much in the way of imagination to work out what his reaction would have been if she'd got his place into this kind of mess. With that thought to inspire her, she set to work.

Tom, still dazzled by the vision of Melanie in her underwear, seemed to have forgotten his hangover, and he made a start on rubbish disposal while she began gathering up the glasses. After that things seemed to go remarkably well. She was beginning to feel a real sense of satisfaction in restoring order out of the chaos, completely forgetting her subservient role as she bossed Tom around without a second thought.

Another hour of hard work and Melanie began to congratulate herself that not even the most discerning eye would be able to tell there had ever been a party.

'Er – there's upstairs,' Tom said, when Melanie suggested they might treat themselves to a cup of coffee.

'Upstairs?'

'The workmen left a bit of a mess.'

'Workmen?' Then she shook her head. 'No, don't tell me. I'll go and have a look.' She climbed the spiral staircase to the upper floor, a simple cantilevered space over the living room, all clean lines in navy, white and chrome.

'They replaced the windows.'

And hadn't bothered to clean up after themselves. They'd probably decided that with all the mess downstairs no one would notice. 'Go and make some coffee, Tom, I'll deal with this.'

A damp cloth dealt with the dust, but the bed needed changing and after a couple of attempts to get a sheet on the huge king-sized bed she gave up and called for help.

Tom, with the recovery power of youth to aid him, sprinted up the spiral stair. 'I'm not much of a hand at hospital corners,' he said, eyeing the bed doubtfully.

'Neither am I,' Melanie admitted, bending to lift

the corner of the mattress. 'But I'll give it a try if you'll help.'

'You're not a real cleaner, are you, Mel?' He stood watching her. 'Are you an out-of-work actress or something?'

Oops. 'Or something,' she agreed, without looking up, as she struggled with the corners. She struggled alone and straightened to discover that Tom was still beside her. He was looking much better and was wearing the stupid grin she recognized as the prelude to a lunge. 'You're supposed to be helping,' she reminded him, sharply. 'On the other side of the bed.'

He shrugged philosophically and two minutes later the job was done. Tom flopped back on to the freshly made bed.

'Hey, don't go undoing all my hard work,' Melanie complained, bending over to smooth the crumpled cover. Tom simply grinned, grabbed her around the waist and toppled her down on top of him.

'I'm shattered. Why don't we lie here and have a little cuddle?'

He had a point, but she'd rather wait until she got home to lie down. By herself. 'Tom, don't be silly, your brother will be back soon,' she warned him, pushing him away and sitting up.

'I've never kissed a Mrs Mop.' It was just a silly game, Melanie knew that, and she laughed as he tightened his grip and put on a ridiculous leer. He was simply feeling better, relieved to be out of a scrape . . . but she wasn't about to humour him.

50

'And you aren't about to,' she said, with mock severity. 'You're in enough trouble already – '

'More than enough.'

Melanie was looking down at Tom but his lips hadn't moved. 'How did you do that?' she demanded.

'Do what?' he asked.

'Speak without moving your lips.'

'He didn't. We're a double act.'

Melanie suddenly realized that Tom had stopped leering at her and was staring instead at something over her shoulder. She turned to see what it could be. And for the second time in a week a shiver of apprehension raised the gooseflesh on her arms.

CHAPTER 3

'Jack,' Tom said flatly. 'You're back.'

'And with my usual immaculate timing not a moment too soon.'

Jack, Mel thought blankly. Jack Wolfe. The cold-eyed man from the travel agent's. She swallowed, hard. It was a bit late to remember where she had heard the name.

Actually, now they were together the family resemblance was unmistakable, but, unlike the boisterous Tom, his brother was the kind of man who would live in the restrained and understated luxury of this kind of apartment. Everything about him murmured *money*, but in a very discreet whisper.

And it didn't take a genius to guess what Jack Wolfe was thinking as his eyes swept her in a comprehensive glance that apparently told him everything he wanted to know. 'Do introduce me to your friend, Tom.'

Except her name. Relief flooded through her. At least he hadn't recognized her. Then she realized it didn't matter. He hadn't recognized her at the travel agent's either. Not a soap fan, then? *Not a chance.*

'Oh, Mel's not a friend,' Tom said, sliding quickly from the bed. 'She's just cleaning up after the party . . .' He stopped, swallowed hard. Despite his rapid recovery, his brain was still working considerably slower than his mouth.

'Indeed?' Jack Wolfe's steel-grey eyes flickered about the apartment and came back to rest upon Melanie as she wriggled out of Tom's grasp and got to her feet. She fielded the look and held it, refusing to be intimidated, but the man was not a bit like his brother. Tom was young, still soft, with an eager puppy-like charm that ensured quick forgiveness of his doubtless many sins. She knew the type, and kept firmly on a training lead he would be amusing company. Jack Wolfe was darker, leaner, harder. A Dobermann to Tom's Labrador. Not amusing at all.

Melanie, used to controlling over-eager young men, discovered that before the insolent assurance of Jack Wolfe her confidence ebbed rapidly and she suddenly found it easier to look anywhere but at him. Apparently satisfied that he had made his point, Jack Wolfe returned his attention to his young brother.

'Cleaning up after the party? Is that why your friend has discarded her own clothes and helped herself to mine?'

'Yours?' The word was jerked from her by the sheer unlikelihood of such a man being seen dead in a pair of threadbare jeans, or a T-shirt from which the sleeves had been hacked to allow ease of movement.

Indeed, from Jack Wolfe's appearance – the severest navy pin-striped suit, the snowy perfection of his shirt, thick dark hair trimmed to a millimetre – she found it difficult to believe that he had ever worn jeans in his life.

'Mine,' he confirmed abruptly, as if reading her thoughts even as she formed them.

And quite unexpectedly Melanie, who hadn't blushed unless she had wanted to since she was thirteen years old, blushed beneath the pale pancake make-up. They were *his* clothes and she was suddenly intensely aware of the way the cloth felt against her skin. Soft, caressing, as if he was in some way . . . touching her. She remembered the electric touch of his fingers as he had steadied her, held her in the travel office. Couldn't he feel it? How could he possibly miss the charged atmosphere?

'I . . . I didn't know,' she found herself stammering idiotically, quite suddenly desperate to get out of them, get out of his flat before he did realize who she was. Heaven alone knew what he would make of the transformation. 'Tom lent them to me to work in –' she began, but he cut her off.

'And since you had finished working, you invited him to help you out of them again?'

'I say, Jack,' Tom interjected. 'Mel isn't – '

'Leave it, Tom,' Mel said, quickly. 'It doesn't matter. I'm just leaving.' She didn't have to justify what had, after all, just been a bit of youthful horseplay – Tom letting off steam because he'd been saved from his brother's retribution. She hadn't encouraged him and she certainly wasn't about to apologize to his big brother, no matter how intriguing his eyes, or electric his touch. Neither had she any desire to stay around and listen to Tom grovel to the man. But as she moved to the head of the spiral staircase Jack Wolfe's tall, broad figure blocked the way. 'If you'll excuse me,' she asked, with studious politeness, 'I have to collect my clothes from the washing machine.' On reflection, not the most sensible thing to have said. But he made no comment, nor did he move. He simply continued to regard her with steely, penetrating eyes that did something not entirely pleasant to her insides, as if she had just stepped off a precipice into empty space and was waiting for the crash.

'Mel?' he enquired, his forehead puckered in the slightest frown, as if he was trying to remember something. She was very much afraid it was where they had met before.

'Melanie,' she elaborated, and immediately regretted it. Her name was none of his business.

'Like the actress?' he asked, and for one dreadful moment she thought he had finally recognized her.

'Like no one,' she replied, forcefully, meeting him head-on and daring another head-on clash with those unsparing eyes. 'Melanie is the name my mother gave me, Mr Wolfe. It's Greek. It means "clad in darkness" . . .' For heaven's sake, what on earth was she doing? She had to get out of there before she told him her entire life story. Well, that would take all of ten minutes; two minutes if she left out her working life. But he hadn't finished with her.

'"Clad in darkness"?' This seemed to amuse him for some reason. 'And what are you hiding from, Melanie . . .?' His inflection invited her to fill in the blank.

Tom leapt in before she could make him ask. Politely. 'Devlin. Melanie Devlin, Jack.'

'Well, Melanie Devlin?'

'Very well, thank you, Mr Wolfe. Now, if that's all?' She said it with all the poise of a princess, intending to put him in his place, but Jack Wolfe wasn't clearly not the kind of man to recognize someone else's idea of his place.

'Not quite all, Miss Devlin. But it will do for now.' Idiot. Putting on the airs of a princess when you were playing the maid was asking for trouble and now the wretched man was laughing at her, not on the surface, but deep down somewhere private. Not that you would have known. Not unless you were standing up close. Close enough to see a little flare of something dangerous gleam in the depths of his eyes, as if he could tell precisely what she was thinking beneath the veneer of politeness and was inviting her to lose her head and let it rip.

No way. As if he saw that, too, in her face, he unbent a little and glanced around. 'It was good of you to stay and help clear up. I know Tom's parties of old; you must have worked very hard to restore this class of order. I hope he thanks you with a suitably large box of chocolates.'

Chocolates? And she thought Luke had been patronizing! 'Oh, he'll have to do better than that, I'm afraid.'

'Oh?' His look was suddenly speculative.

'*Busy Bees* will invoice your brother for . . .' she glanced at her watch '. . . four hours of my time. Plus the extra charge for an emergency call-out.'

'A what?'

'I was desperate,' Tom interjected. 'And you have to admit it was money well spent.'

Jack Wolfe admitted nothing. 'You're from a domestic agency?' he demanded, making no effort to hide his astonishment. She wasn't sure whether to be affronted or pleased. 'From the fun and games I assumed you were left over from the party.'

Affronted. Definitely affronted. 'I've never been left over from anything, Mr Wolfe,' Melanie said roundly as hot colour once more seared her cheekbones. 'Now, pleasant as it is to stand here chatting with you, I do have more important things to do, so perhaps you would be kind enough to let me by?'

'What about my jeans?'

He was concerned about a pair of jeans that should have been put in the dustbin aeons ago? 'Would you like me to take them off now and go home in my underwear, Mr Wolfe?' He looked as if he might be about to say yes. Before he could she hurriedly intervened. 'I'm sorry,' she said, with a firmness that belied the growing sensation of butterflies panicking in her stomach, 'but since my own clothes

57

are wet I'm afraid you'll have to trust me to return them. I will of course wash them first.'

'And my T-shirt. Your agency can send my brother the invoice for that as well.'

She hadn't intended to charge for the service, simply considering it good manners to wash his clothes before returning them. But she was becoming thoroughly sick of her good manners and, looking down at the disreputable T-shirt, she wrinkled up her nose. 'Is it actually worth the cost of the soap powder, do you think? It's barely fit for making dusters.'

'It's old,' he agreed, 'but I'm particularly attached to it. I'm afraid you'll have to buy your own dusters.' And still he didn't move, but instead regarded her thoughtfully. 'What are you, Melanie Devlin? An actress down on her luck?'

The brothers' minds seemed to run along similar lines, Melanie thought, irritated by their apparent lack of imagination. Although she seriously doubted that Jack Wolfe indulged in the kind of harmless horseplay that Tom enjoyed. And innocent she might be, but she was uncomfortably aware that no woman he tumbled into his bed would be in any great hurry to get up.

She caught herself. She had offered to wash Jack Wolfe's clothes merely to annoy him, but the man was winning hands down in that department. He seemed to have the unhappy knack of wrong-footing her, a situation she was not accustomed to. Her suspicions were confirmed when she snatched a quick glance at him and saw the gleam of amusement in his eyes.

It was disconcerting. She was a member of one of the great theatrical families, a West End success, a television star. The men she knew flirted with her, sent her extravagant baskets of flowers, indulged her shamelessly and treated her, without exception, like a lady. Not one of them had ever laughed at her.

Jack Wolfe, however, thought she was just doing a little cleaning to keep the wolf from the door . . . and that she was apparently not above encouraging the wolf inside when she chose.

For a moment she considered telling him just *whom* he was insulting, but some inner sense of self-preservation saved her from doing anything so ridiculous. She had the uncomfortable feeling that even if he knew the truth Jack Wolfe would not be in the least bit impressed.

It was possible that his cynicism was too ingrained to allow him to be impressed by any woman, and since the likelihood of ever meeting him again was so remote as to be negligible, it hardly mattered who or what he thought she was. An actress down on her luck would do well enough. 'Why don't you watch the soap powder ads to see if you can spot me, Mr Wolfe?' she advised him.

'I don't have a television set.'

'Really? Well, that's too bad. Now, since your brother is paying for every moment that you delay me, I think you should take pity on him and let me go.'

'He doesn't deserve my pity, but don't worry, I'll see that your account is paid.' He took a black leather wallet from his inside pocket and removed a ten pound note from it. 'And in the meantime, as a token of my gratitude for doing such a good job, perhaps you'd like to take a taxi home.'

About to tell him to keep his money, that she could pay for her own damned taxi, Mel stopped herself. The suggestion that it was a taxi fare was simply his way of offering her a tip. She might not know much about this kind of work but she was pretty sure that cleaners didn't turn down tips. She certainly didn't want to make him think twice about offering ten pounds to some other girl who might seriously need the money. And if Jack Wolfe wanted to ease his conscience for being so unpleasant to a simple working girl, who was she to deny him that privilege?

'A taxi?' she murmured, forcing herself to simper a little as she took the note, silently vowing that she'd put it in the first charity box she passed. 'Well, thank you.'

His eyes narrowed slightly and for a moment she thought she might have overdone the pathetic gratitude, but he finally stepped aside, releasing her, and she descended the spiral staircase with as much speed and dignity as her ridiculous outfit would allow. But all the way down a prickling sensation at the nape of her neck warned her that his eyes were following her. At the foot of the stairs she paused and glanced upwards. She was right. He was watching her, dark brows drawn together in a slightly puzzled frown.

Melanie bit down hard as she quickly collected her clothes from the washing machine and stuffed them into a plastic bag she found in a drawer. Then, as she passed an exquisite Art Nouveau mirror by the door, she caught sight of her reflection and gave a small exclamation of dismay at a streak of dust swooping across her cheek.

No wonder Jack Wolfe hadn't been impressed by her princess routine. Not that it mattered; she hadn't been employed as a social butterfly but as a cleaner, she reminded herself ruefully, rubbing the dirt off with the hem of the T-shirt.

Richard Latham was right: living someone else's life was an education, but if a wimp like Cinderella could handle it with a smile on her face and a song in her heart, so could she. There was just one difference: she had learned at her mother's knee one basic truth. Not that Prince Charming didn't exist; he did, she'd found him in Edward Beaumont. But that happy ever after was not guaranteed.

As the door closed, Jack Wolfe turned to his brother, regarding him with irritation. 'Can't I leave you here for a few days without you turning the place into a bear garden?'

'I didn't! I asked a mate to bring over a television so that we could watch the match. He suggested a few beers and it just sort of snowballed . . . you know how it is.'

'Do I?'

Tom shrugged. Then said, 'No, Jack. I don't

suppose anyone would dare to crash a party you gave. And if they did you could wither them with a look.'

'Really?' he enquired heavily. 'What a pity it doesn't seem to have the same effect on you.'

'I'm your brother, Jack. You can't fool me.' He grinned. 'Or maybe you're just losing your touch. Mel Devlin wasn't exactly withered either, was she?'

'Miss Devlin . . .' He stopped. For some reason he couldn't quite put his finger on, he preferred not to discuss Melanie Devlin with Tom. 'You'd better give me the name of the agency you used so that I can settle your account,' he said, changing the subject.

'I told you, I'll pay – '

Jack made an impatient gesture. 'I know, I know. But since you will undoubtedly have to ask me for the money eventually we might as well save the bank charges.'

'I'll get a job in the summer, Jack. I'll pay you back then.'

'Yes, you will. I'll make damned sure of it, even if it means having to give you one myself.'

Tom blenched. 'That won't be necessary, really. And – er – I'd better get going. I've a lecture first thing.'

Jack clicked his fingers. 'The name of the agency?'

'I used the one in your book. Busy Bees.' Then he grinned. 'You know, I think you should take that girl on full time, Jack. You need someone who can stand up to you.'

'That's your opinion based on eighteen months of a psychology degree, is it?'

'No. It's my opinion as your brother.' Then, 'It might be fun.'

'Oh, I see. You think I should employ Miss Devlin for *fun*? Whose fun precisely did you have in mind?'

'Mel Devlin? You're joking, she's way out of my class.'

'It didn't look that way when I came in.'

'We were just having a giggle. It's not a crime, Jack. If you tried hard enough you might remember how it's done.'

'More amateur psychology?'

'No, just some more brotherly advice.'

'Thank you. I'll bear it in mind.'

'And underneath all that dust Melanie is quite a dish. She certainly brightened this place up.' Jack looked doubtful. 'You should have seen her when she stripped off.'

'When she did *what*!'

'Just to her underwear,' Tom said, hurriedly. 'I tipped curry over her.'

'You're an idiot, Tom.'

Tom's eyes gleamed. 'Maybe. But being an idiot has its advantages. I promise you, underneath those old clothes of yours she's an absolute poem in satin and lace. And her legs . . . well, they were the real thing, you know, with *shape*.' He was grinning idiotically now. 'She quite took my breath away.'

Jack Wolfe regarded his brother with growing irritation. 'I think you're confusing her with the quantities of alcohol you consumed. And I like my place just the way it is.' Tom was hovering in the doorway. 'To myself.'

'I'm going, I'm going . . .' He gave an awkward little shrug. 'The thing is, I spent the last of my dosh on that curry. If you could just loan me the bus fare . . .'

Jack sighed and opened the wallet he was still holding. 'Here,' he said, handing his brother two crisp twenty pound notes. 'But don't spent it all on beer and pizza. They say that fish is good for the brain. You might try it.'

'Thanks. I will. And – er – sorry about the mess. I won't do it again.'

'That I can guarantee.'

Tom opened his mouth to protest, then hurriedly closed it. House-sitting his brother's apartment was not high on his list of pleasures and it suddenly occurred to him that it wasn't in his best interests to be too convincing. 'Right. I'll be going, then.'

Jack kept up the stern expression until his brother had closed the door behind him, then his face relaxed into a smile as he looked about him. What mess? The place was immaculate.

He wouldn't dream of telling him so, but maybe Tom for once in his young life was right. Melanie Devlin might have a lot more lip than the average daily, but she certainly knew how to do her job, which was more than could be said of the last woman he'd employed, whose excellent references he suspected had been written by employees so desperate to get rid of her that they were prepared to perjure themselves.

It wasn't as if he would have to see much of her.

Not as much as Tom, anyway. Despite the boy's well-meant advice he certainly wasn't about to encourage the girl to strip to her underwear. Not even for the pleasure of a pair of legs capable of taking a young man's breath away. Young men, as he knew from experience, were notoriously easy to please. His smile faded as he walked across to the phone, found the agency number and punched it in before he could change his mind.

'Busy Bees, Janet Graham speaking. How may I help you?'

'Mrs Graham, Jack Wolfe.'

'Oh, good afternoon, Mr Wolfe. What can I do for you?'

'My brother called you earlier for help cleaning up after a party.' He gave the address.

'Good gracious, I didn't realize that was your apartment. The young man . . . your brother? I'm sorry, but he wasn't terribly coherent. To be honest I thought it might have been a hoax.'

'My brother is rarely coherent, except on the subject of rugby.' And having fun.

'Oh, I see. Well, I hope there's no problem?'

'None at all. I'm calling because I would like Miss Devlin to do some general cleaning for me on a permanent basis. Say two hours, three afternoons a week? If that isn't sufficient time we can adjust the hours later.'

Janet Graham hesitated. Jack Wolfe was an important business client and she would do anything to keep him happy. Yet despite an apparently satisfactory performance she had no intention of taking on Melanie Devlin. The only reason she'd given her the job this afternoon was because she had been almost certain that it was a hoax. If she'd had any idea who she was dealing with she would have pulled someone in from another job. Someone she could trust. She certainly wouldn't have sent the Devlin girl. There was something about her. Something that spelled trouble.

'Unfortunately Miss Devlin is not a regular member of staff, Mr Wolfe. However, I could arrange for one of our most experienced ladies to clean for you.'

But Jack Wolfe wasn't interested in one of Janet Graham's 'experienced' ladies.

'By "not a regular", I assume you're referring to the fact that Miss Devlin is an actress?' The girl had been careful neither to confirm nor deny that, he'd noticed. Not that it bothered him; he just liked to know a little more than people thought he knew. It was a philosophy that kept him one step ahead of the game.

An actress? Janet Graham considered the possibility. Maybe. It would certainly explain her flippancy, her couldn't-care-less air of self-assurance. 'Such girls tend to be unreliable . . .'

'But they have to eat, Mrs Graham.'

'. . . and they're always wanting time off for auditions. I wouldn't want you to be let down.'

'I'm relying on you to make sure I'm not. Shall we say Mondays, Wednesdays and Fridays? From two until four. I'll be here on Monday to run through things with Miss Devlin.'

He replaced the receiver without waiting for her to confirm the arrangement. He had made his mind up that he wanted Melanie Devlin and he wasn't taking no for an answer. It wasn't until later, after he'd poured himself a Scotch and taken it with him into the shower, that it occurred to him to wonder why.

Melanie reached the street before she let out a long, slow breath.

Dangerous? Whatever had made her think it would be a bit of a lark to try *dangerous*?

Still far too close to Jack Wolfe's apartment for comfort, she walked swiftly down the street until she was out of sight of the converted warehouse that he called home. Only then did she allow herself the luxury of laughter. Dangerous, maybe, but she'd got away with it. She'd hardly expected him to recognize Melanie Beaumont – he was probably unaware of her existence – but those sharp eyes hadn't spotted the girl who had cannoned into him in the travel agent's either.

Why should he? She looked down at the clothes she was wearing and laughed again. It didn't matter who saw her. Richard was right: no one she knew would give her a second glance dressed like this.

Suddenly the possibilities seemed endless. Could she fool her sisters? Luke even? She remembered Richard's warning about the dimple. Just as long as she didn't smile.

And the reverse of dressing down had its temptations too. Would Jack Wolfe recognize his cleaner if she turned up on his doorstep in full-frontal glamour? Would he even associate her with the distraught female he had held for a moment, close enough to kiss? She hadn't smiled then, had she?

Pull yourself together, girl, she told herself, sternly. You're getting carried away a little here. But it might be fun to find out, to wipe that superior look right off his arrogant face when he discovered his mistake.

She was still giggling when saw a woman standing hopefully shaking a charity box and, remembering the ten pound note, Melanie stopped.

'What are you collecting for?' she asked.

'The local cat rescue people.' She gave Melanie a doubtful look. 'Every little helps,' she encouraged.

'I'm sure it does.' And to the woman's astonishment she reached into the deep pocket of Jack Wolfe's jeans and retrieved the ten pound note he had given her, pushing it into the collecting box. Then she turned to hail a cab passing on the far side of street. For the first time ever a driver failed to notice her. And who, she reasoned, could blame him? With a slightly rueful smile she looked round for a bus stop.

When she finally arrived home, the telephone was ringing. She left it to the answering machine. What she needed right now was a shower.

But when the tape clicked in and she heard Mrs Graham's voice, she stopped to listen. 'This is Mrs Graham, at the Busy Bees Cleaning Service. Please call me back as soon as you – '

Melanie picked up the receiver. 'Hello, Mrs Graham.'

'Oh, you are there.'

'I've just this minute walked through the door.'

'I wondered how the job went this afternoon.'

A personal enquiry? Surely she was the one who should be chasing Janet Graham? 'Fine. No problems.' She pulled a face at herself in the hall mirror, but she didn't think Janet Graham would want to hear about a few minor difficulties concerning curry sauce and the unexpected arrival of the flat's owner.

The woman made a slow job of clearing her throat. 'Mr Wolfe called me a short while ago.'

'Did he?' Tom? Phoning to say thanks for a job well done? How sweet. He was sweet. Unlike his brother.

'Mr Jack Wolfe, that is.'

'Oh!' Well, it was too late to confess what had happened; Mrs Graham obviously knew already. What had he said? she wondered. That she had been fooling around with his brother when he walked in? That she had a lot of lip for a woman who cleaned for a living? No – he couldn't be *that* mean. *Could he*?

'He was quite pleased with your work.' Another major throat-clearing job, as if passing on the compliment might choke her.

'Oh?' *Pleased*? Oh, no, not pleased, *quite* pleased. 'Well, that's good.'

'Yes. While it is not my habit to take on young

69

women who have no real experience of domestic work, particularly girls in your profession, in your case I'm prepared to make an exception.'

'My profession?'

'You are an actress?'

'I have been,' she confirmed. For a moment she wondered if Janet Graham realized who she was and had decided to take her on for the publicity that it would generate for her business if it got out. She might even be planning to put in a call to the diary page herself, anonymously.

'So, I'd like you start work tomorrow. On a one-month probationary basis, of course,' she added. 'Seven o'clock sharp, now. Don't let me down.'

Melanie let out a little gasp. The woman was offering her a job! A proper nine-to-five job. Or rather seven until five, or six, or whatever, job. With no time off for good behaviour. Thanks, but no, thanks. It had been an interesting experience but certainly not one which she was anxious to repeat.

'I'm sorry, Mrs Graham, I appreciate your confidence, but on reflection I really don't think this is the kind of work that I'm looking for.'

The silence at the other end of the telephone had a stunned quality. As if no one had ever had the temerity to turn her down before. 'Are you quite certain? I know the work is hard, but it is regular. It doesn't do to be too choosy . . . I mean, your profession is somewhat uncertain?'

'It has its up and downs,' Melanie agreed.

'Perhaps you'd like to sleep on it.' Stunned and

just a little desperate, Melanie thought, no matter how hard she was trying to disguise it. 'Why don't you call in on Monday morning and pick up your wages? We can talk about it then.'

No way. But she'd forgotten about the money she'd earned. It wasn't much, but she'd worked hard for it. And she'd have to do something about returning Jack Wolfe's clothes too.

'All right. I'll do that.'

It wasn't until Mel had replaced the receiver that it occurred to her to wonder why Jack Wolfe had bothered to telephone Busy Bees. Tom had made the booking, Tom was paying the bill. Why had Jack Wolfe called the office? Surely not to say he was 'quite' pleased with her work. She couldn't imagine him ever being 'quite' anything. Could it be that he wanted to be certain that his precious clothes were returned, properly washed and pressed?

She glanced down at herself. *His* jeans and *his* T-shirt. Who did he think he was kidding? In some other life he might have worn them. But not now. She was almost certain that if she dumped them in the bin he wouldn't even miss them. But not sufficiently certain to risk it. Just in case. She really didn't want him turning up on her doorstep demanding their return. No. That was silly, he didn't know her address, and neither did Janet Graham. Just a telephone number. And she intended to keep it that way.

So, the sooner they were washed and returned, the better. Yet as she gripped the hem of the T-shirt and pulled it over her head, she caught an elusive woody

71

outdoors scent. Oh, no, *really*. Yet as she held the soft material to her face she knew she was right. Beneath the lavender scent of polish, mingling with her own L'Air du Temps, the fresh, sharp resin of new-sawn pine was unmistakable. And without warning she had a vision of the man bent over a saw-horse, sweat beading his brow, immaculate hair ruffled by the wind, the veins and muscles standing proud on his arms as he powered the saw through the wood. A quite different person from the chisel-jawed businessman in the Savile Row suit. A man she might conceivably want to know.

Maybe. Or maybe her imagination was being driven by nothing more exciting than a splash of pine disinfectant.

She snapped out of her reverie and pushed the clothes into the machine, poured in the powder and switched it on. That would deal with his clothes and her fantasies. The sooner they were out of her flat, the better. Then she wouldn't have to give him another thought.

Pleased with herself, she showered, scrambled a couple of eggs to eat with curls of smoked salmon and went to bed early with a book of such complexity that it dealt with any lingering urge to wonder about Jack Wolfe, and what he was doing when he wasn't giving cleaning ladies a hard time.

Yet as she drifted on the edge of sleep, Jack Wolfe bobbed up from the depths of her subconscious, his eyes narrowed as if trying to remember where he had met her before. She sat up with a jolt, her heart pounding horribly fast as if she had just stepped over the edge of some terrifying drop, and she was shaken by a long, deep, shuddering sigh.

She fell back against the pillows, breathing deeply until her heart had returned to some semblance of normality. Wretched, wretched man. It was as if, when he had looked at her with those penetrating grey eyes, he had somehow managed to lodge part of himself inside her brain so that the minute she stopped concentrating on something else her thoughts would keep drifting back to him.

Why? She'd never been hooked on danger. Never been the kind of girl to run after the bad boys, the ones that made your heart beat faster just to think about them. Her heart had beat all right, but she'd had too much sense to lose her head, and her mother to point out just how badly they treated the girls who did run after them.

Or maybe it was having an unmarried mother as an enduring example of what happened to girls who took risks that had made her cautious. Too cautious? Richard certainly thought so. Or was it even simpler than that? Could it be that there had never been anyone dangerous enough to make taking a risk worthwhile?

Well, Jack Wolfe was dangerous, at least for a girl who had no scar tissue over her heart to protect her. He had a careless arrogance, an imperious disregard for what others might think of him that exerted a powerful draw. Even for a girl with enough sense to know better. Which could be why her heart was pounding like a steam hammer at the very thought of him.

She sat up, switched on the light and pushed her hair back from her face. 'Jack Wolfe,' she said, out loud, 'is dangerous. Any girl who got involved with him would be crazy. He's rude, he's arrogant and it is my dearest wish never to set eyes upon him again. And I am not going to waste another second thinking about him.'

And, having given herself a thorough talking to, Melanie beat her pillow into shape and lay back.

Not one? Her subconscious offered the little pin-prick as her head touched the linen. What about when she returned his clothes, dressed to kill in Jasper Conran? And as she thought about it, she finally admitted to herself the reason for her obsession. She had simply never been spoken to like that by a man. In fact, she hadn't been spoken to like that since she had become a pre-pubescent soap star at the age of ten. Obviously her self-esteem couldn't take it.

Well, Richard had warned her about that, too. A pretty face won a lot more friends than a sweet nature.

In recompense, she indulged her idiotic pride by imagining the effect that each of her dresses would have on Jack Wolfe when Cinderella turned out to be rather more than a fairytale. There was a certain pleasure in allowing her mind to construct a series of fantasies in which first uncertainty, and then downright disbelief, would shake Mr Jack Wolfe out of that blade-edged assurance. It might be fun

74

to confront him with his mistake in a way that he couldn't ignore.

It was just a silly game, she knew that. But as she finally drifted off to sleep her final thought was that it was probably a very good thing that she didn't possess a pair of glass slippers. Because whatever else he might be, Jack Wolfe certainly wasn't Prince Charming.

CHAPTER 4

'I didn't think you had the nerve,' Richard said, when she arrived at the wine bar the following evening and told him about her experiment in the world of work. But he had been right about her appearance: despite a different wig, wild and henna-red, her skin dramatically pale, her eyes heavily made up with kohl, he'd stood up and waved the moment she'd entered the wine bar.

Not that he approved. Her clothes were black, aggressive and her boots laced to the knee. She'd been given a wide berth on the Underground and turned a few nervous heads as she strode across the square. It was oddly exhilarating. As was Richard's discomfort. Could it be he'd wanted to go to this actor's workshop tonight with Melanie Beaumont wearing a designer dress and clinging to his arm like some trophy? He always had been vain, wanting to be the centre of attention.

'It was amazingly easy,' she said, just a little amused at his obvious irritation. 'I just walked into Busy Bees and I was handed a job there and then.'

'A permanent job?'

'Not straight away. Frankly, I think Mrs Graham only offered me the post-party clean-up because she was desperate. But the client phoned afterwards and said he was "quite" pleased, apparently. So she offered me a job on the strength of that.'

'The guy must have been a whole lot more than quite pleased. Ma Graham never takes on resting actresses. They're too much trouble.'

'Oh, I didn't *tell* her I'm an actress. I'm not that stupid. Actually, I think Jack Wolfe must have put the idea into her head.'

'Jack Wolfe?' He stared at her. 'Jack Wolfe? As in John Garrett Wolfe? He was the client? Where was this apartment?'

She told him. 'Do you know him?'

'I clean his offices every night after he's gone home.'

She turned and looked across the square. 'You mean he has an office in the same block as Trudy Morgan?'

'In a manner of speaking. He owns the building. That's him at the top.' He pointed to where a light was still shining. 'Working late on his latest scheme to make money. Are you taking it? The job?' he asked, as she continued to stare upwards.

'What?' She turned back to him. 'Oh, no. No.'

'No. It wouldn't do. I mean, it's not that difficult. Just hard . . .' He gave an expressive little shrug, suggesting it would be altogether too much for her.

'Not that hard. And I'm not that soft. I made a good job of Jack Wolfe's apartment, let me tell you.

77

Mrs Graham thinks I'm up to the job. She asked me to reconsider when I turned her down.' He looked sceptical. 'You don't believe me? I'll have you know that she asked me to sleep on it, go and see her on Monday to talk it over.'

'Don't waste your beauty sleep, sweetheart.'

'I won't.' He pulled a face, smiled a little. 'What?'

'Nothing, Mel. You're being very sensible. As always.'

Sensible. Sweet. Dizzy. It was as much as Melanie could do to stop herself from screaming. 'You don't think I could do it, do you?'

'Of course, my darling. If you wanted to.' He was patronizing her. Verbally patting her on the head. 'For a day or two, anyway.'

'For as long as I chose.'

'All right, Mel,' he murmured, reassuringly. 'But why would you want to? You're above all that sort of thing.'

'You mean I'm afraid to get my hands dirty?'

'I didn't say afraid. But you're a Beaumont. If anyone found out what you were doing . . . well, your father wouldn't be very pleased, would he? And as for Luke Devlin! He's worse than ten fathers.'

'This isn't anything to do with them, Richard. I'm twenty-one next month.' Melanie was suddenly overcome with an urge to wipe that superior smile right off Richard's face and she leaned forward. 'I could do anything Janet Graham asked me to. And I'm willing to put my money where my mouth is. How much do you want to bet?'

78

'Don't be silly, Mel.'

'Humour me, Richard. How much?'

'Fifty pounds,' he offered, dismissively.

'You're not taking this seriously.'

'Do you expect me to?'

'If I can't do it, what have you got to lose?' she enquired, in a parody of her much vaunted sweetness.

'A hundred pounds, then,' he said, reluctantly.

She gave him a look that suggested he was the closest thing Scrooge had to kin. 'Five hundred pounds, Richard. For my sister's charity.'

'That's a lot of money.'

'According to you it should be yours within days.'

He gave her a thoughtful look. 'All right. How long will you work for?'

'A month? Is that long enough to prove I can stick it?'

'A month should certainly be long enough. If you're serious?' By way of answer she held out her hand and after a moment he took it. 'Very well. Five hundred. But you have to work a full calendar month.'

'From Monday. There's just one problem. She'll want my address and I daren't give it her or she'll smell a rat. Can I could use yours?'

'Sure, help yourself.' He grinned. 'Move in if you like. I've got a double bed.'

'Thanks, Richard, but I think we've already covered that. You had your chance to make me an offer and you blew it.'

'You weren't serious,' he pointed out.

'Wasn't I? Well, now you'll never know. Besides, I like it where I am.'

'Tell me about Jack Wolfe's apartment.'

'Austere. Uncluttered. Beautiful,' she said, without thinking.

'Ooooh.'

'What?'

'You've been thinking about it. You've been thinking about him. He won't look at you twice dressed like that, you know. He likes his women like his apartment, like his office come to that, pared to the bone, uncluttered to point of – well, austerity.' Did he? Well the man had style. He'd want a partner to match. 'Personally I prefer a bit more comfort.'

'Maybe you just don't have any taste.'

'Definitely smitten.'

'With Jack Wolfe?' She laughed. 'Get real. I cleaned his apartment once, that's all. You said it. Why would he look at me twice?' Actually he had looked. He just hadn't liked what he'd seen. Well, she wasn't blind. She'd seen her reflection in the mirror and on the whole she sympathized with him.

Richard wasn't convinced. 'Have a care, Mel. I promise you he's strictly a bed-and-breakfast lover. There's a whole string of lovely women who thought they could change his mind and have found themselves crying into their pillow.'

'More fool them.'

'More fool you if you fall into the same trap.' He shrugged. 'I'm wasting my breath, of course. He's only got to lift a little finger and women drop into his bed. I can't see the attraction myself. He's got a calculator for a brain and ice where his heart should be.' He leaned forward, touched her cheek in a possessive little gesture. 'When I suggested an affair with someone unsuitable – '

'We're not having an affair! I've only met the man once.' Several people turned around to look at her. 'Well, twice, I suppose, but I can promise you we're never going to have an affair,' she hissed. 'Can we please stop talking about him?'

Richard took no notice. 'He's way off the scale dangerous for an innocent like you.'

'Well, I thought you prescribed dangerous,' she said, crossly.

'There's danger, and then there's Jack Wolfe.'

'Well, you can rest assured, Richard. I have no intention of getting involved with the man. I don't suppose I'll ever see him again . . .' She paused, and Richard instantly picked up on her uncertainty.

'Except?'

'Well, I have to return some clothes I borrowed. Something got spilled on mine.'

'And you had to take them off? You have been having a interesting time.'

'You wouldn't believe how interesting.'

'Well, have a care it doesn't get too entertaining.' Richard leaned forward and stroked one finger down the length of her throat. 'I'd really hate to see a tender little lamb like you served up with a sprig of mint for Mr Wolfe's Sunday lunch.'

81

Melanie grasped his hand and removed it from her neck. 'You're just trying to frighten me off, Richard. You're scared you're going to lose your bet. And you're right.

Melanie presented herself at the offices of the Busy Bees Cleaning Services promptly at seven on Monday morning.

'I've changed my mind. If you still want me.'

Apparently, now Melanie had admitted she wanted the job, Janet Graham no longer felt obliged to be unnecessarily polite. She did not invite Mel to sit and wasted no time in getting to the point.

'I'm taking a chance on you, Melanie. Don't let me down. Auditions are strictly on your own time and if you leave a job unfinished you will not be paid for it.' Janet Graham had the manner of a headmistress lecturing a tiresome pupil; from her own experience of such occasions Melanie knew the woman would not expect an answer. 'And you'll have to take whatever comes along, the bad jobs along with the good.' *Good jobs? What could possibly be good about cleaning?* 'Is that quite clear?'

'Quite clear.' And it was clear that Mrs Graham didn't know who she was. She would have been nicer. She wouldn't have been able to help herself. Melanie was learning quickly about how things were out in the big wide world. 'I don't expect any special favours, Mrs Graham.'

'Then you won't be disappointed. Sit down.' The

lecture was over. 'Now, tell me how you got on with Mr Wolfe?'

'Mr Wolfe appeared satisfied.' Well, he had appreciated her work, if nothing else. He'd telephoned and said so, hadn't he?

'Young men left on their own are a menace, but extremely good for business,' Mrs Graham said, with a glint of satisfaction. 'Was it a terrible mess?'

Young men? She had all but forgotten Tom Wolfe, but of course he was the Mr Wolfe referred to. 'I've seen worse, although I don't think I'd have managed by myself in the time available,' Mel admitted. 'But after I'd made him one of my hangover cures Tom . . . Mr Wolfe . . . recovered sufficiently to give me a hand.'

Janet Graham's shocked expression told its own story. She really would have to keep a rein on her tongue. 'I trust you won't expect the rest of my clients to pitch in and give you a hand?'

'Of course not. But he wanted the job done by the time his brother got home. I simply used my initiative.'

'I discourage initiative, Melanie. In my experience it causes nothing but trouble. Remember that.' She'd try. But she wasn't making any promises. 'In this instance, however,' Mrs Graham continued, 'your quick thinking has had the most satisfactory results.' She picked up a work sheet from the desk. 'As I told you, I had a call from Mr Jack Wolfe, the owner of the apartment. He requested that you be assigned to clean his apartment three times a week until further notice.'

'Oh!' She sat back in her chair. 'How . . . unexpected.' But it made Mrs Graham's eagerness to employ her rather more understandable.

Mrs Graham looked at her sharply. 'Is it? Why?'

'Oh, well.' She floundered momentarily. 'I assumed I would be cleaning offices, that sort of thing. A friend of mine works for you and that's what he does. At night.'

'Who?'

'Richard Latham.'

'Richard?' She gave Melanie a hard look. 'Well, I hope you don't expect to work nights too.'

'Oh, no. No. Really.'

Mrs Graham stared at her for a moment longer before returning to her schedule. 'You'll be part of a team for most of the time, cleaning empty houses after lettings. But since Mr Wolfe has asked for you personally I'm happy to concede to his wishes. Unless you have any particular reason to refuse . . .?'

For a moment Melanie dwelt on the pleasure it would give her to blacken Jack Wolfe's character so thoroughly that for the rest of his life he would have to make his own bed and wash his own dishes. It would serve him right. But Mel was bright enough to realize that Jack Wolfe wouldn't take that sort of nonsense lying down. And she'd made a bet with Richard; more importantly, she'd promised herself that whatever happened she'd stick it out, just to prove to herself that she wasn't the dizzy creature everyone seemed to think she was. So it was time to stop fooling around and start taking it seriously. 'No,' she admitted. 'No reason.'

'Good. This is your schedule for the week. I've given you to Mr Wolfe for two hours on Monday, Wednesday and Friday between two and four o'clock in the afternoon. Starting Friday.' *Given you to*. Mel didn't much care for the expression. 'He just wants you to do general housework. He'll explain more fully this afternoon.' She indicated that the interview was at an end. 'You'd better go and get kitted up now. The girls will be waiting for you.'

'Kitted up?'

Janet Graham regarded the T-shirt Mel was wearing with disapproval. The black outfit had still smelt strongly of curry even after a second wash and had been consigned to the bin. This morning she was wearing a very old sweatshirt that bore the logo of a famous fashion house and a pair of jeans. Standard, classless wear. 'The only advertising my girls carry is the agency name. A uniform is provided, but you are responsible for keeping it clean. Oh, and you'd better let Accounts have your tax form and an address when you have a moment.'

'Yes, Mrs Graham.' She considered asking about the procedure if another client tipped curry all over her. But she had been dismissed. It was exactly like being back at school, Mel thought, and tried not to dwell on just how much she had loathed school.

Ten minutes later she was heading for her first job in a bright yellow mini-van, attired in the agency's distinctive yellow and black striped sweatshirt, black polyester trousers and a snappy yellow and black quartered baseball cap that bore the legend 'Happy to Help'. Last night she had dreamed about making an impression on Jack Wolfe. Dressed like a worker bee, she couldn't fail to.

Paddy and Sharon were bright, lively and inquisitive. 'Why are you working as a cleaner?' Paddy asked her, realizing immediately that she wasn't the usual run of cleaning staff taken on by Mrs Graham. She told them that she was an actress. Resting. They weren't particularly impressed.

'What've you been in, then?'

At something of a loss, Mel invited them to guess, and before they arrived at their destination she had been placed in minor roles in two long-running soaps, one of which she had actually starred in for years, but not as Melanie Devlin, and as the tiresome teenage daughter in an advertisement for frozen food. This humbling assessment of her likely talent was far from flattering and she found herself wondering whether Jack Wolfe had been kinder. Then she caught herself. Mr Jack Wolfe undoubtedly had more important things to do than think about the girl he employed as a cleaner. And she had more important things to think about than him.

But to divert attention from herself she asked Paddy and Sharon about their families.

Mel rang the bell promptly at two that afternoon, her heart giving an odd erratic little beat as she waited, remembering the steel-grey eyes, the jolt of something indescribable that had seemed to arc right through her when he had touched her. Then she gave herself a good mental shaking. His eyes were nothing to do with her. He had called the agency because, looking around his flat after she had gone, he had been impressed with her work. It was a compliment to her professionalism, she thought. To how well she was playing her role. The perfect detached, professional domestic . . .

Jack Wolfe opened the door wearing nothing but a short towelling robe tied carelessly around his waist, his well-groomed hair now dishevelled from the shower. For a moment Mel felt anything but detached as her eyes fastened on the sprinkling of dark hair across his tanned chest where the robe hung loose. And she had stopped thinking anything coherent.

Her appearance seemed to leave him equally bereft of speech. But not for long. 'You – er – had better come in, Melanie.' Then, 'I'm glad to see you're more suitably costumed for the part today.'

Having to wear the wretched clothes was bad enough, but to be the butt of his mordant humour was the pits. 'The only thing this costume is suitable for is playing a bee in *Babes in the Wood*,' she said, with feeling, immediately forgetting her determination to be the perfect professional.

'Well, maybe you'll get lucky this Christmas.'

She smiled through gritted teeth, curling her toes in her DMs to stop herself from slapping him with a

cloth, still damp from her last job. Apparently unaware of Mel's irritation, he stepped aside to let her
into his apartment. So much for detached.

'I've brought back your clothes,' she said. She'd
taken them with her that morning assuming that
someone else would drop them off, either at his
home or office.

He glanced at the bag she was carrying, then at her
face. 'I do still wear them occasionally,' he assured
her.

'Do you, Mr Wolfe?' she enquired, not bothering
to disguise her disbelief. His sharp look suggested
that he was unused to his word being queried, at least
by his employees. But if he chose to make personal
comments about her clothes, she felt quite at liberty
to return the compliment. Ditching the detached
professional persona, she rewrote her part as
saucy, disrepectful, a 'treasure' who had to be humoured. Or, more likely, sacked. *Please.* 'When?' she
asked.

'I'm renovating a cottage near Henley.'

'Personally?' But she didn't have to ask. *The
mingled scent of sweat and pine, the straining muscles
and hair feathered by the wind . . .*

'Who is it, Jack?' A woman's voice drifted from the
interior of the apartment and Mel, instead of relief at
this distraction, felt something else, some feeling that
until then had been entirely alien to her. She could
scarcely believe it. It was jealousy, bile-green and just
as nasty. Oh, good grief.

Until that moment she had simply flirted with a

88

minor need to dress up in her best frock when she returned his laundry so that he would acknowledge his mistake, realize that he had been wrong about her, had been too damned condescending with his ten pound note . . . She hadn't thought beyond that. Richard had seen it, but she had dismissed his concern. Used to flirting with amusing young men who treated her with a great deal of respect, she hadn't seriously considered what a risk this man might be . . .

And as she felt the heat crawl along her cheek-bones, she finally understood what had kept her mind fixated on the man, drawn her thoughts back to him as she had drifted into sleep. His contained masculinity, the dangerous edge to his intellectual muscle was an invitation to the unwary. She had wanted him at her feet, she realized. She had wanted him at her feet so that she could walk away the winner.

Winner? Was she mad? This man had never been at any woman's feet. Yet the challenge was almost irresistible.

Resist, her subconscious intervened with a hurried warning. *Don't get involved. You'll regret it.*

But he had already turned away from her. 'It's just the new cleaner,' he said, and Mel's sharp intake of breath went unnoticed as he headed towards the spiral staircase. *Just the new cleaner?* Well, Melanie Beaumont, she thought, that puts you very firmly in your place. And another black mark firmly against Mr Wolfe's name.

Resist? What was there to resist? He had to be the

most resistible man she had ever met. Probably.

'The cleaner?' A woman appeared in her line of vision. She, too, was a head-turner, built like a crane, tall and angular, with too much bone for real beauty. Mel knew instinctively that the camera would love her. But she wasn't an actress or she would have recognized her, so she had to be a model.

She glanced at Mel, not seeing beyond the hideous black and yellow uniform and not bothering to hide her disdain for anyone who earned her living in such a fashion. Mel, not in the least bothered on her own part, nevertheless fumed on behalf of her new colleagues who didn't have any choice in the matter.

Jack, his back to the girl, didn't notice. 'Make some coffee, will you, Caro, and look after Mel while I get some clothes on?' He didn't wait for Caro's reply, but disappeared up the circular staircase, giving them both a clear view of a pair of large feet, strong calves, a flash of well-muscled thighs . . .

Mel looked hurriedly away. 'I'll make the coffee,' she offered.

Caro, aware of Mel's reaction, smiled with the supreme confidence of a woman who is in possession of what every other woman wants. 'The kitchen is through there,' she said, with a gesture so practised that Mel knew she had been right. The woman was a catwalk model, 'super' class. And as if to confirm the fact she folded herself in a soft leather armchair with the sinuous grace of a cat. 'I'm sure you're far more at home there than I am.'

'Undoubtedly,' Mel said, but under her breath.

Cooking was, for her, a pleasure. Caro, all skin and bone, probably lived on lemon juice and raw vegetables. Ready washed and shredded from a supermarket, she thought, irritably.

Jack Wolfe wasted no time dressing, and was still fastening the links into his cuffs as he came back down the stairs. Caro, curled up in an armchair, didn't bother to look up from the magazine she was reading. Melanie was already working in the kitchen. And there was no scent of coffee. Caro, he decided, was getting just a bit above herself, a little too confident. A bad sign.

'I see you've already made a start,' he said, automatically smiling at Mel as he walked into the kitchen. 'I had intended to sit down with you and discuss what needs to be done, but you obviously don't need telling.'

'No, I don't, and since you're paying for my time I thought I'd better get on.' She was making a performance of wiping down the already immaculate work surfaces so she didn't have to look at him. He noticed that in the same detached way that he noticed everything. Body language told the truth even when people were lying. 'Unless there's anything special you want me to do?' she added, when he didn't speak.

'Special?' he prompted, willing her to turn around. He wanted to see her face. No, not her face, her eyes. They were grey, but there was nothing ordinary about them. They shimmered like watered silk and he had the oddest feeling that he'd seen them somewhere before. On television perhaps? He didn't have

91

a set at the flat, but there was one down at the cottage. He'd bought it for Lisette. Perhaps Tom would like it, he thought. Or then again, perhaps Tom had enough distractions already.

'Shopping, that sort of thing,' she said, still keeping her back turned towards him.

'Oh. I see. Well, yes. I suppose you could keep the fridge stocked for me, pick up my dry cleaning, that sort of thing. I'll organize a float for you. Other than that, just keep the place looking the way you left it the other day. It looked like . . .' *Like home. That was what he had been going to say.* 'Can you cook?' he said, abruptly changing the subject.

'Of course I can cook.' She spun round but, on the point of declaring precisely how talented she was in the kitchen, Melanie realized what was behind the question and, assailed by an unpleasant vision of herself rustling up romantic little dinners for him to share with the pared-to-the-bone, uncluttered beauty of Caro, she rapidly changed her mind. 'Beefburgers. Fish fingers. Pizza.' She ticked them off on her fingers. 'Anything you like,' she declared.

Jack Wolfe was regarding her with a slightly quizzical expression. He was back in pin-striped broadcloth, safer in his clothes, but still disturbing. 'I assume that is frozen pizza?'

'Well, yes.' She switched on a look of surprise, as if unaware that there was any other kind. 'But I always put on a few extra olives. It makes such a difference, don't you think?'

'How very adventurous of you. I would never have

thought of that.' Quite suddenly Melanie wasn't quite sure who was kidding whom and it occurred to her that Jack Wolfe was not a man to fall easily for a bluff. 'Well, I'll leave you to it.'

'Will you be here on Wednesday?' Then, realizing that this sounded just a little too eager, she added, 'I mean, how will I get in?'

'I will give you a key, Melanie.' And, fitting the word to the deed, he took a key from his pocket. About to put it on the countertop beside him, he changed his mind. Without quite knowing why, he reached out and took her hand in his. It was small and unexpectedly white. She couldn't have been doing this job for long. Was that why she was nervous? Because now he was touching her he could tell that she was quite noticeably shaking. All that cheek was an act, he realized with something of a shock; she wasn't nearly as tough as she would have him believe. And, placing the key in her palm, he wrapped her fingers about it, holding it there with both his hands.

Melanie swallowed. She had not imagined the electricity. His touch was like summer lightning, wildfire that ran between them, and as he continued to hold on to her hand, his eyes too seemed to heat from within. They were not, as she had first thought, a steely grey, but were flecked with warm gold lights that seemed to bore into her very soul, and for a moment she was certain that he felt the same charge of excitement. Then steeply hooded lids came down, cloaking his feelings.

'Guard it with your life, Melanie.'

The key was warm from his body, but his hands were cool. Long, slender fingers wrapped around her warm hand and the warmer key.

Hidden layers of heat, like the hidden layers of meaning she sensed behind everything he said. Or was that everything *she* said? Whichever it was, it was horribly disturbing and she wanted it to stop.

'Don't worry. I'll be careful with it.' And she pulled her hand away, but it was shaking so much that she had to stuff it into her overall pocket so that he shouldn't see.

Careful. The word mocked her. No girl would abandon the pampered life she was used to on some ridiculous whim to clean up after a man like Jack Wolfe. Not if she was careful.

'Good.' And he turned to the alarm control. 'I'll just show you how the alarm system works.'

'That would be a good idea.' *Alarm. Warning. Red light*.

Layers and layers of meaning, she thought as she watched while he demonstrated the alarm system.

'Well, you picked that up quickly enough,' he said, after she had demonstrated her mastery of the system a few minutes later. Considering her inability to concentrate, it was perhaps as well that it was the same model as the one installed in her own apartment, so that all she had had to memorize was the number. But she didn't say so. It seemed unlikely that the average cleaner, or out-of-work actress, would have a state of-the-art security system fitted to her home.

Nevertheless she resented the suggestion that her quickness was surprising. 'Just because I'm cleaning for a living, it doesn't follow that I have sawddust for brains.'

He glanced back over his shoulder at her, a frown creasing his forehead. 'I don't recall suggesting that you had. Some people just seem to find these things tricky. Caro has had the police out three or four times setting this off by mistake.' And for just a moment their gaze intersected the same space, colliding in a conspiracy of thought that excluded Caro. It was as if their minds had touched, like a spark leaping a gap to complete an electrical circuit.

And it wasn't just their minds. Mel was standing close enough to identify the brand of soap he had used in the shower, close enough to touch the skin drawn tight across the hard knuckles of his hand still raised to the alarm . . .

For a moment she couldn't breathe as her chest tightened and something altogether strange happened around her midriff, an odd kind of melting that seemed to go right on down, weakening her thighs, sapping their will to hold her up. This time she was the one to drop her lashes, desperate to block out the intensity of that look. Then, without warning, he peeled away from her, putting the width of the room between them.

'Caroline,' he snapped, as he gathered his briefcase from the table, 'if you want a lift into town you'll have to come now.'

* * *

95

Caroline's mindless chatter normally washed over him. Today it seemed as irritating as a buzz-saw and it was with relief that he dropped her at her gym. But his temper improved dramatically once he reached his office.

'Are you sure about this, Mike? It couldn't just be coincidence?'

Mike Palmer had been Jack's CEO for a long time and he understood his caution. 'You're always telling me that there's no such thing as coincidence in business. I didn't believe he'd do it, but he's taken the bait, Jack. Now all you've got to do is play the line a little and then you can reel him in.'

'You make it sound easy. He's hooked, maybe, but Tamblin's been playing this game for a long time; he'll be away at the first suggestion of a trap. But it's a pity about young Latham.' He crossed to the window, watched the clown working the afternoon crowd. 'I feel responsible – '

Mike joined him. 'You're not, Jack. If he'd behaved reasonably when his father's company was taken over instead of trying to cause trouble . . . But then, he always was a drama queen. He should have stuck to what he knew.'

'I know, but he's young and he's hurting. And he's in bad company.'

'He went looking for it, Jack. He deserves everything that's coming to him.'

Jack looked at him sideways. 'Have a care, Mike, you're beginning to sound as callous as me.'

'I've been listening to you long enough; some of it

was bound to rub off eventually.' He nodded down at the square. 'The only reason he's down there now is so that he can keep a watch on who comes and goes from your office. If you hadn't by chance seen him getting into Greg Tamblin's car . . .'

'I know, I know. Two people in the same place the same time . . . a chance in a million.' The same kind of chance that dictated that a man should have a heart attack and fall against the wheel of his car, sending it straight for a bus queue, when for a hundred yards in either direction the pavement was empty . . . He watched the clown for a few more seconds before turning away and crossing to his desk. 'But why should they have taken any more precautions? Latham must have watched me being driven away from the office before he called Tamblin to hand over the latest information he'd found in my wastebin. He couldn't have anticipated a bomb alert, streets being closed off . . . that I would decide to walk back to the office. Chance,' he said, bleakly, 'unlike coincidence, is a force I believe in.'

'You've never left anything to chance in your life.'

'No?' Not in business, perhaps. Business was too important to be left in the lap of the gods. 'Well, let's not this time. I think it's time to throw our shark a red herring; we wouldn't want him to think it was too easy, would we? He might get suspicious.' He touched the intercom. 'Mary? Get hold of Gus Jamieson for me, will you.' He grinned at Mike. 'I feel an urgent need for an island holiday. Or was that a holiday island?'

* * *

'Greg?'

'What is it, Richard? I'm busy right now.'

'Not too busy to hear this. I've had an extraordinary piece of luck.'

'Really. Not too extraordinary, I hope. I distrust luck that seems too fortuitous.'

'Well, it wasn't all luck. I had to work quite hard to get a result, but the thing is, a girl I know is working for Jack Wolfe. Cleaning his apartment.'

'Well, that is certainly interesting. Just how well do you know her'?'

'Not *that* well, Greg. And I don't want to do anything that will leave her vulnerable.'

'You don't want to, but if you have to, you will.'

'You know me too well, Greg,' he said, his voice laughing for the telephone, while his face remained totally impassive. 'I just thought you'd like to know that if the need arises I'll be able to get into Wolfe's apartment.

A few mornings later Sharon took a detour on the way to their first job.

'Where are we going?' Melanie asked, surprised. Their time-sheets were cut to the bone and even a quick stop to buy a bag of potatoes was asking for trouble.

'We're going to pick up Paddy's kids from her mother-in-law.' She said it aggressively, daring Melanie to make a fuss.

Paddy looked uncomfortable. 'I'm sorry, Mel, but

she's got a hospital appointment today and can't take care of them.'

'Don't apologize to her,' Sharon said, angrily. 'She doesn't know what day of the week it is.'

'When I left home this morning it was Thursday,' Melanie said, mildly, before turning to Paddy. 'What's the matter with your mother-in-law?'

'She needs a hip replacement. She's been waiting months for an appointment to see the specialist. Heaven help me when she gets a date for the operation.'

'Couldn't you find a child-minder?'

'What planet do you live on, girl?' Sharon was clearly in no mood to take prisoners this morning.

'Don't tease her, Shar. She doesn't understand.'

She? Girl? Whatever had happened to the two good-hearted women she worked with?. 'Hey, Paddy, Sharon, I'm here. Talk to me, tell me what's going on. Maybe I can help.'

'You? What could you do?'

'Unless I know the problem, nothing.'

'Look, there'd be no point in working if we had to pay a child-minder,' Sharon said. 'We just don't earn enough, OK?'

'I was only – '

Paddy touched her arm. 'Don't worry about it, Mel. It's not your problem.'

But it was clearly a problem for Paddy, a big problem. She was chewing her lower lip to shreds. 'But if your mother-in-law is having a hip replacement she'll be out of action for weeks, months . . .'

99

'I'll sort something out. But today is difficult. It was short notice and there just wasn't anybody I could ask . . . Just don't say anything back in the office, all right?'

'Why not? If Mrs Graham knew about your problems maybe she could do something to help. You can't be the only one who has difficulties with childcare.'

'The only thing Mrs Graham would do,' Sharon interjected, 'is give Paddy the push. She's already been warned once about bringing the children to work. And one warning is all you get.'

Mel was shocked. 'You mean Mrs Graham has threatened to dismiss her?'

Sharon, realizing that Melanie was so innocent it was almost painful, turned to Paddy with a grin. 'Did Mrs Graham threaten to dismiss you, darling?' she asked, in mocking mimicry of Mel's perfectly rounded vowels.

Mel wasn't offended; she knew she was out of her depth in this situation. 'Is she crazy? You both work like heroes; she couldn't afford to let you go.'

'She hasn't a clue, has she?' Paddy said, indulgently.

'Shouldn't be allowed out by herself,' Sharon agreed. Melanie looked from one to the other.

'The girl before you had two children,' Paddy continued, more gently. 'One of them was taken ill at school and she had to leave a job and take her home. Her cards were waiting for her next morning.'

'But that's monstrous. You've rights – '

'Yeah, yeah. Sure,' Sharon said. 'Wash your mouth out with soap before you go back to the office girl. Janet Graham can smell dirty words like "rights" on your breath . . .'

CHAPTER 5

Jack Wolfe stirred at the sound of a key in the lock. Caroline. He stifled a groan. Jet-lagged and bone-weary from crossing the Atlantic three times in ten days, he found that the idea of entertaining Caroline did nothing to revive him. If she had been the kind of woman content to slip quietly into bed beside him, a warm, comforting body against his while he drifted in and out of sleep, he would have welcomed her presence. Just how unwelcome her presence was right now would have shocked her; it came as something of a surprise to him.

Beautiful, sophisticated, emotionally cool, Caroline had seemed until recently his ideal lover. She had no use for meaningless declarations of love; she would much rather have a diamond pendant, and diamond pendants were so much easier to give. However, he preferred a time and place of his own choosing, especially since on this occasion he hadn't had the time for an expedition to a jewellery store. He hoped the consolation of a week in the Caribbean would be sufficient recompense.

He rolled over and lay back against the pillows, waiting for her to bound up the stairs. Bound? Not quite the right word to describe the way Caro moved. Except perhaps when there was the prospect of some little treasure. Well, she *was* beautiful and a man had to pay for his pleasures, one way or another.

But she didn't bound, or even glide gracefully up the stairs. Instead she went into the kitchen and drew some water. He frowned. Miss Caroline Hickey made a virtue out of her lack of domesticity, a virtue he tended to encourage.

There were small noises from the living room, as if she was moving about. He drew his brows together, trying to work out what they could be. Then the strains of the Mozart Clarinet Concerto filled the room. Caroline? Playing classical music? Curiouser and curiouser. Suddenly wide awake, he eased himself off the bed, wrapped a dressing gown about himself and leaned against the polished rail, wondering what else she might do that was totally out of character. Pour herself a large glass of Scotch, perhaps? Make a cheese and pickle sandwich?

No. Nor had she been making coffee. The water had been used to fill a tall jug with a bunch of bright yellow daisies which now stood on a low table behind the sofa. They looked perfect, a vivid splash of colour against the dark, heavy wood, the stark whiteness of the walls. Well, anything Caro did would make a perfect statement. But somehow he didn't associate her with a flower as simple as the daisy. A single spray of black orchids was more her style. And if he was any judge of human nature, she would expect to be the one on the receiving end.

Somewhat unnerved by this apparent shift in her values, he leaned over the rail to see what else she might be doing to surprise him and suddenly the yellow daisies made perfect sense. It was Wednesday. And it wasn't Caro, but his very own Cinderella who had disturbed him, wandering around his apartment totally unaware that she was being observed.

He watched as she twitched the curtains into place, gathered up the things he had abandoned when everything had gone ballistic in Chicago and he'd had to chase across the Atlantic at a moment's notice. A heavy glass, the brandy evaporated and sticky in the bottom, a book face-down on the table where he had left it when the phone had rung late on Monday night.

She had her back to him, yet he knew she had turned the book over, was reading the blurb on the back. Then she flicked it open. Her spiky brown hair was tucked up into her cap and as she lowered her head to read, he was suddenly intimately acquainted with the smooth line of her neck as it curved into her nape. The skin was smooth and white and his hand seemed to tingle with anticipation as, in his mind, his fingers stroked its sweet length before cupping it and turning her towards him so that her head fell back and thick dark lashes drifted down over her eyes as she offered her soft mouth to him. His body stirred at the picture his mind was offering.

Dark lashes? Soft mouth? Where on earth had

those images come from? His jet-lag must be worse than he'd thought.

Unaware that she was observed, or of the effect she was having on her observer, she continued to read, so deeply engrossed in his book that for a moment he wondered if she might decide to stretch out on the sofa, put her feet up and settle down for the afternoon. The possibility of catching her out made him smile.

But no, after a moment she gave a little sigh, closed the book with obvious regret and put it away on the bookshelf. Then she saw the newspaper, folded back to the article featuring his latest corporate clean-up and thrown down on the sofa with his overnight bag. It was a distorted view of what had happened to the company, dwelling on the pain rather than emphasizing the gain; typical of Greg Tamblin's sneering style. He was used to it and normally he didn't care, or at least not enough to do anything about it. But as Melanie picked it up and saw the headline, his smile faded. He didn't want her reading a piece of scurrilous journalism and taking it at face value.

'I like the daisies, Miss Devlin,' he said. 'Where did they come from? Your garden?'

Melanie, believing herself to be quite alone and deep in contemplation of the article about Jack Wolfe, jumped spectacularly. The paper flew out of her hands and landed in a mess at her feet, and her heart, always in a bit of a dither when she let herself into Jack Wolfe's apartment – desperately hoping that he wouldn't be there, then disappointed when she got her wish — made up its mind and behaved like a high-speed lift in a hurry to reach the penthouse. Jack Wolfe, leaning against the polished chrome rail of the mezzanine, all black silk dressing gown and bare legs, was enough to make any girl break out in a dither.

'I'm sorry, did I startle you?' he enquired, with just a touch of malicious humour.

'Startle me?' she exclaimed. 'You could have given me a heart attack.'

He gave her a cool, provoking look. It conveyed, without words, that in his opinion such an event was unlikely this side of a thousand years. 'I thought I heard the kettle,' he said. 'Is there any chance of a cup of tea?'

'Well, you thought wrong,' she declared, indignantly. 'But if you'd like to make that an order?'

'Consider it done,' he snapped, irritated that she was always on the defensive, always hiding herself from him. Even now, the baseball cap shadowed her face. Why on earth did she have to wear the ghastly thing the whole time? But as she crossed the living room, she suddenly stopped and looked up and he thought he saw a flicker of concern cross her features.

'Are you sick?' she asked.

'Sick?'

She gestured vaguely at the rare disorder and said, 'You're not usually in bed at this time of day.'

'Not usually,' he agreed. 'At least, not during working hours.' And he discovered that he enjoyed the pink flush that darkened her cheeks as it suddenly occurred to her that there might be a quite different reason why he was in bed in the middle of the afternoon.

'Is that *one* cup of tea?' she enquired, tartly.

'Unless you'd care to join me? It wouldn't be the first time you've tested my bed springs in the line of work, would it?'

Lord! What on earth had made him say that?

Her lips parted on a little gasp of outrage and he waited for the torrent of abuse he had almost certainly provoked. Certainly deserved.

Her self-control was impressive, although why she should bother when he deserved everything she might throw at him, verbal and physical, intrigued him. Impressive, but not easy. Her fingers were curled up into tight little fists while she struggled to keep her tongue between her teeth. But he was right about the mouth. Soft, full lips. When had he noticed them? His memory, as if it had been waiting for just such a query, immediately supplied the moment. He had been showing her how the alarm worked and she had looked up at him . . .

'How *is* your brother?' she asked, so sweetly that she could have been trickled out of a spoon.

'You haven't seen him since the party?' She didn't bother to dignify that with an answer. 'It was Tom who suggested I should employ you on a regular basis, you know. You made quite an impression on him.'

'That wasn't me, that was the hangover cure I gave him.' She moved towards the hi-fi.

'Don't turn it off.'

'It disturbed you.'

'No, Melanie. *You* disturbed me.' Rather more than she realized, although why, he couldn't have said. If a girl had gone out of her way to look unattractive she couldn't have made a better job of it. Even the possibility of a decent figure was muffled by the awful uniform she wore. Only her eyes danced and shimmered, promising . . . more. And she had the kind of mouth that could give a man seriously sinful ideas. But since she didn't use so much as a trace of lipstick that clearly wasn't her intent. Which begged the question, if he reacted like that when she wasn't trying . . .? He stopped. Some questions were better left unasked. Some answers a man was better off not knowing. 'Rustle me up some breakfast and I'll forgive you,' he said, briskly, turning away.

'Breakfast? It's two o'clock in the afternoon.'

'For you, maybe. I've flown to Chicago and back in the last twenty-four hours and it plays hell with the body clock.'

'And I woke you. I'm *really* sorry.' *Sorry that she hadn't got stuck in with the vacuum cleaner the minute she arrived and made a class job of it.* 'Shall I bring it up on a tray?'

The temptation to say yes, for her insolence, and then to tumble her down on the bed, remove that ghastly uniform and discover for himself what had so excited Tom flickered at the back of his mind. There was something secret about her that seemed to challenge him, and the idea of Miss Melanie Devlin on a tray was suddenly very tempting.

But he had learned not to complicate his life and an affair with a valued employee was a recipe for disaster. It was bound to end in tears and a parting of the ways. A good secretary, or a good cleaner, was worth a lot more than fleeting sexual satisfaction. Caro might not be a warm human being, but the ground rules of their relationship were clearly laid out. It couldn't last forever; eventually all women needed more than he was able to give them. He had learned that with pain and heartache and bitter regret.

But for the time being the relationship suited him, suited her, and he wasn't about to make a fool of himself over a pair of lips that promised the earth. The earth was something he'd made a conscious decision to do without.

Yet as he glanced down at Mel, reminding himself of the unflattering way the black trousers flapped around her legs, the revolting sweatshirt that could have been designed specifically to keep lustful clients at bay, he was swept by a hollow ache for something forever lost.

Then he realized she was still waiting for an answer. 'No, don't bother. I'm awake now. I'll take a shower and be down by the time it's ready.'

As Melanie bent to gather up the newspaper she had dropped, the headline that had first caught her attention leapt out at her. 'WOLFE SLAUGHTERS ANOTHER CORPORATE LAMB.'

It was a crass headline, but she sympathized with whoever had been on the receiving end of Jack Wolfe's mauling. Whenever she encountered him she ended up feeling rather like a neat little row of frilled lamb cutlets herself.

Tested his bedsprings, indeed. Maybe she should complain to Mrs Graham about sexual harassment. She pulled a face as she picked up the kettle and took it to the sink. Fat chance of any help from that quarter. Janet Graham, she had quickly realized, would do anything to keep Jack Wolfe happy. Complaints about him wouldn't be tolerated. In fact, Mel had the feeling that Mrs Graham would happily leap at the chance of getting rid of her if she could do it without offending her most favoured client. Well, she wasn't in the business of making Mrs Graham happy.

She smiled as she turned off the tap and plugged in the kettle. On the contrary. If things went according to plan, she was shortly going to make Mrs Graham very angry indeed. She could hardly wait.

She was still smiling when she took a packet of bacon from the fridge and, using a small knife, stuck the point into the plastic and began to slit it open.

'There isn't any soap.'

As she swung around the knife slipped and jabbed into the base of her thumb and she let out one single but telling expletive. 'Did you have to creep up on me like that?' she demanded.

He regarded her thoughtfully. 'You should take something for your nerves, Mel.'

'There's nothing wrong with my nerves. It's

just – ' She stopped before she said something stupid.

'It's just what?' *You. It's just you. Can't you see that?* Apparently he couldn't, because when she didn't answer he simply shrugged and said, 'Try taking some vitamin B. Here, let me look at that.'

'There's no need,' she said through gritted teeth, backing away. But the countertop dug into her back and she had no escape as he took her hand, steering her across to a bank of drawers where the first aid box was kept.

Vitamin B? It would take a heck of a lot more than vitamin B to calm the butterflies stampeding across her abdomen, Melanie thought. It would take, at the very least, a long contemplative trek across the foothills of the Himalayas. Years and years of navel-gazing at the feet of some guru. Or at the very least on some deserted beach.

It was what she should have done instead of listening to Richard. Maybe it wasn't too late. The minute she got out of here she'd go straight to the travel agent and put ten thousand miles between them. It would be a whole lot safer than a single layer of black silk that wasn't tied with any particular determination about his naked body.

Except that she had already embarked on another plan, one that couldn't be abandoned just because she was having a little trouble keeping her hormones in check.

'I can manage,' she said, tugging at her hand. 'It's nothing. Really.'

111

'Be still,' he said, dabbing the small nick with an antiseptic wipe. You can't be too careful.' *You can if 'careful' means being touched by Jack Wolfe.* 'Here, help me open this.'

He held the individually wrapped plaster in his free hand. To do what he wanted, she would have to brace her hand against his. They were standing very close and as the sharp antiseptic smell faded she was aware of the scent of his skin. It was that special warm-from-bed scent shared by lovers. Intimate, arousing. From somewhere deep inside she heard her hormones groan.

Her eyes were level with his throat and Melanie discovered that she did not need to touch him to know just how it would feel to rub her face against the dark shadow of his beard. It was as if her body was in some way sensitized to his. She simply had to look at his throat and she could anticipate the texture of his skin, the rasp of the stubble, exactly how his hair would feel as the tips of her fingers slid through it. And it was a two-way connection. She knew how his fingers would feel against her face, her shoulders, her breasts; they puckered invitingly beneath the thick, muffling cloth of her sweatshirt as if his touch were real and not just inside her head. She wanted him so much that it hurt.

As if he sensed her quickening, the way the air seemed to stir, thickly, around them, Jack turned his head to look down into her face. For a moment nothing happened and then, it appeared to Melanie, the cold steel of his eyes seemed to soften, melt to quicksilver. And she decided there was nothing wrong with her nerves. Only with her muscles. They seemed to be dissolving, very slowly.

'For God's sake take it,' Jack grated. *Oh, yes, he felt it too!* She heard the reluctant sexual bite in his voice . . . she might be in imminent danger of losing her senses, but she was not alone. 'Melanie . . .'

She quickly caught the corner of the wrapper and ripped it down, dropping the paper and tugging the plaster free. Minimal contact. But the damage had already been done. The dull ache that had invaded her abdomen might be strange and new, but she didn't need telling that there was only one man who could ease it. Or what it would take.

'I can manage,' she protested.

He didn't bother to argue with her. He momentarily released her hand and, taking the dressing from her, peeled back the protective stickers. A tiny crimson spot of blood had oozed from the wound and for a moment he seemed transfixed by it. Then he wiped it away with the pad of his thumb before bending to touch the spot with his lips, kissing it better before sticking the dressing down, as if to seal forever the spot where his mouth had touched her.

'There,' he said. 'All better.' As if she were a child. But as he straightened she realized that he wasn't smiling at all, but that he was suddenly very still, that if she didn't move, say something to stop him, he would kiss her mouth. In a very adult way. And she knew she couldn't let that happen no matter how much she wanted it. For him it would be a quick tumble with a girl who just happened to be . . . handy. He didn't want *her*. He didn't know *her*.

'There's soap . . .' she said, stepping back somewhat abruptly. 'In the cupboard in the bathroom.' Her voice was shaking horribly. 'I put it there on Monday.'

'Soap!' His whole body stiffened.

'You were looking for soap.'

It was a moment before he spoke. 'Yes. So I was.'

'I'll get your breakfast.' She made a move towards the cooker but he was still holding her hand, and as she moved his grip tightened.

'No.'

'What?'

'I said no, Melanie.' He dropped her hand. 'Forget it. Go home. Have the afternoon on me. I won't tell Mrs Graham if you don't.'

'But what about . . .?' *She was going to argue? Was she mad?* A lamb didn't argue with a wolf. Not when the wolf was hungry. She gathered herself. 'Yes. Of course. I'm sorry I disturbed you.'

She was halfway to the door when he said, 'Where did the daisies come from?'

'Daisies?' Then she remembered. 'Oh, an old gentleman I did a job for this morning picked them from his garden for me. I won't be home until late and it seemed a shame to let them die. I hope you don't mind giving them a home.'

Home until late? Was she going straight out after work? Who with? He stared at her for a moment, then shook his head as if to clear it. 'No. No, of course not.'

114

After she had gone, Jack Wolfe walked slowly back upstairs, peeled off his dressing gown and stepped into the shower, letting the sharp needles of water pound at him. It was a long time since he'd felt the need of a cold shower and in the event the effect was negligible.

'Fizz! I didn't expect you so soon.' Melanie had just been going out when the doorbell rang. 'Have you brought it?'

Fizz held up a thick manila envelope. 'As requested.'

Mel peered out in to the hall. 'Didn't you bring Juliet with you?'

'No, I told Luke I had to come up to town for a dental check-up, so he's babysitting. I thought it would keep him busy.' She tilted her head to one side. 'I got the impression that you didn't want Luke to know about this. Or did I misunderstand you?'

'You weren't wrong. Not that I don't want to see him, it's just . . . well . . .'

'You're up to something you don't want him to know about. It's all right, Mel, I do understand.' Fizz noticed her jacket. 'I've come at a bad time, you're just going out.

'No, I was just dashing to the shops, any time will do.' Just as well she hadn't just been dashing to work, although it might have been fun to see how long it would have taken her sister to penetrate her disguise. She shrugged out of her jacket and flung it over a chair. 'Would you like some coffee?'

'Please.'

'Come on through to the kitchen while I make it.'

Fizz perched on a stool while Mel filled the kettle.

'How is everyone? Any news from Beau and Diana?' she asked, politely.

'None whatever beyond the fact that they're cruising somewhere in the Caribbean.'

'And Luke?'

'Ah. About Luke. I feel that I should warn you that Luke has decided that since you haven't gone away he is going to throw a surprise party for your twenty-first.'

'But he gave me one for my eighteenth, Fizz.'

'A surprise party?'

'No, just a fairly simple, straightforward affair, thank heavens.' If three hundred people in Sydney's finest hotel could be considered straightforward, or simple. 'I hate surprise parties. It's all right for men, but just imagine if you hadn't had your hair done? Or your nail polish was chipped?' She tucked her uncharactistically short and unpolished nails out of sight.

But Fizz was smiling sympathetically. 'My feelings precisely. Don't worry, I'll give you plenty of warning. Unless of course you're planning to go away before then?'

'Well, do you know, Fizz, I have been giving serious consideration to a trek through the foothills of the Himlayas . . .' Her sister laughed. 'No, honestly. Then I had a long lie down in a quiet room and eventually the feeling passed.' She turned away to get

116

a couple of mugs from the cupboard. 'The threat of a surprise party might be all it takes to revive my plans.'

'I sympathize, honestly, but I know he misses you. Everyone misses you.'

'Good heavens, it's only been a few weeks. I would have come down to Winterbourne but I really have been busy – '

'So I gather.' She put her hand on the thick manila envelope she had laid on the breakfast bar beside her. 'Are you going to tell me exactly what you've been busy at?'

'Is that the information about the crèche that Luke set up in the Enterprise Park?' Mel replied, avoiding the question.

'Yes, everything you asked for. I got his secretary to copy it when Luke was out of the office. Don't worry, I didn't tell her it was for you.' She paused. 'What's all the interest?' She gave Melanie a long look. 'Are you thinking of booking a place?'

'Booking a place?' Fizz raised a her brows just a fraction and Mel blushed as she realized what her sister was suggesting. 'Oh, for goodness' sake, Fizz,' she protested.

'I just wondered.' She gave an innocent little shrug. 'It's not exactly unheard of.' She hid a smile with difficulty. 'Juliet goes in with Luke sometimes. She loves it. And you said you've been busy. It isn't beyond the bounds of possibility that "busy" involved a man.'

'Isn't it?' Since her last meeting with Jack Wolfe it

117

seemed a very long way beyond.

Fizz, sensing she'd strayed inadvertently into dangerous waters, backed off. 'So, what's the sudden interest in crèches?' she asked.

'My interest is purely practical. I want to know how to go about starting one.'

'Starting one?' Fizz nearly fell off her stool. 'Where? For whom?'

'Is it difficult, Fizz? Are there lots of regulations? Can we get a grant to help with the start-up costs –'

'Whoa! Hold on there. One question at a time. And who is "we"?'

'Does it matter?'

Fizz regarded her thoughtfully. 'You know, maybe Luke is the best person for you to talk to about this after all. He's had hands-on experience, knows all the snags. I'll ask him to call in next time he's in town, shall I?' She picked up the envelope, made a move to leave . . .

'Fizz Devlin, don't you dare move from that stool!' Then, with a certain reserve. 'I really would rather Luke didn't know I'd asked about this.'

'Oh?' Fizz put down her coffee cup. 'You know, I'm sure I noticed a bottle of wine in your fridge. Shall we open it and you can tell me just what it is you're up to, little sister?'

'Up to?' Mel flushed.

'Mmm. Up to. As in . . .' Fizz slid off the stool and headed for the fridge, turning as she opened the door '. . . up to.' She took the bottle of wine from the fridge and set about opening it. 'No rush. In your own time. Or, of course,' she went on, idly, 'as I said, Luke would be happy to drop by . . .'

'Fizz!' Mel begged. 'You wouldn't! Please!'

'Glasses?' Mel opened a cupboard and took out two wine glasses. 'Do you have any cheese? I suddenly feel quite peckish.' And Fizz settled herself back on the kitchen stool and waited.

Mel took some cheese from the fridge, fetched the biscuit tin and then took a deep breath before turning round to face her sister. 'I've got a job, Fizz.'

'Really? I thought you'd turned down the sitcom?'

'What sitcom?' Melanie enquired softly, and it was Fizz's turn to colour.

'Oh, dear. That was careless of me.'

'Very.'

'Well, you know Luke. He likes to keep his finger on the pulse.'

'I know.' And heaven help her if he found out what she was doing. But it was vital that he didn't interfere now, not when she had come up with this marvellous plan. 'I don't want him to know a thing about this, Fizz. It's important to me. It's not anything to do with the theatre, you see. It's just an ordinary job.'

Fizz looked doubtful. 'Luke said you were thinking of doing something ordinary.'

'Yes, well, I'm doing it. Something very ordinary. I'm working as a cleaner, if you must know.' Fizz opened her mouth to say something, then obviously thought better of it and closed it again. 'Oh, for goodness' sake stop looking at me like that and pour out the wine. I'll tell all.' And she did. At least a slightly abridged version of her job that somehow entirely omitted to mention Jack Wolfe. Just in case Fizz had heard the name, she reasoned. After all, Luke was something of a City heavyweight himself. He would certainly know of him, have seen those awful headlines. He would probably object to his niece working for the man in any capacity. He would certainly object to her being employed as his cleaner.

'I don't understand what you think you'll get out of this,' Fizz said, when she had finished.

'Nothing. It's different, that's all. It started off as a kind of as a bet with this actor I worked with in Oz. Five hundred pounds goes to your charity if I win.'

'Oh, well, in that case carry on, you have my full support.'

'It was just for a month. To prove something . . . Then I began to see what was happening. I can't just walk away.'

'Tell me about it.'

Fizz listened sympathetically to Mel's story about Paddy's problems, about the way Janet Graham treated the women who worked for her, but finally she stirred. 'It's a rotten situation, Mel, but I really don't see what you can do. And frankly I don't think Mrs Graham sounds like the sort of woman to start a crèche for her staff.'

'She isn't. The thing is, Fizz, this plan of mine is a whole lot more than a crèche. That was the starting point . . .' She went on, outlining her ideas, her sister's eyes widening as she listened. 'You do understand, Fizz, don't you?' she said, when she had finished. 'I'm just playing at this for a bet; for women like Paddy and Sharon it's a battle every day of their lives just to survive. I can't just do nothing . . . it isn't right, is it?'

'No.' Fizz hesitated. 'No, it isn't right. These women are getting a very raw deal, but do be careful you don't make things worse than they already are. If Mrs Graham finds out that you're stirring things up you might find that you're all out of a job. This might be a game to you, Mel, but for the women you work with – '

A game? No. It was more than that. Far more. 'You don't have to spell it out, Fizz. I'll be careful.'

Fizz nodded. 'Well, I hope the information I've brought is a help and I'll see what else I can find out. I'll get one of those eager young reporters at the radio station researching the need for crèches in the workplace.' She gathered her things. 'And you don't have to worry, I won't tell Luke. Not because he'll fuss. Not because he'll descend on you and insist you give up this job of yours, but because he'll want to take it over and do it all for you.'

'Probably a lot better than I could.'

'Not necessarily. This is your idea, your plan and it's coming from your heart. To be honest, darling, I've never seen you quite so animated about anything.' She reached out and cradled her cheek in one hand. 'If it is just this?' she asked, searchingly.

'What else could it be?' Mel said quickly. 'This is real, Fizz. Not make-believe.'

Fizz tilted her head sideways slightly. 'Umm. Well, if you need any help, just whistle . . .'

'Thanks. You've been a brick.'

'. . . on one condition. You'll let Luke go ahead and organize this party for you.'

'Do I have a choice?'

'There's always a choice, Mel.'

Melanie grinned. 'What kind of party?'

'Anything you like,' Fizz said. 'All the works with a marquee on the lawn? A quiet family dinner? A picnic on the beach?' She paused, for a moment. 'A combination of all three, perhaps? Think about it for a day or two and let me know what you want and when and then I'll let Luke *think* he's organizing a surprise.'

'I don't have to think about it. Let's go with a picnic on the beach.'

'Whatever you say. Now, I'd better let you get on with your shopping.'

'Good grief, yes. I used to wonder why supermarkets stayed open so late. Now I know. I'll come down with you.' She grabbed her jacket. 'Have you seen Heather since the wedding?' she asked, as they made their way down in the lift.

'Mac bailed her out last week after a demonstration in Trafalgar Square and took her down to the cottage to stay with him and Claudia. Thankfully no one realized who she was so it didn't make the papers.'

'Poor kid.' Fizz glanced at her in surprise. 'I imagine getting into the papers was what she wanted. She'll make sure someone knows who she is next time.'

'You think it was a scream for attention?'

'Not a personal one. I imagine she just wants someone to remember that she's the daughter of a Gulf War hero, not some actor her widowed mother upped and married.'

'Melanie – '

'I'm sorry. But everyone seems to be forgetting how young Heather is. Diana and Edward are happy so that's all that matters. And I don't suppose she's got over that crush she had on Mac.'

'Dear God, Melanie, Mac must be nearly twenty years older than her. She's just a child.' Then, 'Oh.'

'Exactly. A child who's lost a much loved father, Fizz. Seeing her mother and Beau married is like her father dying all over again, don't you see? More than a funeral, more than a gravestone, it proves that he's gone, that he's never coming back. Mac was to some extent a substitute, I suppose, but he fell in love with Claudia. You can't blame her for loathing us all.'

She didn't wait for her sister to reply, but stepped forward and hailed a passing cab for Fizz, so that her sister shouldn't see the tears that threatened. That would be too ridiculous. And when she turned back to kiss her goodbye her smile was brilliant. 'She won't stay with Claudia and Mac for long, Fizz. She won't be able to bear it. Especially once she realizes that Claudia is pregnant.'

Fizz stared at her.

'I could be wrong, but didn't you think, at the wedding, that she had a special bloom? That Mac looked like a man walking a foot above the ground?'

★　★　★

123

Melanie was just putting the finishing touches to Jack Wolfe's kitchen when the front doorbell rang. It was Richard and he didn't wait to be invited in, but walked right by her into the apartment.

'Richard!' she exclaimed. 'You can't come in here.'

'Relax, Mel,' he said, with an easy grin. 'Jack Wolfe is in his office. I saw him arrive twenty minutes ago with his lawyer. He'll be hours.'

'That's not the point. You shouldn't be here.'

'Well, you haven't been by lately, so I thought I'd drop in on you and see how you are.'

'Check up on me, you mean. To make sure I'm really working.'

'There's no fooling you, darling.' Richard was wandering around the apartment, his eyes everywhere. 'You're right about this place. It's everything I would have expected.' He picked up a small bronze figure of a dancing girl, examined the signature before replacing it. 'Nice.'

He paused briefly before a large abstract work of art before turning to to take in the simple, uncluttered interior. Melanie didn't know why he had come, but she was uneasy. He seemed . . . hyped up.

'Richard, please. You really must go.'

He had come to a halt in the kitchen and now he turned to her. 'Aren't you even going to offer me a cup of coffee?'

'There isn't time. I've got five minutes and then I'm out of here.'

'Plenty of time for coffee. I'll make it.'

'No, Richard,' she said, desperately. 'Just go. Please.'

Her words finally seemed to sink in and he said, 'Oh, look, I'm sorry, Mel, you're right, this was stupid. I didn't mean to upset you. I just had this feeling that you might . . .'

'What?' He didn't answer and she blushed. 'You thought I might be here with Jack Wolfe. Well, thank you, Richard. As you can see, I'm quite alone, so you can go now.'

'I'm just worried about you, Mel. I feel sort of responsible . . .'

'Well, you aren't. No one is responsible for me. Only me.'

He pushed his hand through his hair, obviously embarrassed. 'I'm sorry. Really. Look let me do something to help – '

'Just go, Richard.'

He glanced at the black sack of rubbish already tied up, ready to be carried down on her way out. 'Well, the least I can do is carry this down for you . . . to make up for being such an idiot.' He picked up the sack before she could object and Mel shrugged. As he said, it was the least he could do. He paused in the doorway, 'When will I see you again?'

'I'll come down to the wine bar one evening,' she said, vaguely.

'Tonight?' he pressed.

'No. Not tonight. I'm having a drink with some of the girls after work.'

'You're joking?'

She was affronted. 'Why should I be joking?'

'Well, this isn't really your scene, is it? In fact I don't really understand what you think you're doing.'

'You know what I'm doing. Relieving you of five hundred pounds in a good cause.'

'I was just winding you up, you know . . .' He seemed exasperated with her. 'God, you're just so gullible. Get out, Mel, before you get hurt.'

'I can't.'

He frowned. 'Of course you can. Just walk away. Or was I right? This is all about Jack Wolfe. That's why you're so desperate to get rid of me. You're hoping he'll come back – '

'No! No, Richard, it's nothing to do with him. Really.' She hesitated. If word was to get back to Janet Graham . . . but Richard was like her, an outsider. He wouldn't tell. He might even help. 'It's this,' she said, taking a leaflet from her pocket. 'What do you think of this?'

He took the crumpled leaflet and looked at it. "*How to Start a Workers Co-op*"? What is this?'

'The first shot in a revolution, Richard. Why don't you come along? I'm going to need all the support I can get.'

He stared at her for a moment. 'You're crazy, do you know that? You'll get them all sacked.'

'Keep the booklet,' she said, as he thrust it back to her. 'Read it. Think about it. You might change your mind.'

'I didn't join this party to start a war, Mel.'

'When why did you join, Richard? You've plenty of talent, so why didn't you just sign on with Trudy or someone and look for some real work?'

'This isn't real?' He hefted the sack in his hand. 'You could have fooled me.'

'Well?' Greg Tamblin demanded, impatiently.

'No need to panic. Carstairs is still the target. This trip to The Ark is simply to distract anyone who might be taking an interest.'

'You're sure?'

'Quite sure. Mr Jack Wolfe isn't going there to sniff around for a soft target. He already owns a very sizeable stake in the place.'

'Who owns the rest?'

'A old friend of Wolfe's called Angus Jamieson; he's in on the whole thing. Just listen to this: ". . . Everything is in place regarding the new acquisition, but as you are aware there is always interest in my movements so I think it would be a wise move to leave the final details to Mike and take a little holiday. A few 'panicky' phone calls from you to the right investment people should be coincidental enough to convince anyone interested that I have more on my mind than sunbathing . . ."'

'The devious bastard. You've done well, Richard. I won't forget this.'

'The only reward I want,' Richard Latham said, with the utmost sincerity, 'is to use Jack Wolfe the way he uses other people.'

'He'll never know,' Greg pointed out.

'I will,' Richard said. And he knew that because Greg Tamblin was greedy and assumed that everyone else was the same, he would believe that the money would be enough.

Revolution? Sitting in a pub near the Busy Bees office, Mel glanced around at her as yet unconscripted army and wondered if she was quite mad.

Probably. She launched into her introduction before she could lose her nerve.

'Right, ladies, I won't keep you long, because I know you've all got more important things to do than listen to me,' she said, handing each of them a large envelope. 'Don't open those now, it'll only waste time. You can read everything when you get home.'

'You must be joking,' someone muttered.

'Lock yourself in the bathroom for ten minutes,' Mel advised, briskly.

'With four kids?'

'Shut up, Jo. I've got a bus to catch. What's all this about, Mel?'

Melanie looked around at the weary faces of the women she worked with. All they wanted was to go home and hopefully find five minutes to put their feet up in front of the television. How on earth could she expect them to find the time and energy for anything more?

'I've got an idea. A plan. I've done some research and with a bit of luck and a lot of hard work –' she looked around them '– and none of you is afraid of hard work – I know it can work. I've written it all down so you can look at it later. But basically what I'm asking you to think about is this. Janet Graham treats you all like garbage. How long are you going to let her get away with it?'

'What do you suggest? Strike action?'

'No.' The idea of organizing a placard demonstration had enormous appeal – and her presence would certainly have guaranteed publicity. But the minute the furore died down the system would be back to normal, except that Paddy, Sharon and anyone else who'd joined in would be out of a job and probably marked as troublemakers into the bargain. 'I know that's impossible – '

'Life's bloody impossible.' This was greeted by laughter.

'Difficult.' Mel summoned another round of drinks. 'But you don't have to lie down and take it.'

'What's your solution, then?'

'Not my solution. Yours. The answer, if you're willing to take the risk, is to form a co-operative and work for yourselves.'

There was a moment of stunned silence. Then Sharon downed her second drink in one swallow and stood up. 'Thanks for the drink, Mel. And the laugh. See you in the morning, girls.' And that was that. Sharon was their natural leader and once she left, the others followed, the envelopes abandoned, unopened on the table. Only Paddy remained.

Mel, stunned at the suddenness with which she had lost her audience, turned to her. 'What did I do wrong?'

'You won't get anywhere until you've won over Sharon; she likes to be queen bee.'

'I don't want to take over the hive, Paddy. I just want to help.'

Paddy's smile was sympathetic. 'I'm still here. Tell me about it.'

'You don't have to rush back to feed your family?'

'Dave was made redundant last week, Mel. He's no Delia Smith, but he can open a tin of beans. So, what's it all about?'

'Oh, I'm sorry, Paddy. You've got troubles enough; you don't want to sit here and listen to my crackpot ideas.'

'I might as well. Laughs are in short supply around our house just at the moment.'

'Then I've got a better idea. Let's get a pile of pizzas and take them back to your house. That way we can get Dave's input too.' Paddy gave her an old-fashioned look. 'The pizzas are on me.'

'It's not that, Mel. They'll be cold by the time we get them home on the bus.'

'Then we'll take a cab,' she said, grinning broadly. 'And when you tell Sharon about it, she'll be mad as hell she didn't stay and join in the fun!'

CHAPTER 6

'Melanie!' Janet Graham put her head round the door and called her into the office. 'I've got a special job for you today.'

'Special?'

'Mr Wolfe, as you may know, has a weekend cottage in Henley,' she said, her tone proprietorial, as if because of her business connection with the owner she had some stake in it. 'He's had a new bathroom installed and now the workmen have left he wants the place cleaned through. His driver is coming to pick you up any minute. It's straightforward enough, but since you have all day, make sure that you do a good job.' She smiled, rare enough to be unnerving in itself, but it wasn't that which bothered Melanie.

'Did Mr Wolfe ask for me especially, Mrs Graham?'

'You? Of course he didn't ask for you.' The smile disappeared as quickly as it had come and Melanie could have bitten out her tongue for giving the woman the satisfaction of lying to her. 'Why should he ask for you?' she asked, suddenly suspicious.

131

'No reason,' she said, as carelessly as she knew how. Just that he had come close to kissing her and she had come perilously close to letting him. If he *had* asked for her . . . That foolish, betraying lift of the heart told her more about her feelings than all the hours and days of heart-searching since. 'I just thought it might be easier to send someone else,' she continued, her fingers crossed behind her back. 'I should be working with Sharon and Paddy today.'

'Leave me to worry about that. Mr Wolfe wants a cleaner for a whole day out of town and you just happen to be more expendable than anyone else.' Janet Graham could look you straight in the eyes and lie. She was lying now, Melanie was certain of it, for no better reason than to make sure she didn't get above herself, begin to think she was important. 'Sharon and Paddy will manage perfectly well without you.'

In other words they'd do three jobs for the price of two while Mrs Graham would get three fees and only have to pay two wages. No wonder the woman was smiling. But Melanie knew better than to say anything. Working for Mrs Graham was, as Richard had promised, an education, and she was learning all about being treated like a nobody, about keeping her mouth shut and taking it. He had thought she would find the work difficult, but that was the easy part. Yet the knowledge that she could, if she chose, walk away at any time gave her a detached view of the situation. For the other women, she knew it was simply take it or leave it.

The sharp toot of a car horn outside attracted Mrs Graham's attention.

'There's your driver,' she said, sharply. 'Don't keep him waiting.'

'Morning, miss,' said the man when she got outside, taking her workbox from her and opening the door of a large, dark workmanlike estate car, so that she could climb into the front passenger seat. 'I'm Geoff, Mr Wolfe's driver.'

'Good morning, Geoff.' The man was pleasant enough, chatting about his wife and family as they drove swiftly along the M4, until beyond Windsor he turned off and headed into the country.

The countryside was fresh and new, there were flowers in gardens and suddenly Melanie wished she weren't tied to London. Well, only another week and she would be able to claim victory in her bet with Richard, although she couldn't possibly take his hard-earned money. Not now she knew just hard-earned it was. Making him admit that he had been wrong about her would be reward enough. Of course, if her plans for the co-operative got anywhere, she would still be needed in London. Paddy had promised to talk to Sharon. Maybe today, when they were on their own, she would have a chance.

'Open the gate, dear, would you?' They had stopped at a five-barred gate marked 'Dove Cottage – Private' and Melanie climbed out of the car, opening and closing it behind the car. 'Thanks. Bit of nuisance, but if it isn't kept shut all those people

133

with four-wheel-drives just charge across the field to get down to the river.'

It was a very ordinary-looking field and there were no animals to stray that she could see. 'Does it matter?'

'Well, it's a site of special scientific interest. Some rare wild flowers grow there – don't ask me what.'

'Oh, I see. Well, couldn't Mr Wolfe just put up a sign?'

'He could. The trouble is, then they'd all be dug up overnight. I don't know what the world's coming to.'

'I'm not sure that I ever did,' Melanie murmured, but they had already pulled up in a walled courtyard at the side of the cottage.

He swung out of the car and crossed to the back door of the cottage, unlocked it and went in, switching off the alarm system. 'If you're making coffee I could murder a cup,' he called back to her, apparently in no hurry to be off.

But Melanie was still outside. The sprawling red-brick timbered cottage faced the river and she had walked round to the front and was staring up at the drunken angles of the pantiled roof where a couple of fantailed doves were strutting their stuff. 'I've put the kettle on,' the driver said, coming out to look for her and saw her staring up at the façade. 'It's lovely, isn't it?'

'It must be really old,' she said.

'Seventeen something, so Mr Wolfe told me once. And the dovecote is really old.' He pointed to a round brick building at the far side of the courtyard. 'The river's down there, through the trees. You should take your lunch down there if the weather holds.'

'Maybe I will.' She turned to him. 'But first I'll get you that cup of coffee.' She was impatient while he drank it, eager to have the place to herself, eager to explore this private, unknown part of Jack Wolfe's life.

Once alone, she walked slowly through the ground floor. The cottage had been furnished for comfort, she decided, a long time ago, and she didn't think there would be a stampede of lifestyle editors beating a path to Jack Wolfe's door begging to do a colour feature on his country home, no matter how enchanting the exterior.

But if the furniture was old, hard-used, too well-loved to be thrown away and replaced by something smarter, the sense of peace and welcome was just as tangible. She stroked the arm of a well-rubbed leather sofa pulled up in front of the inglenook fireplace, then, curious, raised her fingers to her face. Yes. She knew this scent. The Jack Wolfe who wore that terrible old T-shirt was not just a figment of her overheated imagination. He was real, and at the end of a hard day he stretched out in front of the fire on this sofa.

She smiled a little as she opened the French windows to let in the sweet spring air. Away at the far end of the garden a clematis, grown rampant over a woodshed stacked with logs, was flowering its heart out. And there was a saw-horse to the side with a untidy heap of branches waiting to be cut. Jack Wolfe could have paid to have someone cut his logs, but she knew that he didn't and the knowledge warmed her. This was where he came to get rid of the smell of the City. And she would bet a month's wages that he didn't bring Caroline Hickey with him.

The garden, full of secret places, called to her to come and explore, but she resisted the temptation and turned back to the living room.

In the far corner of the room there was an old piano draped in a faded chenille cloth, its surface cluttered with photographs in silver frames blackened from lack of polishing. Mostly they were old, men and women in stiff poses wearing outdated clothes and outdated hairstyles. A few were more recent, a woman who had to be Jack's mother wearing sixties styles, in false eyelashes, holding the arm of a young man and later with a baby, who even then had those same invincible grey eyes. Melanie smiled and moved on. Jack, self-important at ten with his mother and a new baby, which must be Tom.

After that, Tom was the favoured subject and there was nothing more of Jack until his graduation. And then . . .

And then her heart stopped as she picked up a photograph, half hidden behind the others. The girl was lovely, dark-haired, dark eyes luminous with happiness on her wedding day. And the man at her side was Jack. He was married. Had been married? Was still?

She suddenly felt quite sick and, calling herself

every kind of fool for her stupid fairytale daydreams, she grabbed her cleaning kit and hurried upstairs to get on with the job. Start work.

'Jack, are you busy?'

'What is it, Mike? I was just going out.'

Mike Palmer glanced at the wicker hamper in Jack's hand. 'Lunch in the park?' he enquired, with a knowing grin.

'By the river, if you must know.'

'Forget it. It's going to rain.'

'And?'

'And we've just had about fifty feet of fax in from Chicago, following up on your meetings.'

'I should have made my escape while I had the chance.'

'Since when have you wanted to escape from this?' Mike asked, with an expansive gesture.

'"All work and no play", Mike . . .'

'"Makes Jack a dull boy"? I don't think anyone would ever describe you as dull. Besides, there's a rider to that proverb; "all play and no work makes him something greatly worse".'

'Well, that would seem to settle the matter fairly comprehensively. Have you made arrangements for lunch to be sent in?' Jack glanced at the hamper. 'Or shall we picnic in the boardroom?'

'It seems a pity to waste it. Will she be very disappointed?'

'No, it was to have been a surprise. And probably a mistake.' The women who worked for him were strictly off limits; getting involved was asking for trouble. And yet just the thought of Melanie Devlin stirred something deep, something long buried . . . He realized Mike was looking at him a little oddly. 'You did say it was going to rain?'

'Without a doubt.'

Jack turned as his secretary came into the room. 'Mary, get hold of Geoff, will you? Tell him to collect Miss Devlin at about four and take her wherever she wants to go.'

Mike, about to ask who Miss Devlin might be, took one look at Jack's face and changed his mind.

Work was easy. Melanie went through the cottage like a whirlwind, concentrating all her energies, all her thoughts on the task in hand, not even stopping for lunch. She started at the top, resolutely refusing to speculate on which of the dust-sheeted bedrooms Jack had shared with his wife; it certainly wasn't the small single-bedded room he used on his weekend visits. And when she returned to the living room, it was with nothing in her mind but the eradication of dust and cobwebs.

She removed the photographs from the piano without looking at them, took the cloth outside, shook it and hung it over the line to air and after she had finished cleaning she draped it back over the piano. Then she polished every one of the photograph frames until they gleamed before she put them back. To the wedding shot she gave pride of place, in the centre. When she was satisfied, she stepped back

138

to admire her handiwork, just to prove that she was not in the least affected –

'Oh, very nice, miss.'

'Heavens, Geoff, you're early.'

'Mr Wolfe said to pick you up at four o'clock. It's not far short of that.' He looked around. 'The cottage looks a real treat.'

'Thank you.'

He crossed to the piano and picked up the wedding photograph. 'I'd just put that round the back, though, if I were you, miss. He doesn't care to be reminded . . .'

It was a week before Sharon broached the subject of the co-operative again. They'd been cleaning an empty house after it had been renovated by a building contractor and for once had the luxury of a proper lunch break. 'What's all this about, then? You planning on starting up on your own?' she demanded, without preamble.

'An agency of my own? No. I'm an actress, Sharon. This is just a temporary job for me.'

Sharon gave her look that suggested she was living beyond her hopes. 'What's in it for you, then?'

Nothing, except a lot of extra work when she could have been out having fun. But Sharon wouldn't believe that. 'You and Paddy and the other girls could have made life difficult for me. You didn't.'

Sharon shrugged. 'You might talk posh, but you know how to work.'

'Maybe, but I don't like the way Mrs Graham does

business and I don't think you should have to put up with it.'

'Oh, I agree. We agree, don't we, Paddy?' Then she laughed. 'Come on, then, spit it out.'

She spat it out. Or rather, laid out her plan for a co-operative run by the women who did the work. A co-operative with its own crèche and nursery facilities so that no one would have to worry about childcare. A co-operative that could provide after-school care for the older children.

'That would mean employing properly qualified people,' Sharon said.

'Yes. And you'd need properly equipped premises. But with your nursery vouchers you would already be partly funded. And you could offer the facilities at a reasonable price to other working women to help pay for it. The nursery doesn't have to he a profit-making organisation, but it is essential that it covers its running expenses. And the business could be run from the same premises.'

'And where are we going to find somewhere to rent?'

'There's that old house round the corner from you, Paddy,' Sharon said.

And that was it.

Quite suddenly Melanie's idea had taken on a life of its own and become unstoppable. Within a week they had a working business plan, had applied for a start-up loan, enterprise allowance and business training for Paddy's husband. They only lacked one thing. Premises. The house round the corner from Paddy would have been perfect with a little money spent on it, but the council were dragging their feet.

Luke, she knew, could have helped. But she didn't want to involve him. This was her idea and she wanted to carry it through without running home . . .

But who else was there? Her subconscious, right on cue, supplied the image of Jack Wolfe that seemed imprinted on her brain like a photograph. Her subconscious, she told herself, had several screws loose.

Mel was running late. A signal failure on the Underground had put her nearly an hour behind by the time she pushed the key into Jack Wolfe's front door, let herself in and turned off the alarm. He wasn't in and she couldn't fool herself about that niggling sinking feeling any more. It was disappointment.

She shook herself. Who was she kidding? She was his cleaner, for heaven's sake. Nothing more. And not for much much longer. She had given herself a month and that was nearly up. She didn't know what she had proved, but at least no one could accuse her of being boringly sweet any more.

She pulled a note from the fridge door. There was always a note. Sometimes a genuine request for her to pick up his cleaning or to restock the refrigerator. Sometimes it was just an irritation, like today. 'Could you pick up some black olives, Cinderella? Just in case I decide on a pizza.' Was it her imagination, or had the irritating ones become more frequent since he had come so close to kissing her? She crushed the note between her fingers and tossed it in the bin. On her last day she'd leave a little note of her own . . . She caught herself. No, she wouldn't. She wouldn't do anything so ridiculous. She had far more important things to do than tell the man how many beans made five. Any man called Jack should already know that.

She was upstairs cleaning the gallery windows when she heard the front door open. Startled, she turned to look down to the lower floor just in time to see Jack Wolfe stride across the huge open-plan living area and straight out on to the terrace. Someone had obviously seriously annoyed him and he gripped the wrought-iron balcony rail in a determined effort to control the temper that was darkening his features.

She had seen him in a variety of moods, from detached through to withering scorn, but never seriously angry. Whoever had provoked such a reaction had her deepest sympathy.

It was the first time she had seen him since he had sent her home, bewildered, flustered, almost incoherent with feelings so disturbing that she could scarcely think of anything else. So that every Monday, Wednesday and Friday afternoon she was like two separate people: one dreading that when she put the key into the lock he would be at home, the other dreading that he would not.

Not that she needed to see him. His image was so indelibly printed on to her psyche that he was always there just below the surface, waiting to emerge and disturb her if she stopped working, stopped thinking. She wondered, with a sudden insight into her own motives, whether her project to help her colleagues owed more to the effort she put into not thinking about Jack Wolfe than to some high-minded ideal.

The trouble was, there was so much to think about. She was now intimately acquainted with every item of clothing he possessed, she knew the brand of toothpaste he used, that he had a weakness for dark, expensive chocolate, the kind that cracked like a whip when it was broken. He bought books that she wanted to read, would read when she had the time. Worse, she could tell from the music he had been listening to on his stereo system the night before whether he had been alone, or with Caroline. Alone he listened to Mozart, Bach, Oscar Petersen, tastes that she shared. Not that there had been much evidence of Caroline's presence lately which was something of a comfort. But not much.

She had discovered other things too. Richard had told her that he had a reputation for ruthlessness in the City. Well, she knew how that kind of reputation could be distorted. Luke could be thoroughly ruthless when he wanted something. But Jack seemed to revel in it. Actually enjoy it. Why else was he making a collection of newspaper clippings with nasty headlines that played on his name?

And he wasn't just ruthless. He was good at being ruthless, brilliant at it. He lived in the kind of apartment that cost telephone numbers and owned a cottage on the river at Henley. And cottages on the

143

Thames at Henley didn't come cheap. Even if it had been a family home that he'd inherited, not many people could afford to just keep it.

She always knew when he had been there. The jeans and T-shirt would be waiting for her to wash and she had to fight the urge to hold them to her face so that she could remind herself of the sharp intermingled scent of pine and sweat . . .

Occasionally she relived her fantasy of meeting him at some smart gathering, wondering how he would react when he saw her dripping with diamonds and designer silk, how he would react when their hostess introduced them. *'Melanie, may I present Mr Jack Wolfe? Jack, this is Melanie Beaumont. Edward Beaumont's youngest daughter. Did you see her in the West End last year with her sister, Claudia? No? Well, of course, seats were like gold dust.'*

And he would say, *'Don't be ridiculous, her name isn't Beaumont, it's Devlin. I should know; I employ her as my cleaner.'*

The fantasy faded as he was ignominiously requested to leave.

Looking at him now, all constrained temper, she gave a little shiver as she dragged herself out of her daydream. Ridiculous, of course. She had never dripped with diamonds in her life and Jack Wolfe probably wouldn't bat so much as an eyelid even if he met her in the Royal Enclosure at Ascot. He'd certainly never do anything as crass as exposing her as his cleaner. But she doubted he would miss the opportunity to mark the event with a little note on his fridge door . . .

'Last week you couldn't wait to spend a few days in the West Indies with me.' His voice startled her from her musings, warning her that he was not alone.

'Surely we can go the week after next? A week in the sun is hardly a matter of life or death, after all.' Caro's voice as she followed Jack on to the terrace was so reasonable, so sweet, that it made Melanie's teeth ache. And her sympathy evaporated like desert rain.

He didn't bother to confirm or deny the justice of his cause. 'If it's the money that's bothering you,' he said, cuttingly, 'I'll cover your wretched fee.'

'Darling, I'm going to be on the cover of the world's most glamorous magazine.' Her voice was honeyed, rich, amused at such foolishness. '*Money* can't buy that.'

'No?' As he turned on the woman Mel almost flinched. Was Caro mad? Couldn't she hear that razor-edge to his voice? Or was it so sharp that you wouldn't know you'd cut yourself until you were bleeding? 'Perhaps you'd better tell me what could, Caro.'

But Caroline Hickey merely smiled, apparently oblivious to the danger, her smiling scarlet mouth inviting him to supply the answer for himself. Mel, motionless above them, an unwitting and most reluctant eavesdropper, was all too horribly aware what the woman was trying to do. But she had no desire to witness a marriage proposal, particularly not one extracted by blackmail.

In desperation she dropped her duster out of the window she was polishing and it landed in a little puff of powdery pink cleaner that dulled the shine on Jack Wolfe's handmade shoes. For a moment he stared at it, then bent to pick it up, and Mel found herself looking down into his upturned face.

'Good afternoon, Cinderella,' he said, extending his arm to return the large, and inevitably yellow, cloth. 'It appears that your skill with a duster is exceeded only by your tact.'

'We're hot on both at Busy Bees,' she informed him.

'But not so hot on timekeeping. You shouldn't be here.'

And neither should you, Mel thought, but being hot on tact she didn't say so. Not that she had the opportunity.

Caroline, furious that her big moment had been ruined, was momentarily unable to disguise the fact. Her comment was brief but scatalogical and she glared at Mel as Jack took the opportunity to re-treat, tugging at his tie as he disappeared inside. 'If you'll excuse me, Caroline, I've no doubt you've got things to do before you leave for New York and I've got to make alternative arrangements for my own trip . . .'

For a moment Mel lost sight and sound of him, then his feet were clattering up the spiral staircase. He was rapidly followed by Caroline, paler than she had been. 'You mean . . . you'd take someone else?' she demanded.

'I explained the situation when I asked you to go with me, Caroline,' he said, tossing the tie on to the bed and flinging his jacket after it. He began to unfasten his cufflinks. 'I need a woman with me for camouflage.'

Camouflage? Whatever had happened to romance? Mel wondered.

'But darling, I look terrible in khaki . . .'

Caro's attempt to make him laugh failed. 'I doubt if you could look terrible in a black plastic sack, but if you're not available, I'll have to find someone who is.'

But Caroline wasn't ready to give up. 'Look, Jack, can't we talk about this?' She indicated Melanie, trapped in the corner by the window, with a dismissive wave of her hand. 'Send her away and – '

'And what?' he demanded. Melanie began to noisily pack her cleaning stuff back into her yellow carrying box. Neither of them took any notice. 'I asked you to join me for a few days in the Caribbean. Two days ago you were bubbling over with excitement at the prospect; now suddenly you say that it's impossible.'

'But I've told you why.'

'Indeed. And since you have more important things to do – ' He lifted the telephone receiver. She had been dismissed, forgotten as he began to punch in a number. Mel, unable to escape, was riveted by the sheer force of wills that was making the air vibrate with tension.

Caroline snapped first. 'More important than

sitting about while you're working on some grubby little scheme to make money – '

His jaw tightened imperceptibly. 'Hardly little, darling. And as for grubby . . . tell me, does the dirt magically rub off when the money crosses the jeweller's counter?' Mel, sensing a full-scale row brewing, murmured that she had some shopping to do. But drawing attention to herself was a mistake. Jack, dropping the telephone back on to its receiver, reached out and, by the simple expedient of fastening his fingers about her wrist, stopped her from going anywhere. 'No, don't go, Mel,' he said, not taking his eyes off Caroline. 'I have a proposition for you.'

'No, really,' she began, desperate to stop this before it got out of hand. 'I must go.'

But he didn't let go. He didn't even turn and look at her as he put it to her. 'I'm offering a week in the Caribbean, Mel, with nothing to do but lie in the sun all day. What do you say?'

Say? *Say?* She was lost for words. She knew he didn't mean it, that he was trying to force Caroline's hand, but she refused to be used as a pawn in their games. No way.

'That's very kind of you, but I'm not owed any holiday,' she said, through gritted teeth. Somehow she managed to sound regretful, a remarkable achievement considering she wanted to hit him with her big yellow workbox. Very hard.

'It won't be a holiday, Mel. You'll be working; I'll be paying the agency for your time.'

His gall stunned her. 'I doubt if Mrs Graham

would consider it . . . proper,' she said carefully. 'If you'll excuse me?' He wouldn't; he didn't. His hand remained firmly attached to her wrist.

'It's strictly business, Mel. I'm confident that I can persuade Mrs Graham of the urgency of the situation.'

'But what about the propriety of it? Could you convince her of that too?'

He turned then to look at her properly. It wasn't any better, Mel decided. 'Propriety?' he repeated. She wasn't quite sure which surprised him more, the fact that she knew the word, or that she thought it mattered.

'Correctness of behaviour or morals,' she supplied, in case he wasn't sure. She'd learned more than good manners and how to vacuum a carpet at her mother's knee. Juliet Devlin had been hot on vocabulary too.

'I'm aware of the meaning, Mel. And I have no doubt that your character speaks for itself.'

She wasn't about to argue with that. No matter what she said, he'd claim some kind of victory. 'Won't it be terribly expensive?' she asked, stalling, trying to think.

'Don't worry about the expense.' He smiled faintly at her apparent naïveté. 'Paying for your time by the hour has got to be cheaper than paying by Caroline's reckoning.'

Seeing the game slipping away from her, Caro retreated a little. 'Darling, can't you see that Cinderella has no desire to go the ball? You're making the

149

poor creature blush. Let her go and I'm sure we can sort something out.'

Poor creature? Cinderella? And as for blushing . . .

Heartily sick of playing piggy in the middle, she placed her free, less than clean hand on Caroline's immaculate cream jacket, Emporio Armani without a doubt, and forced a sickeningly sweet smile to her lips.

'Oh, please, don't worry about me, miss,' she gushed. 'If Mr Wolfe can arrange things with Mrs Graham, I'll be happy to help.' She pointed to the legend emblazoned on her cap. 'It's our motto, see?' She forced a giggle. 'And I've never been to . . .' She turned to Jack Wolfe who was now regarding her through dangerously narrowed eyes. 'Where was it again?'

'The British Virgin Islands.' And he tilted a brow just sufficiently to suggest that the name positively guaranteed propriety.

Caroline regarded her with open dislike for a moment, then with a small laugh dismissed her, turning back to Jack. 'Her nails would give her away in a moment, darling. Look, I don't want to be unreasonable . . .'

'But you're not being unreasonable, Caroline. I'm the one being thoughtless, for which I sincerely apologize. Of course your magazine cover must come first. You mustn't think of sacrificing your career on my account.'

Caroline Hickey made a brave attempt at a laugh. It wasn't particularly convincing but, considering that her carefully laid plans to provoke a proposal had just been sabotaged by the cleaner, Melanie had to give her nine out of ten for effort.

'All right, darling. You win. Take the poor girl if it pleases you to make a fool of yourself and of her. No doubt she'll be only too pleased to hang up your clothes, clean your shoes and offer any other little services you ask of her in return for a free holiday.' Caroline gave her a swift assessing glance. 'A day at a beauty salon, some decent clothes and who knows, she might convince someone that she's actually your partner. Who, I couldn't say. And if she doesn't,' Caroline gave a dismissive little shrug, 'I'm sure that whatever desperately secret takeover bid you're planning isn't *that* important . . .' She was too clever to spell out the possibilities, instead leaving the threat dangling. 'Bye, darling. Give me a ring when you get back.' Her lips lingered for just a moment against his cheek, leaving a waft of Poison to remind him of what he was giving up, then she was gone. A classy exit, Mel had to admit. And doubtless she expected Jack to be regretting his rash decision before she had reached the ground floor.

She might well be right. Jack, with what had undoubtedly been a bluff well and truly called, turned and regarded Mel with what was undoubtedly a frown. Mel could hardly blame him. Dressed in a uniform with about as much sex appeal as cold porridge, her ill-cut wig sticking out from beneath a baseball cap, there was nothing about her to attract a man whose choice in feminine company, like his taste

151

in furniture, favoured the expensive and the beautiful if Caroline was anything to go by.

But if he had hoped to change Caro's mind by his tactics, he had misjudged the girl. She wasn't about to give up the top slot in the cover stakes for less than a wedding ring and who could blame her? She might not be happy about the cleaner taking her place but had obviously decided that it was a whole lot safer than leaving Jack to choose someone more exciting, someone who might pose more of a threat to her long-term plans.

Melanie could almost hear the cogs in the other girl's mind ticking over. She who fights and runs away, lives to fight another day. And Jack would undoubtedly fall into her arms, chastened and obedient, after a week in the enforced company of his charlady.

But now she was left alone with Jack Wolfe, the apartment suddenly seemed very quiet. Why didn't he say something? That it was all right? That he didn't mean it? He was going to, surely?

'Well, that appears to be settled, Melanie. You have a passport, I take it'?'

He was that desperate? 'Yes, I have a passport.'

He nodded. 'If you'll give me your address I'll get my secretary to pick you up first thing. She'll organize a hairdresser – *This was ridiculous; surely he didn't expect her to go with him to some place she'd never heard of?* – and some clothes.'

'There's no need.' Because she wasn't going.

'Indulge me.'

Indulge him? Some devil prompted her to say, 'I can borrow some clothes.'

'It might be better . . .'

'And I promise I'll give my nails a good scrub. I had some handcream for Christmas,' she added. 'I expect that will help.' *What on earth was she playing at?*

'Do you think so?' Jack didn't think her hands needed any help at all. They were small, he remembered, and very white. Or had they already begun to show the wear and tear of her job? Lifting the hand he was still holding, he spread her fingers across his palm. Her nails were shorter than Caroline's and unpainted, but beneath the dust her hands, like her eyes, were unexpectedly beautiful. What else about the girl would surprise him? He glanced up, as if her unguarded face might tell him more.

Mel was beginning to see through a red mist. *How dared he?* How dared he be so insensitive? She knew he didn't want her. To toy with her like this was intolerable. Well, two could play at that game.

'And of course it will be very good experience for me,' Mel said, removing her fingers from his hand.

'Experience?' He now gave her the full benefit of those slaty dark eyes. 'What kind of experience?'

She gave a little gasp. He wasn't playing, he was being totally serious about this. And for a heartbeat she couldn't decide whether that was better, or worse. Then she knew. It was worse. In fact it was just about as bad as it could possibly be.

'Acting, of course,' she said, with studied carelessness. 'If I'm to provide – what was it? Camouflage? That is the whole point of this exercise, isn't it? You need a female companion to cover up your real reason for going to this place. So I'll have to pretend that I'm in love with you. Just in public, of course.'

'I suppose you will.' He voice was tight as he said it. He didn't sound exactly overwhelmed by the idea. Scarcely whelmed, if she was honest with herself. Well, she hadn't expected him to be. Had she?

'I could even provoke a lovers' quarrel if you like?' she offered, prolonging his agony – and hers.

'Somehow, Cinderella, I have the feeling that you could provoke a war, given sufficient time.'

'Thank you.'

'That wasn't a compliment.' He regarded her thoughtfully. 'What about in private? Have you any ideas about how you'll manage that? Bearing in mind your concern for – what was it? Propriety?'

'Private?' She hoped he didn't detect the slight wobble in her voice as the tables were turned and it was his turn to tease a little.

'In the intimate seclusion of our suite.'

She was right. This was not a man to be taken in by a bluff. Oh, well, she'd never thought . . . she hadn't intended . . . 'Can't you afford two bedrooms?'

'That would rather defeat the point of your presence, I'm afraid.'

Her heart was suddenly beating like a drum. 'Not even twin beds, then?'

'Just one large and extremely comfortable four-poster bed.'

154

She thought it was time she stopped playing games. With him and with herself. 'I think you're a bit tall for a sofa, Jack Wolfe. I think perhaps you'd better find someone more accommodating . . .'

But he wasn't going to let her go that easily. 'You were happy enough to accommodate Tom,' he reminded her, 'and all he was offering you was hard work. I'm offering you the chance to lie in the sun and relax and I promise you it will be a lot more fun – '

He stopped as her face flamed. Damn! What on earth had made him say that? He'd never intended . . . Or did his mouth know more than his brain was admitting?

Melanie, her cheeks painfully hot, suddenly realized just how stupid she was being. She had thought she was in control of the situation, but she wasn't, and remembering Richard's warning she felt unexpectedly vulnerable, quite at the mercy of a ruthless man who was capable of using anyone if it suited his purpose. Well, not her. *Not her!*

'If you believed that, I wouldn't be working for you,' she said, attempting to wrest back her advantage by attack.

'Really? Are you sure?' He knew he was behaving like an idiot, but Melanie Devlin did something to him, stirred something vulnerable in him that he had thought dead and buried. His only defence against her was attack. 'Maybe it was Tom's description of your striptease that made you so appealing.'

'I didn't – '

'Strip?'

'Tease!' She glared at him. 'And why all the sub-terfuge, anyway? Is another poor lamb being prepared for ritual sacrifice on the altar of commerce?'

His expression froze. He didn't like that. Not one bit. 'That, Melanie Devlin, need not concern you.' He raked long fingers through his thick, dark hair, suddenly wishing he'd never started any of this nonsense. He should have explained, asked for her help. She might even have said yes. 'Look, I know this is a little irregular, but I promise you that all you would have to do is look good and enjoy yourself.' It wasn't going to work. He'd blown it. Maybe. 'Or couldn't an actress of your apparently limited talent manage that?'

'You don't think I could do it?' Reckless, stupid. Anything but careful. *Oh, Richard, she thought, is this dangerous enough for you?*

'I don't know, but I suppose if you were any kind of an actress, Mel, you wouldn't be cleaning for a living.'

'There are a lot of good actresses out of work, you know. Would you like an audition? I do a truly amazing Portia. "The quality of mercy is not strained . . ."' she began.

Jack held up his hands in surrender. 'Enough. I'm convinced. Although I really don't think this is a job for Portia.'

'No, neither do I. She wouldn't approve at all.' Melanie was horribly, ridiculously close to tears. She shouldn't have allowed things to go so far, allowed him to get to her . . . 'In fact, on consideration,

156

neither do I. I suggest you get out your little black book and start dialling,' she threw at him. 'I'm sure there are hundreds of women who would just jump at the chance of a few days in the sun with you.'

'Are you? And just what evidence have you for thinking that?'

That he was not only rich, but had the kind of looks that would turn any girl's head, not just poor Cinderella's. She considered saying so, but decided she'd already said more than enough. 'Yes?' he prompted, then, when she still remained silent, he continued. 'I work for a living, Mel. I don't have time to run a harem. My threat to call someone else was simply that – a threat. Unfortunately I underestimated Caro's determination.'

'Why don't you give her a call? I'm sure she's in a forgiving mood.'

'I'm sure she is. However, I am not.' He gave her a sideways look. 'I guess it's you or nothing.' His lack of enthusiasm was decidedly galling. She wasn't begging him to take her with him, for heaven's sake. In fact, it was time to put him straight.

'Then I guess nothing is what you've got.' She bent and picked up her workbox. 'I'm sorry, Mr Wolfe, but I've got a hundred and one more interesting things to do this weekend than go to the West Indies with you. Wash my hair. Cut my nails. Defrost the fridge.' His image swam just a little through her bright, Busy Bees smile. 'Oh, and since you've now had more than two hours of my time you'll have to shop for your own olives.'

CHAPTER 7

Jack remained perfectly still until the front door banged behind Melanie. Banged hard. She was angry. Well, what had he expected? That she would fall into his arms and say thank you? She'd known he'd simply been trying to jolt Caroline into changing her mind and no girl with an ounce of spirit would have said yes. She would have to put up some kind of resistance, no matter how attractive the offer. Perhaps Melanie was right. Perhaps he should call Caro. She might have come to her senses. Unfortunately he already had.

Besides, the idea of taking Melanie to The Ark, despite every particle of common sense telling him that he was crazy, seemed more and more attractive. He needed someone who looked the part, someone decorative who would lie on the beach all day, dance all evening, giving the casual observer the impression that he had left business behind him to indulge his passion for a beautiful woman undisturbed . . .

Undisturbed? He smiled wryly at that. Melanie Devlin could disturb a sloth. She disturbed the hell out of him in a way that Caro could never hope to. But beautiful? No one who paid close attention to such matters would be convinced. And that was really the whole point. It had never been his intention to be too convincing.

She would be perfect. If only he could convince her. He glanced at his watch. It was gone five. Would she go straight home, or on to another job? He'd have to speak to Mrs Graham either way. And then he smiled. That was it. He wouldn't have to do a thing. He'd leave Mrs Graham to convince her.

He crossed to the phone and picked it up, but his first call was to Mike Palmer.

'Mike, there's a slight change in plan. Caro won't be coming with me tomorrow. I'm taking Melanie Devlin.'

'Jack!'

'Yes?'

The word was the gentlest of queries. The most dangerous kind, as Mike knew well enough. 'Nothing. But the *Courier* is running with the story tomorrow morning . . .'

'Well, this will cause an extra *frisson* of excitement in their gossipy little hearts. Ensure their attention.'

'All right, I'll get on to them. Who is Melanie Devlin?'

'My cleaner.' And Jack held the receiver away from his ear as Mike proceeded to issue a string of warnings. 'Have you quite finished?' He didn't wait for an answer. 'Now this is what I want you to do.'

'She'll kill you,' Mike said, when Jack had finished.

'Caroline or Melanie?'

'Both, in all probability.' Jack laughed and hung up. Mike shook his head, scarcely able to credit that a few days ago he'd been concerned that Jack was losing his ruthless streak.

When Melanie finally staggered into the office just before seven that evening, Mrs Graham, looking horribly pleased with herself, called her straight into her office. 'Melanie, you're late. You should have been here an hour ago.'

'I was delayed up on the Underground. I've been late all day.' But she wouldn't be bothering to put in for overtime. She'd learned a lot in a few short weeks.

'It's been most inconvenient. I've had to wait for you.' Melanie stared at her. Did she expect an apology? 'Mr Wolfe telephoned.'

'Oh?' Mel, who had had quite long enough to dwell on her idiotic behaviour, thought she knew what was coming. Well, she'd asked for it . . . begged for it.

'Apparently he needs you all next week to help his mother packing and cleaning before she moves house.' She bestowed a somewhat grudging smile. 'I have to admit that you've turned out rather better than I had expected. Melanie. This will be a nice little job for you.'

Mother? Moving house? What was the woman talking about? What had happened to being dismissed at a moment's notice?

160

Mrs Graham looked up from her schedule of work. 'I've already rearranged your other jobs.'

'Have you?' Mel enquired, faintly. Well, that was all right then, wasn't it?

'Mr Wolfe sent this over by courier for you. It has all the details you'll need.' She handed over an envelope. 'He wants you to telephone him after nine and arrange about transport. He's laying on a car for you, apparently.' She sounded impressed. She had a right to be. Mr Wolfe was an impressive man. He was also arrogant, dictatorial and cavalier. And, like the rest of his kind, he couldn't bear not to get his own way.

'Actually, Mrs Graham, I'm not in a position to leave London right now. Perhaps Paddy could do it, I'm sure she'd welcome the extra work.' And let Mr Wolfe talk his way out of that one.

'I'm afraid that won't be possible. I'm going to have to let Paddy go. She's been causing trouble – '

'Trouble?' Mel had a terrible sinking feeling in the pit of her stomach. 'What kind of trouble?'

'Oh, demanding crèche facilities, that sort of thing.' Janet Graham didn't even look uncomfortable as she lied with with sickening unctuousness. Paddy had demanded nothing. Janet Graham had obviously found out about the co-operative somehow and this was her way of keeping the rest of her staff in line. Better the job you have than some airy-fairy nonsense . . . Well, Fizz had warned her. Richard had warned her. 'You're not going to let me down, are you, Melanie? Mr Wolfe is an important client. A

161

lot of jobs around here depend on being able to keep him happy.' Lies and moral blackmail. She had to hand it to the woman, she didn't mind getting her hands dirty in the cause of profit. And, as always, she held all the cards.

Melanie wanted to tell Mrs Janet Graham exactly what to do with Jack Wolfe, her job and Busy Bees. But she couldn't. She'd lost Paddy her job and as yet had nothing better to put in its place. She would have to do something about that. Or rather, Jack Wolfe would. If he'd gone to such lengths he must be really desperate. She'd just have to take a leaf out of her employer's book and try her hand at a little blackmail. 'I'll have to make a phone call.'

'If you must. Use the one in the main office.'

Jack Wolfe answered the telephone at the second ring. She didn't waste time on preambles. 'This is Cinderella. If you want me to come to the ball you're going to have to grant me the statutory three wishes.'

'Can I be Prince Charming *and* the Fairy God-mother?' She heard the laughter in his voice. He thought he'd won. Well maybe he had, but he would pay for his victory.

'You'll never be Prince Charming, Jack Wolfe, but this is your opportunity to wave your magic wand. Unless a lifetime of bliss with Miss Hickey suddenly seems desirable?'

'Are you blackmailing me, Melanie?' He sounded amused.

'Is the pot calling the kettle black?'

He laughed out loud. 'What do you want? Money, fame, a new wardrobe?'

'Those things I can manage by myself. Right now Mrs Graham is just about to sack an employee named Paddy Rorison. I want you to stop her.' Well, that wiped the smile of his face, she thought as the sudden silence came in shock waves down the phone.

'And how do you propose that I do that?'

'It shouldn't be difficult for a man with your track record of getting his own way. You must know that she'd do anything to keep you happy. Even employ me.'

'Who is Paddy Rorison? Your boyfriend?'

Melanie gritted her teeth. 'Paddy is a charming lady with a husband who has just been made redundant and four children who right now are relying on her to keep a roof over their heads. She works like a demon, but Mrs Graham has decided she's a trouble-maker . . .' She was, she discovered, practically incoherent with rage.

'Is she?'

'A troublemaker? No. She's just the scapegoat.'

'I sense a guilty conscience at work here. Correct me if I'm wrong?'

'No,' she admitted. 'You're not wrong. At least not entirely.'

'Mmm. I think you'd better let me have her address, just in case Mrs Graham isn't quite as smitten with me as you seem to think.'

Melanie told him. 'But it would give me enormous

pleasure to think that Mrs Graham was having her arm twisted.'

'Is that right? Well, I'll do my best to appease your conscience, Miss Devlin. Second wish.'

'I've persuaded some of the women who work at Busy Bees that they should form a co-operative and work for themselves – '

'That's the troublemaking, I take it?' The laughter was back in his voice.

'Personally I'd call it initiative, but I have to confess Mrs Graham warned me on my first day that she wouldn't stand for that either. The thing is, there's a property that's absolutely perfect for them but the local authority are not at all keen to let them have it.'

'Maybe they've got it earmarked for something else. Or maybe they just think you're off your head.'

'Maybe you're right. Maybe I need someone to inspire a little confidence.'

'You mean you want someone to apply a bit of pressure.'

'Is *that* how it's done?' she breathed, with apparent admiration.

'It won't be easy.'

'If it were easy, I wouldn't be asking. And Paddy's plight has lent a certain urgency to the situation.'

'I'll need to see some kind of business plan, Mel.'

'That's no problem. Our business plan is a work of art.'

'So long as it's not a work of fiction.'

'Give me your number and I'll fax it to you this

164

evening. You'll be astounded by its clarity of vision, its determination of purpose, its sheer brilliance.' Fizz had helped her and her accountant had gone through it with her, line by line. 'I wrote it myself,' she said, crossing her fingers.

'Then how can it possibly fail?'

'You'll help?'

'If it lives up to its sales pitch I'll be delighted to. Third wish.'

That was just a little bit more difficult. A little bit more personal. It might not even be necessary. 'I think I'd like to keep that in reserve.'

'If I'm being blackmailed I think I have a right to know the full extent of my commitment.'

'Surely that's the whole point of blackmail. It's open-ended.'

'Not in this case.'

'I'm not blackmailing you, Mr Wolfe. Nothing awful will happen to you if you say no. But you played dirty, so if you want my help you're going to have to pay for it.'

'How much?' he insisted.

'I just want to be sure you'll remember that I'm your cleaner. Nothing else.'

His soft laughter was unexpected. And under the circumstances not very flattering. 'Save your wish for a rainy day, Miss Devlin. I make it a point of principle never to play house with people who work for me. Now, have we got a deal?'

'Yes.' She hadn't hesitated. There had been no need to hesitate. After all, she had his word, didn't she? Disappointment that it had been given without a second thought seemed ridiculous under the circumstances. Foolish, almost. Even just plain idiotic. Yet it was the second time she had backed away from danger and she was perhaps more disappointed with herself than with him. What was it Claudia was fond of quoting? Three's a charm. Like all smart sayings it was double-edged, but suddenly she had an inkling of what her sister meant. 'Yes, Mr Wolfe,' she repeated, more firmly. 'We have a deal.'

'Then you'd better let me have your address. I'll send a car for you first thing.'

'It's absolutely forbidden for staff to give their addresses to Busy Bees' clients, Mr Wolfe. They might get ideas about employing them first-hand and saving the agency fee.'

'You gave me Paddy's.'

'That was different. And I really don't need someone to hold my hand when I visit the hairdresser. Just give me the flight number and time and I'll meet you at the airport.'

For a moment there was silence. 'It's all in the envelope I sent to the office. Don't let me down. Melanie. I'm sure Mrs Graham would be quite happy to break her rules if I were to explain what you've just asked me to do.' He didn't hear the word she called him, because he had already hung up.

'Is everything settled?' Mrs Graham asked her when she returned to the office.

'Yes.'

166

'Excellent. I'll see you when you get back and you can tell me all about it.' Then, as if regretting this unaccustomed warmth, 'Just make sure that neither Mr Wolfe nor his mother has reason to complain about your work.'

His mother! She seriously doubted whether the man had ever had a mother. No, that wasn't kind. Even rats had mothers. 'No, Mrs Graham,' she said, as she shut the door behind her. 'Thank you, Mrs Graham.' Then she said something else, but under her breath. Her headmistress had kept a bar of carbolic soap especially for pupils who used bad language. Mrs Graham was too much like her to take the risk.

Richard Latham picked up an early edition of the *Courier* on his way home from a late-night shift and he turned automatically to the gossip page as he waited in an all-night cafe for a bacon roll.

A photograph of Jack Wolfe and Caroline Hickey immediately caught his eye; the caption riveted him to his seat.

Jack Wolfe, financial wizard and eminently eligible man about town, has apparently swapped partners for his trip to the Caribbean. Until as late as yesterday he was planning to take the lovely Caro Hickey to The Ark, a romantic paradise island in the British Virgin Islands. But last night Caro jetted off to New York for a photo-shoot and Jack's

*surprise choice of holiday companion is a young
actress by the name of Melanie Devlin. No,
folks, I haven't heard of her either. But watch
this space.*

His tea grew cold beside him. Jack Wolfe might
have an ice-chip where his heart should be, but it
seemed that under the right kind of heat even
permafrost would melt. He'd always recognized that
Melanie was a blow-torch just waiting to be lit, but
there was a quicksilver quality about her; he'd put
down lures in the past, but she had always eluded
him, always kept him just at fingertip length. He
laughed out loud.

'What's so funny?'

Richard turned to the man behind the counter.
'Life.' It all had such a wonderful symmetry about it.
Everything was just falling into his lap.

First that idiot Tamblin had fallen for his plan.
Well, he was greedy and greedy men were easy to
fool. When he sold his Carstairs shares at a big fat
profit when the takeover went ahead he was going to
find out just how big a fool he had been. Richard
knew that the TSC would fall over themselves to
offer him immunity from prosecution when he went
to them with a well-rehearsed attack of conscience
and told them how Wolfe and Tamblin had been
insider-trading; that Tamblin had recruited him as a
go-between to carry information from Wolfe. It all
sounded so believable. And it would be so hard to
disprove. And Melanie, working in his flat, would be

involved. He'd already taken steps to see that she would.

Sooner or later Wolfe might be able to convince the TSC that the evidence was false, but he'd be long gone by then and Jack Wolfe's business would be in ruins. He smiled at the thought and then looked down at the paper. And now this. This would be the icing on the cake.

Wolfe couldn't possibly know who Melanie really was or that piece in the paper, so obviously planted to boost the illusion of a man with his mind on anything but business, would have been a whole lot bigger. And there would have been pictures, not just of Melanie, but the whole Beaumont clan. Well, it would be a pity to keep the man in the dark about who he was bedding.

He used the payphone on the countertop to call directory enquiries. 'Broomhill, Sussex,' he said, when the girl answered. 'I need the telephone number of Devlin Enterprises.'

If you wanted to hurt someone really badly, he reasoned, you wouldn't use a peashooter like Greg Tamblin. Not when someone kindly handed you a cannon.

Janet Graham discovered her secretary giggling over the piece when she arrived for work. Telling the girl to get on with her work and not waste time on such trash, she bore away the post, relishing the thought of sacking the Devlin girl the moment she returned. And let Jack Wolfe complain after the lies he'd told her. Helping his mother, indeed! And then she realized that the letter she was holding was Melanie's resignation.

In New York, Caroline Hickey received a fax marked urgent from her publicist and held up the cover shoot long enough to dash off a furious reply.

Trudy Morgan didn't see the paper until she arrived at her office, but when she did her first thought was to call Claudia and warn her just what kind of Grade A heartbreaker her baby sister was involved with. Her second thought was that it might be better to do nothing. Getting involved in her clients' love-life was not her idea of a good time. And Jack Wolfe was her landlord. Her third thought made her smile for the rest of the day.

Luke Devlin didn't read gossip columns. Fizz did when she had time, but she was busy and Claudia never read the papers until lunchtime. She called her sister as soon as she saw the piece in the *Courier*, but when Fizz tried to get through to Luke his line was engaged.

'Mr Devlin? Richard Latham. You won't remember me, although we did meet at Melanie's eighteenth birthday party.'

Luke recalled that there had been several hundred young men at Mel's eighteenth . . . 'Yes, of course. But if you're looking for Melanie, Richard, I'm afraid – '

'No, Mr Devlin. That's the whole point of my call. I *know* where Melanie is. Or rather where she's going right at this moment.' He hadn't called too early. The last thing he wanted was to have the love-birds stopped at the airport, the affair hushed up. 'I just wondered if you do? Or the kind of man she's going with?'

Luke tried to get hold of Melanie. All he got was her answering machine but the hall porter was happy to tell him that his niece had just left for a short holiday. And that she expected to be away for a week.

Five minutes later Luke was calling Edward Beaumont on the other side of the Atlantic. 'Edward, have you heard of a place called The Ark?'

Heathrow was heaving with travellers but Melanie saw Jack Wolfe at once. Hard to miss, standing a head and shoulders above the crowd, he was looking about him, impatiently seeking her out amongst the milling mass of people eager to be away on holiday. Casually dressed in a lightweight jacket, he was attracting more than his fair share of attention.

Once his eyes swept over her but although they paused momentarily on the girl crossing the concourse as if she owned it, they did not linger. Instead he glanced at his watch with growing irritation, evidently a man not used to being kept waiting, and she paused, wickedly, to keep him on tenterhooks just a little longer.

Which was why she hadn't given him her Chelsea address. Or one of the reasons. Overlooking Chelsea

Harbour, her apartment was way out of the reach of a struggling actress, let alone one reduced to cleaning to make ends meet; besides, having decided to dispense with her disguise and make a grand entrance, she didn't want to give him any clues to her true status before she handbagged him with her appearance. He'd played a low-down trick on her; it wouldn't do him any harm to let him sweat a little on whether she was going to turn up.

She had spent a long time considering the impression she wanted to make. She could have gone for old-fashioned head-turning film-star glamour, rented some furs, borrowed a Peke to tuck under her arm, and with a chauffeur in tow with her luggage she could have made an entrance that would have stopped the traffic. She was sorely tempted, but she had forsworn furs years before and besides, there might just be a photographer hanging around in the hopes of spotting someone worth snapping. Even if he didn't recognize her, he would certainly take photographs on the off-chance that she was someone with a price on her head and she didn't want Luke reading about this little escapade over his morning toast. It would certainly give him indigestion.

Besides, glamorous clothes would be uncomfortable on a long journey and she had, too, the suspicion that Jack might be expecting something tackily over-the-top from his 'out-of-work-actress'. No, she would simply be herself.

No wig. No unflattering pancake make-up. No ghastly Busy Bee workclothes. The transformation was simple enough, but the effect was stunning.

The light make-up she was wearing made a serious difference to the way she looked, giving her face definition, lighting the clear grey depths of her eyes. And the understated elegance of classic simplicity was her preferred alternative to the yellow and black outfit. She gathered herself, took a deep breath and swept forward. It was time to find out if Jack Wolfe was impressed with her efforts on his behalf.

Her luggage, a well-worn but good matching set, was placed directly on the scales, the pale gold curve of her hair swinging over her cheek to obscure her face as she tipped the porter and thanked him quietly before approaching the desk.

'Good morning, miss. Your ticket and passport, please,' the clerk requested, with an appreciative smile.

That was when Mel turned to Jack Wolfe, once again consulting his watch. 'The young man is asking for my ticket, darling,' she murmured, softly. Then she smiled.

There was moment, a still, very quiet moment in the bustle of the airport, while Jack Wolfe took in the stunning transformation of his cleaner.

She didn't flinch but waited while his narrowed eyes absorbed the delicately applied make-up; while he absorbed the glossy sleekness of hair that, released from the confines of the badly cut brown wig, fell to her shoulder in a shining golden curve; while he absorbed the casual elegance of a loose biscuit linen jacket, softly gathered trousers a shade or two lighter

173

that emphasized the length of her legs and a cream silk shirt that she had bought in a sale, but even so would have cost the worker bee a week's wages.

Had he recognized the girl who had so nearly bowled him over at the travel agent's? For a moment Melanie held her breath. Apparently not, because without a word he turned to the clerk and handed over her ticket.

'I was beginning to think you were going to miss the flight,' he said finally, returning his attention to Melanie once he had been handed their boarding passes.

'The traffic was terrible.'

'I came by helicopter from the City airport. You could have saved yourself an uncomfortable journey,' he said, placing his hand at her elbow before heading purposefully towards the escalator.

She turned and looked at him as they rose smoothly to the departure lounge. 'I didn't want to put you to any bother.'

'Is that right?' He gave her a slightly quizzical look. 'And here was I thinking you just wanted to keep me guessing whether you'd turn up or not.'

She hoped that was the effect she had achieved, but since he had made no noticeable alternative arrangements it seemed unlikely. She lifted her shoulders very slightly in the merest suggestion of a shrug. 'Why should I let you down? We've both got everything to gain from co-operation.'

'Everything,' he agreed, smoothly.

'And Mrs Graham is really strict about the address

rule,' she added, as if that settled the matter.

'Your address is hardly a secret,' he replied. Mel frowned. Mrs Graham would never disclose an employee's private address and was about to tell him so when she caught the sardonic glint in his eye. 'You obviously live in the wardrobe department of the BBC. I saw that very outfit in a television drama last week.' Undoubtedly he was teasing but it took all her self-control to ignore the irrational desire to slap him that swept over her. This is me, she wanted to shout. Can't you see that?

Idiot. The man couldn't see beyond the role she played three times a week at his apartment. She was an actress down on her luck and doing a cleaning job to keep body and soul together. And she had played her part so well that he hadn't even considered the possibility that she might be anything else.

She had a momentary glimpse of Paddy and Sharon's lives. Bright, lively woman judged forever by what they did for a living. No one would ever give them a chance to be anything else. Unless she, or someone like her, made that chance happen for them.

'Well? Am I right?' Jack Wolfe was still regarding her with a look that told her she was doing a good job, but she wasn't fooling him. But she didn't scream. Instead she lifted the corners of her mouth into the slightest of smiles.

'No, you're not right. Worse, Mr Wolfe. You're lying.' He stared at her, clearly taken aback by her attack. 'You don't have a television,' she pointed out with considerable satisfaction. 'And I may be wrong, but I'm sure you don't visit Miss Hickey to watch hers.' *Miaow.* 'However, you will be getting a bill for costume hire.' She was sure Fizz would be grateful for a donation to her children's charity. And it would make up for losing the bet with Richard. She wasn't prepared to count this week.

'How big?'

'It will be cheaper than buying me a whole new wardrobe,' she promised. 'But everyone needs working clothes and somehow I didn't think you'd appreciate my overall and cap?'

His eyes swept over her once again. 'You thought right.'

That was heartfelt and Melanie smiled. 'You approve of my choice of costume?'

'I can't wait to see what else you've brought with you . . . darling,' he added, provocatively, echoing her own taunting remark at the check-in desk. There was no doubt about which particular garment he was referring to and a slow blush seared her cheekbones. Well, if he expected sexy nightwear he could think again. 'And you can while away the long, tedious hours of the journey explaining why you found it necessary to make quite such a point of changing your appearance.'

'That's simple enough. I prefer to keep my two lives entirely separate.'

'Each clad in darkness?' It was her turn to stare at him. 'Did I get it wrong? Clad in darkness. That is what you said your name meant?'

'Oh, yes. Yes.'

He shrugged. 'Why?'

For a moment she didn't understand what he was asking. Then, as the penny dropped, 'Oh, I see. My appearance. I should have thought that was obvious.' She'd known he would ask that and had her answer ready. 'When I'm a star I won't want every Tom, Dick and Jack running to the papers saying I was their cleaner, will I?'

'Isn't that a little unkind? Robbing us poor men of such a small thrill. Darling.'

Melanie's smile was an essay in insincerity. 'Darling?' she repeated with distaste. 'Don't you think that is such a false term of endearment? Almost as if you've forgotten my name.' Before he could answer, she indicated the bookshop with the smallest gesture. 'Do you mind if I look for something to read on the plane? What with the hairdressers and packing, I didn't have time to shop this morning.' And a book would avoid the need for unnecessary conversation during the long haul across the Atlantic.

Taking her hand, he ignored her question, instead he spread her fingers out over his to admire the pale pink ovals of her nails. A slightly crooked smile lifted one corner of his mouth. 'I see the hand cream worked.'

'That, and the judicious use of rubber gloves. I never saw myself playing in kitchen sink dramas. I have enough of that in my day job.' She attempted to pluck her fingers from his, but before he let her go he lifted her hand, touching it lightly with his lips. They were cool, dry, electric and the tingle that shot from her hand to every part of her body warned that he packed the kind of voltage usually carrying a danger sign. What on earth was Caro thinking, letting him off the leash?

'We're not in the West Indies yet, Mr Wolfe,' she reminded him.

'Every role needs rehearsing, Mel. And it's time you started calling me Jack, don't you think?'

'It's certainly an improvement on darling,' she agreed.

He looked at her thoughtfully, then dropped her hand. 'Did you say you wanted a magazine to read on the flight?'

A magazine. What else? A book would certainly be too much for a mere cleaner with pretensions to a stage career. Especially a book without pictures. 'Yes,' she replied, coolly, heading for a display of the kind of magazines that offered true life stories of such horror that she almost flinched. Bravely she picked up two of them. Jack plucked them from her fingers and replaced them. After consulting the shelves, he took down a couple of thick glossy magazines.

'You look the part, but you'll have to try harder than that to keep in character,' he said, mildly.

'Character?' To Melanie, hovering on the brink of madness, it suddenly seemed possible, just possible that she might just derive some amusement from the situation if she could keep her head. 'Oh, I see . . . you want me to behave like Caroline?'

'There's no need to go quite that far.'

'You'd better keep an eye on me,' she said, throwing a look of regret at the abandoned magazines as she carried the glossies to the checkout. 'In case I do anything silly.'

'I intend to. A very close eye. Fortunately it won't be difficult,' he said, as he paid for the magazines.

Melanie swallowed hard and turned away. 'Aren't you going to choose something?' she prompted.

'I think I have pretty much everything I need,' he said, recapturing her hand and holding it possessively enfolded in his.

His fingers were cool, strong. She snatched her hand away. 'Not quite everything.' Despite his assurances, she was determined to make that quite clear at the outset; after all, he had been dealing with the worker bee when he'd made those. Now he'd seen what lay beneath the yellow and black horror of her uniform, she didn't entirely trust him to keep his word. He might not play house with his staff, but there was nothing to stop him from sacking her. Not that she had the slightest intention of resuming her job on her return to London. 'For "everything" you need Caroline Hickey,' she reminded him.

'Oh, I think we both know that Caro blew it. But she'll have her career to keep her warm on long winter nights.' The smile that had momentarily brightened the slaty darkness of his eyes abruptly vanished and he lifted his head as the public address system called a flight departure. And she recalled Richard telling her that the moment any woman showed signs of seeking something more permanent

179

than bed and breakfast, she was dropped. It seemed that Richard was right.

'That's our flight. Come along . . . darling. Paradise is waiting.' And taking her by the elbow, he led her towards the boarding gate.

The aircraft seemed to be overflowing with couples who were about to get married in the exotic beauty of one of the endless string of islands that made up that much-blessed area known as the West Indies. The excitement even overflowed into the more sedate first class section of the aircraft as one couple attempted to press champagne on their fellow travellers.

'Maybe Caroline made a mistake after all,' Melanie remarked drily, as the excited couple were ushered back to their section of the aircraft by a grinning stewardess. 'Wedding fever could be catching.'

Jack raised his head from the file he had been studying since they lifted above the grey English skies and out into the sunshine. 'Like measles?' he enquired.

'Oh, no, you can be vaccinated against measles. Marriage is more like the common cold. Immunity is much harder to come by.'

'I've been vaccinated, Melanie.' His face betrayed nothing. 'But then you already know that, having thoroughly polished the family picture gallery.' Including the wedding photograph which he preferred tucked away out of sight. 'But it was a long time ago. Maybe I should have a booster shot. What do you think?'

'I think your reaction to Caroline would suggest your immune system is in perfect working order.'

'Maybe. Or maybe I'm just immune to Caroline.' He reached across and rubbed the side of his thumb gently against her cheek. His touch made the fine down of her skin prickle and she jerked back.

'You don't have to worry about me, Jack,' she said, quickly. 'I'm not contagious.'

The look he gave her was long and thoughtful, as if he might be tempted to put that assertion to the test.

Melanie quickly buried herself in her magazine and stayed there. Just in case.

They left the big jet at Antigua, joining a small charter plane, and Melanie watched as the British Virgin Islands gradually appeared out of the haze, a broken necklace of small islands thrown down by some careless giant hand in a jade and emerald sea.

'Which one are we going to?' she asked, as excitement overcame her growing apprehension about what would happen when they arrived at their destination.

Jack leaned across her as the plane began to bank, his shoulder pressing firmly against hers as he surveyed the horizon. 'That one,' he said, pointing out one of the larger islands. 'At least, that's where we're landing.

It's called Virgin Gorda. Columbus is supposed to have said it looked like a young woman in early pregnancy. What do you think?'

As she turned to answer him her cheek brushed

181

against his chin and once more that dangerous tingle of electricity sparked through her. 'He . . . he wasn't looking at it from the air.'

'I suppose not. The Ark is that small island beyond it.'

She swiftly redirected her gaze to the window but his chin, roughened with the day's regrowth of dark beard, remained tucked up against her cheek as he abandoned work in favour of the view and she was right about the way it would feel. Harsh and exciting. It took every ounce of willpower to remain staring out of the window when all she wanted to do was turn her head so that their lips tangled and instead of playing games with words, they played something altogether more dangerous. Madness.

'It's an island? I thought it was just the name of the hotel.' There had been telephone numbers and a contact address in the envelope he had sent over to Mrs Graham, but no further details about their destination.

'Oh, it's more than a hotel. It's a resort. Very exclusive, very expensive and it can only be reached by boat, so we'll have a Columbus-eye view ourselves shortly. I hope you don't get seasick.'

Unfortunately not. Throwing up over Jack Wolfe might just have made the whole trip worthwhile.

A taxi took them from the airport along the narrowest part of the island, offering tantalizing glimpses of the sea and distant islands on either side of them. And yachts everywhere. This was, she realized with a sudden niggle of apprehension,

182

a playground for the rich and famous, and she sent a heartfelt prayer to whatever saint was responsible for such things, that no one she knew sailed by. Then, as they climbed to the highest point of the island, the setting sun turned the whole world to gold dust and she forget all about her problems, turning to Jack, wanting to share the beauty of the moment with him. It was then that she realized he had been watching her rather than the view.

'Aren't you glad I forced your hand?' he asked.

Irritated by his smug assumption that he knew what was best for her, she snapped back, 'No one likes to be left without a choice.'

'Even when the choice is between this and scrubbing floors?'

She had annoyed him and Melanie told herself that she was glad of it. 'Scrubbing floors is honest work,' she declared, and turned back to the view, but the magic had gone and by the time they had descended to the creek to board the launch that would take them across to The Ark the sun had slipped into the sea leaving only an afterglow to light their path.

Lights began to string out along the shoreline, reflecting in the water and the gentle rhythm of the steel pans drifted out across the water. As they headed across the bay, Jack made his way to the rear of the launch and she wondered if her last remark had been one too many. He'd been abstracted all through their journey, apparently engrossed in figure-covered papers. But the papers, like her magazine, had been there as a barrier between them. An excuse not to talk. She wondered if he was beginning to wish he'd coaxed Caroline to give up her magazine cover, no matter what he'd had to promise. He surely wouldn't worry overmuch about breaking his word once he'd got his way? Or was she maligning him?

As if he could sense her thoughts he turned suddenly, the breeze feathering a dark lock of hair that fell across his forehead, and for a moment it seemed that everything stood still, the sea, the spray, the lock of hair . . . then he held out his hand to her in an invitation to join him.

It was as if he was saying, Come on, this is going to be great. Relax. And without hesitation she went to him and he looped his arm about her shoulders.

Relax. Why not? With the soft Caribbean air warm against her face, the heady evening scent of tropical flowers mingling with the fresh salt tang of the sea it was easy. Then the launch hit an eddy and as she staggered slightly, his grip tightened.

'All right?'

'Fine,' she murmured, as he drew her back against his lean, hard body. Absolutely fine, she told herself, refusing to acknowledge the flutter of nerves that rippled over her stomach, the fact that it was increasingly difficult to breathe as she found herself drifting under the romantic spell of the place. Romantic spell? Listen to her. This wasn't romance, it was jetlag. She was just tired. She glanced at her watch, but it was no help. She had already changed it to local time and real time was hours later than that. She should be in bed.

Her mind backed rapidly away from that disturbing thought.

It was *ages* until bedtime. There was dinner first and, having refused food on the plane she was hungry. Terribly, terribly hungry. And then they would have coffee and perhaps a brandy – she rarely drank anything more than half a glass of wine, but anything to spin things out – maybe even a walk along the beach . . . There were hours and hours to fill before she had to worry about bedtime. But still, in an effort to forget about sharing a room with the man, about the way his chest was pressed firmly against her back, the way his hands were linked about her waist and his breath was stirring the down on her cheeks, she said, 'I think Caroline was crazy to miss out on all this.'

'You would have given up the offer of a starring role for me? I'm touched.' That was a tricky one and, as if he knew, he laughed at her predicament. 'Shall we agree not to mention her again, Mel?' he continued, his voice unexpectedly soft. She turned and looked up at him but his face was in shadow. 'You really don't have to constantly remind me that you're not Caroline. I can see that for myself.'

She stiffened, pulling away from him. 'I wasn't . . .' she began. Or maybe she was. Maybe she had brought up Caroline's name simply to remind him of the boundaries to their relationship. But he was probably still smarting from the girl's attempt to twist his arm. 'I'm sorry. It was tactless of me to mention her. I won't do it again.'

'Thank you.' There was a certain wry humour in his voice. 'Apart from anything else it would sound odd, don't you think?'

'Odd?'

'If every time I touch you, you mention another woman.' *Every time he touched her*? 'It might be noticed, don't you think?'

'Are you planning to touch me that often?' she asked.

'As often as appears necessary. Taking your arm as we enter the dining room. Your waist as I help you from the boat. And I like to dance up close, don't you? All in the line of business, of course,' he added, reassuringly. At least she thought he meant to be reassuring.

'Of course,' she repeated. Melanie discovered she was rather hoarse and cleared her throat. 'It's just the sea air,' she explained, when he enquired if anything was wrong, and she looked determinedly ahead as they approached the island, turning into a creek formed by two long shoulders of land.

The lights of the The Ark were getting closer; The Ark, where she had been hired to play this man's lover with sufficient conviction to ensure that his real reason for being there was not discovered. She had just said that Caroline was crazy to miss out on all this, but she was the one who was crazy, not Caroline. Had all that hot soapy water she'd been in up to her neck for weeks softened her brain?

Suddenly, despite the warmth, the scented tropical air, the gentle swell of the ocean beneath the hull of the launch, she wished she were back in London, wearing that ridiculous outfit and scrubbing someone's floor. Anyone's floor. But it was too late; his arms were fixed firmly about her waist and there was no escape.

She stared numbly ahead as the impressive waterfront entrance drew ever nearer. The central stone building of the hotel, part of an old fortification, glowed in the floodlights, looking rather like something that might have been built by Blackbeard to house his plundered treasure, if Blackbeard had been the kind of man to settle down.

Lights picked out small cottages tucked away amongst the hibiscus and bougainvillaea that scrambled everywhere, lights that reminded her that she would shortly be tucked up in one of them. With Jack Wolfe. How on earth were they going to manage? She could sleep on the sofa, always assuming there was a sofa, but they would have to share a bathroom, would undoubtedly encounter one another half dressed. Half dressed? She realized with a sinking feeling that she had never seen a pair of pyjamas when she stripped his bed and remade it. But then, he really didn't look like a pyjamas kind of man.

Oh, pull yourself together, Melanie Beaumont. You wanted a bit of danger. If that's as dangerous as it gets, what's your problem? If he so much as lays a finger on you all you have to do is scream and you'll blow his cover wide open.

But what about the arm, the waist, the dancing? Her

187

subconscious seemed to smile. But Melanie couldn't be quite sure.

Around them the tropical night enveloped them in warmth, tree frogs chirruped and the rigging of moored yachts chimed a reassuring welcome. Then the launch bumped against the jetty and her Nemesis turned her to face him.

'Well, we're in paradise, Mel,' he said, looking down at her, his eyes unfathomable in the half-light. 'What do you think of it?'

'It's . . . um . . . beautiful,' she said, her voice as stiff as her body, which she was holding rigidly as far from him as possible.

'I'm glad you think so, because very soon it'll be time to prove just how good an actress you are.'

'Good?'

'Perhaps we'd better have a run-through. Just to be sure.'

'What –?' He didn't give her time to think, breathe, utter the protest that formed on her lips. He bent and kissed her so convincingly that her response required no acting ability. None whatsoever.

CHAPTER 8

'Welcome.' Broad stretched vowels turned themselves into warm laughter as Mel, reeling, breathless
and flustered, broke free. 'Welcome to The Ark.'
The face of the man tying up the launch split into a
grin as he offered a huge hand to pull her up on to
dock. She seized it before Jack could take it upon
himself to further demonstrate his possession. But he
was beside her in a second, his hand in hers, leading
her along the jetty.

'Why did you do that?' she demanded, through her
teeth.

'Just establishing our credentials, darling,' he said,
smoothly. 'We must start as we mean to go on.'

'I don't remember you mentioning anything about
kissing. Only elbows and waists.'

'And dancing. We're on holiday, remember.'

'You're on holiday. I'm working. I've got a time
sheet to prove it.'

'You can fill it in now. Twenty-four hours a day
until further notice.'

'I get time and half after six o'clock.'

'Do you? Well, I never expected paradise to come cheap.'

'You can't buy paradise, Jack.'

'No? Just watch me.'

They entered the cool bright reception area, open on one side to the sea to catch the breeze coming in from the ocean, and were immediately enfolded in a Caribbean welcome by the smiling receptionist. 'Come along through to the office, Mr Wolfe. Mr Jamieson is waiting for you,'

'I can deal with the formalities,' Jack said, turning to Mel. 'Why don't you go and settle in? I'm sure you'd like the place to yourself while you unpack and sort yourself out.'

Mel didn't argue, but gratefully seized the chance he offered her to take a shower and change undisturbed. A maid was summoned, a large woman with a sense of humour to match, and, taking a key, she escorted Melanie along a well-illuminated path.

'I'm Sarah,' she said, 'and I'll be looking after you while you stay here.' She continued to chatter brightly, pointing out the facilities as she went, while Mel murmured in what seemed like the right places until they reached the cottage. Sarah swept through the sitting room and threw open the French doors that led on to a veranda. 'You'll get the breeze here because this side of the island faces the Atlantic ocean. It's never too hot.'

Melanie moved across the veranda and looked down at the long white curve of beach frilled with white foam where the waves ran up on to the sand. Out at sea were the lights of distant yachts, and above them the stars. It was bewitching, enchanting. Paradise indeed. She sighed, she wasn't quite sure why, before turning back to Sarah.

'It's quite lovely.'

Sarah beamed with pleasure. 'I'll leave you to settle in now, but if there's anything you want, please just pick up the telephone and ask for me.'

'I will. Thank you.'

Once Sarah had departed, Mel turned to explore the cottage. The sitting room was furnished in dark gleaming woods and brilliant prints that no doubt in the daytime would echo the garden it overlooked. There was a fridge containing anything she could think of in the way of drinks. And to her relief an absolutely enormous and comfortable-looking sofa. She opened the bedroom door.

'Oh, good grief,' she exclaimed, halting in the doorway. It wasn't so much a bedroom as the kind of honeymoon suite that appeared in glamorous movies. He'd promised a four-poster bed and he hadn't been kidding. This one had been created from the same dark tropical wood as the rest of the furniture, but the bedroom was not furnished in the brilliant print textiles used in the living room. The carpet, acres of it, was pale honey and with her recently acquired consideration for chambermaids she hardly dared to step on to it. But it was the bed that continued to hold her gaze. Positively king-size, it was hung with exquisite cream lace lined with honey-coloured silk. The coverlet and curtains had been made to match.

She took a deep steadying breath and decided there and then that she would certainly surrender it to Jack and stick to the safety of the sofa. She didn't stop to examine the luxury of the honey-veined marble bathroom, or to dwell on the slightly disconcerting discovery that the shower was open to the dark tropical sky. Instead she plunged gratefully beneath it to wash away the grime of travel. And, aware that Jack would be close on her heels, she didn't linger as much as she longed to; instead, wrapping herself in one of the bathrobes provided by the hotel, she returned to the bedroom, determined to be dressed for dinner by the time Jack returned.

She was too late. Having discarded his jacket and shoes, he was already stretched out on the bed, legs crossed, hands clasped behind his head, eyes closed.

'I didn't hear you come in,' she said, accusingly, clutching at the front of the bathrobe.

He opened one eye. 'Would it help if I whistled?' He began to whistle tunelessly.

'Don't be ridiculous.'

'Then stop twittering about like some virgin schoolgirl, Mel. This is business.' He rolled off the bed in one smooth movement and suddenly the room didn't feel anywhere near as huge as he stood over her, daring her to contradict him.

'You could have fooled me,' she retaliated, glaring up at him. She was making a fool of herself. She knew she was and yet she couldn't stop. 'I've been carried off here without so much as "by your leave" . . .'

'If you didn't want to come, why didn't you tell Mrs Graham the truth?'

'What is the truth? That you're a liar? A financial Assyrian hunting down defenceless –' Mel stopped, a little vague on the subject of the Assyrian's intended victims.

Jack appeared unmoved by this attempt to shame him. 'Why didn't you tell Mrs Graham the truth?' he repeated.

'Mrs Graham wouldn't have believed the truth.' She shrugged. 'And she wouldn't listen when I tried to get out of taking the job you were *supposed* to be offering.'

'Don't tell me she threatened to fire you if you didn't take it? The woman seems hell-bent on self-ruination.'

'Hardly. There are always women desperate for work.' But although the threat had hovered it had remained unspoken and, since Melanie had just accused Jack of lying, it would be hypocritcal to do it herself. However, she could hardly tell him the truth. She was, she realized, the unhappy possesser of any number of explanations, explanations that no one in their right mind would take seriously. 'Actually, because of you I'm her blue-eyed girl at the moment, but I don't kid myself, Jack. If she found out about this little side trip, I'd be out on my ear.'

'Would you? Poor Cinderella. Never mind, there's always the co-operative.'

'Once we've got suitable premises.' She stared up at him. 'How could you tell her that your mother had insisted on me working for her? Your mother has never met me.'

'No, but since she's living in Connecticut with her third husband she's not about to tell.'

'You are impossible,' she said, sternly.

'Oh, I'm much worse than that.' And, hooking his thumb beneath her chin, he deposited a searing kiss on her upturned lips. 'But then you already know that.' Then he released her, and before she could think of something suitably cutting to say in reply, the bathroom door had closed firmly behind him.

Subsiding on to the stool in front of the dressing table, Melanie admitted that it was true. She knew it. She'd always known it. And as she applied her make-up she tried to remember why, when Paddy had rung her last night to tell her that Mrs Graham had gone to the extraordinary lengths of calling at her house to ask her to take on a new job as a special favour, it had all seemed such a very clever idea.

What had been so clever about it? Surely she could have found Paddy a job herself if she'd put her mind to it? And who could say whether Jack Wolfe could help with the lease for the co-operative? Whether he would even try? If he said he hadn't been able to do anything, who could challenge him?

Clever. Ha! It was perfectly obvious that her brain cells refused to work properly when in close proxi-mity to Mr Jack Wolfe. They behaved like a compass put too close to a magnet and her thought processes

194

became confused, distracted, out of focus. And it wasn't just her mind that went haywire . . . her body seemed to take on a life of its own too. That kiss, for instance . . . nobody ever kissed her unless she wanted them to. She paused in her application of mascara to stare at her reflection. Had she wanted him to? Her cheeks were slightly pinker than usual; her eyes had an extra sparkle. Was that what he had seen and responded to? If so, she was in serious trouble.

And if she was in that kind of trouble, why was she smiling from ear to ear?

But she already knew the answer to that, recognized the perilous excitement of not being totally in control. It was as if Jack exerted some power over her. Maybe he was an alien . . . Her reflection grinned idiotically back at her from the mirror and she finally gave in to the impulse to giggle. He was working for an intergalactic holiday company who were planning to take over The Ark and use it for package holidays for wealthy interstellar travellers.

Still laughing, she turned to her suitcases and began to unpack, wondering what to wear for her first dinner in paradise. With the serpent. She'd just have to make sure she avoided apples. And used a long spoon. It was all very well coming over all giggly, but it was quite obvious that clothes were the least of her problems.

Then she held up the oversized purple T-shirt that was her favourite sleepwear. She didn't go in for glamorous nightwear and she hadn't given it a thought when packing, but this garment was certainly not the stuff of honeymoon suites. More the kind of thing worn by the average virginal school-girl . . .

She stopped worrying about her nightwear as a sudden silence warned her that the shower had stopped. She stuffed the T-shirt under a pillow and began to scramble into her clothes.

Melanie was sitting on the sofa, idly turning the pages of one of the magazines Jack had provided for her entertainment at the airport and making a brave effort to appear totally at ease with the world, when a shadow across the doorway indicated that she was no longer alone.

Assuming what she hoped was a bored expression, she glanced up. Jack Wolfe, wearing nothing but a towel slung about his hips and rubbing vigorously at his hair with another, was standing in the doorway, watching her.

The corded column of his neck, the naked expanse of tanned shoulders bedewed with water from the shower, the dark cruciform of hair that patterned his chest and dived disconcertingly in an arrowhead beneath the whiteness of the towel were disturbing enough. But as he roughly towelled his hair, the towel knotted carelessly at his hips worked looser and looser and she stared at it with fascination, the tip of her tongue against her upper lip, quite unable to avert her eyes in spite of the inevitability of what was about to happen.

196

She blinked as Jack retrieved the towel the moment before it finally unravelled, tucking it more tightly about him, and she looked up to discover that he was regarding her with the kind of smile designed to make maidens blush. Her cheeks flamed obligingly.

'Are you going to stand there all night parading yourself?' she demanded, irritably. Irritation was as good a disguise as any to keep her true feelings to herself, to deny that for a moment she had wanted the towel to fall, to see this man who had haunted her thoughts ever since she had first set eyes upon him in all his naked glory. 'I'm hungry,' she continued, in an effort to blot out the disturbing emotions that trickled through her veins, making her go first hot, then cold. It didn't work.

'Is that why you were in such a hurry to dress?' he asked, sliding his fingers through his hair in an effort to tame it. Her fingers itched to do it for him. 'In my experience it usually takes women hours.'

'Does it?' She didn't want to hear about his experience with women. 'I'm sure your experience is extensive, Mr Wolfe, but frankly, the length of time some women take to get dressed baffles me.' Her shrug was so casual, so dismissive that it deserved a curtain call of its very own. 'I mean, what is there so difficult about putting on a dress?' She glanced down at the exquisitely simple scarlet gown she was wearing. 'You just step into the thing and zip it up.' Her gesture, like her dress, was an essay in elegance. 'Ten minutes. Tops.' She smiled up at him. 'Why don't you see if you can beat it?'

'If you insist, but to be honest I don't think red is my colour.' His smile was slow and oddly seductive. She should have quit while she was ahead.

'Very funny.' She waited but he seemed to be in no hurry. 'Do you think you could get a move on?' she encouraged.

'Perhaps you should show me how it's done.'

'I'm not *that* hungry.' *Who was she kidding?*

'No?' *Not Jack Wolfe, evidently.*

But he clearly wasn't convinced by her hunger and he was right to be sceptical. Her only reason for speed-dressing had been a very real desire not to be caught her at the dressing table in her underwear when he vacated the bathroom and an absolute determination not to share the bedroom whilst he dressed. And if that made her look like a virgin schoolgirl . . . well, it couldn't be helped.

'I'm sorry if I've disappointed you,' she apologized with saccharine-sweet insincerity.

'Could you say that with a little more conviction?'

'Since I'm not part of the cabaret, Mr Wolfe, but here for the sole purpose of lending you probity, that's about as sorry as I get.'

'Probity?' Jack repeated the word thoughtfully. 'Now that's a word to conjure with.'

'And from my experience of you to date, conjuring with it is what you do best,' she replied, with every outward appearance of calm, although her insides were having a full-scale fit of the jitters. She felt a whole lot safer around Jack Wolfe when he had his

198

clothes on and she wished he would cut the verbal fencing and just go and get dressed.

'Best?' His mouth straightened in a smile. 'Stick around, Cinderella. You ain't seen nothing yet.' He indicated the fridge. 'Now, since we're supposed to be on holiday and having a good time, why don't you pour us both a drink while I'm dressing? I'll have a gin and tonic. You could take them out on to the terrace . . .' His smile suggested that he understood all about her need to put some distance between them, but he didn't let her off the leash for long. 'I'll join you in a minute.' Then he demonstrated that he was no slouch in the shrug stakes himself. 'Ten at the most.'

Feeling safer as he retreated into the bedroom, she called after him, 'Wouldn't real lovers be inside, behind closed doors?' He turned back, giving her a slow, thoughtful look that travelled the length of her body, making her skin tingle every inch of the way until it reached her cheeks. Silly question. Stupid question. And she wasn't silly, or stupid. Usually. 'I . . . um . . . I just want to do justice to my role . . .' She cleared her throat. 'That's all.'

He held the bedroom door open and stood aside, inviting her in. 'If you're that enthusiastic, Melanie, come on through and I'll be happy to co-operate,' he said, very softly, his voice rasping over her skin like a cat being rubbed the wrong way.

'Um . . . no . . .' she breathed, pressing back into the sofa in an effort to increase the distance between

199

them. 'I . . . um . . . I think I'll pass on the practical. Thanks all the same.'

'In that case I'd advise a little caution, darling. Put the serious flirting on hold until there's someone around to appreciate your performance.'

'Flirting! That wasn't flirting. I was just . . . entering into the spirit of the role . . .'

'Is that so? Well, try it again, lady, and I promise you you'll get a spirited response.' Then he carefully shut the bedroom door.

Melanie stood up, her legs shaking a little from the intensity of an emotional crossing of swords that she shouldn't have allowed to happen. She'd been alone with the man for less than an hour and was already sending out all the wrong signals. She had thought she was the one in control here, but she had been fooling herself. When he had kissed her, her insides had done an impression of an ice-cream in a heat-wave; giving him the wrong impression, she decided, would be very easy.

It was just as well that Jack Wolfe was not interested in her. Not really interested. Oh, sure, he was human enough to welcome her into his bed if she decided to play her part for real, despite all that high-minded stuff about keeping his hands off the staff. His invitation might have been a tease, but there had been nothing playful about the threat that followed it. Nothing. And she shivered, despite the soft warm breeze lifting the curtains.

Jack Wolfe might turn up the heat whenever he looked at her, touched her, but she would do well to remember why she was here. The man was as calculating as they came, and he and Caro Hickey deserved each other. She sighed a little, any inclination to giggle evaporating, and she acknowledged that they had got each other.

Then she crossed to the mini-bar. A drink, he had said – well, why not? A drink suddenly seemed like a very good idea.

Jack Wolfe closed the door behind him and waited. Heard her move around as she mixed a couple of drinks, then go out on to the veranda. Only then did he take his cellphone from his travel bag and call Mike.

'What is it, Jack?'

'We've got a problem.'

'And it couldn't wait until morning?'

'Morning?'

'Never mind,' Mike said, smothering a yawn. 'Go on.'

'It's Melanie Devlin.'

'Well, don't say I didn't warn you – '

'She knows Richard Latham. I saw her talking to him about three or four weeks ago, before she started working for me. She'd changed her appearance and I didn't realize she was the same girl until she turned up at the airport.'

'Changed her appearance? You mean she's been working for you under false pretences and you still took her with you?'

'I didn't have any choice. If she is working with

him, I don't want them to know they've been rumbled.'

'If?'

'It could just be a coincidence.'

'There's no such thing as coincidence in business, Jack. Remember?' *Never*? 'How the hell did she explain the change in her appearance.'

'Adequately.'

'Then let's hope you don't talk in your sleep.'

'No one's complained yet.'

'Who the hell would dare?'

Jack stared at the phone. It was true, he thought, Mike Palmer was getting a harder edge to his character, pushing more. Another year and he'd be thinking of stepping into his shoes. 'I thought you liked working for me, Mike.'

Mike laughed. 'Oh, I do, Jack. Where else would I get this quality of entertainment and be paid for it? Is she chasing you around the bedroom yet?'

'Not so that you'd notice,' he replied, somewhat wryly. 'The arrangement is still that one of us sleeps on the sofa.'

'You haven't decided who yet? That sounds promising.'

'Not from here.'

'She's playing it coy? Well, I'd advise you to do the same. If she is planning to extract all your secrets using the art of seduction it'll drive her to extreme inventiveness. If you're going to sacrifice your body for the greater good of the finance market, you might as well enjoy yourself.'

'Thank you, Michael, I think I can handle things at this end without any advice from you.'

'I don't doubt it. It should make for an interesting week.' Jack thought that 'interesting' understated the situation somewhat, but Mike was already far too amused by the whole situation for him to say so. 'And we can use this to our advantage.'

'Thanks, but I had planned a quiet week in the sun, leaving you to do all the work for a change.'

'I've a pretty good idea what you have planned, Jack. And a cottage at The Ark will be a whole lot more conducive to your purpose than a damp afternoon in a boathouse.'

'If you believe that, Mike, then it's clear that you've never spent a rainy afternoon in a boathouse. Now, I've briefed Gus and he's keen to do his bit, but what I need from you is everything you can discover about Melanie. And her connection with Latham.'

It was odd, she should be tired but she was too restless to sit down. Instead she walked across to the low wooden rail that surrounded the veranda. Below her the gardens dropped away to the beach where the palms were rattling in the warm, moist breeze coming in off the sea like a caress, moulding the silk chiffon of her dress to her legs.

The soft drag of the surf against the sand had a soothing quality, the mingled scents of frangipani and the sea had a heady, exotic beauty, and on the breeze she caught the plaintive melody of a steel band being played a long way off. Mel leaned against the rail and, despite everything, smiled a little.

What on earth was she complaining about? This morning she had been in London. A cold, wet London that refused to buckle down to a serious attempt at summer. Now she had the warm tropical night, a beach of pure white sand just yards from her door and the sea to rock her to sleep.

OK, so she had Jack Wolfe, too. But all she had to do was play her part. Smile, flirt a little when there was anyone around to see. What did it matter if the wretched man thought she was deluded into believing she could act? She grinned. He should talk to Trudy Morgan; she would tell him that the part might have been written for her.

Jack stood in the doorway for a moment, quietly watching her. Watching the way she pushed her hair back from her face, the way the breeze moulded the cloth of her gown to her body. Hired finery? He considered the way the low, scooped-out back hugged her skin as if it had been made for her. No, not hired. Second-hand clothes never fitted like that.

It was extraordinary how beautiful she was, much more than the simple transformation wrought by the change of hairstyle and designer clothes. How could he have been so easily deceived? He was usually so quick to spot any kind of pretence. Yet how closely had he looked? If he was honest with himself he knew he had avoided her, made sure he wasn't at home on the days she came in to clean, because right from the beginning there had been something about her that he had recognized as dangerous. Her spirit, her sense of mischief and an air of mystery that had made his pulse beat just a little faster. It was beating faster now.

Melanie didn't hear him until it was too late to turn and put some distance between them and she twitched nervously as, slipping his hand about her waist as if it were the most natural thing in the world, he leaned beside her against the rail. 'Enjoying the view?' Jack asked.

'I was.' She tried to move away, but as he turned towards her, his arm still about her, they were closer than ever.

'Jack . . .' Her voice begged him to release her, but her eyes were saying something quite different and he could see a tiny pulse hammering in her throat as she looked up at him.

'What is it?' Then, before she could answer him, he shook his head. 'Not now. There's someone on the beach looking this way.' She glanced out into the darkness but he hooked her chin back so that she was facing him. 'You're not interested in them, only in me.'

'Am I?'

'Who else? Why don't you put your arms around my neck and show them just how much?'

She tipped her head back to look him full in the eyes. 'Do you mean kiss you?'

Did he? Mike had suggested that it would be an interesting week. It would certainly be interesting to see what she made of this opportunity to disarm him, seduce him. How long would she play the reluctant *ingénue*? Maybe all she needed was a little encouragement, permission to be bad. 'Is it so difficult, Mel? It's the sort of thing actresses do every day, surely? Pretend? Don't you have classes in that sort of thing?'

'Classes?' The only lessons she would need to deal with Jack Wolfe were in self-defence. No, that was unfair. But a few lessons in basic common sense might not be a bad idea.

'At RADA, or somewhere?'

'I don't believe I've ever had classes that would cover this situation,' she replied, her voice dangerously soft. 'Anywhere.'

'In that case, I suggest you call on memory. It really can't be that long since you kissed a man?'

That depended on what you meant by kissing. 'I don't make a life's work out of it.'

'You're stalling.' His eyes gleamed provokingly and, challenged, she lifted her arms, pale in the starlight, to link her hands behind his head. His hair was still slightly damp from the shower, she could smell the shampoo he had used and the faint woody top-note of his cologne mingled with the scent of tropical flowers. It was, after all, not in the least bit disagreeable being kissed by Jack Wolfe. She had tried it, and honesty compelled her to admit that she had liked it.

It was the pretence she objected to. Or maybe it was his lack of pretence. If he had made an effort to meet her halfway it wouldn't have seemed quite so cold-blooded . . .

Horrified by the turn her mind was taking, she closed her eyes. Cold-blooded was exactly right and, stretching up on her toes, she pressed her lips against his. They were cool and dry and unresponsive.

Confused, humiliated, she attempted to pull away from him, but he held her close, refusing to let her escape. 'It couldn't have been that long, surely?' he said, regarding her from beneath heavy-lidded eyes.

'I believe I did more than enough to fool anyone walking along the beach,' she replied, stiffly.

'Maybe.' He looked down at her for what seemed like an age, his eyes unreadable in the starlight. 'But you know what I had in mind was something more like this.'

His lips on hers were light, hardly more than a teasing breath, reassuring her that this was nothing but a game to fool the curious eyes of any passing onlooker. Nothing to cause more than a minor flutter in her midriff, a stir of uncertainty as his hands spread over her waist and back, drawing her closer so that she could feel hard muscle beneath the smooth cloth of his shirt where her neckline swooped to hint at the soft swell of her breasts, his body enticingly warm against her skin.

She gave a little gasp of pleasure and the stir of uncertainty quite suddenly deepened to a realization of the danger she was in as a rare heat flared deep within her, jolting her senses into pounding life. But it was too late. Her negligent lips had been suborned into parting to the teasing touch of his tongue and now she was drowning in pure sensation, sinking deeper and deeper with no thought of ever coming up for air, no thought of anything but the seductive delight of being kissed by a man who knew how to give pleasure just as surely as he knew how to take it.

'You can open your eyes now, Mel. The lesson is over.' Her lids snapped open and she found herself looking up into an expression that was a whisper away from an insult. For a moment she could not believe it, then she wrenched herself free and turned away, blushing furiously. 'But you will let me know if you need me to show you again, won't you?' he added insolently as he moved away to collect his drink from the table, turning to hold out hers.

'I don't need anything from you, Jack Wolfe,' she declared, taking the glass. The man was arrogant, rude and she had had about enough of his games for one day. 'I'd like to remind you that bringing me along was all your idea and that I'm here for your benefit.'

'Not just my benefit,' he reminded her.

'If you're talking about the co-operative, we're leagues apart. You're playing for higher stakes than I could ever dream of, Jack Wolfe, so if you want me to keep your secrets it might be wise to try a little politeness.'

'You don't know my secrets.'

'I can make a pretty good guess.'

'Can you?' He took a drink from his glass. 'That sounded very like a threat.'

208

She hadn't intended it to be, but it was too late now to withdraw. 'You can take it any way you damned well please,' she said, and turned away, determined to put as much distance between them as the veranda allowed.

But he grasped her wrist before she had gone half a metre. 'Well, I can threaten too, so listen to this, lady. If you want my help with your precious co-operative . . .' co-operative! Dear heavens, he'd actually fallen for all that rubbish. He'd bent over backwards to do everything Melanie had asked, inventing a job for her friend, instructing Mike to pull all the strings he could find at the local authority '. . . I suggest you keep your mouth shut about why I'm here and behave yourself.' Well, he had to make it look good, didn't he?

'I don't give a damn about your secrets and I can assure you that behaving myself is what I do best.' For a moment they glared at one another, then quite suddenly his mouth twisted in an ironic smile.

'Is that so? Well, shall we keep that fact just between ourselves? I imagine it's so rare around here that it might give rise to gossip.'

'And that would never do.' She gave a stiff little shrug, refusing to answer his smile. 'I'll play your game, Jack. Just as long as you remember that's all it is. Even if we were married I wouldn't want you to kiss me in public.'

'Is that right? Well, call me a cad, sweetheart, but I wasn't planning on giving the impression we were married.' And he lifted her wrist, touching it lightly to his lips before tucking her hand in his arm. 'Now, shall we go and see what the dining room has to offer? Or, in the interests of keeping up appearances, do you think we should have an intimate dinner, alone, here?'

'After you've gone to so much trouble in order to look this place over? That is what you're doing, isn't it? Looking it over, seeing what it's worth before you make a move? You can't do that if you never leave the cottage.'

'That, of course, is true,' he said, his voice edged with irony, because if Mel was a plant there was a certain irony to the situation. In fact it was possible that his smokescreen was about to burst into flames. 'Shall we go?' She turned and pulling away from him swept across the terrace, but he caught her before she reached the door. 'Together, Mel. It's really too soon to be acting out the lovers' tiff, don't you think?' He reclaimed her arm and linked it through his. 'Relax, darling. Smile. You're in paradise, remember?'

She grimaced. 'It would help if you would stop calling me "darling".'

'You really don't like it?'

'I loathe it. I'm not overstruck on "sweetheart," either. And when it's so patently false it does nothing to help the romantic image you seem so keen to foster.'

'I'll do my best to remember. Honey?' He was teasing her again, Mel realized, and she gave him a look that assured him she didn't find it in the least bit funny. 'Oh, come on, Mel. Relax, enjoy yourself. Just think, you could be back in England, battling with the Underground after a hard day at the mop and bucket.' His smile deepened. 'You're not honestly going to tell me you'd prefer that?' His gesture took in the thickly clustered stars and as Mel raised her eyes to heaven and breathed in the warm scent of the tropical night folding itself about her, alive with the stridulation of a million unseen tiny insects singing in the darkness, she did at last manage a smile.

'Honestly?' Well, no. But she had the feeling that she'd be a lot safer on the Underground. 'You don't want to know what I'm thinking. Not honestly. You just want me to look good and behave myself so that no one suspects you're not all you seem to be.'

'Look good, yes. But if you plan on behaving yourself . . .'

'I know. Keep it to myself.'

His grin was as disconcerting as it was sudden. 'You're getting the hang of it. Come on. Let's have something to eat before you faint from hunger.'

With that he swept her along the path, so that by the time they arrived at the dining room she was slightly breathless and more than a little flushed as she anxiously scanned the other diners.

She had expected the other guests to be around their own age, but some of them were considerably older. Romance, it seemed, was not just for the young, at least not at these prices. And just for a moment the memory of her father and Diana at their wedding slipped into her mind. They were probably dining somewhere just like this, right now.

But there was no doubting the romantic ambience of the place. The dining room was intimate, softly lit with candles flickering in the gentle breeze that came off the sea, and their arrival attracted indulgent glances from nearby tables.

And Mel discovered, at that moment, that while it was one thing to play a part, it was quite another to have everyone believe that part to be the truth. Not that she would have cared if she and Jack really were lovers. If that had been the case, she doubted if she would have even noticed the other diners.

'I feel as if I'm the centre of attention,' she said, uncomfortably, as they were settled at their table.

'Looking like that you'd be the centre of attention wherever you went,' Jack said, as they were settled at their table. The *maître d'* immediately summoned a waiter to open the bottle of chilled champagne that was waiting for them and left them to peruse the menus.

'In the circumstances I'd rather not be.'

Jack shrugged. 'Does it matter?'

It would matter if Luke heard about this jaunt. She wondered if her uncle knew Jack Wolfe? He must know of him. He certainly wouldn't take it kindly if he discovered The Wolf had stolen away his little lamb. But that was her problem, not Jack's.

He leaned forward. 'I don't think you need worry too much. Somehow I don't see this as Janet Graham's kind of place,' he assured her, confidentially.

His undisguised amusement annoyed her, but then he wasn't to know that she had friends who were as familiar with the Caribbean as their own back yards.

'I didn't imagine for a moment I would meet Mrs Graham, but you're not the only person I clean for. I mean, would you want to meet *your* domestic in an exclusive holiday resort?'

'It wouldn't bother me in the slightest.'

'That's very noble, but I can assure you, Jack, that some of the ladies I work for don't have your egalitarian principles.'

He finally got the message. 'Relax, Mel. Out of that ghastly uniform no one will recognize you, I promise. I didn't recognize you myself at the airport. In fact if it hadn't been for your voice I don't think I'd have believed my own eyes.'

'My voice?'

'Those perfectly rounded vowels,' he explained. Her voice. Of course, *that* was why they had all leapt to the conclusion that she was an actress. 'You look like a lady and you talk like one,' he said, in confirmation of her sudden enlightenment. He gave his attention to the menu and missed the dark and angry flush that flooded her cheeks.

'And do I act like one?' she enquired, coolly.

'You're doing fine. Don't worry,' he muttered.

'On what authority do you base that opinion?'

He finally looked up, saw the spark of anger that darkened her eyes. 'Have I offended you?' he asked.

'You seem surprised. Did you think it would be impossible to offend a girl who is forced to earn her living by cleaning up after you, Jack?' Her voice had a clear, carrying quality and several heads turned in their direction.

Jack Wolfe sat back in his chair and gave her his full attention. 'In answer to both your questions, I base my opinion on the way someone behaves, not what they do for a living. Now, is there anything else you'd like to broadcast to the rest of the dining room while you're in the mood?' he enquired, his own voice matching her own. A couple at a nearby table immediately found the contents of their plates intensely interesting. He waited. 'No? Then if I apologize for being less than a gentleman, perhaps we can both forget that you have just behaved like less than a lady.' Mel, utterly confused at having the ground swept from beneath her, blushed deeply. Apparently satisfied by this indication of her contrition, he continued. 'Now, what would you like to eat?'

CHAPTER 9

Despite her earlier declaration that she was starving Melanie had quite lost her appetite. 'I'm not sure,' she said, glancing at the menu. 'I'm not as hungry as I thought.'

'Grilled fish and a salad, perhaps?' he suggested, in the resigned manner of a man used to ordering for a weight-conscious model and then watching her pick at her food.

Well, she wasn't a model. She wasn't in the least bit like Caroline in any way, shape or form, Mel thought crossly as she considered the menu more carefully, looking out for dishes that Caroline wouldn't have touched with a bargepole. 'The local seafood in puff pastry sounds good.' Absolutely laden with calories. 'Or the chicken breast in rum cream sauce. Or dorado cooked in a breadcrumb and banana crust.'

'Do you know what dorado is?' he enquired, gravely, almost as if he knew what she was doing.

'No,' she admitted.

'It's a kind of fish.'

'Is it? Oh, well. Perhaps not with banana.' Her smile was as wide as it was insincere. He appeared not to notice. 'I'll have the seafood in pastry.'

'Nothing to start?' She shook her head. Jack conveyed their choices to the waiter then, when he had gone, he lifted his glass. 'So, what shall we drink to?'

Mel shrugged. 'Your nasty little business deal, perhaps? Caroline's rising star? You decide,' she said, carelessly.

With one hand he reached across the table and placed his hand over hers. With the other he picked up his glass and raised it to her. To anyone watching it would have appeared their closeness was total. His eyes, as he challenged her, belied it.

'I thought you were going to behave yourself,' he said, quietly. For a moment she remained motionless in her chair, transfixed by the unexpected charge of his touch as he continued to hold her hand, waiting for her to respond. Very slowly she picked up her glass and for a moment it was a toss-up whether she threw the wine at him or drank it. He apparently read the thought in her face even before she herself was aware of it. 'I wouldn't advise it, Mel,' he warned, softly.

She leaned towards him, to any onlooker absolutely captivated by the good-looking man opposite her. 'Why? What would you do to me?' she asked, her voice equally low, sorely tempted despite his warning, or perhaps because of it, to put him to the test.

He smiled, very slowly. 'You could risk it and find

216

out. But I understood that you had serious objections to being part of the cabaret.' His fingers tightened on hers and he tilted his glass, touching it against her own. 'May I offer instead a toast to life, love and the wit to enjoy both?'

'To life and to love,' she repeated. Then, 'I'll leave it for you to decide which you'd rather have this week.'

'Not both?'

'Not both,' she confirmed, with a firmness that belied the tremor that emanated from the region of her abdomen.

'It does seem a pity to waste that bed.'

The tremor intensified. 'And I thought *you* were going to behave yourself. Caroline had a choice, Jack. As your cleaner you didn't consider it necessary to give me the same privilege.'

He had inadvertently invited Mata Hari along as his personal guest and she was objecting? Well, in the circumstances he supposed she would have to put up some kind of token resistance. It wouldn't do to be too obvious. Besides, Mike was right, it might be more fun to let her do the seducing.

'Frankly, I thought it would be easier for you that way,' he said, seriously.

'Easier?'

'I'm not a complete idiot, Mel.' No? Then where were those gales of hollow laughter coming from? 'I understood why you felt obliged to reject my proposition. But it's just a job.' He regarded her thoughtfully. 'You don't feel threatened when

217

you're in my home, do you?'

'You're not usually in it,' she pointed out. 'Just
look what happened when you were.' She had meant
the scene with Caroline, but as their eyes met she was
certain that he too was remembering what had so
nearly happened the day she had woken him. 'I'm
afraid that when we get back to England you'll have
to find someone else to do your dusting,' she said
briskly and, detaching her hand from his grasp,
removed it from his reach.

'Because of this?' he asked, his face, his voice quite
unreadable. She had no idea whether he was shaken
by this announcement, or relieved. Not a man to play
poker with. Not a man to play any game with. A wolf
in the clothing of sophisticated, urban man. But a
wolf nevertheless.

'You think I would allow myself to be put into the
same position again?'

He could scarcely believe the gall of the woman.
'You're being given a holiday in the lap of luxury,' he
pointed out. 'What is there to complain about?'

Melanie remained silent. If he was that insensitive
there wasn't any point in trying to explain it to him.

'You're really that angry with me?'

'Congratulations, Jack. You've finally got there.'

'Perhaps I was a little high-handed,' he admitted,
suddenly not quite so sure of himself. If she was
acting, she was good. Very good.

'Perhaps you were.' She waited, but that was
apparently the extent of his apology. Her shrug
was more mental than physical. 'The next time

218

you need female companionship I suggest you call one of any number of young women of your acquaintance who, despite your insistence to the contrary, would undoubtedly have leapt at the opportunity to come along on this trip with you.'

'If by that you meant to be flattering, Mel, let me tell you you failed.' He emptied his glass. It was immediately replenished by a discreet waiter. 'Besides, that would be inviting romantic complications.'

And according to Richard he avoided romantic entanglements like the plague. 'Which is why Caroline let you get away with bringing me. She doesn't consider me a threat.'

His gaze swept over her sleek hair, delicate make-up and beautiful clothes in one all-encompassing glance. 'If she could see you now I don't think she'd be quite so confident.' He didn't wait for a response to his back-handed compliment. Instead he offered her a smile of such unexpected sincerity that she almost gasped. 'If I assure you that I won't coerce you into anything else, will you forgive me?' he asked.

It was as if he was two different people, Melanie thought. One was a tough businessman who didn't care whom he stepped on when he had a goal in sight. But when he smiled, really smiled, he was quite different. And that haunting mental image of him in a pair of jeans worn soft with use, his torso slicked with sweat as he bent over a sawhorse, flickered disturbingly into her mind. He was still tough, but it was an appealing toughness, all in his body, the rope-like sinews of his forearms, the paired muscles as they tightened down his back. It was odd how she could see him so clearly, almost taste the salt of his skin . . .

'I'll consider it,' she conceded quickly, looking down at her glass, avoiding his eyes. 'But I'm afraid you'll still have to find someone else to do your dusting.'

'And if I won't have anyone else?'

The image faded. Did the wretched man really think he could always have what he wanted, just for the taking? She looked up. His expression hadn't changed. He was still smiling, but suddenly she could see right through it. This was a man who took what he wanted without thinking twice about the consequences for anyone else. It would give her the most intense pleasure, just this once, to disappoint him. 'Then I'm afraid you'll have to do it yourself, Jack. I put my resignation in the post before I left for the airport.'

Jack Wolfe leaned slowly back in his chair. He was still smiling with his mouth but his eyes were hooded, so that she could no longer tell what he was thinking. 'You've resigned?'

'Yes.'

'So you are no longer working for me?'

There was something about the way he said that that sent a tiny shiver of apprehension whiffling down her spine. And then she remembered. He didn't play house with people who worked for him. But he'd said that to the worker bee. Would he have taken the same line if he'd known that beneath those horrible clothes, the wig, the unflattering make-up, she was someone else entirely? And she'd just given him the perfect get-out. But it wasn't too late to retrieve the situation.

'Why would you think that? I gave Mrs Graham a week's notice.' That should cover it. 'One has to be considerate.'

'To Mrs Graham? I thought you were planning to undermine her business?'

'I am. But there's no reason to give her advance warning.'

'A week?' She nodded. 'Well, that should do it,' he agreed, smiling to himself. Melanie was reminding him that she expected him to stick to his own rules, but she wasn't thinking things through. It should have been obvious to her that once she had given notice the reason for them no longer existed. But it was academic, anyway. He'd decided the moment he'd set eyes on her in the airport that there was no way he was going to spend the whole week on a sofa. Not when he had Mata Hari along for company, no matter how amateur. And when, on the launch, he had taken her into his arms and kissed her he'd known he wouldn't have to.

He wasn't fooled for a moment by her outraged modesty. He didn't believe for a moment it was genuine. And if it was? Well, it was the classic symptom of a girl who wanted to throw caution to the winds, but whose instincts were telling her she was a fool. Her instincts were good, of course, but in the end they would be no match for a warm sun, a little wine, and the enforced intimacy of the situation. He'd make sure of that.

'A week is going to have to do it, Jack, because it's all you've got. But I haven't forgotten that you're doing me a favour too, so for the next seven days I'm prepared to appear to be . . .' He raised a pair of questioning brows at her hesitation. '. . . *appear to be*,' she repeated, carefully, 'everything you want.'

Nicely put. 'I'm very grateful.'

'How grateful? Have you had a chance to look at my business plan?'

'Briefly. And you were right, it's well done.' He regarded her thoughtfully. 'Very well done. In fact, it's so well done that I'm beginning to wonder just who you are, Melanie Devlin. You come into my apartment, clean up after me, wash my clothes, do my shopping when I ask you. You probably know more about me than anyone since my mother . . .'

'Surely not more than Caroline Hickey?'

'I can assure you that Caroline has never felt the urge to wash my socks . . .'

'Really?' She did a very good feigned surprise. 'What urges *does* the delectable –?'

'. . . and until today you chose to masquerade behind an unattractive brown wig as a rather plain girl no one would bother to look at twice,' he continued firmly, cutting her off before she could say something totally outrageous.

It was odd, Melanie thought. Being outrageous had never been her thing; that was Claudia's forte.

222

Fizz was the smart one of the family, the girl who'd started her own radio station, married a millionaire and made motherhood look like a piece of cake, while she . . . well, she had somehow slipped into the role of the baby of the family. Indulged, humoured, and just a little bit spoiled.

Suddenly *outrageous* seemed very tempting. But before she could try it, Jack added, 'I have to ask myself, why?'

Melanie wasn't fooled for a moment by the lightness of his remark. He hadn't been convinced by her excuse and now he was digging a little.

'Camouflage?' she offered. That was the reason he had given for bringing her along on this jaunt. 'It's a jungle out there.' She lifted her shoulders in a gesture far too elegant to be described as a shrug. 'But then I'm not telling you anything you don't already know, Jack. Am I?'

Jack Wolfe felt a warning nudge somewhere beneath his belt. He had a gut instinct for trouble and suddenly, now, when it was too late to do anything about it, he had the uncomfortable feeling that he had stepped out of Caroline's frying pan right into the fire. *I'm not telling you anything you don't already know* . . . What the hell *did* he know about the girl? The only concern on his mind when he had forced her hand had been that she might not quite look the part, might not be convincing enough. Where had his famous gut instinct been then?

Kicked into touch by rampaging hormones? That had to be ridiculous. Yet there had been a fillip of

223

excitement when the idea had taken hold, the kind of excitement that he had kept at arm's length for so long that he had almost forgotten how it felt. That alone should have been enough to send up a storm-warning.

What was it Tom had said about her? She had knocked his socks off. And he had dismissed the boy as muddle-headed. He didn't quite know why, because even dressed as Cinderella she had been quite capable of stirring something in him, touching some part of him that Caro had never even got near to.

But then, that was part of Caro's attraction.

Then Melanie had arrived at the airport looking like a million dollars and he knew he'd been taken for a fool. And there wasn't a thing he could do about it. But he would. No one took him for a fool and got away without paying for the privilege. He just intended that the payment should be pleasurable.

'Jack?' she prompted.

'Yes, it's a jungle,' he agreed, bringing his attention firmly back to the problem in hand. And the problem was that if she wasn't who or what she had seemed, then who was she? Really? Not just some girl who had ideas of being an actress, that was certain. Or maybe she was; maybe Latham had convinced her that he could find her work if she did this for him. Or was that what he wanted to believe? If so, he was a fool. But he didn't have to keep on being one. He smiled at her. She smiled back a little uncertainly, took a rather large swallow of champagne. Despite her careful veneer of self-assurance, she was nervous.

He raised a finger and the waiter refilled her glass.

'What is it?' she asked, when he continued to smile at her.

He shook his head. 'Nothing. But it just occurred to me how little I know about you. Apart from your name.'

'Are you sure you even know that?' she enquired, archly.

'It was on your passport.' There was no reason to believe it was anything other than genuine, but he'd already given Mike the number and asked him to check it out. Just in case.

'That's true,' she agreed. Up to a point. Born Melanie Devlin, acted for years as Melanie Brett, but since her London début she had taken her father's name and become a Beaumont. It had been a little late for Edward to adopt her; she was already an adult. But he had been keen for her to change her name formally. She'd think about it when she got home. Maybe Heather would like to add it to her name, too. Or there again, maybe she wouldn't. Jack, she realized, was waiting for more. 'You've never wanted to know anything else,' she said, somewhat abruptly.

Jack swivelled the glass between his fingers, watching the delicate trails of bubbles rise to the surface. Then he looked up, caught her staring at him. 'In that case I've been a fool, Miss Devlin. You are clearly a very remarkable young woman and I'm seriously interested in everything about you. We have all evening so why don't you tell me about

225

yourself? I want to know . . . well . . .' and he smiled again '. . . everything.'

And it was obvious that he did. Mel wondered why. Why *now*? Surely he should have asked her that before hauling her across the Atlantic? She returned his smile, took another sip of champagne and then quite deliberately kept him waiting.

'I really should know a few details,' he prompted, 'in case anyone asks.'

He hid his irritation well, Mel thought as she watched him. But he *was* irritated. He wasn't used to being kept waiting. He didn't like it, while she, conversely, had begun to enjoy herself.

'Make it up,' she invited.

'We might give different answers to the same questions,' he pointed out quite reasonably.

She raised her brows a notch. 'Who's going to be interrogating us?' He didn't offer an answer and she leaned forward, lowering her voice to whisper. 'The *camouflagee*?'

'The *what*?'

'The camouflagee. If I'm camouflage, there must be someone around trying to spot the join, or what's the point?'

He stared at her for a moment, then he laughed. She was good. Very good. 'You're a bright girl, Melanie,' he conceded. 'So I don't have to explain why it's so important that we get our story straight. Where do you live, for instance?'

'Not with you?' she asked, lifting a well-shaped brow into a delicate arch. 'How very old-fashioned.'

'I am old-fashioned.' Then, almost as an after-thought, 'Would you want to live with me? If we were lovers?' Melanie blushed and quite suddenly Jack laughed. She wasn't that good, not with skin that blushed like a ripe peach to betray her. She was glaring him at him for laughing at her blushes. 'I'm sorry. That was unkind. But as I'm sure you've realized, I prefer to live alone.'

'Yes, I realized. Poor Caroline.'

'She knew, Melanie. Don't waste your pity on her.'

'You're a cold-hearted bastard.'

'You are not the first person to have made that observation.' Why did people say cold, he wondered, when they meant unfeeling? His heart wasn't cold; it had simply stopped functioning as anything but an efficient pump the day Lisette had been mown down . . . And they called him cold because he had channelled all his passion into making money. At least he had been able to use it to do some good. He realized she was staring at him and he straigh-tened slightly. 'I thought we'd agreed not to mention Caroline again. It's your life story I'm interested in.' There was a long pause while he waited for her to continue. She didn't. 'So where *do* you live?' he was finally driven to ask. 'If not in the wardrobe depart-ment of the BBC?'

The sweet reason was beginning to sour, Mel noticed, and, twirling the stem of her glass between her fingers, she considered what to tell him. Bearing in mind she'd have to live with whatever she said for the next week.

Stay in character and never lie when you can tell the truth was a good maxim and it would certainly make more sense than inventing a lot of nonsense about living in a bedsit in some part of London she barely knew.

That decision made, Melanie raised her lashes and looked him full in the eyes. 'I live in Chelsea,' she said.

'Chelsea? What part of Chelsea?'

'I have an apartment overlooking the harbour.'

His mouth twisted slightly; apparently he was unimpressed with her inventiveness. 'Isn't that rather expensive?'

'Extremely expensive,' she agreed, driven by a deep, dangerous need to make him see her, really see her instead of the idea he had built up in his mind. 'Are you sure that you can afford me?'

'It would seem so. At least by the hour.' She bit back the urge to tell him that he was paying seriously bargain basement prices for her time. Instead she took a long swallow of champagne. 'Do you live alone? Or with your family?' he asked, after another pause during which he must have realized that nothing further was going to be volunteered.

'There are a number of other possibilities,' she pointed out.

'That you're living with a man?' Latham? The idea was not pleasing. Then he shook his head. 'You wouldn't be interested in the kind of man who would have let you come away on this jaunt with me.'

'Wouldn't I?' She was surprised he had given the

matter any thought, and that, having thought about it, he was so perceptive. 'But it's just a job.' It was his turn to remain silent, hers to shrug. 'Perhaps you're right. But I don't live with my family, either. Like you, I prefer to live alone.' And Melanie smiled. Sticking to the truth, she discovered, was rather fun.

'I see. So there you are,' he continued, apparently deciding that this was after all a game and since she was making up the rules, he might as well play along with her for the time being, 'an out-of-work actress, reduced to cleaning to make ends meet, living in an expensive apartment in Chelsea. May I ask, if it isn't incredibly rude of me, just how you manage to pay the rent?'

The mockery was gentle enough, but it was there. Mel wondered what it would take to make him doubt himself. Just for a moment. After all, divested of her ghastly uniform and dressed in expensive clothes, Melanie knew she looked the part for the simple reason that she *was* the part. And she would take great pleasure in denting that unwavering confidence.

She wrinkled her forehead in a delicate little frown. 'Rent?' she repeated, as if she wasn't quite sure what the word meant. 'I'm sorry, Jack, didn't I make myself clear? I own the apartment.'

There was no outward sign of his irritation. No outward sign that he was anything other than slightly amused by her silliness. And yet his growing annoyance came back at her like radar waves, so strong that she could almost feel the shock of it. 'You own an apartment in Chelsea,' he said, slowly, 'and you scrub floors for a living. Could it be that I was right all along? That you are, indeed, Cinderella?' The teasing smile that played about his mouth didn't quite make it to his eyes.

'With you as Prince Charming? I don't think so.' Her own smile rivalled candyfloss for sweetness and had about as much sincerity as that of a hungry crocodile. 'And who scrubs floors these days? Although I don't suppose you'll be keen on my broadcasting details of my brilliant career. I'd probably better stick to the actress part. We needn't mention that I'm out of work.' She glanced pointedly around at the softly lit restaurant, the well-dressed couples. The whole place oozed money.

He took no notice. 'Even without rent, the expenses . . .' He was being sucked in, she realized, enjoying the sensation of being in control, at least for the moment.

'It's kind of you to worry, Jack, but honestly, it's not a problem. I have considerable assets. A large, well-managed portfolio of shares. Some property – '

'Apart from the flat in Chelsea?' he enquired.

'Apart from the flat in Chelsea.' She took another drink. 'In Australia, actually.'

'Australia,' he repeated. 'How original.'

'Do you think so? It's where I lived until quite recently.'

'Is that a fact?' He sat back in his chair and regarded her thoughtfully. 'And all these . . . assets

230

. . . they bring in a suitably large income, I hope?'

If he had believed in their existence, this question would, indeed, have been incredibly rude, but since he plainly didn't believe one word of what she was saying she answered him.

'I'm certain that your hope is vastly exceeded by reality, Jack.'

'Are you indeed? So where did these assets come from? Were they inherited?'

'Some, from my mother. And my uncle gave me a lump sum on my eighteenth birthday. But over the years I've earned quite a lot too.'

'Not that many years,' he pointed out. 'How old are you?'

'It isn't polite to ask. But since you have, I'll tell you. I'm twenty.' But not for much longer.

Twenty. The same age as Lisette when she died. 'Your mother . . .' He cleared his throat. 'Your mother couldn't have been very old, Mel.'

'No. She wasn't old.' Not quite forty, still beautiful, still with the possibility of a wonderful life ahead of her with the man she had loved all her life . . . 'She died in an accident a couple of years ago. A flash flood.'

He said nothing for a moment. She wasn't sure if he was simply being quietly sympathetic, or trying to work out if she was telling the truth. 'Tell me about the rest of your family, Mel. You *do* you have family?'

'Doesn't everyone?' But he was no longer playing. 'Well, let me see. I have a father, but I didn't know him until last year. He and my mother weren't married,' she explained. 'I'm afraid he was married to someone else . . .'

'Was?'

'She died too.'

'Quite the Greek tragedy.'

'Sophocles would have had a field day,' she agreed. 'My father's first wife was a natural . . .' That, she thought, reproaching herself, was an awful thing to say even if it was the truth. 'And when I finally met my father I discovered I had two half-sisters, both married now, one with a baby daughter who is named Juliet after . . .'

'After the Shakespearean heroine?'

'Who?'

'Juliet. I thought perhaps the theatre ran in the family.'

'Oh, I see.' She shook her head. 'No, actually she was named after my mother.' *Her mother. Edward's first grandchild had been named for his lost love. How on earth could she have thought that her father, or Luke, had forgotten her?*

'*Your* mother?' She looked up to discover Jack regarding her with the faintest suspicion of a frown and she rapidly blinked back the threatened brightness. 'Isn't that rather unusual, given the circumstances?'

'Not in this case. Fizz – the half-sister with the baby daughter – is married to my uncle, my *mother's* younger brother. No relation. In case you were wondering. People do, you know,' she said, pertly, to cover that sudden moment of revelation. 'And then my father remarried a few weeks ago and I now have a stepmother and stepsister,' she added, and then stopped.

'That's it?'

'Isn't that enough?' He didn't immediately answer. Obviously not. Oh, well, in for a penny . . . 'You might also like to know that it's my birthday next week. In the circumstances . . .' she made a general gesture to take in their surroundings '. . . you would be expected to know that, wouldn't you? But please don't feel that you have to buy me a present,' she added. Still no response. Melanie wrinkled her brow, thoughtfully. 'When is your birthday, by the way?'

Jack Wolfe shifted uncomfortably. 'Stop it, Mel.' She managed to look puzzled. 'I think you've demonstrated that your imagination is in full working order, but the joke has gone quite far enough.'

She regarded him from beneath lowered lids. Not quite. Not quite. 'That's why *you're* wooing me, of course. For my family connections. And my money. You've lured me to paradise in the hopes of getting me to say "I will" beneath a tropical moon before anyone can convince me of the error of my ways. I know they do beach weddings here,' she said. 'I saw some photographs in Reception.'

Jack almost choked. 'You're worth marrying for your money?'

'Would you doubt it?'

'I hope I'm gentleman enough to believe that your body would be inducement enough.'

'How sweet,' she said, thoroughly enjoying herself

233

now. 'But I'm afraid it's definitely the money. After all, I'm here with you, sharing a romantic beach cottage, so you see as far as the world is concerned my body is already yours.'

She spread her hands in a gesture that indicated she had finished, inviting his response. She rather hoped he would be lost for words, but he wasn't.

'I think you'd better tell me more about your very interesting family, Mel. If they're to come racing to the rescue I'd like to know what to expect. Your father, for instance. Is he likely to be wielding a shotgun?'

She leaned forward and lowered her voice in a confidential manner. 'It's my uncle you'll have to watch out for. He's been *in loco parentis* for as long as I can remember and is inclined to be protective. As for Dad, well, he's still on his honeymoon, so you're safe from him. For the moment.'

He held up his hand, finally reduced to laughter. 'That's enough. You'll be telling me next that you're pursued by every impoverished young man in the land.'

'Will I? Actually, you'd be amazed at the really rich ones who quite fancy me too.'

'I'm beginning to think I'm beyond further surprises. Tell me, have you never been in the least bit tempted by any of them?'

'Heavens, no,' she declared. 'I'm an only child – '

'Apart from the two half-sisters and a stepsister?'

'– and shockingly spoilt, which is why, despite all the dire warnings of my family and friends, I've

234

chosen to risk my heart on a scoundrel who will undoubtedly break it. Any man who used a girl to cover a doubtful business enterprise would have to be a scoundrel, wouldn't he?' she asked, very gently.

His jaw tightened slightly and suddenly he wasn't laughing any more. 'Doubtful?'

'Why else would you need camouflage, Jack?'

'That's enough, Mel.'

'You don't like your role?'

'Make up your own stories if you like. Leave me out of it.' He had begun to enjoy her game until he was cast as the villain, she realized with interest. Had she struck a raw nerve?

'But all the best stories have a villain,' she explained. And the best villains were dangerous, exciting men who could curl a girl's toes with a twitch of a brow, the suspicion of a smile.

'Maybe. Perhaps you should consider a career writing dizzy romances instead of trying to make it on the stage.'

Dizzy, eh? Mel laid her hand on her heart. 'But it was the truth,' she said, earnestly. 'Every word. Didn't I convince you?'

'To be honest, Mel, it's frightening how convincing you were.' He regarded her with something like pity. 'For a moment there – ' He looked up as the waiter approached with their food.

'Yes?' Mel encouraged, her eyes sparkling at this evidence of her success.

For a moment he said nothing as doubt gnawed at him. Then he shrugged. 'It seems that you're a far better actress than I gave you credit for.' Good enough to blush on cue? He turned away as the waiter began to serve them, unwilling to let her see how much her charade had irritated him. Then his frown deepened. 'Don't look now, but someone's staring at you.'

'One of my many fans, I have no doubt,' Mel said, flippantly enough, but nevertheless a nervous quiver rippled her spine. A fan was a complication she could do without. 'What does he look like?'

'Mid to late fifties, hair greying at the temples, exquisitely tanned. One of those thoroughly distinguished English gentlemen that you wouldn't trust with your daughter.'

'As bad as that?'

'Don't look,' Jack said, catching at her wrist as she began to turn. Mel jumped as if branded and for a moment their eyes locked. Then, very carefully, Jack opened his fingers and let her go. It made no difference. The heat was still there, burning right through her. 'He's still staring,' he said, with studied carelessness. 'You wouldn't want to give him any encouragement?' *Or would she? Was this her contact?* 'Would you?' he pressed.

'Perish the thought.'

'My sentiments exactly.' He indicated her plate. 'That looks good,' he said, as if determined to return the conversation to the mundane.

'It is,' she replied, wondering whether a comment about the weather would help. She didn't risk it, but tucked in in a manner intended to suggest that she could manage without conversation of any kind for the time being.

For a while he respected her silence, but it was too good to last and when she shook her head at the offer of a pudding, he obviously considered he had been quite forbearing enough.

'Would you like to dance?' The question was obviously rhetorical since he stood up without waiting for her answer. For a moment she considered declining so that he would have to sit down again, but that would be petty and besides, she liked dancing.

'Will I have to brave my fan?' she asked.

'No. He didn't stay. You're quite safe.'

That was a matter of opinion, but as they danced on the terrace to the lively rhythm of a local band she decided to forget everything but the fact that the music was good, the night beautiful and by the time the music had changed tempo and Jack drew her closer, Mel had no difficulty at all in laying her head against his shoulder.

'You know, I rather like it here,' she said, as she nestled sleepily against him.

'I'm glad to hear it.'

'I could almost like you, too.'

He drew back and looked down at her, his shadowed face masking a thoughtful expression. 'The feeling is mutual, Cinderella, but if you don't get to bed soon you'll be asleep on your feet.'

Mel *was* tired. It had been a long day. 'Horses sleep on their feet, did you know that?' she asked him as, with his arm about her shoulders, he led her from the terrace.

'I had heard. I wouldn't advise it in your case.'

'Can we walk back along the beach?'

'I don't think so.'

But she giggled and, standing on tiptoe, whispered loudly in his ear, 'But isn't that just what lovers would do?'

He stared down at her. 'Just how much champagne did you drink, Mel?'

'Two glasses,' she replied, without hesitation.

He was sceptical. 'And the rest.'

'No.' She was adamant. 'I never drink more than two glasses. It goes to my head, you see.'

'I do see. Especially when combined with jet-lag. I'll make a note for future reference,' he said, turning her firmly in the direction of the path back to the cottage.

Mel resisted. 'No, it's this way to the beach.'

A couple passed them, throwing them an indulgent glance as they went. Jack Wolfe was not accustomed to being indulged and he didn't like it. Besides, walking along a beach hand in hand with a girl as desirable as Mel Devlin when he was sleeping on the sofa was, in his opinion, above and beyond the call of duty. Not that she was in any state to stop him sharing the bed. But until he knew a little more about the girl, he preferred to wait until she did the inviting before he climbed into the four-poster beside her, even when sleep was the only item on the agenda. 'Forget the beach,' he said, roughly, and without warning he picked her up and strode towards the cottage.

Mel opened her mouth to protest, then, deciding that being carried was every bit as enjoyable as walking on the soft sand, she changed her mind and, wrapping her arms about Jack Wolfe's neck, she closed her eyes and fell asleep.

Jack Wolfe, his arms full of the most unexpectedly enchanting creature he'd met in years, gave a wry little smile. They might be in paradise, but Eve was apparently beyond temptation. At least for tonight.

CHAPTER 10

Melanie, opening her eyes to early morning sunlight, was, for just a moment, lost. Then, remembering where she was, she smiled and stretched beneath the luxurious canopy of the four-poster, secure in the knowledge that she didn't have to scramble out of bed this morning and fight her way across London in a crowded tube train.

'Do you always wake up happy, or is it the prospect of a week in my company that makes you smile like that?'

Her smile was rapidly replaced with an expression of horror as, sitting bolt upright, Mel discovered that she had an audience, had apparently had one for some time judging by the relaxed manner in which Jack Wolfe was stretched out across the foot of the bed, his back propped against one of the posts, his bare legs crossed, a cup of tea balanced on the palm of his hand.

'What the devil do you think you're doing in here?' she demanded.

Jack grinned. 'Taking refuge. I didn't want to be

caught sleeping on the sofa by the maid when she brought the tea. A thing like that causes gossip.' He raised his cup. 'Can I pour one for you?'

'Isn't it a bit early, even for early morning tea?' Mel asked, pulling the sheet up to her chin, quite unnecessarily in view of the demure nature of her nightwear. 'In the circumstances.'

'There's no compulsion to get up but, since the circumstances would seem to preclude all the more entertaining possibilities of spending the time, I thought you might like a swim before breakfast.'

She relaxed a little. 'That's the first good idea you've had since I dropped that duster at your feet.'

'I don't know about that,' he demurred. 'When it comes to thinking on my feet I believe I've had a unexpectedly good week so far.' *Of course, he could be kidding himself.*

She watched uncertainly as Jack eased himself off the bed and poured her a cup of tea from the tray, handing it to her before retrieving a bathing slip from a drawer and heading for the bathroom. He reappeared a few moments later wearing it and a towel around his shoulders, nothing else, and Melanie decided that all her fantasies about his body had been right. It was sun-darkened and teak-hard.

'I'll see you on the beach,' he said, heading for the door. Then he turned and paused in the opening. 'Oh, and before you join me, please hide that thing you're wearing.'

'Thing?' Mel looked down at her T-shirt, anywhere to avoid the almost magnetic lure of the black strip of cloth bisecting his narrow hips. She swallowed. 'I'll have you know that this is my favourite nightshirt.'

'Really? Well, it takes all sorts, I suppose, but I'd hate to frighten the chambermaid.'

'Why would it frighten the chambermaid?'

'It frightened the hell out of me.'

'You?' She glanced down at it, her forehead creased in a tiny frown.

'Don't be long, darling. It's a beautiful morning.' With that he was gone and the room seemed suddenly very empty.

Mel sipped her tea slowly, then, knowing she wouldn't be disturbed by her very disturbing companion, took her time about covering as much of herself as she could manage with a high factor suncream. It was pure luxury not to be rushed. A simple pleasure, one that she could never have anticipated when every morning had begun in this leisurely manner. She hesitated for a moment between two bathing suits, then chose a demure one-piece in colours like those of the beckoning sea, pale turquoise at the shoulders, darkening to midnight blue at the hips. She brushed out her hair, slipped her feet into a pair of sandals and, taking a towel from the bathroom, followed Jack down on to the beach.

The sand was soft and white and she immediately abandoned the sandals, longing to feel it between her toes as she walked, lifting her face to the fresh breeze coming in off the sea. After the weeks of mind-numbing drudgery she felt suddenly released, foolishly grateful to Jack for his trickery. Not that she was about to tell him that.

Jack hadn't waited for her on the beach. She could see his dark head as he cut through the water in an economical and decisive overarm stroke. So, the wolf could swim as well as bite. The thought disturbed her for a moment, then, as the warmth of the sun began to heat her shoulders, she dropped her towel and ran across the sand, eager to throw herself into the curling Atlantic rollers. For a few minutes she swam vigorously, enjoying the warmth and clarity of the water.

After a while she paused for breath, treading water, looking about her for Jack. He was nowhere to be seen and she looked towards the beach, half expecting to see him standing there, laughing at her. Somehow he was always laughing at her. It was empty but for a couple of youths raking the tide line. She turned in the water, looking about her, seized by a sudden anxiety at his disappearance. That was when something gripped her ankle and pulled her under.

For a panicky, heart-stopping moment she struggled. Then she saw him, grinning at her, his hair standing on end as they floated down. For a moment relief was the overwhelming sensation; this was rapidly overtaken by fury at the fright he had given her. She kicked free and flew at him. The water slowed her and he caught her, his hands on her shoulders, holding her off without difficulty. She would have sworn it was impossible to laugh underwater. Apparently not. And suddenly she wanted to laugh too.

They erupted breathless. At least, she was breathless. He was still laughing. Mel gasped in some air and, brushing aside his hands, she lunged at him, determined to give him the serious dunking he deserved. Jack made no effort to avoid her and this time he didn't hold her at a distance but looped his arm about her waist and pulled her close, letting the water absorb the shock of their collision. And as they collided, the sea wrapped itself around them, holding them close so that their legs tangled beneath the water, wet skin against wet skin, and the dark hair across his chest grated against the swell of her breasts. She gasped again, but not from lack of air.

Then quite suddenly Jack stopped laughing, his eyes darkening as he looked down into her face, and Mel watched, mesmerized, as his mouth descended with agonizing slowness.

It was just a kiss, she told herself. Despite his unkind comments on her abilities as a kisser, Melanie had long ago lost count of the men she had kissed on stage and for the television cameras during her career, but that had just been acting. It hadn't meant anything. *This* didn't mean anything. It was simply another role . . .

She kept telling herself that as his sea-washed mouth began to tease hers, but the trouble was that none of her previous encounters had been with men as expert in the subject as Jack Wolfe. Or with men as eminently kissable. As her clumped wet lashes crashed down against her cheeks, she found herself wondering if his talent was simply happy chance, or

244

the result of long and serious practice. And since it meant absolutely nothing, did it matter? Seriously? Then who was she trying to kid?

Without prompting, she opened her lips to his sweet invasion. Wrapping her arms about Jack Wolfe's neck, Melanie let the movement of the water wash her against him and began to kiss him back. Seriously.

Drifting down beneath the surface of the water, her heart thundering in her ears, her blood singing, Melanie stopped reasoning and instead her entire being centred on Jack's long fingers as they slipped through her hair to cradle her head, his hand at her waist turning her, so that she was below him, held there by the pressure of water forcing her upwards. And the pressure of his body holding her beneath him, moulding her against him.

The tender skin of her thighs grated against his hair-roughened legs, tangling with them in a kind of dance; her pelvis offered an eager frame for his hips; the softness of her breasts crushed against the un-yielding barrier of his chest made her long to discard her costume, let him know how she tightened to his touch; and his hand behind her head, his mouth on hers was so sweetly seductive as they began to drift slowly to the surface that she wanted it to last forever.

Instead, seemingly endless minutes later, they erupted breathlessly from the water, his arm still holding her against him, his fingers still teasing the smooth skin at the nape of her neck while the water poured from her hair.

And for a moment Jack regarded her through steeply lidded eyes. 'You look like a mermaid,' he said, at last.

'Do I?' Her lids flickered up so that she was looking directly up into his eyes. 'I'm a little overdressed to be a mermaid, surely?' She was completely relaxed in his arms, boneless, and he suspected that if he peeled away her costume he would meet no resistance. The thought aroused him, a fact she must be aware of, but mermaids were dangerous creatures, sirens luring unsuspecting sailors to their doom. And he wanted to be certain who was doing the luring.

He abruptly disengaged himself, putting a yard of distance between them. 'I appreciate your enthusiasm, Mel, but it would be a pity to waste such a seductive performance when there isn't an audience to appreciate it.'

For a moment Mel didn't understand what had happened; she was floundering and out of her depth, but it had nothing to do with the twenty feet of ocean beneath her.

'Audience?' The boys had finished sweeping the sand and the beach behind Jack was now totally deserted. Then the slightly acerbic tone he had used penetrated her addled wits. 'Audience?' she repeated, suddenly furious with him for reducing something beautiful to his own miserable standards. 'For your information, Mr Jack Wolfe, seduction was the last thing on my mind,' she added. 'I was simply . . .' She stopped as she realized that she was making a grade A fool of herself.

'What?'

'Practising,' she said, crossly.

'Oh, I see.' Hands linked behind his head, he lay back in the water and began to float away from her. 'Then I'm happy to confirm that you're a very apt pupil. In fact I'd have to say you're making excellent progress.'

She didn't waste breath on a reply; instead she threw herself on him, swamping him, pushing him beneath the waves, and when he was submerged to her utter and complete satisfaction she turned and left him, swimming back to the beach faster than an extra from *Jaws*.

It was only minutes later, standing beneath the shower, bathroom door securely locked, that it even occurred to her to wonder why he hadn't turned the tables on her. He could have done it quite easily. Dunked her, made her beg for mercy. She'd seen it a dozen times, a hundred times, as couples had fooled around in the water. Couples. She blushed at her own stupidity.

They weren't a couple. For one crazy moment out there, as they had ridden the emerald waves locked in each other's arms, she had forgotten that. But he hadn't.

Melanie wrapped herself in a towel, returned to the still empty bedroom and sank on to the stool in front of the dressing table. She picked up her comb, it snagged in a knot and she tugged it irritably, making tears start into her eyes. 'Damn!' she said, beneath her breath. Why on earth had she ever allowed things to get to this state of affairs? Why on earth had she ever thought . . .?

She swivelled on the stool as the door began to open. 'Would you please knock before you come in here?' she snapped, blinking back the tears.

'I did,' he said, in an equally ill temper. Then he stopped as he saw the overbrightness of her eyes. 'I assumed you were still in the bathroom. Do you mind if I use it now?' he continued, more gently.

'Help yourself.' Jack made no immediate move to avail himself of the invitation, but continued to look at her as if he wanted to say something but wasn't sure how she would respond. Unsettled, she finally broke the silence. 'What are your plans for today?'

'Nothing very strenuous. Recover from jetlag, sunbathe, explore a little perhaps.'

'No clandestine meetings beneath the palm trees?'

'Not today,' he said, solemnly.

Was he laughing at her? 'Just checking. I wouldn't want to be in the way,' she said, in a manner that let him know she didn't think it was at all funny.

'I'll tell you when you're in the way.' He dragged his fingers through his wet hair. 'There are a couple of bikes outside the cottage; we could ride down to the other beach if you like.'

'We?'

'You and I.'

She looked doubtful. She'd seen the bikes, but it hadn't occurred to her that she would be expected to ride one of them. The last time she'd been confident on a bike, it had had training wheels. 'I thought you'd

248

be busy,' she said, turning back to the mirror.

'I'm sorry to disappoint you, but I'm afraid you can't get rid of me that easily. But you can have another shot at drowning me tomorrow. I've chartered a boat for the day. You don't suffer from sea-sickness, I hope?'

'Just don't wear anything you're fond of,' she warned him, still tugging the comb through her hair. Then, realizing she was being silly, she shook her head. 'No, Jack, I don't suffer from sea-sickness.'

'I'm glad. There are some coves you can't get to any other way. I'm reliably informed that they shouldn't be missed.'

'I'm sure it will be lovely,' she said, unenthusiastically. 'The whole island is lovely. Why else would you be interested?'

'Why else?' Then, 'For heaven's sake, Mel, you're supposed to be an actress, can't you at least pretend to be having a good time? Why are you making such a drama out of this?'

Her eyes flashed. 'Drama is what I do for a living.' Correction – wanted to do. What a pity her agent didn't take the same attitude. 'Of course this isn't anything as grand as a drama. It's more your below-average sitcom.' Well, there, maybe Trudy was right after all. Maybe she should have taken that sitcom; at least that part had a decent fee.

'I'd have said the weather is rather better. And the scenery. And there's no reason we shouldn't have some fun.'

'Fun? This is supposed to be fun?'

'Of course. If I'm not having a good time, no one will believe that we're – '

'It's all right, Jack,' she interrupted, hurriedly. 'I get the picture. You want fun. Fun you shall have.'

'I can't see why it should be so difficult to try and enjoy yourself.'

Oh, but it wasn't. It wasn't difficult at all. That was the trouble. She had been enjoying herself out there in the sea, enjoying herself rather too much, though she wasn't about to admit it. 'Why? Because by rights I should be back in London cleaning someone's greasy oven?'

'I didn't say that.'

'You didn't have to.'

He folded up his long legs, balancing easily on his toes as he took her hand and looked her straight in the eye. 'Look, maybe I didn't play quite fair with you – '

'*Maybe*?'

'But I really appreciate the way you're helping me out. I know it can't be easy, but you're here now, Mel, and I'd like to think you'll have just a fraction more enjoyment here with me than might be extracted from a greasy oven.'

A fraction? She looked down at his hand on hers. His skin was darker, as if he spent a lot of time in the sun, the hairs on his wrist already turning gold. If it was *just* a fraction she would feel a lot happier about the situation. 'I think I can say with perfect truth that this is a whole lot more fun than cleaning an oven,' she conceded. But then you knew where you were with a greasy oven. 'Jack?'

250

'Yes?' His voice was softer now. Dangerously lulling. She refused to be lulled.

'It must be one hell of a deal you're trying to pull off if you're willing to go to all this trouble.' He didn't deny it. 'Wouldn't it have been easier to have done what Caroline wanted than take a risk with me?'

'Is it a risk, Mel?' He regarded her steadily. 'If you've anything you think I should know, maybe this would be a good time to tell me.'

Mel had the disconcerting feeling that she was being invited to confess. But what to? He couldn't possibly know . . . She frowned, then shook her head. She was just feeling tense. 'I might make a mistake, mess up everything for you.'

'You might,' he agreed, regarding her with a certain edge to his expression. Then, when she said no more, he rose to his feet. His expression was doing all the right things on the surface, but beneath the smile she had the sense of shutters coming down. 'But any girl who can think on her feet as quickly as you can should be capable of handling almost any situation.'

'When did I think quickly?'

'When you rescued me from a fate worse than death with your fluffy yellow duster. No business deal is worth that kind of sacrifice.'

'Would it have been such a sacrifice? Really? She's very beautiful.'

'Isn't there an old saying? Beauty is as beauty does. It's something we would all do well to remember.' He nodded slightly before turning away to stride across

251

the room. 'I won't be long, so if you want to get dressed without an audience I suggest you get a move on,' he said, before closing the bathroom door behind him with a quiet, decisive click.

Melanie didn't need telling twice. She was into a pair of wide-legged, sizzling pink cotton shorts and a matching vest top before he had reached for the soap. Then she pushed her feet into a pair of white espadrilles, tied her hair back with a scarf and was carefully applying another layer of sun-cream to her nose when Jack reappeared a scant ten minutes later.

Their eyes met briefly through the mirror before she turned away, scooping up her sun-cream to dump it into her soft leather shoulder bag.

'It's all yours,' she said, shortly, heading for the door. 'I'll meet you . . . somewhere.'

He didn't try to stop her. 'By the pool,' he said. 'I won't be long.'

'Take all the time you need.'

He waited until she was gone and then dialled his office. 'Mike?' he said, after a few moments. 'Have you managed to discover anything?'

'This is ridiculous,' Melanie muttered, as she walked along the path to the main hotel building, blind to the sun and the sea and the brilliant flowers spilling from every bush and tree. 'I could be lying on a beach anywhere in the entire world right now. Instead I'm . . .' Head down, she had blundered into another figure before she realized that she was no longer alone.

The man caught and held her and then, as she was

252

about to let out a startled scream, he clamped his hand over her mouth. As she stared up in shocked recognition of her assailant, he took her hand from her mouth. 'Beau?' she muttered, faintly. 'What on earth are you doing here?'

Her father smiled down at her with a slightly ironic twist to his mouth. 'That's funny, Mel, I was just about to ask you the same question.'

Melanie's cheeks flooded with colour. 'It's not what you think, really ...' she began, then stopped. Some things were beyond explanation and she had a feeling this was one of them.

'No? Well, I suppose it isn't really anything to do with me. You're all grown up. At your age Claudia...' He stopped. 'But you're not Claudia. It was quite a shock to walk into that dining room last night and see you sitting there with a total stranger.'

'He's not a total stranger to me.'

Beau grinned unexpectedly. 'I didn't imagine he was. So, who is he?'

But Melanie's thoughts were elsewhere. 'Last night?' she queried, recalling Jack telling her that someone was staring at her. 'That was you?'

'Your boyfriend spotted me, did he? I wasn't sure. I hope it hasn't put a damper on your fun.'

Boyfriend! Fun! Why was everyone so hooked on *fun*? 'Jack mentioned someone was staring at me, but he doesn't know who you are.' Or surely he'd have said something? Well, he had said *something*. But something more like, 'Isn't that Edward Beaumont ...' or even just '... that actor ...'

'Doesn't he? How lowering to my self-esteem.'

'Not really. I don't think he's much of a theatre-goer. And he doesn't own a television.' She glanced nervously behind her. He'd be along in a few minutes and she'd rather he didn't find her in deep conversation with her father. 'And even if he had recognized you, he wouldn't have known that you were my father. You see, he doesn't know who I am, either.'

'You're joking?' *She wished.* 'Who does he think you are?'

'Melanie Devlin.' She shrugged. 'It's the name on my passport. Believe me,' she hurried on before he could ask any awkward questions, 'it seemed like a good idea at the time, and for the moment I think I'd rather keep things the way they are, so, if you don't mind I'd be happier if we got off this path.'

'Surely. Diana threatened me with all kinds of mayhem if I interfered but now that I've run into you, quite by chance, you understand, I know she'd love to say hello. We're down at the marina. It's this way.'

She wasn't particularly eager to pay a call on Diana, but she could hardly refuse. 'You're on a yacht?'

'Luke and Mac chartered it for us as a wedding present. Didn't you know?'

'Your honeymoon was the subject of enormous secrecy.'

'Was it? Oh, well, the papers can be a nuisance. Although why anyone would be interested in me these days, I can't think.'

'Perhaps they were thinking of Diana. The tabloids are bound to be interested in the lady who has finally broken the spell of the lovely Elaine – '

She broke off. Mentioning her father's loathed first wife when he was on honeymoon with his second had to be shockingly bad manners. Her mother would have been appalled.

He stopped on the narrow path and turned to her, a slight frown creasing his tanned forehead. 'I suppose you're right. We didn't have a moment's peace from the moment we announced the wedding.'

'It must have been difficult for her.' Edward looked at her more sharply, picking up the edge in her voice. 'It's bad enough when you're used to it,' she said, quickly.

'Yes.'

'It couldn't have been much fun for Heather either.'

'Personally I consider Heather and fun to be mutually exclusive. She gave Diana a really hard time.'

'You mean she refused to lie down under the Beaumont charm? You can't win 'em all, Beau.'

Again that sharp look. 'Maybe not. But it's miserable for Diana.'

'She doesn't look all that unhappy.' Melanie paused on the path to look down at the marina. Diana was stretched out on the deck of a sleek yacht, soaking up the early morning sun.

'Well, no one could be miserable in a place like this.' He looked around at the gardens, the marina, the distant islands swimming in a pink, hazy mist. 'Isn't it just out of this world?'

'I'm reliably informed that it's paradise,' Melanie agreed, a touch wryly.

'Someone we met in Barbuda told us the food here was fabulous so we thought we'd sail over and try it.'

'Did it live up to your expectations?'

'You tell me. Diana refused to embarrass you last night even if it meant I had to starve.'

Diana had been misguided, Melanie thought, irritably. It would have been worth any amount of embarrassment just to see the look on Jack's face when she introduced her father. Especially after such an unflattering description . . .

'If you starved, it suits you. You're looking good, Beau.'

'I feel wonderful. I haven't felt so happy since . . . Well. It was a long time ago, Melanie. You can't bring back the past.'

She almost flinched as he put his hand on her arm and patted it gently. That was supposed to be some sort of comfort to her? 'Of course not.'

'Melanie – ' She heard the hurt in his voice as she pulled away.

'This is a beautiful yacht, Beau,' she said, quickly.

'Yes, well, you'd better come aboard.'

Diana, gilded by the sun, her ash-blonde hair perfectly groomed, rose from the sun-bed. 'Edward!' she scolded, pushing her sunglasses down her nose and peering over the top of them. 'I told you not to bother the child. How would you have liked it if your father had gatecrashed some romantic dalliance.'

Dalliance? Yuck.

'I didn't. I ran into her quite by chance, didn't I, sweetheart?'

'Quite by chance,' Mel repeated, through gritted teeth.

'Mmm,' Diana murmured, doubtfully, looking behind them. 'You're on your own?'

She coloured and that made her feel stupid. Diana was so cool, so sophisticated. 'Jack is . . . that is . . . I needed a bit of fresh air before breakfast.'

'There's a bit of a mystery, Diana,' Edward said. 'Apparently Mel's young man doesn't know who she is. What do you think of that?'

Mel's teeth remained firmly gritted. She had no wish to encourage Diana's views on the subject.

But Diana shrugged. 'I don't blame her keeping her name a secret if she can get away with it. It must be rather refreshing to be certain that someone is interested in you for yourself, rather than for who you are. I haven't been part of this family long, but I've seen enough to understand how things can be.' She glanced at Melanie. 'You cannot believe the number of blue-rinsed matrons we've met who think they own a piece of your father simply because they saw him in some play twenty years ago.'

'Diana! They don't have blue rinses.' Then he grinned. 'Well, not all of them.'

257

Diana ignored this. 'Jack who?' she asked, peering over her sunglasses at Melanie.

'Wolfe. Jack Wolfe.'

'Is he an actor?'

'Heaven forbid.' Diana's brows rose an immeasurable amount. 'They aren't all like Beau. Actually Jack's something in the City.'

'Well, that covers a multitude of sins, too,' Diana replied.

'He's a friend of Luke's, is he?' Beau asked, butting in, clearly puzzled by the hostility that had flared so quickly between the two women. 'Is that how you met?' Melanie frowned. 'Did Luke introduce you?' he elaborated.

'Oh, no.' They might both be financial wizards, but they were so utterly different . . . at least, she supposed they were different. She'd never really thought about how Luke went about the business of making money. Now she came to think of it, there had been some bother when he took over the Broomhill factory the previous year . . . 'No,' she repeated. 'We met quite by chance.'

'Lucky chance. He's quite something.' Diana grinned as her husband pointedly cleared his throat. 'How long are you staying?'

'Just a few days.'

'But you'll be home for your birthday? We're flying back especially – ' Beau began.

'Darling, that was supposed to be a surprise,' Diana chided, gently.

'It will be even more of a surprise if the guest of

258

honour doesn't show up,' Beau pointed out.

'I'll be home by then,' Melanie assured them.

'Well, make sure you bring Jack. You can't hide your family from him forever, no matter how tempting that might be. It can't possibly be any worse than the first time Claudia and Heather met. My darling daughter called Claudia a mindless bimbo to her face.'

'I heard. That she lived to tell the tale was undoubtedly due to the fact that Claudia was too busy falling in love at the time to take offence.'

'It was the fact that Mac was falling in love with Claudia that caused the fracas in the first place,' Diana pointed out. Edward, who hadn't heard the story before, looked first at Diana, then to Melanie for an explanation.

'Heather had a schoolgirl crush on him,' Melanie explained.

'Good God. He's old enough to be her – '

'Father?' Melanie offered. 'Well, some girls go for father-figures. And some men, like Mac, know better than to be tempted.' Her father paled and she realized she had to get off the yacht before she said something she really regretted. 'I must go, or Jack will be sending out a search party for me.'

'What a pity he's let you out of his sight this long,' Diana said, pointedly. 'Tell me, have you seen Heather?'

'No. But I understand Mac bailed her out for causing an affray at a student rally a week or so back. No need to worry, though, it didn't make the papers. No doubt she'll make a better job of it next time.'

'Melanie!' Beau stepped towards them.

'It's all right, darling. Melanie is quite right. Heather is in the mood to cause maximum embarrassment. I seem to remember you telling me about Claudia going through a similar phase.' She was regarding her stepdaughter thoughtfully. 'And now, it seems, it's Melanie's turn.'

'My turn?'

'To be embarrassing. Sweet, innocent, delightful Melanie. Always so charming, so well-mannered. A credit to her poor mother . . .' She made a broad gesture at their surroundings. 'Isn't all this just a little out of character? A holiday with your lover, the press doubtless on standby for the topless pose on the beach . . . Or is he your lover? Frankly I'd have put you down as a professional virgin. A bit like your mother really. She tried it once and never bothered again – '

'Diana!' Edward, horrified, tried to intervene but was ignored.

'She was a sweet, innocent little thing too by all accounts.' Melanie felt a rush of hot fury as Diana continued, 'Edward told me all about her – '

'He told you, did he? Well, gosh, that must be all of what – let me see – golly, that must be at least eight people who know how much he professes to have loved her.' The fury erupted. 'You know, I can't think what Heather's making such a fuss about. At least *her* father was mentioned in dispatches, got his

260

picture in the papers for heaven's sake, and she even got to go to the Palace with her "*poor mother*" for a posthumous medal.'

'I know how Heather is feeling, Melanie. She's working through it in her own way. It isn't pretty to watch, but she isn't burying her feelings. Your mother could have had Edward any time she chose after Elaine's death but she was too scared to go for it, and if you want my opinion you're a whole lot like her.'

'Diana, for goodness' sake,' Edward said, clearly shocked by the suddenness of the scene, 'that's enough.' Then he turned to Melanie. 'I think you'd better go.' He was looking at her as if he didn't recognize her. She could hardly blame him; she didn't recognize herself. Without another word, she turned and fled.

'Would you mind telling me what the hell that was all about, Diana?' he demanded, as he watched his youngest daughter run along the marina decking.

'It's quite simple, sweetheart. She's angry with her mother.'

'With Juliet? Why?'

'For dying so that the fairy-tale could never end happily ever after.' She followed the figure flying up the path into the shelter of the gardens. 'But good girls don't get angry with their dead mother, so she's decided she's angry with me instead, which is a lot more acceptable.'

'Great. And now she's got herself mixed up with some crook. What the hell am I supposed to tell Luke?'

261

'Tell him his informant was right. She's here with Jack Wolfe.'

'He won't like it.'

'I don't suppose he will. But he can hardly expect you to shanghai her and carry her off in the hold.'

'You don't know Luke.'

'She's a grown woman, Edward. You can't protect her from life. All you can do is be there for her when it hurts. But if you don't mind, I think I'd like to get out of here before you call Luke and tell him that.'

Oh, God, that had been so horrible. She had been so horrible. Melanie stared down from her rock perch above the marina at the yacht, willing her legs to take her back down there and apologize, make her peace.

'Good morning. It's a lovely day, isn't it?'

'Is it?' she asked, discouragingly. There was nothing lovely about it as far as she was concerned. It had started off badly and was going downhill fast.

'Haven't you noticed?' The man sounded concerned, as if somehow her happiness was important to him. He certainly wasn't about to go away. 'You were so intent on the view . . .'

Melanie had scarcely noticed the view, but short of being downright unpleasant . . . She gave a little shiver. She'd already been unpleasant enough for one day, and with a determined smile she concentrated on the scene before her.

The sea on this side of the island was every shade from palest aquamarine to purple with the misty shapes of distant islands, some so vague that she wasn't sure whether they were really there, or just figments of her imagination. And just offshore some comical grey pelicans were diving from the rocks for fish. He was right, it was a lovely day, and her problems were her own and not to be inflicted on anyone else. She turned, with a belated smile.

'You're right, it's a lovely day, the view is perfect, and so is this island.'

'I'm very glad you think so.' He grin broadened at her puzzled look. 'Angus Jamieson. Gus to my friends. And I'm glad you like my island.'

'Your island?'

'Like Noah, I built an Ark.'

'All by yourself?'

'Well, no,' he admitted. Then, 'And come to think of it I suppose the bank owns a pretty big chunk of it . . .' He looked pensive for a moment before his grin returned, as if it was a permanent fixture that even the thought of banks could not defeat. 'But not this particular bit,' he said, indicating the few square feet they occupied, 'so you're in no immediate danger . . .'

Melanie tried to ignore the tiny chill that settled around her heart. Danger from what? 'Except perhaps from the animals? Where do you keep them?'

'Animals?' Then he laughed. 'Oh, no, this is an Ark for people. They're more profitable.'

His grin was infectious and Melanie found herself responding. 'And do they come in two by two as well?'

263

'They usually come in that way, but I take no responsibility for how they leave.'

'I'll bear that in mind.'

'I'm sorry, I didn't get the chance to say hello when you arrived last night,' he said, hunkering down beside her and offering his hand.

'Hello,' she said. 'Melanie Devlin.' Gus Jamieson seemed very young to own anything as important as a whole island, even one in hock to the bank. Late twenties, tanned and fit as a athlete and with the kind of easygoing smile and fair, boyish good looks that invited confidence. 'Mel,' she invited. 'I arrived last night.' Then she laughed, too. 'But if you own the place you already know that.'

'Yes, I do. May I?' She moved up a little so that he could sit beside her. 'I hope you're settling in? Finding everything you need?'

'Oh . . . yes. Yes, thank you. The cottage is quite beautiful.'

'You're sure?' He looked slightly concerned, as if somehow picking up on her uncertainty.

'Absolutely wonderful,' she affirmed, making more of an effort.

His mobile face creased into a broad smile. 'Well, if there's anything you need, anything at all, please don't hesitate to ask.'

He looked so eager to do her bidding that she felt obliged to put him to the test. 'Actually, I wondered, do you have a shop? I would like to try my hand at snorkelling but I haven't any equipment.'

'There is a boutique in the main building and a

kiosk for film and the usual holiday essentials, but you don't need to buy sports equipment. Just ask at Reception and they'll loan you anything you want. It's all part of the service.'

'Really? Well, that's great.'

'I'm glad you think so.' He turned and leapt to his feet as someone came up behind them. 'Good morning, Jack.'

'Gus.' He nodded curtly. 'I see you've already met Melanie.'

'I was just explaining that she could borrow any sports equipment she wants, snorkelling gear, tennis racquets, whatever, from the hotel,' he said, enthusiastically. 'And if you feel like – '

'If we feel like doing anything as dangerously energetic as playing tennis, we'll bear it in mind,' Jack replied, discouragingly, his long fingers curving possessively beneath Melanie's elbow, urging her to her feet. 'I thought we were going to meet at the pool, darling?'

'Right. Well, enjoy your breakfast,' Gus said, his easy manner suddenly less certain.

'I'm sure we will,' Jack said, dismissively.

'That wasn't very friendly,' Mel said, as Jack propelled her towards the dining room.

'Why should I be friendly?'

She gave a little shrug. 'I thought you would have wanted to get to know the man . . . if you're planning a takeover.'

His brows arched. 'Is that what I'm doing?'

'I'm sorry, Jack, but it doesn't take a lot of working

265

out. You're not really here on holiday, so you must be giving the place the once-over for one of your famous lightning raids.'

'You've been reading too many financial journals,' he said, drily.

'No, just the press cuttings piling up on your desk.' His brows rose slightly at that. 'I have to move them to dust. "Lightning raid" seems to figure fairly frequently.'

'Well, I'm afraid Gregory Tamblin has a very limited vocabulary.' She stared. 'Surely you must have noticed that they were all written by the same man? Since you read them all so carefully.' Then, somewhat disconcertingly, he smiled. 'You're a bright girl, Mel, but I promise, whatever I'm planning, I can manage without putting you to the trouble of flirting with Gus Jamieson.'

Mel barely hesitated as she reached for a jug of freshly squeezed orange juice from the buffet and filled two glasses. 'Oh, it was no trouble at all,' she assured him, passing him a glass of juice. 'He's very good-looking – '

'Is he? I hadn't noticed and frankly, my dear, neither should you. Not on my time. If Mr Jamieson wishes to flirt with you he must invite you to stay at his own expense after you've worked your notice. For the purposes of this trip, I reserve all rights in that department.'

'– and he has enormous charm,' she continued as if Jack hadn't spoken. She took a sip of juice, smiled appreciatively and sincerely hoped he'd get the message that she considered him severely lacking in that department.

'Charm isn't everything, darling. It certainly doesn't make him worth pursuing. He might own this island now . . .'

'But not for much longer?' He shrugged. 'I don't believe you,' she said.

'Why should I lie?' he enquired, evenly. He didn't want Tamblin to believe in his red herring. But it was essential to convince the man's spies that he did want him to. That way, Tamblin would feel pleased with himself for seeing through it and not look any further.

'Well, look at the place . . .' She made a vague gesture at their surroundings and he watched as Melanie looked about her at the rich panelling of the dining room, the furnishings made from exotic tropical woods and the buffet laid out with a variety of fruits to tempt even the most jaded palate. 'It's fabulous.'

'I agree. The island is a prime piece of real estate developed to the highest standards. Unfortunately, the handsome and charming Mr Jamieson has a lot to learn about business. He's expanded beyond his means, always a mistake. Fatal during a recession.'

'I thought the recession was over. Besides, there are always people with money to spend at a place like this.' She knew loads of people who would absolutely love it. Her father and stepmother to start with. Although right now they were probably wishing they had chosen any other resort in the entire Caribbean to drop in on.

'I agree. But the competition is fierce. Look around you, darling, The Ark isn't exactly over-loaded, is it?' In contrast to the night before, the dining room was almost empty.

She refused to concede the point. 'It's early. And I imagine a lot of guests take breakfast in their cottage. If Gus had the vision to build this place from scratch he can't be entirely stupid.'

She seemed genuinely concerned, Jack thought. Maybe she wasn't deeply involved enough to know what was going on. It had to have been chance that brought her to his flat to clean up after his brother. And no one could have anticipated the turn of events that would have ended with her accompanying him to The Ark itself. Yet she knew Latham, worked for the same firm. And Latham would certainly take advantage of the situation whether she knew she was being used or not.

Well, so would he. The harder he seemed to be trying to distract them with his left hand, the more determined they would be to follow his right.

'It takes more than vision to build an empire, Mel. Good judgement and an element of luck are needed. Mr Jamieson's judgement was always in question and his luck has just run out.' He didn't cross his fingers; he knew that Gus would cheerfully forgive him for such slander in a good cause.

Although if he found Gus gazing into Melanie's eyes with quite such enthusiasm again it was doubtful if he would feel much like returning the compliment.

'. . . *his luck has just run out.*' The headline on the

268

newspaper clipping Melanie had picked up in his flat swam unbidden into her head. The journalist had described Jack as a lone wolf hunting down companies in trouble and devouring them without compassion. 'While you're going to hit the jackpot. Again.'

'I make my own luck and I've never allowed sentimentality to hamper my judgement. Gus Jamieson would have been wise to have sold out last year when a major chain made him an offer . . .' Well, the offer had been real enough, but he'd had the good sense to come to an old friend for advice. 'Now, well, I'm afraid he'll probably have to settle for considerably less.'

'That's immoral!'

'Shall we sit down?' he suggested.

'You don't have to do this. You could help him.'

'I am helping him.'

'By stealing everything he's worked for?'

His jaw tightened ominously and he had to make a conscious effort to remember why he was at The Ark. Why she was with him. 'Stealing is an emotive word, Melanie. I imagine The Ark will come pretty expensive even at a cut-down, bargain-basement price. But maybe you would prefer me to walk away and leave him to the sharks?' He smiled mirthlessly. 'Perhaps you think they'll be less ruthless than a wolf.'

CHAPTER 11

Melanie gave him an old-fashioned look. 'Waste all that time and money for nothing? Do you think I'm a complete fool?'

No, anything but a fool. There was only one fool sitting at this table and it wasn't Melanie Devlin. 'I think you've got a soft heart and an equally soft head when it comes to business.' *And he was beginning to think it was contagious.*

There was something about the way Jack said that that drove any immediate concern for Gus Jamieson from her head. 'Do you mean the co-operative? You said you were impressed with my business plan. You said you'd help.'

So much *concern.* 'It's an elegant piece of work, I grant you.' *That alone should have warned him.* 'You didn't really write it all by yourself, did you?'

'It was my idea. I admit I had a little help with the plan.'

'A little help?'

'A lot,' she conceded.

'Yes, well, whether the women you are trying to

270

help will appreciate what you're doing for them I take leave to doubt. I'll give it six months before it all falls apart in chaos.'

'I see. You've got me here under false pretences. The minute we get home you're going to back out, aren't you? Forget everything you said about helping us – '

'Not at all. I'm not risking my time or money. I've done everything you asked. I've found your friend a temporary job and my CEO is investigating the situation regarding the property you want to lease. We have a bargain, you and I, and I won't renege on it. But remember what I said. Six months. At the most.'

Jack took his seat opposite her, ordered coffee and eggs Benedict for both of them, without troubling her for a decision. Normally that kind of high-handedness would have irritated her, but she was too deep in thought even to notice.

Could Jack be right? Could she be making a serious mistake? Paddy and Sharon were totally convinced, raring to go, but what about the others? After all, someone had ratted on Paddy . . .

'Well?' Jack finally asked. She sipped her orange juice, raised her left brow a quarter of an inch and waited for him to elaborate. 'I'm right and you know it.'

'Nonsense. In six months the whole thing will be up and running like clockwork.'

'If it is I'll give you a contract.' Something about the way that Jack was looking at her suddenly that

271

made her nervous. As if he knew he wouldn't be troubled. As if he knew something that she didn't.

'I'll hold you to that.' Then, changing the subject, looking around the dining room so that she could avoid his eyes, she said, 'Do you know what Gus needs here?'

'Yes, but I have the strongest impression you're going to tell me anyway.'

She made a dismissive gesture. 'Publicity. He needs publicity. Some really good publicity.'

Jack nearly choked. Yesterday's *Courier* would have dealt with that, although whether Melanie would be so eager to help out when she knew what he'd done was a moot point.

'Publicity takes time to get results and he hasn't got time.' He had no objection to discussing the situation. If Melanie was thoroughly convinced she would call Latham and tell him. When? She couldn't use the phone in the cottage or the number would show up on the bill. After breakfast? From Reception. Well, Gus would make a note of any numbers she called. 'And advertising is expensive,' he added, apparently as an afterthought.

'I wasn't talking about advertising. I meant the kind of publicity that money can't buy. You just have to know the right people.'

How true. 'Then we must assume he doesn't know the right people. Whoever they are.'

'But I do.' Melanie stopped. About to explain that she knew just how to get The Ark into the papers, get people talking about it, she suddenly remembered

272

that she was supposed to be a seriously out-of-work actress, incapable of helping herself, let alone anyone else. Jack was swift to remind her of that.

'I think it would take more than a photograph of you topless on the beach to bring the fashionable hordes clamouring for room at the inn,' he suggested, rather too complacent about the idea for Mel's liking.

'You haven't seen me topless,' she said, tartly, remembering Diana's horrible remark. Well, she had doubtless deserved it. She had said some pretty horrible things herself. She glanced out at the marina but there was no sign of Beau or Diana. Just the crew readying the yacht to move out.

'No? Then who do you think put you to bed last night?'

Melanie turned and stared at Jack for a moment. Then she dismissed his implication as ridiculous. 'I don't need to think about it. I'm quite capable of putting myself to bed,' she declared.

'Last night? Are you sure?'

She regarded him sourly over the rim of her glass. 'Do you actually remember?'

'Of course I remember. Vividly.' They'd had dinner, danced. Elbows, waists, even cheek to cheek, she remembered, her face growing warm at the way she had clung to him, begged him to walk along the beach . . . Then –

Then? She frowned. Then what? She looked up and saw the way he was looking at her and she knew. 'You didn't . . .' But even as the words left her mouth she knew it was the truth and she felt herself blush all

273

over as he sat back and regarded her with an insolent grin. 'How could you?'

'It seemed a shame to spoil your pretty clothes. I'd hate you to get into trouble with their rightful owner.'

She gritted her teeth. 'My underwear was my own.'

'And very pretty, too. Although a touch on the expensive side for a cleaning lady, I would have thought. I recall that Tom was rather taken with it, although I have to say that he would have been thoroughly disappointed with your taste in nightwear.'

'My nightwear is none of his business. Or yours.' She wanted to slap that self-satisfied grin right off his face . . . She gave a little gasp. What on earth was the matter with her this morning? It was as if there was some nasty little demon inside her . . . besides, Jack would have stopped her before her hand made it halfway across the table. But he was still grinning. 'We seem to have strayed somewhat from the point,' she said, tartly.

'Have we? What point?'

'The Ark. Shall I tell you something about it?'

He sighed. 'Is there any way to stop you?'

'No, Jack. But I think you should reconsider your plans. I have a feeling that this particular lamb isn't quite ready to lie down on your barbecue.'

He didn't exactly reel back. He merely looked bored with the whole subject. 'None of them comes willingly, Mel. But in the end it makes no difference.'

'Never? Well, of course I could be wrong. I just hate to see anyone who's worked hard to make something special forced to hand it over to the fat cats.' She smiled. 'In this case, for fat cat you can substitute lean wolf.'

'Mr Jamieson didn't waste his time talking to you, did he? Maybe he's heard all about your assets. Perhaps you should be careful he doesn't try to charm them out of you,' he warned, with the kind of smile a cat has when it's just spotted the canary making a break for it.

'Assets?'

'You hadn't forgotten your well-managed portfolio?' he prompted. 'You really must try and keep a track of your story or you'll end up in all kinds of trouble.'

Story? Oh, good grief, her *story*. She laughed – at least she hoped he would think it was a laugh. It was more a little collapsed sort of noise that escaped from her as she remembered the way she had teased him over dinner the night before. She must have been mad. Without a doubt stark raving mad. Why else would she be here, playing all kinds of dangerous games with Jack Wolfe?

'I won't forget,' she said.

'It must be difficult,' he continued, apparently enjoying a little retaliation for her remark about fat cats and lean wolves, 'never knowing who has your best interests at heart and who is just after your money. Of course if you gave it to Gus Jamieson it wouldn't be trifled away by your fortune-hunting

275

lover.' He raised one dark brow in a quizzical expression. 'Would it?'

'Oh, really!' she exclaimed, heat flying to her cheeks as the whole of the previous evening's conversation came back like an X-rated nightmare to haunt her. How much champagne had she drunk last night, for heaven's sake? She'd definitely be sticking to orange juice for the rest of this trip, and as if to impress herself with the necessity, she took another sip from her glass.

'Of course trifling might be more fun.' He was openly laughing at her now.

'Then what a pity you're here on business, Jack,' she said, as the exquisitely prepared eggs Benedict was laid before her.

'Can I take it from that, Miss Devlin,' he replied, his voice as slow and smooth as treacle pouring from a spoon, 'that you'd be more than willing to trifle with me if it would save young Mr Jamieson from ruin?'

Well, Melanie Devlin, you walked right into that one. It was definitely time to put a serious curb on her tongue. Time to change the subject. 'Gosh, this does look good,' she said, brightly, picking up her fork. But that didn't work. She had to put it down again immediately, or betray just how much her fingers were shaking. It wouldn't have been so bad if it had just been her fingers . . .

'Well, Miss Devlin? Nothing more to say on the subject? Could it possibly be that it's Mr Jamieson's lucky day?' He didn't wait for her response, which was just as well; she was utterly speechless. Apparently satisfied, he regarded his own breakfast. 'You're right, Cinderella,' he said, 'this does look very tempting. And swimming before breakfast certainly does something for the appetite.'

Swimming? She didn't think swimming was responsible for the hollow feeling in the pit of her stomach. As she stared at her breakfast Melanie wished vehemently that she were back in a rain-soaked London gulping down a simple piece of toast before rushing off to scrub any number of floors.

She stirred. 'I thought I might try snorkelling this morning.'

'Is that what Mr Jamieson suggested while you were cosied up together on that rock? Did he offer to teach you?'

'Gus?' She suddenly realized he thought she had been with Gus all that time, although why he should assume she was flirting . . . Was that why he had been so abrupt with the man? Could it be that he was just a tiny bit jealous? Of course not. Stupid thought. 'Sadly, no. Perhaps he would have done if you hadn't arrived just then.'

'I'm sure he would. But it isn't a problem, Mel – you have me. All day.'

'I wouldn't want to put you to any bother, Jack.' She smiled. 'I'm sure you have far more interesting things to do than play nursemaid to me.'

He smiled right back. He wasn't planning on playing nursemaid. Now, doctors and nurses . . . 'Why should it be a bother, darling? You're doing

277

me the most enormous favour. The very least I can do is ensure that you have a good time while you're here.'

'Oh, I intend to.' As she began to eat her breakfast, something occurred to her. 'Did you know that people come here by yacht?'

'There wouldn't be much point in spending a fortune building a marina if they didn't,' he pointed out.

'No, I mean just to eat at this restaurant? Apparently it's known all over the Caribbean.'

He frowned. 'Gus told you this, did he?'

Not Gus, but somehow she didn't think Jack would be amused if he knew her father was anchored just a few hundred feet away from where they were sitting. She glanced down at the marina and saw Beau standing on deck talking to one of the crew as they prepared to cast off. They were just going to sail away . . .

It was too late to make her peace. Or was it? If she ran . . . She half rose . . . 'Mel?' Jack was looking at her a little oddly. 'Is everything all right.' As she watched, the yacht edged out into the creek. 'Mel?'

'Fine,' she said, subsiding into her seat. She'd see them at her birthday party. It was only a few days. No problem. They'd laugh about it probably . . . She turned back to Jack. He too was staring at the departing yacht and to distract him she said, 'It's just, I thought, if the restaurant is so well-known, why is the hotel in trouble?'

Something inside Jack snapped. 'You're the bright

278

one, Melanie; you tell me when you've come up with an answer.' He pushed back his chair, tossed his napkin on the table as he stood up, abandoning his breakfast. 'In the meantime I'll go and organize the snorkelling gear. Just in case there's a sudden rush.'

Startled by Jack's sudden loss of temper, Melanie watched him stride off in the direction of Reception. What on earth had she said? Then she grinned. She had got to him. She'd really got to him. Could it be that he wasn't quite the wolf he liked everyone to believe? Then she pulled herself together. If he wasn't on the prowl, what was he doing in a place like this with an unwilling girl he'd dragged along to give him cover?

Unwilling? And a wave of guilt unexpectedly overwhelmed her. She had called Jack unscrupulous, but what about her? She was aiding and abetting him simply by her presence. If wasn't as if she had *had* to come along with him. She could undoubtedly have found some other way to help Paddy. And if the local authority had remained difficult about letting them have the old house they wanted as a base for their co-operative, they could surely have found somewhere else? Not quite so perfect, or convenient maybe . . . Yet she hadn't even hesitated. It had all seemed so neat that she hadn't even questioned her own motives for agreeing to the deception.

She stared out at the clear bright sea. It was a question she had been avoiding ever since she had been faced with the choice. And it had been easy to avoid in the rush of getting her hair done, having a manicure, packing. Then there had been the need to cancel the milk and the papers. All those desperately important things that George would have happily done for her if she had asked . . .

Now honesty compelled her to confront the situation, face up to the truth. She had accompanied Jack Wolfe to the West Indies for no other reason than that she had wanted to. From the moment in his flat when he had fastened his fingers about her wrist to stop her from leaving and, without even turning to look at her, had suggested it. All right, so she had turned him down, walked out on him. But she had regretted it the minute the words were out of her mouth. And when he had given her a second chance to say yes, she hadn't hesitated.

For a moment she held her breath, half expecting the world to come crashing down about her ears. But nothing happened.

Right.

OK.

So?

So anyone could understand the appeal of an opportunity to seize her moment of triumph, let him see that Cinderella had been the Princess all along . . .

She drew in a sharp breath. *Stop kidding yourself, Mel. That was nothing.* It hadn't even worked, for heaven's sake. Not really. Oh, she'd given him a surprise, but not enough of a surprise to justify this. And she could have set it up any time she wanted.

This was truth time. She hadn't wanted to show herself in her true colours because once she had, she would have burned her boats. No more visits to his apartment. No more possibilities of flirting with danger. No more Jack Wolfe . . .

Ever since she had crossed Jack's path she had felt the attraction even as she recognized the danger. But she had kept on crossing it.

But was it the danger she was addicted to? Or Jack Wolfe?

Silly question. She had been standing in the path of a runaway truck for days, weeks, just waiting for it to run over her . . .

Now she realized that at some point it had, so how come she hadn't noticed?

How on earth could she have been so stupid?

Easily. It had been happening since the dawn of time. Except then it would have been a runaway woolly mammoth.

Well, it was too late to do anything about that. But falling in love didn't have to make her an accessory to Jack's business deal. She didn't have to stand idly by and do nothing while he destroyed a young man's dreams. Not when she could do something about it.

One phone call to a journalist who would fall over himself to betray the secret honeymoon destination of Edward Beaumont would provide Gus with all the instant free publicity he could handle. Jack would be none the wiser, nor would Gus. And Beau and Diana's yacht was already disappearing into the distance. They would be long gone before the news

281

hit the streets, so it couldn't possibly hurt them. It was perfect.

And once her conscience was clear she could concentrate on playing chicken with her own personal truck.

Professional virgin? *I don't think so, Diana.*

Jack had the right of it. It might just be Gus's lucky day. It might just be everyone's lucky day.

An hour later, Jack, perched astride an old and somewhat battered bicycle, one foot on the ground, was waiting for her to follow his example and Mel had suddenly lost all desire to sing.

'You *can* ride a bicycle, Mel?' he asked, as she hesitated.

'I don't know. I haven't tried for quite a while.'

'Oh, come on,' he said, taking her swimming things and putting them in her basket, impatient to be off. 'No one ever forgets. Just get on and push off. The minute you start it'll come back to you.'

'Will it?' She pushed back her hair and regarded the machine with distrust.

He looked back over his shoulder and straightened in the saddle when he saw that she had made no effort to do as she was told. 'What's the matter?'

She gave an awkward little shrug. 'The last time I was on a bike it was pink. And it had training wheels.'

'Training wheels?' His grin displayed a lot of teeth. Not a bit wolf-like, though. Rather nice, straight, white teeth. But then everything about the man gave an impression of the same well-groomed strength, of rock-steady reliability. He had the look of a man you could turn to if you were in trouble. It was a look that had undoubtedly contributed to his success in the treacherous waters of the financial world. Well, he wouldn't be getting his hands on The Ark at a cut-price, knock-down rate. Not this time. And it would all seem like chance – he would never know, or at least he could never be sure – that she had had anything to do with it. So why was she shaking? *Her subsconscious gave a hollow laugh.* 'How old were you,' he asked. 'Three? Four?'

'What? Oh, four.'

'Well, you're a bit big for training wheels these days.' He propped his own machine against the wall and came back to her. Thankfully she prepared to abandon her own machine. Too soon. He took it from her, placed it firmly in the centre of the path and said, 'Come on. You'll soon learn.'

Melanie regarded the bicycle with loathing. 'I'd rather not, if you don't mind.' Just how far could it be to the other beach? 'Why don't we walk?'

'Don't be silly, Mel. Everyone should know how to ride a bike. It's cheap, green – '

'In London? With all those traffic fumes? I'll stick to the Underground, thanks, it's safer.'

'There isn't any traffic here,' he pointed out, taking hold of the handlebars and the rear of the saddle. 'I won't let you fall. Come on, climb aboard.'

'You're being horribly bossy.'

'I'm allowed to be. I'm the boss.' Jack regarded her a certain detachment. No girl who had decided to make a fool of Jack Wolfe could be frightened of a mere bicycle. Could she? And if she was, maybe she should have a taste of what was in store for her. He grinned. 'You're not afraid, are you, Mel?'

Absolutely petrified. Suddenly a runaway truck seemed safe by comparison. 'You'd better run me through the basics,' she muttered, unwilling to display her lack of courage in the face of something as unthreatening as self-propelled transport.

'Put your right leg through there,' he said, releasing the saddle so that she could do as she was told. He patted the saddle. 'And your bottom on here.'

She placed her right leg as directed and slid up on to the saddle, balancing herself on tiptoes. 'How's that?' she asked, looking up at him.

Such touching trust. Such innocent eyes.

'You're doing fine so far, Mel, but you're going to have to take at least one foot off the ground and put it on a pedal if you want to actually go anywhere.'

'I'm happy here,' she assured him. 'This is good.'

'Well, it's up to you, of course. But you'll get hot and uncomfortable if you stay there all day. And I thought you wanted to . . . snorkel.'

'I could do that in the pool,' she said.

'There isn't anything to look at in the pool. This will be more fun.'

'Says who?'

'I do.'

For just a moment she thought she detected a note of something more than simple encouragement in his voice. What was it? Anticipation? Mel gave a little gasp and looked quickly down at her left foot, small, neat, sandalled in soft leather. She tried to lift it to the pedal; it remained firmly on the ground, refusing to co-operate. 'You'd better remind my foot that you're the boss,' she said, with a slightly edgy little laugh, 'it can't have been paying attention.'

'I can do better than that.' Keeping one hand on the handlebars, he bent and, grasping her ankle, lifted her foot up on to the pedal. The bike wobbled and she squeaked nervously but he retrieved the saddle and held it easily, grinning at her as he stood up. 'You see?' he said. 'It's easy.'

'As falling off a log.' The foot on the pedal was shaking like jelly. In fact quite a lot of her was shaking like jelly, not least because of the way she was now cradled by his arms as he gripped the machine fore and aft, taking its weight. With her shoulder and arm and hip pressed close against him, staying where she was looked more and more attractive. After all, if they were going to play these dangerous games, they might as well do it in comfort, right here in the cottage . . . 'Jack – '

'Push off with your right foot,' he instructed.

Oh, well. 'You'll hold me?' she demanded. 'You won't let me go?'

'Trust me.'

Trust him? Was he kidding? But he didn't wait to see if she trusted him or not, giving her a firm push-start before she could change her mind. The pedals went round, the wheels went round. Her right foot caught up with the free pedal and he released the handlebars, running alongside her as she gathered speed, still holding on to the saddle. She caught her breath, laughing as she half turned to him. 'I can do it!' she exclaimed. He wasn't there. He was about twenty feet behind her, grinning with a self-satisfied 'I-told-you-so' expression.

Melanie began to wobble. Then she gave a little scream as her foot slipped from the pedal. After that everything happened very fast. From a distance, the clipped glossy leaves and huge pink flowers of the hibiscus gave an impression of cushiony welcome. The cushion, she discovered to her cost as the bicycle tossed her into it, was stuffed with sharp little twigs.

'You rat!' she exclaimed, furiously, trying to push him away as, making no attempt to hide his amusement, he picked her effortlessly out of the bush, set her on her feet and dusted her off, examining her for damage. 'You let go!'

'You were doing fine without me. Are you hurt?'

'Yes,' she declared. 'I'm scratched to death.'

'Really?' He looked her over, apparently unimpressed. 'Well, your vocal cords seem to have survived intact.'

As if to prove him right, she yelped as he plucked a leafy twig from the front of her vest. 'Don't do that!'

He broke off the slightly battered hibiscus and tucked it behind her ear. 'Ready for another go?'

'No.' She glared at him and then at the bike. Her initial reaction had been more than justified.

'No one is born knowing how to ride a bike, Mel. Everyone falls off. The trick is to get back on again,

286

straight away.' And he picked it up, holding it for her, apparently expecting her to do just that. No argument. She approached the loathed machine with the utmost reluctance, but it had now become a challenge, something personal between them, and she remounted without a word. For a moment he stayed with her, his arm behind her, his chest hard against her back until she was away, wobbling a little as she realized she was on her own; then, as she picked up speed and steadied, she gave a whoop of sheer exhilaration.

The path curved through a thick plantation of jungle-like vegetation, a minefield of unexpected obstacles for the unwary. A bright lizard shot out in front of her and she screamed. A couple of chickens squawked nervously and flapped furiously along the path in front of her, desperate to escape but not quite sure how. She would have stopped, but was having the same trouble as the chickens. Her feet and her brain were not connected. 'Jack,' she pleaded desperately as she began to wobble again. 'How do I stop this thing?'

'Use the brakes,' he called, from his own machine a few feet behind her.

Brakes? She looked down at her feet. What brakes? He caught up with her as the path dipped towards the cove, grabbing for the back of her vest to slow her down. 'The brakes,' he repeated, guiding his bike alongside her as the path widened. 'They're on the handlebars. Just squeeze them gently.' And suddenly her mind unlocked and she remembered, the bike slithering to a halt just inches before she ran out of path. She put a foot down, but her leg was shaking so much that he had to catch her. 'Fast learner, aren't you?' he said, holding her against him. She looked up and he was smiling. Not laughing at her, but truly smiling with eyes that crinkled up at the corners, a mouth that widened into tiny creases. 'If there were any cars on this island I could be persuaded to teach you to drive.'

It was her turn to smile. 'I don't have any trouble with cars. They have a wheel at each corner and stand up all by themselves. I learned to drive when I was ten. Truly,' she said, as she saw his disbelief. 'Luke put blocks on the pedals of an old mini as a present for my tenth birthday and let me loose in the bush.'

'Luke?'

'My uncle. I passed my test first time.' She snapped her fingers carelessly. 'No problem.'

'Only with bikes.'

I wish, she thought. 'I broke my arm when I was little and no one made me get back on.'

'That was a mistake.'

'Well, I did tell you I was spoilt.'

'So you did.' And his look changed subtly, the smile no longer teasing, but searching.

The trembling had long since ceased; there was no good reason for her to continue to cling on to him no matter how much she might want to, so she stepped back, pushing her hair back from her face. She encountered the hibiscus and, laughing awkwardly, removed it. It was as if she was thirteen again, awkward, shy, out of her depth when a good-looking boy smiled at her but wouldn't make the first move because she was already famous.

'Well,' she said, twirling it between her fingers, 'I can't say I'll be making a habit of it, but thanks for showing me how it's done.'

'Any time, Cinderella.' The thoughtful, penetrating look continued for a moment more, then he turned to the beach. 'Well now, isn't this something?'

For a moment she continued to regard his profile, but his face guarded his thoughts too well and she finally followed his gaze. The beach was extraordinary. Nothing like the long white beach that stretched endlessly in both directions in front of their cottage, the small horseshoe of sand was flanked on either side by the strange natural sculptures of ancient boulders. More huge rocks littered the beach, providing quiet shade. And out to sea the sleek lines of a yacht slicing through the water half a mile or so offshore provided an elegant counterpoint to the blue of the sky and the sea.

It was idyllic. Quiet and peaceful, with none of the commercial razzle that usually went with a holiday resort, only a discreet bar beneath the wide shade of a thatched roof, and a stone-built barbecue where locally caught seafood would be grilled in the open air at lunchtime. Both were deserted this early in the day.

Jack had been right when he had said this was paradise. 'This is far more than something,' she said, after a long pause. 'But even paradise had its serpent.' She turned to him. 'Or in this case, wolf.'

For a moment Jack regarded her with irritation, almost as if he wanted to say something, but knew she would never understand.

'You know, you have a beautiful mouth, Mel. There's basically only one thing wrong with it. It just keeps on working when your brain has switched off.' He propped the bikes in the shade of the palm grove and turned back to her. 'Now, pick your spot, lie down and if you're good I'll rub your back with sun-cream.' She opened her mouth to protest, indignation rescuing her from that stupid tongue-tied awkwardness.

He stopped her by the simple expedient of kissing her; for a moment she went rigid, pushing against his chest with the flat of her hands. He simply hooked his arm about her waist and pulled her hard against him. Then, with the other hand framing her face, he took his time about teaching her the only use for her mouth he was prepared to countenance.

And as the warmth of his lips began to stoke up her internal thermostat her stiff fingers began to bunch handfuls of his shirt, pulling him closer. Why did she persist in fighting him when this was what she wanted? This and a whole lot more . . .

But, apparently satisfied that he had her full attention, he raised his head to look at her. 'And when I've finished with your back, I might just let you loose on mine. Have you any problem with that?'

She swallowed hard. The only problems she had were with a heart that was beating erratically, skin that was flushed with more than the heat of the sun and a pulse that pounded in a way not entirely attributable to her recent exertions on the bike. He did that to her every time. How?

No one else had ever managed it. Why should she suddenly start lusting after a man whom common sense told her to steer clear of? She'd never been short of common sense. At least, she had thought so until now. But maybe she'd been fooling herself about that. Maybe it was simply that no one had discovered the 'on' switch before.

'Say, "No Jack",' he prompted.

'No, Jack,' she repeated obediently, but just a touch breathlessly. 'No problems.'

'I'm glad to hear it,' he said, turning to retrieve the snorkelling gear from the old-fashioned basket fixed to the front of his handlebars.

'Jack . . .'

'Yes?' He glanced back at her, a pair of well-honed eyebrows daring her to risk another lesson in obedience.

'Nothing. Except . . .' Except what? Forget everything I've ever said about not wanting to kiss you. Kissing you has become my number one priority and I can't wait to try a little trifling . . . 'I think that would be a good place,' she said, turning swiftly away to point to a shaded part of the beach where a couple of sun-loungers seemed to be waiting for them. 'My complexion is a little tender for too much sun.'

'Your complexion, like your mouth, is beautiful, Mel.' His gaze swept from the creamy white expanse of skin above the scooped neckline of her vest, via her throat, her chin, her small, neatly proportioned nose, coming to a halt when their eyes finally met. 'You should certainly take care of it.' He smiled. All of a sudden he kept on doing that. Why the sudden change? He tossed up a bottle of sun-block, catching it without difficulty, and pointed with it to a huddle of palm-thatched *cabañas*. 'Why don't you go and change? Then it'll be my pleasure to do everything I can to help you achieve that goal.'

If it had just been *his* pleasure, surely breathing wouldn't be this much trouble? What on earth was she getting into? 'There's no hurry,' she said, with a little gasp.

'I thought you wanted to go snorkelling.'

'I do, but . . .' Apparently he wasn't interested in buts, handing her her costume wrapped in a towel without another word. 'Right. I won't be long.'

Mel had rinsed out her swimsuit and left it to drip over the balcony after her early morning swim. In the privacy of the *cabaña* she unrolled her towel and extracted the tiny white bikini that was her alternative. In the friendly atmosphere of her London club, where she was among friends, the bikini had seemed unexceptional. But now, as she tied the shoestring straps behind her neck, she was suddenly aware of her body in a totally new way, the way Jack would be looking at it. At least the way she hoped he would be looking at it. Because that was the way she was looking at him.

She wrapped the towel around her for the sake of modesty, but that just made her look stupid. And she

292

didn't want to be modest. She wanted him to look at her, every bit of her. She took off the towel, slung it over her shoulder and let herself out of the *cabaña*.

Jack had pulled the loungers deeper into the shade of a couple of huge rocks. He'd peeled off his T-shirt and shorts and was already stretched out as if he had nothing else to do in the entire world but work on his suntan. His eyes were hidden by a pair of dark glasses, but she knew he was watching her as she crossed the deserted beach; she could feel him following every movement. But who was she to criticize? As she approached his prone figure covered by nothing but the narrow strip of his black Speedo, her own eyes were focused with equal intensity on the spare, sinewy lines of his body. It was hard and exciting and it suddenly occurred to Melanie that, while a girl who prided herself on common sense would not choose to spend the day on a deserted beach with such a man, a girl who thought that flirting might be fun could not have chosen a better spot.

As she came alongside him she experienced an intense longing to reach out and touch him. Tell him exactly what she was feeling.

Her insides tied up into knots at the thought and instead she flopped down on to the lounger with her back to him, looking out to sea. What a coward! He could only say no . . .

'Lie down, Mel,' he said, his shadow falling over her as he sat up. 'I don't want you to burn.'

'I won't. It's still early and I've already given

myself a thorough coating – ' she began, and could have kicked herself. What was the matter with her? Where was the girl who had wanted to take a risk, court danger? The girl who, an hour ago, had cleared her conscience and was now ready to throw caution to winds.

She should be encouraging Jack Wolfe, not putting obstacles in his way. But on this occasion obstacles were apparently pointless and she jumped as he touched her with the tip of one finger, right between the shoulder-blades.

'You managed to reach here?' he asked.

'Well . . .' she said, glancing back at him.

He was regarding her with scarcely veiled amusement. 'Of course, if you're a contortionist, along with your many other talents . . .' He raised a pair of dark brows, inviting her confirmation that this was indeed the case. She considered telling him that she was – except that he would undoubtedly demand a demonstration.

'No, but – '

'But me no buts. Forget you were once a spoiled four-year-old and for once just do as you're told.'

Somewhere deep inside her brain an alarm was sounding, red lights were flashing. Danger! Danger! But the sun was beating down on her skin, the sea sparkling an invitation. Why was she even hesitating? Mentally she switched off the alarm and without another word she stretched out on her stomach, burying her face in her arms.

He took his time, lifting the heavy weight of her

hair sideways to expose her shoulders before pulling on the bow at her neck to leave the field clear for his ministrations. Mel considered protesting that this was unnecessary. Before she could make up her mind about that, he began to unclip the back fastening. That was too much and she half rose in protest just as it fell away; she subsided with a little yelp that escaped before she could do anything about it.

A hot flush of colour raced to her cheeks, colour that wasn't cooled by Jack's soft laughter, or his hand slowly smoothing a broad band of cream over her warm skin in one single caressing stroke that began at her nape and didn't finish until it encountered the lower half of her bikini. His touch was gentle, intimate, deliciously seductive.

A tiny squeak escaped her and she hung on to her breath as his hands spread out over her sides, his thumbs pressing down her backbone as he encircled the sensitive skin at her waist.

'What's the matter, Cinderella?'

'Nothing.' Her voice was husky, she cleared her throat. 'Nothing,' she repeated. 'I'm just fine.'

Fine! What was she saying! She was far from fine. Oh, lord, he was off again, stroking the cream along the width of her shoulders, across her shoulder-blades, down her sides, nudging his fingers against the soft swell of her breasts, sliding his thumbs beneath the cloth of her bikini bottom to make certain she was protected in the vulnerable strip that would be exposed as she bent down. She should be pleased that he was taking so much trouble. She *was* pleased, she decided. Deliciously, entrancingly, exquisitely pleased. In fact she was beginning to wish he'd take the wretched thing off altogether and make a thorough job of it. She considered suggesting it, but then decided to leave it to him. He obviously knew what he was doing.

Each touch was a new delight, a new torment that unravelled undreamt-of desires deep within her, provoking a slow build-up of heat that made her mouth throb, her breasts ache to be touched, stroked, kissed . . . oh, lord . . . he'd stopped . . . no . . . a little gasp of relief as he began to apply the same magic to her legs.

The pads of his fingers began a series of long, caressing strokes and she shivered as he applied the protective cream to the pale, tender skin of her inner thighs, her calves, her ankles. It was blissful, and as the cream melted against her skin, her entire being followed suit and began to turn to warm jelly beneath his hand.

Then he stopped. She gave a little moan of disappointment that she was too far lost to disguise. But no, there was no end to bliss, it seemed, as, his voice coming from deep within his throat, Jack murmured, 'Turn over, Mel.'

For a moment she remained perfectly still. If she turned over there would be no going back. But she didn't want to go back. She'd tossed her coin, made her choice weeks ago. She should have an affair with someone totally unsuitable, Richard had said. Someone who would break her heart. The part might have been written for Jack Wolfe. It was time to ditch the sweet little *ingénue* forever. Time to grow up. She couldn't wait.

And as she obeyed him and turned over, the white bikini top slipped off the lounger and fell on to the sand.

Warmed by the sun on the outside, her insides heated to the core by Jack Wolfe's fingers, Melanie knew she had been right. In the shadow cast by the great rocks she and Jack were so entirely alone that they might have been the only two people in the world.

CHAPTER 12

Melanie had longed for the look she could see in his eyes as he stared down at her. No man had ever looked at her in quite that way before, with a desire so raw that her breath caught in her throat.

As if he knew, he reached out and touched her there, gently teasing his knuckles down her neck, into the small hollow at the base of her throat before turning his hand to run the tip of his thumb along the line of her breastbone. She held her breath, waiting, knowing that she was a heartbeat from some great secret. For a moment it seemed she would gain her heart's wish, then without warning he stood up, dropping the bottle on the sand beside her.

'You don't have to be a contortionist to finish the job, Melanie,' he said, tightly. And snatching up the snorkelling gear he walked swiftly away, leaving her to cope alone with feelings that had spiralled so swiftly out of control, taking her on some blazingly new emotional rollercoaster. For a moment they had been poised together at the pinnacle; now she was crashing back to earth alone.

Shivering, she sat up, bunching her legs up to her body as if attempting to hide her naked breasts from Jack, from herself. But it was too late. And she had exposed more than her body. Jack knew now that he would only have to click his fingers and she would be his. He'd probably always known it. That day when she'd cut herself, if he'd kissed her then there would have been only one place it could ever have ended up. He'd known it even if she had not quite understood what had hung in the air between them. And he'd made his choice. Sent her away.

He had no intention of getting involved with the girl who came in three times a week to clean his sink. No matter how much she turned him on. And he'd just made it plain that he still felt the same way. There was some consolation to be gained from the fact that he was as angry with himself as he was with her. But not much.

She wrapped her arms about her legs and rested her cheek on her knees. What on earth was the matter with her, anyway? It wasn't the first time a man had rubbed her back with sun-cream, for heaven's sake. There had been a time when she'd spent half her life on a beach and her back had been the subject of some very assiduous attention indeed.

But Jack Wolfe hadn't just been rubbing sun-cream on her back. He had caressed her with it, stroked her, deliberately arousing her with every touch. He'd had seduction in mind and she couldn't have made her response plainer. So

why, having quite deliberately torched those indescribable feelings, had Jack walked away?

Because he didn't get involved with women who
worked for him? Somehow she didn't think so. A
man who made his own rules could break them any
time he wanted. And for a moment there it had been
touch and go.

Maybe if she refused to work out her notice? Quit
now?

Maybe she needed her head examining.

Mel looked towards the rocks that tumbled into the
sea but she couldn't see him, and with a tiny sigh that
she would have liked to have been relief, but was very
much afraid was regret, she retrieved her top from
the sand. But her fingers were shaking so much that it
took a lot longer to fasten than the first time. And she
took a long time about coating the front of her body
with the sun lotion. She needed time, and she
suspected he did too.

Jack plunged into the water, desperate to cool the
heat that was hammering through his veins.

Leave her to do all the running, Mike had advised.
Play it cool. He'd thought he had been doing exactly
that.

Last night it had been easy. She had suggested a
walk along the beach, although he had the feeling that
had had more to do with too much champagne than
any serious intent at seduction. Not that it would
have mattered if she had. She was so tired that she
was asleep long before he had put her to bed. And

undressing a woman who was asleep was not, despite what he had said to her this morning, a major turn-on. He preferred a little cooperation.

Not that she hadn't been infinitely desirable as she had lain tumbled against the sheets in that ridiculous purple T-shirt, and the temptation to slip in beside her, to be there when she woke, was almost overwhelming. Perhaps that was why he had taken himself so determinedly off to the sofa.

But then, this morning, as he had watched her walk across the beach, lithe, fresh, full of life, something had caught at him, stirring a memory of how he had been, once. And the man who had caught at her ankle hadn't been the cold-hearted bastard with a name that was a gift for lazy journalists; it had been someone he had almost forgotten existed. Until sanity had reasserted itself.

And sanity had reasserted itself with a vengeance when he had heard what Mike had discovered. Mrs Graham might have unbreachable rules about disclosing the address of an employee, but Mike Palmer could extract blood from a stone with nothing more forceful than the power of his smile. Janet Graham didn't have a chance.

But it turned out that Melanie Devlin's address was already well known to him. It was the same as Richard Latham's.

Which was why it had taken him so long to bring himself to follow her up this morning. He'd needed that time, every minute of it, to eradicate all trace of what he was feeling.

He stopped swimming and hauled himself up on to a flat slab of rock.

Feeling. He turned the word over in his mind, testing it. There was an awful fascination about it, like probing at a painful tooth. You were aware of it for days, weeks before action became imperative. And he began to wonder just how long these feelings had been creeping up on him.

Since that moment when, giggling in his brother's arms, she had turned and looked at him. Her eyes were extraordinary. He'd thought then that there had been a flash of recognition . . . but had assumed she must have seen his photograph in the press. Caroline loved to have her photograph taken with him.

But the minute he saw her at the airport he knew it had been before then. That moment in the travel agent's doorway when he had held her shoulders, wanting to hold so much more. Was it her eyes that had driven him to his office window, seeking her out, distracting him? And then he had seen her talking to Latham and he had blanked her from his mind. It wouldn't be so easy a second time.

He leaned back against the hot rock. This was not a good moment to rediscover feelings. Not a good moment to discover that his heart was still capable of pulling a few tricks, reminding him that he hadn't always been the cold, unfeeling bastard that Melanie had accused him of being.

Nor was it a good moment, he'd discovered, to come across Gus doing exactly what he had asked him to do. Making Melanie like him. Enlisting her sympathy, hinting at money worries. Jealousy had grabbed him by the throat. Jealousy and anger. Poor Gus. He hadn't known what he'd done wrong. But it wouldn't take him long to work it out. He was good at relationships, understood people; they liked him, warmed to him on sight. And he had taken to Melanie. He'd seen the disapproving look Gus had given him when he'd asked him to make a note of any phone calls she made, when he'd told him to make sure everyone stayed off this beach for the morning.

And, like Gus, Melanie Devlin had a talent for making friends. Tom, Gus, they had both fallen under her spell. Well, so had he. Even when she was telling him to take a running jump he wanted to laugh and pull her into his arms and invite her to jump with him. He had warmed to her without even noticing it, but, like icy fingers encountering sudden heat, the only thing he was feeling right now was pain.

And this morning he had intended to have his revenge on her for that, take his hurt out of her hide. Except that when it came to it, he found he couldn't do it. Not in cold blood. Because his blood had been very hot indeed, and that was not the same thing at all.

He turned as he heard Melanie approach, rolling up into a sitting position. God, but she was lovely. How on earth could he have missed it? Then he recalled his determination to have her work for him, a moment that first day when something had shimmered in the air between them. And the day he had surprised her, made her jump like a startled kitten – how close he had come to making love to her then . . .

He hadn't missed it. He'd known. Somewhere inside his head he'd always known that she was more, much more than she was prepared to let the outside world see.

'What kept you?' he demanded, irritably. The swim hadn't helped much. The water was too warm. Or maybe his blood was just too hot.

Melanie was not in the best of moods either. 'I'm sorry, Jack,' she said, with uncharacteristic sarcasm. 'I didn't realize you were in such a hurry to go swimming. If you'd stayed to give me a hand with the hooks and bows I wouldn't have kept you waiting.'

'If I'd stayed . . .' He regarded her with more than a touch of exasperation. 'I'm not made of wood, Mel. What with having to put you to bed last night and that little stunt you just pulled . . .' he looked away, screwing his eyes up against the distant horizon, unable to face her with the blatant lie '. . . well, you're not making it exactly easy.'

'Stunt?' Stunt that *she* had pulled? The nerve of the man.

'It's difficult. Your mouth says one thing and your body says something quite different. It's the kind of combination that could get a man into a lot of trouble.'

'So you walked away?' Not made of wood, huh? Personally, she'd have said he was mahogany right through. But maybe it was all an act. Maybe they were both acting their socks off. And she was the one who'd been giving out the 'hands off' message left, right and centre. How was he to know that she'd had a change of heart?

'It seemed wise.'

'Then I'll have to make myself a whole lot clearer in future,' she said, with what she hoped sounded like a careless lack of concern. 'I'll put it in writing if you like.' She pulled herself up on to the rock beside him, her thigh brushing lightly against his, the dark hair on his leg acting like static on the invisible down of her skin. He didn't appear to notice. Considering his complaint that she had been leading him on, that he was finding it difficult to resist, that had to be just a little suspicious. Didn't it? Just how good was he at hiding his feelings? 'And I'm really sorry about last night. I must have drunk a lot more than I thought.'

'More than two glasses of champagne, anyway.' He was obviously a past master at careless concern himself and that irritated her. *She* was supposed to be the actress around here.

'And just now. I wasn't teasing.'

'Weren't you?' Just how calculating was she? Just how far was she prepared to go for Richard Latham? 'Weren't you trying a little pay-back for being forced into this situation? You can look but you mustn't touch? It's what you've been saying ever since we arrived.'

She didn't know how she managed to prevent herself from hitting him. She hadn't been the one with her hands all over *him* a few minutes ago, doing things with sun-cream that not even Factor 20 could protect you from.

'I haven't noticed you listening.'

'Perhaps it's time I started.'

She turned to meet his gaze head-on. The sun was bringing out the little gold flecks in those slaty dark eyes, making them sparkle disconcertingly. Like fool's gold, she thought. Was she a fool?

'Don't be sore, Jack. A girl has to play a little hard to get. Especially when she isn't being given a lot of choice.'

'You mean that the reluctance was all an act?' He didn't sound convinced.

'I am an actress,' she pointed out, gently.

'Then you're a whole lot better than I gave you credit for.'

'Thank you.' He gave her a look that suggested he hadn't been paying her a compliment. She refused to take offence, lifting her shoulders a little, forcing a smile as she leaned back, propping herself on her hands, lifting her face to the sun as if the matter was closed.

But Jack could see the tension in her body, giving the lie to her apparent dismissal of the situation.

Had she really thought that he would leap on her like some damned caveman? Or had the invitation to walk along the beach in the moonlight been her plan all along, scuppered in the end by jetlag and too much champagne? If so, Mike was a better judge of the situation than he was and she must be getting desperate. Somehow the thought was more arousing than it should be. *She* was a whole lot more arousing than any man could be expected to resist when he was being offered her on a plate. And there was no other way to take that little scene.

Her body was so lithe, so very desirable, and as she tilted her head back her hair fell away like a skein of pale gold silk. The breeze lifted a strand across her face and he wanted to brush it away, feel the smooth skin of her cheek as he cradled it beneath his hand. She turned her head, as if conscious that he was staring at her, and he felt control slipping away from him; it always did when she looked at him like that. It was like trying to stand up in a earthquake.

'Don't do that!' he growled.

'What?'

'Pretend.' Her eyes widened and suddenly he found himself staring at the small pebbles beside him on the rock. He picked up a few, tossed one into the sea. 'I'm sorry. I'm not making much sense this morning.'

'I'm sorry too, if I've confused you. It was my intention to make everything quite clear.' *It's burn-your-boats time, girl. Now or never. Have you got the guts?* 'I'm trying to seduce you, Jack. Maybe it's because I haven't had a lot of practice that I'm making such a hash of it. Is there any chance of a little help around here?' She regarded him through a lowered fringe of lashes. 'There are a few gaps in my education.'

'Gaps?' He swung round to look at her.

307

Melanie knew her cheeks were heating up, but she refused to back down. 'It seems such a pity to waste paradise, and kissing you turned out to be . . . well . . .' Her shoulders seemed to be working overtime. She was becoming positively Gallic in the shrugging stakes.

'To be what, Melanie?' he enquired, softly.

Everything her midnight fantasies had promised? Worth the risk of heartbreak? No. Burning her boats was bad enough; exposing herself so completely would be madness.

'You don't seem to be *that* busy working on your important deal. But of course if you'd rather not,' she said with a very small sigh, 'I'll understand. I'm sure you believe that it's as much a mistake to mix business with pleasure as it is to get involved with your staff. I suppose that doing both at once would be quite impossible – '

'Melanie?'

Was it her imagination, or was he closer? She hadn't seen him move and yet . . . 'And there's Caroline to consider,' she said, by now fully into her stride. 'I know you said – '

'Caroline is history,' he said, continuing to regard her with curiosity. 'She has been for weeks.' *Ever since he had tangled with a girl in a doorway.* 'Tell me about the gaps.'

Mel wriggled her shoulders. She hadn't bargained for him to come right out and ask . . . But he was still looking at her, waiting for her answer. Oh, well. The worst thing that could happen was if he fell off the rock laughing. 'You were the one who said I was behaving like a schoolgirl virgin, Jack,' she said, finally.

'But you're not a schoolgirl.'

'No. I'm not a schoolgirl. But it's amazing the way everyone treats me as if I were one. Even my new stepsister. She's nearly three years younger than me, you know, but she treats me as if I were some Goody Two-shoes straight out of convent school.'

'I don't think Goody Two-shoes would have come on this little trip, do you?'

'She might. If she had a good enough reason.'

'A job for your friend, perhaps? A home for your co-operative?'

She turned to him. 'Those things are important, but on consideration I hardly think they would be enough.'

'I wouldn't have thought so. So what would be enough, Mel?' *To help your lover pull off a financial coup?*

She shrugged. 'Maybe I just felt like doing something outrageous for a change. Something shocking. Maybe I was regretting turning you down the moment the words were out of my mouth. But don't worry about it. Put it down to too much sun. A dip will probably do the trick.'

'I doubt it. I've already tried.'

'Really?' She glanced at him. His skin had quickly dried in the sun, but his hair was still damp, tangled. Her hands were shaking as she sat up and seized one of her flippers, attempting, without much success, to

309

push a foot into it. 'Oh, well, I'll give it a go; it'll give the fishes a laugh if nothing else. I've never actually done this before, you know . . .'

'Another gap in your education?'

'I was a child-actress. I missed a lot of school,' she said, rather crossly. She had rather hoped that he might have been touched by her declared innocence. She had rather hoped that he might offer, very tenderly, to do something about it. She risked a quick glance, but his face was like the rock she was sitting on. Two refusals in as many months, then. Could it be that she had suddenly developed bad breath?

The way he keeps kissing you? No chance. Then why? Was he still, despite his denials, regretting that he hadn't conceded to Caroline? There was nothing like absence to put things into perspective. His first marriage hadn't been bad enough to put him off the institution for life, surely?

She concentrated on the strap, but her fingers, along with her common sense, seemed to have lost contact with her brain some time during the morning. Messages weren't getting through. The bikini had been bad enough but the horrible rubber strap had a mind of its own – and it appeared to be in better working order than hers. She would have given up, except that would have meant looking up, meeting that rock-wall of resistance. But Jack had pushed himself off the rock, jumping down into the thigh-deep water. Without waiting for an invitation, he grasped her ankle and propped her flippered foot

310

against his chest while he fastened it for her.

She kept her lashes firmly lowered. She'd said enough. More than enough. She'd invited him to the party, but if he was determined not to boogie she wasn't going to make any more of a fool of herself than she had already.

But refusing to meet his eyes made not one jot of difference. She knew he was looking at her; she could *feel* him looking at her. The air around them was charged with electricity, the touch of his fingers as they brushed against her ankle relaying glorious messages to her brain, firing new, explosive synapses that set off an unstoppable chain reaction of awareness.

It was as if for the last twenty-one years she had been asleep. And now when everything was wrong, when it was impossible, she was quite suddenly wide awake to a whole new world of possibilities. Jack Wolfe had hit the 'on' switch and she was lit up like the Trafalgar Square Christmas tree. The trouble was, it wasn't Christmas.

He had finished the first foot and let it go. Then he took her other foot, holding her firmly around the ankle as he pushed it into the second flipper. Once more her heel was pushed firmly into his abdomen as he tightened the strap. It was as hard and flat as an ironing board, the skin warm against her heel . . .

She held her breath as he straightened, fastened his hands about her waist.

'Ready?' he said. She nodded, unable to make her mouth form the words, and he lifted her from the rocks, for a moment holding her against him, her feet inches from the bottom, their bodies touching – warm skin against warm skin in the cool water. The messages grew thunderous and she clutched almost desperately at his smooth, muscle-packed shoulders. Well, heck, she wasn't *that* innocent. Maybe, just maybe, Christmas was coming early this year. Maybe it was time to send Santa a list . . .

'Kiss me, Jack,' she murmured, sliding her arms up and around his neck. 'I want you to kiss me.'

'I can see that.'

Could he? Of course he could. She was flashing out signals like a June bug in heat. Oh, lord! 'Then what's stopping you?' *Who said that?*

'I'm still not sure why you should want me to kiss you.' *Jack couldn't believe he'd said that.* 'I know you said you were acting your socks off. But why? If you were looking for a little excitement, why did you make such a point of insisting you didn't?'

Why? He wanted to know *why?* For Pete's sake, the man had been kissing her left, right and centre whether she wanted him to or not ever since they arrived on this damned island. Now she wanted a piece of the action and he was asking *why?* If he didn't know . . .

Her eyes snapped open as the haze of sexual desire cleared. 'Actually, Mr Wolfe, I can't remember. In fact I've quite suddenly gone off the whole idea.' She tried to wriggle free, but he continued to hold her, the wide space between his eyes puckered in a frown as he regarded her with a slightly puzzled look. It was as if he was trying to weigh something up, almost, she thought, as if trying to decide whether he could trust her. But that was ridiculous.

Or was it? Damn the champagne for running away with her tongue last night; she'd said too much and now he was suspicious of her. Well, if she was honest, he had every right to be. But she didn't have to dangle there and take it.

'Could you please put me down? I'd like to swim now.'

She blinked back a stupid self-pitying tear that trickled down her cheek as he obediently released her. He didn't have to do that . . . she hadn't meant it . . . oh, damn! She pushed herself away from him, lunging at the water before he could see, but she hadn't gone a yard when his hand clamped about her ankle, bringing her to an abrupt halt.

Floundering, unable to put a foot down and right herself, she was at his mercy, unable to tell him to get lost, or even shout for help without swallowing half the Caribbean. He took full advantage of the situation, hauling her back towards him with deliberate slowness. Then he caught her around the waist, flipped her over and pulled him hard against him, the cool wetness of her skin against his warm, hair-spattered chest.

'What the hell do you think you're doing?' she demanded.

'You didn't mean that, did you?' He seemed taken aback. As if he'd just stumbled across the key to some unbreakable code and now he knew all the answers.

Suddenly the gold flecks were blazing and there was no mistaking his intention, but even before she opened her mouth to tell him that she wasn't interested, that she'd meant every word, she knew it was too late. He hadn't waited for an answer, because he didn't need one. And as his mouth sparked off a mark ten earthquake somewhere in the region of her midriff, Melanie realized that whatever she had been about to say couldn't possibly have been important.

Important was the way he tasted of the sea and the hot sun; the way the warm musky scent of his skin filled her mouth; the way his fingers were cupping the nape of her neck, his thumb stroking against the pulse hammering in her throat and turning her bones to warm putty.

She already knew that he was a major league kisser, that he could kiss for Great Britain, captain of the team, Olympic gold medal material. But it was obvious to Melanie that until now he'd simply been toying with her, doing exactly what he had said he would, just enough to convince anyone who was interested that they were the lovers they seemed to be. It had suddenly stopped being a game and the difference was . . . staggering.

As his arm tightened around her, his tongue ravaging the softness of her mouth until breathing was no longer an option, Melanie finally understood why they called him the Wolf in the City. It was more than an easy play on his name by the headline-writers. This man was dangerous. And she'd been flirting with him, making it plain that she'd welcome any advances he cared to make. Whatever had happened to sensible? She was behaving just like the dizzy girl in the sitcom she'd turned down. At least that had been make-believe, while this . . . she ought to be kicking him, not kissing him . . .

'Jack –' she pleaded faintly into his mouth, but there was no escape. She'd asked him to kiss her and she was getting the full treatment whether she wanted it or not. And oh, dear God, she wanted it. Wanted his teeth nibbling at her mouth, wanted his tongue sliding seductively inside her lower lip, bringing her slowly to melting point. His name became a groan and then even that was lost as his fingers opened across her waist, across her back, drawing her tight against him so that she was left in no doubt about the way he was feeling. And for the first time since they'd met they were in total agreement.

'Well?' he murmured, when he had finally made any point she'd care to think of, and quite a few she'd never even considered until now. 'Shall we continue this somewhere less public, or shall we swim?'

Melanie froze. *Why on earth did he have to ask? Didn't he know? Did he expect her to say, Carry me to the nearest cave, strip me naked and make a woman of me, darling? It was like being asked by a boy if he could kiss you. Only a hundred times worse. And there could only ever be one answer.* 'Go to hell, Jack Wolfe,' she said.

'All in good time, sweetheart,' Jack said. And he laughed. The sound was like something strange, unreal. When had he last laughed out loud, for sheer happiness? Too long ago. She might be playing some deep and devious game, but there was nothing cold or calculating about Miss Melanie Devlin. Calculating would have seized its opportunity. Calculating would have given him the green light. Calculating would not have sent him to hell but would have said, 'Let's get out of here, fast . . .'

It was plain now that Melanie was working on a purely emotional level. What was happening between them had nothing to do with takeovers, or commercial espionage, or anything he gave a damn about right now. She had wanted him. Even the most experienced seductress could not pretend that kind of arousal. Melanie didn't know enough to pretend anything. But it hadn't been her all too obvious desire that had convinced him. It had been her eyes. Her beautiful eyes had smoked with anger that he could have been so insensitive.

He *laughed*. Melanie couldn't believe it. He had been leading her on, tormenting her, driving her crazy . . . she ducked out of his arms and kicked away from him. But not fast enough. Not even with the flippers.

He was still laughing as she righted herself, spluttering with rage from her second dunking. 'I know, I know,' he said quickly as she opened her mouth to tell him exactly what she thought of him. 'Hell. In a handcart, no doubt. But first I have to give you a snorkelling lesson. Or have you changed your mind about that, too?'

316

She was speechless, utterly speechless.

'Right, since you've obviously made your mind up, shall we begin?' And without waiting for her reply he proceeded to demonstrate the use of the snorkel and mask, calm as you like; as if the earth hadn't just moved; as if a tidal wave of emotion hadn't just swept her off her feet; as if kissing someone like that was nothing out of the ordinary, nothing to get out of breath about. Well, maybe for him it wasn't. 'Now, have you got that?' he asked, glancing up.

She was staring at him as if he was a being from another planet and he discovered that the urge to kiss her again was almost overwhelming. But making love on a beach was for masochists. An hour ago he wouldn't have cared . . . Now he wanted it to be a pleasure, for both of them. First they would swim and afterwards they would shower together and use that bed for the purpose it had been intended. It would, he knew, be worth the wait.

'Melanie?' he prompted.

'Yes,' she said, dragging her mind back to the task at hand. 'I think so.'

'Try it, let me see.' Cool as a cucumber? Oh, no. Not a cucumber. More like a great big prize-winning marrow. Well, she'd do her best to respond in kind. Except that as she lowered her face beneath the surface, trying to remember everything he'd said about breathing through her mouth and not all the other things she would rather be doing with it right then, he placed his hand at her waist, keeping her at his side in case she got into difficulties.

But the snorkel was the least of her worries. All her difficulties involved far simpler things, like the way her leg would keep brushing against his, the way that he held her so that his hip and thigh pressed against hers.

Considering that simply remembering to breathe was something of a problem, the snorkel was a doddle.

And then, while she was still trying to work out what exactly was going on between them, he used his other hand to take hold of hers and lead her out into deeper water. As if she wasn't already dangerously out of her depth!

At least the fish were a diversion. Jack led her around the deep pools created by the huge rocks, startling shoals of brightly coloured fishes that turned and flashed and then crowded round them curiously. The sea was mysterious and cool and beautiful. Another world, but she was scarcely aware of it. All her senses were concentrated on those small portions of it where Jack's fingers curled around her waist and her hand, anchoring her to him.

She dared a glance at him and behind his mask he might have been smiling, or he might not. Why was it so difficult? Why did men and women play these games when the rest of the animal kingdom seemed to have the whole sex thing down to fine art?

They swam into a shoal of vivid blue and yellow parrot fish that for a little while stayed to explore these strange new beings, and before she knew it Melanie was staring cross-eyed at one of the fishes peering in at her face mask as if she were the one in the goldfish bowl. She caught Jack's eye and she could see he was thinking the same thing, and suddenly there was no doubt that he was smiling at her, or that she was smiling back.

For a while they drifted over starfish and crabs scuttling over the sand and then Jack tapped the stainless steel watch strapped to his wrist and turned them back towards the shore. Instead of heading for the sand, he released her waist and, leading her by the hand, headed into a gap between the rocks, where they had tumbled to form sea-caves. Melanie grasped his hand nervously, hating to be in dark, enclosed spaces, but these caves were not like that. They weren't dark. Inside, the sunlight seeped through the gaps in the roof to lend a translucent green light that rippled the surface of the water and reflected back against the roof.

'Wow!' she said, as she pulled off her mask, her voice echoing in the dim cavern. 'This is beautiful.'

'I thought you might like it.' He tugged off his flippers and tossed them with his mask on to the small bar of sand where the beach had been sucked through the rocks. 'Here, hop up and I'll take those things off your feet.'

Melanie hauled herself on to a small boulder that protruded from the water, offering each foot in turn while she raked her fingers through her hair, pushing it back off her face.

Jack looked up and suddenly he was very still. 'All you need is a shell comb, Melanie,' he said, the words

319

echoing softly off the rocks. 'Then you'd look like a proper mermaid.'

She too was still. 'There's nothing proper about mermaids, Jack. They sing strange songs and lure sailors to their doom . . .'

'I remember. You said that you were overdressed for the part.'

Her heart was hammering now. 'I am.'

His eyes were dark, shadowed as he straightened. 'Why don't you show me?'

'Are you quite sure you're prepared to take the risk? Once you've heard the mermaid singing – '

Softly, she began to sing an old folk song from the Auvergne; the strange acoustics of the caves picking up the lilting melody lent it an awesome mystery and as Jack stared at her, mesmerized by the sudden realization of what she was going to do, Mel reached up and pulled at the bow fastening her bikini at the neck.

It was like holding an audience in the palm of your hand, she thought, that magic moment when a thousand people held their breath as one and waited for permission to breathe again.

She flipped the clasp that held the top in place and then, after a pause that seemed to last forever, she lowered her lashes and let it go. It dropped away from her, catching momentarily on the rock before slipping into the water and drifting away.

Still, it seemed, he was waiting. So Melanie raised her arms, and as she pushed her fingers through her hair a soft expletive finally escaped Jack's lips.

She stopped singing but the notes seemed to echo on and on as she remained poised, waiting, on the rock, her arms akimbo, the small, dark buds of her breasts pouting with anticipation beneath his stunned gaze.

'Who the hell are you?' he asked, his voice little more than a hoarse whisper.

She raised her lashes then and looked him straight in the eyes. 'Does it matter?'

Jack Wolfe felt desire explode within him. Nothing mattered. Nothing but this moment. Nothing but Melanie Devlin sitting in a shaft of sunlight that shimmered over her hair and turned her wet skin to liquid gold. She could have been anything. Siren. Mermaid. A magical creature who had woken him, like some enchanted princess, from a deep torpor of the spirit to fill his being with a forgotten longing. A desperate need to hold her, to feel her arms about him finally shattered the ice cage of his heart and sent him surging towards her, driving out the last vestige of concern about motive or intrigue. She was his saviour, not his enemy.

He reached out to her and she came into his arms with a little sigh, a shiver of anticipation, and as he lifted her from the rock she uncurled herself and slid down him, wrapping her arms about his neck as she kissed him with a boldness that lent a fierce urgency to his need.

He sensed the change in her, the utter bonelessness of her body as she moulded herself against him, her breasts flattening against his chest, her belly hard against the surging heat in his loins. This was no uncertain flirtation with danger. She wanted this as much as he did, and by taking the lead she was showing him how much.

Melanie's lips deserted his mouth and, although he made a move to recapture her, set off on a tour of exploration that promised to make a man feel like a god. She nuzzled the tender skin beneath his chin, drawing an involuntary sound from deep in his throat. She lapped the hollow at the base of his throat like a hungry kitten before her tongue slid along his collar bone, nipping at his skin. There was something animal about the way she seemed to be tasting him and he groaned her name as she slid lower, seeking his nipple, teasing it to hardness with the tip of her tongue, her own nipples hard and thrusting against his stomach, her hands sliding over his back, fingers wide and eager against his flesh.

'Melanie, sweetheart,' he murmured, dropping to his knees, so that the sea lapped around his thighs, cooling his heat.

Circling her waist with his hands, he drew her to him, kissing the soft swell of her stomach, tasting the salt drying on her skin. His tongue eased slowly along the line of her bikini and she whimpered softly, letting her head fall back, offering herself to him, and with a kind of wonder he slipped his hands inside the white cloth of her bikini and eased it down her legs, lifting each foot in turn so he could remove it, wanting her entirely naked, entirely his. Every part of her. He devoured her with his eyes, his hands, his mouth, stroking the smooth white skin of her thighs with the tips of his fingers, trailing them with his lips until the seaweed scent of the sea was obliterated by the sweet muskiness of her desire and he dipped his tongue into the honeypot, drawn irresistibly by the dizzying, addictive essence of her.

There was a shuddering, ragged intake of air as she fought for breath and he looked up. But she didn't want him to stop. Her eyes were glazed with something beyond desire, something new and undreamt of. *New.*

Before the realization hit him, before he could begin to think about what that might mean, she slithered down into his arms and, wrapping her arms about him, she kissed him again.

Her tongue was demanding, insistent now, driving everything else from his head, and as he matched her growing ardour she began to push frantically at the cloth of his swimsuit, her hand boldly seeking the rearing, almost painfully intense arousal that she had provoked, an arousal that it seemed no amount of cold water could extinguish. And as her fingers found him, held him, it was his turn to gasp.

CHAPTER 13

Jack knew they should move, get out of there and back to the cottage. He tried to pull away from her, tell her, but even as he attempted to frame the words Melanie covered his mouth with hers once more and the languorous exploration of her tongue, hot and slow and deep, took him far beyond any capacity for rational thought. She was a siren and her song had captured his heart even as it set him free.

Despite his experience and her lack of it, it was Melanie who led the way, lying back in the water, her hair fanning out around her face as she drifted back towards the sandbank. 'Make love with me, Jack,' she murmured, and lifted her arms to him in invitation. And, as with the sirens of myth, he had no defence against such sweet temptation.

He went to her arms and held her, kissed her, made sweet love with her, knowing that for Melanie it was new, special. Despite the clamouring in his loins he held himself in check, wanting to give more than to take . . . And the slow and tender exploration of her body reawakened forgotten needs, lost desires so that he too trembled, weak with desire so that when she whimpered softly into his mouth, 'Now, Jack, please . . .' the fragile control snapped and he came into her with a fierce passion that seemed as new for him as it was for her. And when they finally soared together in that meteoric oblivion of pleasure, it was for him, too, as if it were the very first time, so that he felt reborn, remade, full of wonder.

Afterwards, when he opened his eyes and looked down at her, he saw that her eyes were luminous, reflecting the green light of the sea, shimmering with more than their silken beauty. And as he bent to kiss them he tasted the salt of tears on her lids. But she was smiling, too. Tears of joy, then? He rolled on to his back, pulling her down on to his chest, stroking the damp hair back from her face as it lay against his heart.

'Thank you,' he said, scarcely able to form the words, so deep was his gratitude.

She raised her head to look down, her smile catlike in its satisfaction. 'It was entirely my pleasure,' she assured him, huskily.

'Not entirely, I can promise you.' He thumbed away the tears that she seemed unaware of, touched her mouth, and as her lips parted to his fingers, her tongue lapping each one in turn, he felt invincible, godlike. 'Was it worth waiting for?' he asked.

'I *think* so.' She looked at him seriously.

'You're not sure?' For a heartbeat he felt the sudden gripe of uncertainty and then, as he saw her teasing smile, a deeper, more compelling need for her bucked through him. 'Well, I wouldn't want you to be left in any doubt, my love. You only have to say the word.'

'And what is the word?'

It was his turn to smile. 'You get three guesses, sweetheart.'

'And if I don't get it right?'

'I disappear in a puff of smoke.'

'Is that so?' Melanie enquired, thoughtfully. 'Well, I'd better be careful not to make a mistake.' Apparently deep in thought, her fingers began to stray, absently sliding through the rough, dark hair that shadowed his chest, her thumb-tip brushing against the flat tip of his nipple, extracting an involuntary groan. She raised herself a little so that her breasts brushed against him. 'Did you say something?'

'No,' he gasped.

She ran her hands more purposefully over his chest. 'Sure?' And when he didn't answer she let the tips of her nails slide across the taut plane of his belly so that he had to bite his lip to keep from yelling out loud with pleasure. He wanted to see how far she would take her game, how long he could hold out against it. 'I thought you might be cold.' Before he could answer she sat up, straddling him with her legs so that her buttocks nudged against the growing heat of his manhood. She looked back over her shoulder and then turned to face him, a small smile deepening the dimple at the corner of her mouth. 'No, definitely not cold.'

'Mel . . .' She eased herself back, lifting herself

over him, taking care not to touch the evidence of his need for her. Then, slowly, she lowered her head to swirl the tip of her tongue around his navel. 'Please. . .' he moaned, louder now, and she lifted her lashes to look up at him as her tongue began to slide down across his abdomen until the word became a growl.

Slowly she raised her head. 'Please?' she enquired.

'Yes,' Jack begged. 'Please.' And without waiting for her to register her triumph, he grasped her around the waist, holding her above him for a moment when their eyes said all the things that were beyond words before slowly lowering her on to him.

'Yes,' she moaned, and then laughed softly. 'Yes, please.'

Afterwards they swam naked in the clear, sun-spangled water, touching each other, holding each other, not wanting to leave the magic, knowing that outside, in the brilliant sunshine, it wouldn't be quite the same. But it couldn't last forever. Clinging to Jack, holding on to him as if he were the rock at the centre of her being, Melanie laid her head against his chest

'If I don't get out of here soon, Jack, I really will become a mermaid.'

'I thought you already were,' he murmured, nuzzling her cheek.

'A very wrinkly mermaid. Pickled in brine.'

'A cold one at any rate,' he said, holding her, reluctant to let her go. But she *was* cold; they had been in the water far too long. Well, warming up would be another pleasure to share. They would go back to the cottage, take a warm shower together, send for lunch and eat it in bed.

He gathered her bikini and handed it to her, lending his shoulder as she steadied herself to put it back on and trying not to dwell on the way the water and sun reflected on her skin, the way that she had felt against him . . . If he started thinking about that, they'd never get out of the cave. He turned away as she fastened her top, tugging on his own swimsuit.

'How do we get out of here?' Melanie asked, when she'd finally managed the clasp. 'Do we have to swim back to the beach?'

'No. No more swimming. We can walk through here.' He extended his hand and they splashed through the light-barred caves, gathering their snorkelling gear as they went.

'Can we do this again tomorrow?' she said, as they emerged into the late morning sunshine.

'Tomorrow?' He turned to her. 'I hadn't thought to wait that long.'

Melanie blushed, or maybe it was just the sudden heat. 'I meant . . . Oh, you're an idiot, Jack Wolfe,' she said, laughing.

'You know that's really no way to speak to your employer,' he reminded her, with mock severity.

Her employer! 'Oh, I beg your pardon,' she said, with equally insincere humility. Then, 'You're an idiot, Mr Wolfe. Sir.'

His mouth twitched. 'That's better.' He leaned

forward, kissed her mouth taking care not to touch anything but her lips.

'Make the most of it, Mr Wolfe. I resigned. I gave Mrs Graham a week's notice, remember?'

'I remember, but I'm afraid I fired you, about an hour ago.' The kiss began to heat up. 'Without notice. Did I forget to mention it?'

'No hanky-panky with the staff, huh?'

'An unbreakable rule. Any complaints?'

'None whatsover. This way I can get you for unfair dismissal as well as sexual harassment . . .' She let out a squeal as he grabbed her.

'In that case, I'm certainly going to make the most of it.' He pulled her into his arms and for a moment simply held her. Melanie expected him to kiss her, but he didn't. 'Come on, let's get out of here.'

'Jack . . .'

'What is it?'

'There's something I have to tell you.'

'Not now.' Whatever she wanted to tell him, he didn't want to hear.

'It's important.' He straightened, looked down at her and she knew that he was right. The cave was special, magic. And what she had to tell him would take some time. She pulled a face. 'I'm afraid there's no way I'm going to be able to ride that bike again.'

'Oh, I see. Well, that isn't a problem.' He tossed the snorkelling gear on to a nearby rock and swung her up into his arms. 'I'll carry you.'

And despite her giggling protestations that it wasn't necessary, he carried her all the way back to the cottage. 'Everyone will think I've lost the use of my legs . . .'

'It's more likely they'll think you're a lazy cat, but if that worries you, we could always stop and explain – '

'Jack!'

'God,' he said, 'I love it when you blush.'

'You're the only man who has ever had that effect on me.'

'Plan on keeping it that way.'

Plan? Melanie let her head fall against his chest. She knew better than to make plans . . . This affair had nothing to do with plans or reality.

What had happened in the sea-caves had been entirely her decision. She had wanted him and she had sung her siren song, luring him into her arms, knowing full well the consequences. It had been beautiful, but as for plans, she wasn't fooling herself.

Richard had warned her that Jack liked his women on a bed-and-breakfast basis without any messy emotional complications. And love was a pretty messy complication by any standard. If she wanted to hold on to him she would have to keep that well hidden.

It shouldn't be that difficult. Like Caroline, she had a life of her own, a thriving career, a beautiful apartment to go home to. Of course she would have to be careful to keep it light, watch any tendency to cling, to scare him away . . .

She stopped the treacherous thoughts.

She had promised not to fool herself and already

she was pretending. She could act and act and act all she liked, but pressed again the warmth of his flesh with the steady thump of his heart beneath her ear she knew that kind of relationship would never be enough for her. Like her mother, she would have all or nothing.

But unlike her mother she refused to spend the rest of her life looking back, wondering, regretting . . . and in the end afraid to take a chance at happiness in case the man she had spent all those wasted years yearning for had forgotten her.

She would have the rest of this week and then she would say goodbye. Somehow she would manage to brush the whole thing off as a holiday romance; something to be cherished, but not extended beyond its natural span so that it ended, like his relationship with Caroline, in humiliation. He would probably be relieved and he would remember her, if at all, with a hazy fondness.

'Hey, are you going to sleep?'

She opened her eyes and smiled up at him. 'It's been a pretty energetic morning.'

'Then I have the perfect answer. A siesta.'

'Before lunch?'

'No, not before lunch. Before lunch we'll have a warm shower. Then we'll have lunch in bed. After that we'll have a siesta.'

A siesta. We. The two of them. She would sleep in Jack's arms and it would be heaven. And she wasn't about to waste heaven worrying about next week, or agonizing over whether to tell Jack her life history.

The Ark was a moment out of time. The outside world didn't matter.

'You've got it all worked out, haven't you? Did anyone ever tell you that you've a managing disposition, Mr Wolfe?'

'I believe the odd comment has been passed, Miss Devlin. But then, it's what I do best.' He stopped at the cottage. 'Would you like to open the door?'

'You could put me down now,' she pointed out.

'I could,' he agreed. 'But why don't you just leave the details to me? You open the door and I'll carry you through to the shower. After that, if you have any other plans for my hands, I'll be happy to accommodate you.'

'Not managing,' she reflected, happily. 'Just plain bossy.'

'In that case I suggest you do as you're told first time.'

'Yes, sir,' she said, snapping off a salute before reaching for the door handle. Who was arguing?

'Mike?'

'Jack, for heaven's sake, where have you been?'

Jack regarded the telephone with a slightly quizzical expression. 'Swimming, relaxing. The things you do on holiday. Then, because I'm always concerned about my employees, I thought I'd check in and see how things are going. So how *are* things going?'

'Which particular things did you have in mind?'

'Chicago?'

332

'No more problems. Will you stop over on your way home?'

'I might. Tamblin?'

'Vacuuming up the shares as if there's no tomorrow. The TSC are watching him.'

'Anything else?'

'Melanie Devlin does not live with Richard Latham. She just uses his address.'

'Anything else?'

'You're not surprised?'

'No. I don't believe she knows anything about Carstairs or insider trading.'

There was a pause. 'She was *that* good?'

Jack didn't reply. He simply disconnected the call and switched off the phone.

Mike Palmer regretted the words the minute they were out of his mouth. Yet he knew he was right to be suspicious. And once Jack came to his senses he would be the first to admit that he'd been wrong. Yet in all the years he'd known Jack Wolfe he'd never known him to miss the obvious. Even when Lisette had been killed and he was so racked with guilt that he couldn't eat, or sleep, he had never lost that edge. It was what had made him so dangerous.

He replaced the receiver slowly. Or maybe this girl was just another symptom. He'd sensed a change in Jack over the past few weeks, a restlessness, as if work was no longer enough. The sympathy he had shown towards Latham had been a case in point. And the day he had planned to leave the office without saying a word, to picnic with this girl, that had bordered on the

333

romantic. It was then that Mike realized exactly what was different about Jack Wolfe. He hadn't taken this girl to the West Indies because Caro had let him down. He'd taken her because he was in love with her.

He groaned. He would have been glad for the man, if he wasn't so certain that he was being duped. Made a fool of, but couldn't see it. Well, it happened to everyone once in a while and if Jack wasn't thinking clearly enough to worry why Melanie Devlin had given a false address, somebody else would have to do it for him.

He flicked the intercom on his desk. 'Get hold of Geoff, Nicki. Last week he collected a girl from the cottage at Henley. See if he remembers where he took her.'

'I'll get right on to it. Bob Gibson from the *Courier* called you a few minutes ago. He wants to know if its true that this girl Jack has taken on holiday with him is not an actress, but his cleaner.'

'What!'

'Apparently he's had a call from Caro's publicist. She says Jack's planning some takeover and he's taken this girl as cover because Caroline was too busy to go with him. According to her, Caro and Jack are still an item. Please tell me it isn't true.'

'It's not true. At least the part about them still being an item.' That was the one thing he could be certain of. And he'd warned Jack that Caro wouldn't take public humiliation lying down, but somehow he didn't think calling him back right now and saying 'I told you so' would be a healthy move.

'So, what's the cleaner like?'

'She's an actress, Nicki. An out-of-work actress.'

Nicki laughed. 'You don't have to sell the story to me. Tell it to Bob Gibson, he loves a good fairy-tale.'

Fairy-tale? Well, that was a thought. 'Oh, I think I can top anything Caroline Hickey can offer. Get him back for me.'

'Aren't you going to call Jack first?'

'Jack is too busy to be bothered with this kind of nonsense.' It would be better handled by someone thinking with his head rather than his heart . . . or any other part of his anatomy. The phone rang. 'Bob? Mike Palmer. I heard Caro's stirring things up? Nothing like a woman scorned for vitriol,' he said, with a laugh.

'Vitriol sells newspapers.'

'And I thought it was true love.'

'True love needs an angle.'

'Is that right? Well, how about a cross between Little Red Riding Hood and Cinderella?'

'You're telling me the cleaner story is true?'

'Well, you know how it is, Bob. The girl's an actress but she's between jobs and she has to pay the rent – '

'So Cinderella's scrubbing the big bad Wolfe's floor and when she kissed him he turned into Prince Charming. Is that about it?'

Mike swallowed. Jack would murder him. 'You could put it like that.'

'Can I quote you?'

'Quote me? What did I say?'

335

Bob chuckled. 'So this actress: tell me something she's been in.'

'Well, there you've got me. Can't Equity help? Even if she's only done walk-on parts she must be a member. She might even have an agent who can let you have a photograph . . .' He crossed his fingers. 'I think you'll find it will be worth while finding one.'

There was a long pause. 'What are you telling me, Mike?'

'Nothing. I'm telling you nothing.' Even he couldn't bring himself to go that far. Then, with sudden inspiration he said, 'Have you ever seen the brochure for The Ark, Bob? It's really a very romantic place. I'm trying to think who got married there last year. Some American film star . . .'

'They do weddings?'

'Just a few – ' Bob Gibson couldn't get off the phone quickly enough after that and Mike grinned as he hung up. Sometimes he thought Jack too ruthless, and he never hesitated to tell him so. But he'd got a real buzz out of that: doing exactly what Jack would have done . . . if he hadn't been otherwise occupied.

'Geoff says he took Miss Devlin to Chelsea Harbour,' Nicki said, coming in and distracting him. 'He says she's a really nice girl. He carried her things in for her and the porter at this really classy block of flats where she lives told him that she really is an actress. She used to be in one of those Aussie soaps. I'll have to ask my girls if they know her; they love them.'

'An Aussie soap?' Mike demanded. 'Have you any idea which one?'

'No. She came to England last year, apparently.'

Well, it didn't matter. The coincidence was too great to be ignored. She and Richard Latham might not live together, but they clearly went back a long way.

'Are you going to throw yourself on to your sword,' Nicki asked next morning as Mike stared in horror at the full-page spread in the *Courier*.

'Melanie Beaumont?' he said. 'It can't be true. I mean . . .' he stared blankly up at his secretary '. . . what the devil was she doing *cleaning*?'

'Maybe she's kinky. I can see that washing Jack Wolfe's socks might have a certain attraction.' Mike glared at her. 'Personally,' she went on, undaunted, 'my favourite part was the bit about her father and stepmother being on honeymoon at the same resort. How would you rate that on the embarrassment scale? Eight? Nine? No? Well, maybe you're right. A full-blown ten.'

The phone beside him rang. 'Answer that, Nicki,' he snapped.

'Don't worry. Jack won't have seen this. Yet. It's only four o'clock in the morning where he is.'

She was right. It wasn't Jack. It was worse. It was Luke Devlin.

Melanie stirred and smiled as Jack kissed her throat. 'Mmm. That's nice.'

'Wake up, sleepy-head. It's our last day. We don't want to waste it.'

Five blissful days had flown by and tomorrow they would go back to London. No, she wouldn't think about that. Not a moment before she had to. 'I agree. We shouldn't waste a minute. Come back to bed,' she said, resolutely keeping her eyes closed.

'Behave yourself,' he murmured, kissing her lids.

'Not today,' she said, reaching for him.

'Not ever again, if I have anything to do with it. But a man has to eat,' he reminded her, easing himself out of bed.

'Call room service.'

'Not this morning. I've got a treat for you. Gus spotted a pod of humpback whales yesterday. He's taking us out to see them this morning.' Melanie stretched, opened her eyes and he laughed. 'Lady, you look exactly like a cat who's just had a saucer full of cream.'

'I have,' she said, softly. 'Now all I need to make me purr is to be stroked.'

'Not a chance. Come on, up you get.' He pulled her to her feet and for a moment held her before releasing her with something like a groan. 'I think you'd better shower on your own, or we'll never eat.' He turned her around and slapped her bottom. 'Don't be long.'

'If you're sure you'd rather look at a bunch of old whales – '

'A pod,' he said, firmly. 'Old, young, babies. I promise you you'll be sorry if you miss them.'

'I expect you're right.' So why was every bone in her body telling her that she should get back in bed and stay there, keeping him beside her?

'I'm always right.'

Melanie paused at the door of bathroom and looked back.

'Hurry, sweetheart.'

'Come with me.' She knew she was being foolish, that the sense of an ending was because everything they did today would be for the last time. Yet even as she extended her hand to him he seemed to hesitate. 'How will I manage without you to scrub my back?'

Jack knew he should resist. He wanted to ring Mike, put the guy out of his misery. He'd kept promising himself he would. Today was a day for putting the world straight and starting anew.

He felt bad about hanging up on a man who was only doing his job. But what could he have said? It doesn't matter what you tell me about her? In her arms I've discovered how to be human again? Mike would have been kind, but he would have thought him a fool. Well, maybe he was. But, fool that he was, he knew with each hour that passed that he loved her more.

And as the days had passed he'd grown more certain that what had happened between him and Melanie hadn't been anything to do with The Ark, or anybody but themselves. Since that first morning neither of them had mentioned the resort, or why they were supposed to be there. They'd swum, they'd danced, they'd walked barefoot along a starlit beach and made love as if there was no tomorrow. But tomorrow was suddenly upon them. And it was time to set everything straight. Because when he went back to London things were going to be different.

But the difference was about putting his life before his work. His love before anything. So he went to her. 'I don't know how you ever managed your back without me.'

She took his hand, suddenly laughing. 'Easily. But it's not as much fun.'

The whales were majestic, huge grey mottled shapes that slid through the water with a silent power before turning and flipping their tails, as if inviting the watchers to leave their silly boats and join them. Melanie stood at the side of the launch in silence watching them.

'Well?' Jack said, after a while.

'They're beautiful.'

He looked down at her, then, cradling her cheek, turned her face so that he could look at her. 'Then why are you crying?'

'Because they're so beautiful and because people are so cruel.' She leaned against him. 'I don't think I can bear to watch any more.'

'I know. I felt the same way the first time I saw them; a sense that you've touched something from the past, something that you might never see again.' He turned back to Gus. 'This is far enough,' he called over the sound of the engine. Gus waved and turned the launch back towards the island.

Melanie glanced back at the whales. It wasn't just those great doomed creatures that had made her feel sad. All morning the feeling of impending loss had being growing deep inside her. And it wasn't all imagination. Jack had been distracted. With her in body, attentive, loving even, but she had sensed that his mind had been elsewhere. Already moving on to other things. Then she looked up at Jack. 'The first time? You've been here before?' He didn't answer. 'How silly of me not to have realized when it was obvious that you knew your way around . . .'

Melanie's heart seemed to crumble. She'd thought this was new and special for both of them but she'd been fooling herself. He'd brought Caroline here, made love to her in the sea caves, walked with her on the beach holding her hand. Gus must have known. Everyone must have known and she suddenly felt sick. Her whole world was falling apart as she realized what a fool she had been. He had lied to her. Lied with his body when he made love to her. Lied even about why he was at The Ark. This was no clandestine visit . . . there had been no meetings . . .

She had planned to walk away with a smile and a careless wave so that this would always be a lovely memory for both of them. Memory! In a week he wouldn't even remember who she was . . .

And she wouldn't be able to forget. And this feeling, this sick feeling of betrayal was how it was going to be tomorrow. Forever.

She turned away from him to dash away a stupid tear as the boat began to turn into a small cove and slowed. 'Why are we stopping?'

'I asked Gus to lay on a picnic for us. We'll have the cove to ourselves.'

'When do you want me to pick you up, Jack?'

'About four?' Jack suggested, and without waiting for an answer jumped over the side of the boat. He smiled up at Melanie, offering a hand. 'I believe this might be the world's most perfect spot for a picnic. What do you think of it?'

She looked at the tiny cove, its perfect crescent of white sand cradled by tumbled boulders and palm trees. 'It's beautiful,' she said. And it was. Heart-breakingly beautiful. And because her mind was numb, because she couldn't think of anything else to do, she let him lift her out of the boat.

'Everything's waiting for you,' Gus promised. 'I'll see you later.'

'He's going to leave us here? Alone?'

Jack laughed at her concern. 'What's the matter, sweetheart? You don't think I'm going to suddenly turn into the big bad wolf after all and gobble you up?'

'You've already done that,' she said, slightly disturbed by a sudden air of purpose about him. Something that reminded her of the man she had run into in a travel agent's doorway weeks before . . . 'Why did you bring me here?' she demanded.

'Because . . .' He turned her to him, his hands resting lightly on her shoulders as they stood ankle-deep in the surf. 'Because I think it's time we talked. Don't you? The last few days have been wonderful, Melanie, but before we go home we need to – well, talk.'

'What about? About the lies you've told me?' *No! No! This wasn't how it was supposed to be. Play it cool. Mel. Be a lady. To hell with that!* 'To tell me thanks, it's been great and let's do it on this great beach just for old times' sake? Forget it!' She turned and splashed blindly through the surf, breaking into a run as he reached for her.

'Melanie, for heaven's sake, what on earth brought this on?'

She clenched her fists, stared at the sky. *Wasn't it obvious?* 'You have lied to me, haven't you? You've been here before. And whatever you're doing here now, it certainly isn't sussing out some slimy take-over of The Ark.'

'No. It isn't,' he agreed. 'But – '

'But what?'

Jack's eyes darkened. 'But you've lied too.'

She glared at him. 'I have never told you a lie.'

'Maybe not directly. But not telling the truth comes a pretty close second in my book.' He lifted the collar of the linen shirt she was wearing. 'The designer clothes you wear aren't borrowed, are they? They fit as if they've been made for you, which they undoubtedly have. You don't have to work as a cleaner.'

'I haven't had any complaints.'

'I didn't say you were bad at it. Only that you don't have to do it. And who produced that beautifully costed business plan for a co-operative?' She didn't answer. 'And then there's the clincher. You told Mrs Graham that you lived at the same address as a man called Richard Latham. But you don't.'

'You checked up on me!'

'Your sudden change in appearance was unnerving. Especially when I remembered where we'd met before. And that you were a friend of Latham's.'

'Richard? What on earth has Richard got to do with anything?' She was standing beneath a shelter thatched with palm fronds on an exquisite horseshoe beach. There were sun-loungers, cushions, towels. A huge cool-box. Snorkelling equipment, even. Everything they could possibly need to enjoy the day together. One last day that might have been as perfect as all the others they had shared. And they were having a row. She sat down suddenly. 'You wanted to talk, Jack. I think perhaps you'd better get what you wanted to say off your chest.'

'Last year Gus was in trouble. Real trouble, unlike the fake bother I cooked up for the benefit of Greg Tamblin.' He saw her frown, but could have sworn she didn't know the name. 'The bank was threatening to cut their losses and sell their stake to a holiday chain that were making interested noises ... I persuaded them to sell it to me instead. I think it was money well spent, don't you?'

'You *helped* him? Last year? But what are you doing here now?'

'Ah, well, sweetheart, one good turn deserves another. This time he's helping me.'

'How?' He wanted to kiss her. He wanted to coat her with sun-cream and then make love with her and swim naked with her in the cove, but she was sitting rigid as a board, half-turned from him, refusing to meet his eyes. 'How?' she insisted. Then, 'Tell me about Gus.'

He stretched out on the lounger, hands behind his head. 'Gus is a man with a vision. When he inherited this island it was derelict. The farms were deserted, the buildings falling down. With the sweat of his brow he's turned it into something special. Local people are coming back because there's work and land. Visitors love it because it's not commercial. It's beginning to turn round, start to pay back for all the work and investment, but it takes time, too long for the bank. When they finally twigged to the fact that he wasn't going to turn it into the mass tourist resort they had fondly imagined, they decided to pull the plug. Like you, Melanie, I couldn't bear to see him lose it.'

'So why are you here now?'

'I rather think you know that, Mel.'

She looked round at him. 'Me? I thought you were here to carve the guy up. It's why I told – ' She stopped.

'Told who, Melanie? What? The only person you've rung since you've been on this island is Paddy. Or did you get her to pass a message on to Richard Latham . . . I suppose it would have been easy enough; you all work for the same charming lady.'

'Richard? Why do you keep bringing up Richard Latham.'

'Because you know him.'

'Of course I know him. We worked together years ago in Australia. But what on earth has he got to do with this?' Then, 'And why the hell have you been checking up on my telephone calls?'

'Call. You have only made one call. To Paddy. Were you checking up on me? Making sure that I'd carried out my promise?'

'No. I knew you had. But . . .' Her shoulders slumped. 'Oh, God, this sounds so silly now.'

'Why don't you let me be the judge of that?'

'I wanted to get a message to the gossip page at the *Courier* and I didn't have their number so I called Paddy and asked her to pass it on.'

Jack rolled up into a sitting position. 'The *Courier*?'

'You remember what I said about publicity? For The Ark?' He waited. 'Well, I saw someone here. Someone they would be interested in. I thought if I told the gossip page The Ark would get a mention.'

'That wasn't very kind. People come here for privacy.'

'Oh, they'd already gone by the time I called. They just stopped overnight at the marina. I didn't want to be any part of what you were doing here, Jack. What you told me you were doing. I thought I could help Gus without anybody knowing . . .'

He opened the picnic box, extracted a couple of sodas and opened them before handing one to her. 'It was a kind thought, but unnecessary. The *Courier* have already run a story on The Ark in the last few days.'

'Oh, well . . . it was just a thought. Every little helps.'

'Maybe you should hear the full story before you make up your mind about that.' And he explained about Greg Tamblin's and Richard Latham's plan to make a fortune from insider trading. 'When I realized what they were up to I laid a trap. But I didn't want it to be too obvious. If it had been too easy they might have smelt a rat. So when they were in too deep to pull back without losing money, Gus helped me set The Ark up as another target. Then I allowed them to find out it was just a red herring so that they would feel very clever at spotting the blind, and wouldn't notice the trap until it was sprung.' He was sitting with his elbows on his knees, staring at the sand.

'So, how does that affect me?'

He looked up. 'Mike Palmer, my CEO, had already informed the *Courier* diary page of my plans to come here with Caroline. But Caroline was famously going to New York and, gossip pages being what they are, I didn't want any speculation of the wrong kind. So Mike called again and said there had been a change of partners.'

'You mean it was in the paper? About us coming here together?'

'Yes.' He saw her face. 'Mike said you would kill me.'

She shook her head. 'It can't be helped, you weren't to know . . . but I can't believe that Richard could be so devious. He came to your flat once, when I was working there. I thought he was behaving oddly.'

'Why, what did he do?'

'Nothing much. But just coming to the flat was odd. I thought he was checking up on me . . . making sure I was actually working. We had a bet, you see, that I couldn't stick it a month.'

'A bet?'

'Five hundred pounds to him if I couldn't take it. The same to charity if I won.'

'Oh.'

'I told him to get lost and he came over all contrite and carried the rubbish down for me.' She groaned. 'That was what he came for, wasn't it? To check out your rubbish!'

'He wouldn't have needed to come to the flat. I made sure he found everything he wanted at the office.'

'Maybe he thought that was too easy.' Jack frowned. 'He's in real trouble, isn't he? Why? Why would he do that?'

'After his father's company was taken over I was called in to sort the place out. It was a mess. Out-of-date equipment. Top-heavy management. Richard was supposed to stay on the board to keep the family connection but he was so obstructive that the new company decided he was more trouble than he was worth – '

'And then his father had a heart attack.'

'The heart attack came before the takeover, Mel. In fact it provoked it.'

So he'd lied right from the beginning. 'And this man Tamblin? Is he the journalist . . . the one whose cuttings you keep?'

348

'Yes. I caught him insider trading a few years back. Instead of exposing him I suggested he find some less tempting form of work. It was a mistake. He used his contacts to get into financial journalism and has been on my back ever since. And now he's up to his old tricks again, using Richard.'

'I think it's possible that Richard is using him, Jack.' He waited. 'He's enormously likeable, bags of charm when he's getting his own way. But he's manipulative, too. I've seen him pull some strokes with the director when we worked on the same soap, just for a bet, just to prove he could make people do things.' And she'd let him do it to her. He'd known about the post-party clean-up; she'd told him about Jack's call to the office and he must have realized immediately what that meant, why Mrs Graham was so eager to give her a job. 'I'd forgotten how he liked to do that,' she said. Then she looked up. 'But if he held a grudge, Jack . . . You really ought to warn your office. You think you've been fooling him all this time, but it's quite possible he's been fooling you.' She stood up. 'Look, do we have to wait for Gus? Isn't there some other way we can get back?'

'Not unless you fancy a long, hot hike. Besides, we're only halfway through this session of true confessions. It's your turn.'

'I told you, Jack. I was working for a bet, I didn't know anything about Richard's plans. And I certainly didn't tell him I was coming here with you.'

'If he reads the *Courier* he knows now.'

'Well, that's hardly my fault.' She wrapped her

349

shirt around her a little tighter as the wind began to rise, kicking the sand up from the beach.

'Will it cause you problems?'

She glanced at him.

'I had assumed that you were an out-of-work actress who might welcome a little publicity. But you're clearly something else entirely.'

'Not entirely. I am an actress and I'm not working. But out of choice, not misfortune.'

'I should know who you are, shouldn't I? That's why you changed your appearance. Who are you, Melanie?'

'We've already covered my life history, Jack. I wasn't lying about that. I've done some television, a West End play. I'm not offended because you haven't seen me in anything. Tell me about your life,' she said, eager to change the subject.

'Oh, you know. The usual story. School. University. The City.'

'And marriage.' If they were clearing the decks, they might as well make a good job of it.

'Marriage,' he repeated, but he was no longer paying attention. Instead he was staring out to sea.

Melanie turned to see what had caught his attention, shading her eyes from a sun that was suddenly brassier, angrier. 'What is it?'

'I don't know.' He stood up. 'But it's getting very dark over there. I think we might be in for a storm.'

As if to confirm what he said, the wind caught at her hair as she rose beside him and she put up her hands to hold it back from her face. For a moment they stood together, watching the darkening edge of the sky where the front seemed to be coming lower and closer at an alarming rate. 'Will Gus come back for us?' Melanie said, grabbing hold of Jack's shirt as a sudden gust buffeted them and she staggered against him.

'I think perhaps it's too late for that, Mel. I'm afraid we're going to have to make a run for it.'

CHAPTER 14

The wind hit the beach like a rocket, tearing the thatched shelter to shreds and tossing the sun-loungers aside, streaming out the palm fronds as it came after them.

The rain hit before they were halfway up the shallow rise behind the beach as they battled to breast it and make the lee. Great drenching sheets of the stuff that ran down their faces, leaving them gasping for air.

By instinct, Melanie had grabbed her bag as she ran, but now it was filling with water, weighing her down, and Jack grabbed it. 'Is there anything important in here?' he shouted above the almost unimaginable noise. She shook her head and he dumped it. It was immediately caught by the wind and bowled away, spilling its contents as it went. Jack caught her hand, hauling her after him.

She stumbled along the path, barely able to keep up as her canvas shoes too began to fill with water and soak it up, weighing her down.

Behind the hill, the wind was less of a problem, but

it still sucked the breath from them and the rain made breathing doubly difficult. After a few hundred yards they were both struggling for air and Jack stopped while Melanie clung to him for a moment. 'There's an old sugar mill up here somewhere. If we can get there, we can get out of this.'

'It won't blow down?'

'It's stood a lot worse than this in its time.' He leaned back. 'Ready?' But she was staring out at the grey and angry sea. Beau and Diana were somewhere out there. And she was remembering another storm, just as sudden, that had killed her mother. 'Melanie?'

'Yes. Come on, let's go.'

Ten minutes later they almost fell into the old stone sugar mill and it seemed to take forever, battling against the wind, to close the door behind them. Eventually it was done and they leaned back against it, their chests heaving in unison as they recovered their breath. 'The next time you decide to take me on a picnic,' Melanie gasped out, 'think again.'

'I'll do better than that. The next time you suggest we spend the day in bed, I won't argue.' Then he straightened and looked about him. 'But in the meantime we'd better make ourselves comfortable.' He looked at her. 'You're shivering,' he said, taking her into his arms.

'So are you. I can't believe how the temperature's dropped.'

'We might be able to make a fire.'

'And send out smoke signals so that someone will come and find us?'

'Not while this wind is blowing.'

Melanie crossed to the old stone chimney. 'There's plenty of kindling and wood, but nothing to light it with.' She rubbed at her arms. 'I suppose you could try rubbing two sticks together.'

'You've obviously never tried to light a fire that way.' He reached up to a shelf where there was an old candle stuck in a jar and his hand dislodged a box of matches. 'I suspect we've stumbled on a lovers' tryst,' he said, looking around. There was a rug on the floor, an old sofa draped in a clean white sheet with a couple of bright cushions.

'Thank heavens for lovers,' she said, as he lit the candle and began to pile up small scraps of wood shavings, then bigger pieces of dry kindling and, when it was well alight, began to place small logs carefully over it.

'Why don't you get out of those wet clothes?' he advised. 'Wrap yourself in that sheet and you'll soon warm up.'

Melanie didn't need a second invitation, peeling off her sodden clothes and draping them near the fire. 'This is big enough for two of us,' she said, sitting on the sofa. 'Come on. Your clothes will soon dry.'

Jack made up the fire and then peeled off his T-shirt and shorts before joining her on the sofa and tucking the other end of the sheet about him. 'Now we wait.'

'No. Now we talk. We'd got as far as marriage,' she reminded him. He put his arm around her, easing her on to his lap so that they could lie together on the sofa. 'What happened, Jack. Are you divorced?'

'No, not divorced. Lisette was killed in an accident.'

'Oh, Jack. I'm sorry. If you don't want to talk about it – '

'No, it's all right. It's time I did.' But it was still a while before he began to speak. 'She was killed standing at a bus stop.'

'A bus stop?' she prompted after another long silence.

'I know. It was quite stupid. I mean, why on earth would the wife of a relatively wealthy man be standing at a bus stop?' She didn't think he expected her to offer an answer. 'I'll tell you, Melanie. She was catching a bus because I was so wrapped up in work that I'd forgotten her car had a flat battery. She'd asked me to put it on charge. She never could work out how to do anything like that herself. And I forgot. She didn't have anywhere desperately important to go. But she wanted me to know that I was neglecting her. So instead of ringing for a taxi she decided to catch a bus. She wouldn't have complained about the car refusing to start, simply yelled at me for forgetting to do something about it. She wasn't like that. She would have told me about how she'd waited for hours for a bus, the screaming children, the dirty seats . . .'

'What happened, Jack?'

'A man, a good family man, driving quietly along the road going about his business, simply collapsed and died at the wheel of his car. He fell against the

355

steering wheel, his foot stuck on the accelerator and three people died. Lisette was one of them.'

'And you blame yourself.'

'Wouldn't you?'

'Accidents happen, Jack. Stupid accidents. I know. My mother was killed in a flash flood a couple of years ago on the way to the theatre. We were all going. It was Luke's idea. He bought the tickets, called my mother, offered to drive up and fetch her. But she said no, she didn't think she'd come. Then, at the last minute, she changed her mind. And she died. Luke blamed himself for not realizing sooner . . . It was my father, you see, playing Shylock. We didn't know then. But it wasn't his fault. Everything we do has some unforeseen consequence.' She stirred uneasily. 'I shouldn't be here now.'

'Where should you be, Mel? Doing some old biddy's ironing?'

'No. I should be lying on a beach somewhere in Australia. I was going to book the first flight out of London when I bumped into you. But you said, "Slow down. You'll hurt someone." And that made me stop and think. Then I met Richard and he . . .' She gave a diffident little shrug. 'You stopped me, Jack, and then Richard wound me up like a clockwork toy and sent me on my way again.' She turned to look down into his face. 'And I ended up cleaning your apartment. Did you love her very much?'

He didn't even have to consider his answer. 'I thought I did when I married her. She was fresh, lovely; she seemed the obvious choice. And I was something of a catch, I suppose. It didn't take me long to realize . . . Instead of taking the brave decision, admitting I'd made a mistake, I simply buried myself in my work. But she didn't have a job. She sat at home and brooded. And her bitterness drove her out to bus stop when she could have picked up a telephone and called a taxi.'

'So that's why you prefer bed-and-breakfast partners like Caroline.'

'Is it?'

'Plenty of style, not much content. You didn't even have to pretend to stop thinking about work when you were with her, did you?'

'I suppose not. Now you, my love, in that horrible wig and that ghastly uniform, had no style at all, and you weren't particularly lovely to look at. Yet ever since I met you work has seemed less and less important. In fact I haven't called my office for days. Poor Mike will think I've been swallowed by a shark.'

She grinned, eased herself more comfortably against him as the warmth of the fire made her feel drowsy. 'Gus would have phoned him if you'd been eaten. It might even have made the front page of the *Courier*.'

'You may be right. But he certainly thinks I'm not talking to him.' She looked surprised. 'We had a bit of a disagreement. About you. He thinks you're the Mata Hari of commercial espionage . . .'

'And what do you think?'

'I know what you are.' She waited expectantly for

357

him to tell her, but instead he pulled her down and kissed her.

When she finally lifted her head, she said, 'This thing with Mike – don't let it fester, Jack. Call him as soon as we get back to the hotel. Make your peace.' She turned to listen to the wind howling outside the sugar mill and shivered. 'You should never part on hard words. Always say goodbye as if it was the last time . . .'

'That was heartfelt.'

'It was. One way or another I have a lot of calls to make. And my father and his new wife are out there somewhere on a yacht. I wouldn't want to have to live with the way we parted . . .'

'Hey. Come on. This is just a squall. It'll be over in no time.' He eased her head down on to his shoulder, put his arm around her. 'Are you warm enough?'

'Mmmm.' He kissed her again as she nuzzled against him and closed her eyes.

Melanie woke to silence. For a moment she couldn't place where she was, only that she was with Jack, that his arm was around her. And then she remembered the storm.

He was asleep and he looked so sweetly vulnerable that she couldn't resist kissing him. His chin, the corner of his mouth, the tip of his ear. He stirred. She continued her mouth's butterfly assault on his temple, an eyelid . . . At some point she became aware that although his eyes remained closed he was awake, but she didn't stop, visiting his throat, the hollow of his collarbone, easing down his chest with little flickers of her tongue until she felt the unmistakable stirring of his body against her thigh.

'You know, a girl could get into serious trouble that way.'

'A girl might just be wondering long it would take – '

Without warning he grabbed her, and as she laughed they overbalanced and fell on to the floor with the sheet twisted about them. 'Now, lady, what were you saying?'

'I was saying that it isn't nice to lie there lapping up attention while a girl is getting desperate – '

'Desperate? Well, that won't do.' He began to kiss her.

For a moment she surrendered utterly, then she began to wriggle. 'Jack – '

'It's too late to change your mind young lady,' he began. 'You can't just lead a man on and expect to get away with it – '

'*Jack!*'

The urgency with which she said his name finally penetrated his sleepy arousal. 'What?' She was looking up towards the doorway and he turned his head. The three men standing in the doorway were more or less upside down. One was Mike Palmer; the second looked vaguely familiar; the third, he had never seen before in his life. He didn't remember inviting any of them in. 'Did you want something, gentlemen?' he enquired, his voice less than friendly. 'As you can see, we're rather busy.'

'Please don't rush, Mr Wolfe,' the vaguely familiar one said. 'Any time in the next sixty seconds will do. We'll be waiting outside.' And the door closed.

Jack turned and looked up at Melanie. 'Who the hell was that?'

She swallowed. 'Do you remember me telling you about my uncle? The one you'd have to worry about if your intentions were less than honourable?'

'The one who's married to your half-sister? Luke?' She nodded. 'That was him?' He sat up as the names finally connected and memory slammed back. '*Luke Devlin*? Luke Devlin is your uncle?'

'Yes, Jack. And I'm afraid he's brought reinforcements. The guy built like a brick outhouse is Gabriel MacIntyre – Mac – he's married to my other sister, Claudia. I think perhaps it might be a good idea to get dressed now, my love. I don't imagine Luke was kidding about the sixty seconds.'

Their clothes were dry but crumpled and they didn't possess a comb between them. 'How do I look?' Melanie asked.

Her hair had dried into tiny waves, her skin was burnished by the sun. Jack thought he'd never seen her looking lovelier. 'You look like an angel.'

'Kiss me.'

'The condemned man's last comfort?' he suggested. But he held her for a moment, kissed her sweetly. Then he took her hand. 'Come on. Let's get this over with.' He opened the door and ushered her through, closing it carefully behind him. There were two buggies pulled up on the path. Gus was sitting in one with Mike, taking care to look anywhere but at Jack and Melanie. Luke Devlin and his brother-in-law were standing by the first. 'Go with Gus, sweetheart. I'll see you back at the cottage,' Jack murmured.

'Oh, but – '

But he was already walking across to Luke Devlin and he slid into the driver's seat of the buggy. 'Shall we go, Mr Devlin?' he said, starting the engine. Luke's eyes narrowed and he glanced back to Melanie. 'Melanie will be quite safe with Gus . . . why don't you go with them, Mr MacIntyre? What Mr Devlin and I have to say to one another doesn't need an audience.'

Melanie watched the two men drive away and then smiled at Mac as he crossed to her, raising herself on tiptoes to kiss his cheek. 'Hello, Mac. This is an unexpected surprise.'

'Luke was a bit concerned . . . about the storm.'

'Really? He heard the weather forecast and he flew all the way from London?'

'I'm sorry, Mel,' Gus said. 'Your uncle turned up this morning. I thought he'd go crazy during the storm and there was no way I could stop him from coming with me to pick you up when I saw the smoke from the mill.'

'It's my fault, I'm afraid.'

Melanie turned to the man in the back seat.

'Mike Palmer. Jack's number two.'

'The man who thinks I'm Mata Hari? Why are you here?'

'Would it help if I said I'm sorry?'

'I'm not quite sure what it is you've done, Mike.' He glanced sideways at a stony-faced Mac and began to explain. But nothing could prepare her for the two-page spread the *Courier* had devoted to her fairy-tale romance with Jack. Or rather her entire family's romantic history. They were all there.

Her father and his first wife, the actress Elaine French. There was a picture of her mother, years old. Heaven knew where they had found that. And of course there was the recent wedding photograph of Beau and Diana.

Side panels were devoted to wedding pictures of Fizz and Luke, Claudia and Mac.

The centrepiece was a blown-up image of a heart-shaped locket. In one half was a picture of Jack, in the other one of herself. And the banner headline, running across two pages and decorated with bells and horseshoes, read '*THE BEAUMONT BRIDES*'.

They'd missed nothing. Even speculation that the newlywed Mr and Mrs Edward Beaumont on honeymoon in the Caribbean had called at The Ark and encountered Jack and Melanie. It was salacious, intrusive and perfectly horrible and she didn't know how she was ever going to be able to look Jack in the face again.

'Okay, Mike. What happened?'

'Latham saw the first newspaper piece and telephoned Devlin. He told him that you were the one doing the insider trading. Devlin called the TSC and they put him in the picture about that. But it meant we couldn't hang around. Tamblin has been arrested. Latham was picked up at the airport.' He paused.

'Come on, there's more.'

'Latham had all the papers and tapes he'd stolen from the office listed and dated ready to hand over to the TSC.'

'Mike!' Jack protested impatiently. He had more important things to do than discuss business.

'One of them was apparently from your apartment. The draft of the letter you wrote to Gus. He'd clearly labelled it as being given to him by Melanie Devlin on your instruction.'

'But we both know that draft was never at my apartment, Mike.' He leaned back. 'He meant to implicate her.'

'Why?'

'The man is clearly as twisted as a corkscrew. He probably always fancied her. This was to be her payback for not falling under his charm.'

'I suppose so.' Mike glanced at the newspaper. 'What can I say about that?'

'You did what you thought was right. You didn't know she was one of the Beaumonts. I didn't know until Uncle Luke spelled it out in words of one syllable.'

'Devlin descended on me like a ton of bricks. I couldn't convince him that you weren't about to marry the girl. When he said he was coming here to find out what was going on, well, I thought I'd better come too.'

'I bet that was a jolly journey.'

Mike said nothing.

'Well, I'm glad you did come. How do you fancy being my best man?'

'You're kidding me? He's not put a shotgun at your back?'

'Not exactly. I put one to his.' Jack grinned. 'He was all for whisking his darling girl away from me until I reminded him that there are no pockets in a Speedo.' Mike looked confused. 'Where do you keep your condoms when you go snorkelling, Mike?'

'You're telling me that you looked Luke Devlin in the eye and said that?'

'He wasn't quite as slow as you, Mike.' Jack frowned. 'Actually he said something rather odd. He said if that was how it was there was no point in fighting it; it was in the Beaumont genes.'

'What do you suppose he meant?'

Jack had a very good idea what Luke meant, but he didn't say so. He simply shrugged. 'Who can say? But he's married to one of the Beaumont girls himself so I guess he knows what he's talking about. Now, tell me about the co-operative.'

'I would have thought you had more important things to think about.'

'I'm clearing the decks, Mike. Then I'm handing the whole lot over to you for the foreseeable future, so I suggest you pay attention.'

Melanie showered, washed her hair, laid out her clothes for the evening and the following morning and packed the rest. She had just closed her suitcase when she heard the cottage door opening.

'Jack?'

'Hi, sweetheart. Feeling better?' he said, as she appeared in the bedroom door.

'Yes, thank you.' She looked at him anxiously. *No black eyes or broken nose.* 'Luke didn't beat you to a pulp, then?'

'Certainly not. Two civilized men can always settle their differences without resorting to violence.'

'Oh? How?'

'Well, first I pointed out that you were a grown woman, capable of making your own decisions. I agreed that the publicity was not only unfortunate but in extremely bad taste, but that circumstances had combined in a way quite impossible for anyone to foresee.'

Her eyes strayed to the table, the newspaper. 'I'm sorry. Truly. I should have told you who I was . . .'

'Don't worry about it. It makes a change to be described as Prince Charming instead of the big bad wolf. Although whether Luke would agree with the character change is a moot point.'

'It wasn't that civilized, then?'

'There were one or two moments when things could have gone either way. But as you see, I'm here, in one piece and unchaperoned.'

'Well, Luke isn't a fool. We're going home tomorrow and this will all be nothing but a nine-days' wonder. You'll see.' She pulled her hands free. 'Is Luke having dinner with us?'

'That was the plan.'

'That is very civilized.'

'I hope so.' For one terrible moment he had thought she had truly meant it. That after tomorrow she would go her own way and never think about him again. But her smile, so slight, so full of sadness, told another story. He would have asked her to marry him right then, but he was sure she would decide that Luke had put pressure on him and refuse.

'I'm going to get dressed, Jack. And then I'm going down to the marina. I'm worried about Diana and Beau.'

'They'll have put into shelter somewhere. The islands have a thousand safe places to ride out a storm,' he reassured her.

'I'm sure you're right, but I tried to get them on the radio earlier and there was no response.'

He briefly cradled her cheek, kissed the top of her head. 'Wait for me, darling. I'll come with you.'

She watched him cross to the bathroom, close the door. A week ago she had thought 'darling' the most careless of endearments. But the way Jack had said it then . . . She turned abruptly away, settled herself at the dressing table and began to apply her make-up, brush out her hair.

She had just discarded her towelling wrap and was standing in her grey silk teddy when Jack opened the bathroom door. He paused for a moment, struck silent by the sheer beauty of her. It was more than her slender, lovely body, her wide eyes, thick glossy fair hair. It seemed to shine from somewhere within

366

her and he wanted to go to her, tell her how much he loved her and then show it in every way he knew how.

But now wasn't the time and after a few seconds he moved to help her with her zip as she stepped into a grey watered silk dress. It was straight, stopping well short of the knee, and the neckline was cut square across her breasts, with broad pleated straps falling into tiny cap sleeves.

'You look lovely,' he said. Then, 'Can you wait long enough for me to give you something? I know it's not your birthday until the day after tomorrow, but everything will be a rush tomorrow.'

And after that it would be over? 'A present?' she said, brightly. 'How lovely.'

'I hope you think so.' He opened a drawer and removed a leather-covered jeweller's box. The pendant and long drop earrings were delicate white gold filigree glittering with diamonds, glowing with tiny seed pearls.

'Oh, Jack. How lovely.' She lifted one of the earrings from its velvet bed. 'Can I wear them now? They'll go with my dress.'

'I thought so.' He fastened the pendant for her, while she fitted the earrings. And then he stood behind her, looking at her reflection in the long oval mirror. 'Mmmm.'

'What?'

'I'm thinking about making love later, with you wearing nothing but that pendant, those earrings. In fact I'll be thinking about it all through dinner with your uncle.'

'You won't!'

'Yes, darling, I will. And now I've told you, you'll be thinking about it too. Every time I catch your eye you'll blush.'

'Jack, that's scandalous,' she said, laughing despite the telltale glitter of tears. 'I won't look your way.'

'You will. You won't be able to help yourself.' And as if to prove him right she spun round to face him. 'You see?' And he kissed her forehead so as not to mess up her lipstick. 'Now stand right there where I can see you while I'm dressing.'

His movements were spare, economical, and he was dressed too soon.

'Do you want me to tie your tie?'

'Not if you plan on leaving this room in the next hour.' He slipped into his jacket. 'Come on.' He was not particularly looking forward to the evening that had been planned, but he had delayed her as long as humanly possible.

The marina was full of craft that had run in before the storm. Now children ran up and down the jetty, while harassed mothers and nannies tried to control them. Melanie craned to see any sign of a familiar figure. But Jack restrained her when she wanted to run along the decking.

'You'll break your neck in those sandals. Come on up to the hotel. If she's docked, Gus will know.'

But Gus was not in evidence. 'He might be through here,' Jack said, heading for a door marked 'Private'. He opened it. 'Gus?' he called.

'Yes?' Gus's voice answered from somewhere within.

Jack turned back and grasped Melanie's hand. 'Come on, we'll ask him.'

'But it's dark.'

'Switch on the light, Gus.'

Gus obeyed and lit up a room full of people who with one voice shouted, 'Surprise!'

Melanie stared, unable to believe the sight before her. Her entire family. Friends. Fizz. She glared at Fizz. 'You promised,' she said. Everyone laughed, apparently in on the joke.

'I would have told you, sweetheart. But you weren't around to tell.'

'And what about the picnic on the beach?'

'I don't remember you specifying which beach . . . and when we left England it was bucketing down with rain . . .'

But Melanie had already seen Beau and Diana and without hesitation she ran to them both and hugged them. 'I'm sorry. Oh, Diana, I'm so sorry,' she said. But Diana was holding her and suddenly everything was all right and everyone was talking and hugging her.

Claudia swept down on her. 'Don't let this man out of your sight, sweetie,' she said, eyeing Jack. 'He is gorgeous.' She flicked a teasing smile at Mac. Mac smiled right back, sliding his hand possessively about her waist.

'Don't flirt with the man, Claudia; one Beaumont is as much as any man can handle at a time.' He

369

extended his hand to Jack. 'We missed out on the introductions earlier. Gabriel MacIntyre. Everyone calls me Mac. You've already met my wife.'

'Claudia,' Jack said. 'The glamorous sister.'

Claudia laughed delightedly as she took his hand, stretching up on her toes to kiss his cheek. 'Absolutely gorgeous,' she repeated. Then she turned to Fizz. 'This is Felicity, the clever sister.'

'The clever one?'

Fizz blushed, but Claudia answered for her. 'She chose not to be an actress; she owns and runs a successful radio station, she married Luke Devlin and she has a gorgeous baby daughter. Girls don't come cleverer than that.'

'I'd say you're running her a close second,' Melanie said, glancing meaningfully at Claudia unusually loose-fitting dress.

Claudia smiled right back at her. 'And then there's Melanie.' She linked her other arm through Mel's. 'What would you like me to tell you about Melanie?'

'You couldn't tell me anything I don't already know,' Jack said.

'Is that right?'

'Heather didn't come?' Melanie intervened before her sister decided to say something utterly outrageous.

Claudia wrinkled her nose in distaste. 'Heather is up a tree in Berkshire being revolting.'

'You mean staging a protest, Claudia,' Mac corrected her, gently.

'I know what I mean.'

'Melanie.' Melanie turned at the sound of Luke's voice and he leaned forward, kissing her cheek. 'You look lovely.'

'Thank you.' He took her arm, led her away from Jack, from the crowd. 'I only want you to be happy, you know that, don't you?'

'Of course.'

'I mean there's no need to rush into anything. No matter what.' She stared at him. 'I know Jack thinks he ought to marry you – '

'Ought to marry me? Why?'

'Because of all the publicity. Because, well . . . in case . . .'

Melanie blushed as she understood the reason for Luke's unusual diffidence. 'Oh, I see,' she said. 'Well, you don't have to worry. I'm not marrying him or anyone. No matter what.' Furious with him, with Jack but most of all with herself, she turned and walked quickly away, blinking back the foolish tears. 'Come on, Beau. Dance with me,' she said, slipping her hand through her father's arm, dragging him away from the buffet.

'What's the matter?' Fizz said a moment later, seeing her husband watching Melanie as she danced some silly new dance while her father looked on, slightly bemused. 'You look bothered.'

'I am. I think I've just said something incredibly stupid.'

'Have you? Well, it's been that kind of week. Come and dance with me and I promise you, you'll forget all about it.'

371

He smiled down at her. 'Is that a promise?'

Melanie stood it for a long as she could, pretending, smiling, being the life and soul of the party. Then suddenly Diana was at her elbow. 'This is a bit hectic, isn't it? Come on, Claudia's flirting with Jack so he won't miss you for at least a minute. Let's get some fresh air.' Mel gratefully followed Diana down into a small garden and joined her on an ornate wooden bench.

'Do you want to tell me about it?'

'Oh, heck, Diana, there's nothing to tell,' she said, defiantly. Then a little sob caught her out and her stepmother put her arm around her.

'Tell me anyway.'

'It's just so ridiculous. According to Luke, Jack thinks he ought to marry me because of all this nonsense, all this publicity. In case I'm pregnant. It's positively medieval.'

'I don't know. Marriage may be a touch old-fashioned these days. But it's hardly medieval. Anyway, what Luke thinks doesn't matter. What do you think?'

'Jack isn't into long-term relationships. His first wife died in an accident and he blames himself. Now he keeps clear of commitment, emotional ties.'

'People change.'

'Not really. And why should he? He has his life exactly as he wants it. Tidy, uncomplicated. There's no way I can be a part of that.'

'Love is certainly complicated,' Diana said, sympathetically. 'And you are in love with him?'

She didn't need to think about her answer. 'Yes, Diana, I'm rather afraid that I am.'

'And you want the whole thing? Love, commitment, children, "till death us do part"?'

'It's a lot to ask.'

'You've a lot to give, sweetheart. Come on, dry your eyes. The night is young. Anything might happen.'

'I don't think I can go back in there. And I can't go back to the cottage.'

Diana didn't argue. 'All right. Here's what you do. Go down to the boat, stow away. I won't even tell your father where you are.'

'But Jack will look for me – '

'I'll tell him you've got a headache, that you don't want to be disturbed.'

She was still doubtful. 'I'll need my things. My passport. It's in the hotel safe.'

'I'll get Gus to give me a hand. Go on now. The *Silver Dragon's* moored about halfway along on the right. Someone will make you a cup of tea and tuck you up. We'll be moving out at first light, so don't worry if you feel all at sea when you wake up. You will be.'

Diana watched her for a moment as she hurried down the path, stopping to take off her sandals as she reached the marina and then running along the decking. Only when Melanie was safely aboard the yacht did she turn around and go in search of Gus.

CHAPTER 15

Melanie woke to the gentle swish of water against the hull, the flickering light of the sea against the cabin walls, and she gave a long, shuddering sigh. Last night had been a nightmare. That party, all those people. Jack looking rather grim. She'd turned into her pillow, still damp with the tears she had shed, until, exhausted, she had finally fallen into a troubled sleep.

Something was digging into her neck. She reached up. It was one of the earrings that Jack had given her and just touching it threatened another deluge. He had promised that he would think all evening of her naked in the jewellery he had given her. Making love with her.

Her knees came up against her stomach as she thought of that, as she instinctively curled up to protect herself against the pain.

There was a tap on the cabin door. 'Diana?' Then, 'Who is it?'

'It's your breakfast, Miss Beaumont.'

Beaumont. It was so long since anyone had called

her that. 'Oh, thank you.' She'd locked the cabin door last night. Now she wrapped a sheet around her and opened it.

A young woman brought in a tray and put it down beside the bed. 'I've got your bag here. I'll fetch it.'

'Thank you. Is Mrs Beaumont awake?'

The girl looked at her a little oddly. 'Mrs Beaumont?'

'Diana. Oh, never mind. Thanks for breakfast.'

'You're welcome.'

She poured herself some tea. And drank it leaning against the side of the yacht, looking at the islands as they drifted gently by. She ate some papaya but couldn't face anything else. When was the last time she had eaten properly. Breakfast yesterday? Did it matter?

She showered. Dressed in a pair of shorts and a shirt that she tied around her midriff. Her face was pale and blotchy after all that crying, but there was nothing that could be done short of a full make-up, and she didn't think either Diana, or Beau, would expect that. But she tried to smile. Diana was being enormously kind. Being miserable would not do.

And having given herself a stern talking to, she opened the door and went up on to the deck. Waiting for her, stretched out on a sun lounger, dark glasses hiding his eyes, was Jack.

She opened her mouth, couldn't think of a thing to say and closed it again.

'You left without saying goodbye, Melanie. I knew you would regret that.'

'I – ' Still nothing. Only a helpless little gesture that betrayed her misery. 'Yes. I just needed to get away.'

'Always say goodbye as if it were the last time. So that if anything happens you'll never reproach yourself with harsh words. That was the general drift, I think, of your argument?'

'Jack. Please. You must know why I left and I'd rather not discuss it.' She looked around. 'Where are Diana and Beau?'

'Having breakfast at The Ark, I imagine.' He patted the lounger beside him. 'You might as well come and sit over here. There's no escape.' Short of jumping overboard. He certainly didn't look as if he'd be put off by a locked cabin door. So she walked stiffly across the deck and eased herself down beside him. He took her hand before she had the wit to take it out of his reach. 'That's better.' Yes, it was. Infinitely better. But then it was infinitely worse too. Because nothing had changed. 'Now, would you like to tell me why you ran off last night? It couldn't just have been that terrible surprise party, or presumably you'd have invited me to run off with you.'

'No. It wasn't the party that was terrible.' She paused. 'Well, actually it was, but I suppose in any other circumstances it could have been fun.'

'Everyone else certainly seemed to be enjoying themselves.'

'But it had been a hell of a day. The storm. Finding out about Richard. That horrible newspaper article.'

376

'And?'

'And then Luke said something.' He waited, patiently, the pad of his thumb gently caressing the delicate skin on the inside of her wrist. 'He thought you felt you had to marry me. That you felt honour-bound or something . . .'

'Honour-bound? Because your reputation is in ruins? Your good name torn asunder? Because your entire life is blighted because we've spent a few days together in the sun? I don't know why he didn't suggest you join a convent.'

'Don't be ridiculous.'

'You mean your life isn't blighted? Wouldn't be even in the admittedly unlikely event that you are pregnant?'

Having his child, she thought, might just be the one thing that would save her. 'No. It would be infinitely worse if you married me because you felt you had to.'

'And bearing in mind my past determination not to become emotionally involved in any way with another woman after the death of Lisette – '

'Jack please!'

'– and my well-known success in achieving that aim, do you honestly believe I would do that? Did I race back from that man-to-man stuff with your uncle and immediately offer the emotional sacrifice of marriage?'

'No.'

'No. This week has been wonderful, Mel, but no one in their right mind would marry someone they'd

377

only known for a week.' She gave him a sharp look. 'All right, a month,' he conceded. 'I thought we needed time to get to know one another. Discover the things we had in common, the things we don't.'

'You're right. Anything else would be madness.' Her eyes, as she turned to him, were uncertain, shadowed.

'Madness,' he agreed. 'And since we've agreed on everything so far, I know you must also understand that the only reason I would ask you to marry me now, or ever, is because I cannot conceive of life without you?'

'Must I?' She wished he would take off those wretched dark glasses so that she could see what he was really thinking.

'Let me put it another way. Just to establish the principles. What would induce you to consider marrying me? Now, or ever?'

'Just to establish the principle?'

He nodded.

'It would have to be because life without you would be . . .' Just living. A life empty of love or purpose. 'Unimaginable.'

'Unimaginable. That's it. So we have love first. You do believe that marriage is important? I know some women think it's an anachronism – '

'Marriage is a statement of intent, Jack. A public commitment. A haven in which to bring up children . . .'

'So you would want all that? A home, children, a working partnership between – '

378

'– two people who care enough about each other to never knowingly cause hurt to each other,' she finished.

'Able to give each other space, yet always being there – '

' – and still, in forty or fifty years' time, still being able to reach out for a hand and feel – '

His hand gripped hers more tightly. ' – a touch of fire.' He raised her hand to his lips and set off an inferno. 'Well, now we've established the principles, I have a question to ask you.' He removed the dark glasses so that she could see his eyes, know his heart. 'On the terms and conditions set out above, will you marry me, Melanie?'

Her leaden heart seemed to kick-start into life. 'Can I have that in writing?'

'In blood if you want.'

'No. In kisses. From here . . .' she pointed to her forehead and he obligingly kissed it '. . . to there.' She wiggled her feet.

'That's going to take some time,' he pointed out. 'And I have to go and tell the captain to turn this thing around and head back to port.'

'Port?'

'The Ark. Or are you really set on a long engagement? It just seems such a pity to waste the licence when Gus has gone to so much trouble to get it. And since the congregation is ready and waiting.'

'Licence? When did you get a licence?' Her eyes widened. 'Before Luke arrived?' He didn't answer, simply crossed his fingers behind his back, hoping that Gus had been able to arrange it in time. It was the smallest white lie, and the way Melanie's face lit up was reason enough. 'Whatever happened to the advisability of getting to know one another?'

'Oh, that. It went the same way as my belief that making love on a beach was for masochists.' His eyes blazed. 'You've turned me into a mushy old romantic. So, what do you say?'

'But shouldn't Tom be here? Or your mother?'

'Those are your only objections?'

Melanie held her breath for just a second. 'Yes, they are my only objections.'

'Then you'll be happy to know that they will be arriving on the afternoon plane.'

'You asked them to the wedding before you asked me to marry you?'

'I love you, Melanie. I wasn't going to take no for an answer. I think a much more interesting topic of conversation would be where we should spend our honeymoon.'

'Oh, but – '

He leaned across and placed his finger over her lips. 'Before you ask, Mike is babysitting your co-operative.'

'Is he? How kind.' Then, 'Oh, I don't suppose you gave him any choice.'

'Let's just say it's the equivalent of doing ten thousand lines for that revolting newspaper article. Now, where shall we start? You were thinking of Australia?'

'There's an amazing island I've been told about. There are only about fourteen cottages. There's diving on the reef . . .'

'That sounds good. And I'd like to visit Tahiti.'

'To see the dusky maidens in their grass skirts? Forget it. Japan. I've always wanted to go to Japan. And Thailand.'

'India? The Taj Mahal by moonlight. And what about Petra?'

'Oh, yes, Petra . . . Oh, no. Jack, we can't do it all.'

'That's only halfway round the world. Luke said you were planning to take a year off; that gives us plenty of time to go the rest of the way. Of course, we don't have to spend it all travelling.'

'No. There must be something else we could do.'

'Give me a minute, I'll think of something.' He stood up, suddenly. 'Come on.'

'What?'

'I've thought of something.' He bent and swept her up into his arms and began to carry her below deck. Then he stopped. 'That's if you can remember the word.'

She laughed and let her head fall against his shoulder. 'Just one word? I seem to recall that there were two. "Yes". And "please".'

Above them, on the bridge, the girl who'd brought Melanie her breakfast tray handed a cup of coffee to the yacht's captain and nodded down at the two deserted sun-loungers. 'It looks as if the wedding's on. I guess we'll be heading back to The Ark.'

He turned and smiled down at her. 'Those were

my instructions. But the ceremony isn't until sunset, so I wouldn't say there's any rush, would you?'

Heather leaned back into the dark shadows of the branches as the sky began to pale in the stillness of pre-dawn. She felt safer in the darkness, but she knew it was only an illusion of safety, a brief reprieve. An hour, two at the most, and this would all be over. Yesterday they had come with their loud-hailers and warned her, giving her the chance to climb down, admit defeat and walk away.

The others had all gone, disappearing in ones and twos as the futility of their protest had become obvious. The middle-class supporters in their Barbours and green wellies who had flocked to the road site when the television cameras had been in evidence at the beginning had long since drifted away to join some new cause.

But at dawn the cameras would be back, eager to get pictures of the last protester being dragged away by the sheriff's officers, knowing that she would put up a struggle, give them a hard time. Although if her mother hadn't been married to Edward Beaumont they probably wouldn't even have stayed for that.

She felt in her pocket, hoping that she might find an overlooked sweet, anything. Her food had run out two days ago; she had half a bottle of water. Even without the sheriff's men today she would have been forced to surrender.

She knew that it was stupid to have stayed so long. She wished now that she had slipped away with the others so that she wouldn't have to see the machines rip through the trees. She let her head fall against the trunk of the great oak that had been her home for the last few weeks, feeling the rough bark beneath her cheek growing wet with her tears.

It was so stupid. She hadn't meant it to be like this. She'd only come along to the demonstration because she'd wanted to infuriate her mother, get her name in the papers, embarrass everyone. She'd never expected to actually *care*.

And the stupid thing was, she knew her mother would understand, would care too.

'Oh, Dad,' she said. 'I miss you so much. And I miss Mum too. I wish she'd come home.' Maybe that the real reason she'd stayed in the tree so long. Because there was nothing and no one to come down for.

She stiffened as a soft noise reached her from the ground. Nights and days watching and waiting had honed all her senses, but since she had been alone they had become so highly attuned that she was alert to the slightest movement, the softest footfall.

She peered down through the branches but could see nothing. Were the sheriff's men planning a pre-dawn raid before the newsmen gathered for the final act? It was the publicity they hated most. And there was nothing worse for a company's image than to see four of its burly henchmen manhandling a young girl. She just wished she could have been cleaner, washed her hair, been wearing a dress just to make herself look more vulnerable.

Below her she heard the crack of a twig, the almost imperceptible vibration through the trunk and branches as someone began to climb. Her mouth dried as fear clutched at her.

What was going on? This wasn't the way it was supposed to be. Had they decided to get her out of the way before the newsmen arrived? She edged back further into the shadows, uncertain which way the attack would come.

'Oh, Mum!' she whispered, feeling more alone and afraid than she had in all the last few days since everyone else had deserted the protest. Even in the daylight with a dozen cameras trained on them, the rent-a-thugs the contractors had hired to evict them wouldn't care about the bruises they inflicted. In the dark, with no one to see . . .

'Heather?' The voice was low, barely discernible. 'Heather, are you there?'

She flinched back against the trunk, not recognizing the voice, fearing a trap. 'Mac said to tell you he would have come himself but he dared not risk his knee.'

'Mac?' The name was startled from her. 'You know Mac?' A man hoisted himself over the branch and grinned at her, only his teeth and the whites of his eyes showing against his blackened face, the dark balaclava.

'He sent this. So you'd know I was on the level.' He offered her something small and bright.

'His medal!' She looked back at him. 'Who are you?'

384

'Jack. Jack Wolfe. I'm a brother-in-law of sorts.'

'Of sorts? What does that mean?'

'If I tell you that I married Melanie last week, does that give you an idea?'

'Married.' She had forgotten to whisper. 'Wasn't that rather sudden?'

'Very. We would have sent you an invitation but we didn't know the number of your tree. Now shall we go before we both end up in jail?'

'They'll have to carry me out,' she declared defiantly.

'Oh, they will,' he assured her. 'Melanie just thought it would be rather fun if you gave them the slip. While they were gearing up to storm the citadel, you could be giving a press conference somewhere plush in London, nails manicured, wearing a designer suit . . . You know, confound the image of the grubby professional protester. It would make people take you more seriously.'

She stared at him. 'Are you for real?'

'Believe it, sweetheart. But it's been a while since I climbed a tree, so if you could make up your mind . . .'

'Is Melanie with you?' she asked.

'She's keeping watch at the bottom of the tree. We haven't got much time before the security patrol comes back. If you'd rather stick it out to the bitter end, just say . . .'

'No. No, I'll come with you.'

They slithered down the tree and ran for a battered minibus with the contractors' logo on the side. There were half a dozen of them lined up in the compound.

She'd seen them arriving day after day bringing site workers to work. She glanced at Melanie. 'We faked it up,' she said, sliding back the door. Then as headlights swung across the far side of the site they rolled onto the floor of the van, heads down, out of sight while someone closed the door behind them.

'Close call,' Jack said, as the security patrol continued on its way without stopping. Then, as the handbrake was released, the van began to slide quietly out of the parking bay.

'Did she come, Jack?' someone said.

Heather blinked and moved in the direction of the voice. 'Fizz?'

'Dear God, Heather, you smell awful,' she said, reeling back.

'So would you if you'd been living up a tree for a month,' Heather returned defensively, and then, as they reached the main road and the engine started, a couple of bulky figures climbed in beside them. 'Mac!' She flung her arms about him. 'And Luke,' she said, with more restraint.

'Hey, kid, what about me?' Claudia grinned from the seat behind the door.

'You all came!'

'Couldn't miss out on the fun.'

She looked around. All except her mother and Edward. Still on their honeymoon, no doubt. There never had been such a family for getting married, she thought. Then, 'Who's driving?'

'I am. They wouldn't let me climb the tree and they said I was too old to push the van,' Edward

Beaumont said, glancing at this newest and most troublesome addition to his family. 'And it's true. I'm too old for this kind of thing. Is there any more coffee in that flask, Diana?'

'Just a drop. I thought perhaps Heather would appreciate it.'

Diana turned in the front passenger seat and passed the cup back to her daughter. 'Hi, darling. Been having fun?'

'Fun!' Heather wanted to laugh and cry and fling herself at her mother all at the same time. Instead she did what she always did and yelled at her. 'Fun! Have you any idea what's been going on while you've been swanning about the world? The sheer, wanton destruction – '

'Save it for the press conference, darling. We'll all be there. Edward's booked a room at the Grosvenor House. If they'll let you into the place smelling like that.'

'Just let them try and stop me.'

Diana leaned back and kissed her daughter's cheek. 'That's my girl.'

Claudia said, 'Go for it, kid.'

Fizz reached out and held her hand briefly.

Melanie slid down beside Jack, took his hand into hers and squeezed it. 'Interesting family you have,' he murmured into her ear.

'Thank you,' she murmured.

'I'm not sure it was a compliment.'

'No, I meant . . .' She looked up into his face, saw that he was teasing. 'You know what I meant. Thank you for doing this, organizing the van, going up that tree.'

'There's a price to pay, darling.' His voice was low and full of laughter.

'Oh? And what's that?'

'I haven't decided.' His teeth appeared as he grinned in the darkness. 'But I'll think of something.' He bent and kissed her. When he looked up again it was to discover that he was the object of six pairs of eyes. Only Edward was intent upon the road. 'I think,' he said, 'it's time we went somewhere a long way from your family.'

'We could go back to – '

He placed a hand over her mouth. 'Don't say another word. Don't even mention which continent it's on. Surprise parties and family gatherings in the dead of night are all very well . . . but we've got some unfinished business, you and I.'

'Oh, you mean Tahiti and Japan and India –'

'I do.' And this time, when Jack Wolfe kissed his wife, he didn't care who was looking.

THE EXCITING NEW NAME IN WOMEN'S FICTION!

PLEASE HELP ME TO HELP YOU!

Dear *Scarlet* Reader,

Good news – thanks to your excellent response we are able to hold another super Prize Draw, which means that **you could win 6 months' worth of free *Scarlets*!** Just return your completed questionnaire to us **before 31 January 1998** and you will automatically be entered in the draw that takes place on that day. If you are lucky enough to be one of the first two names out of the hat we will send you four new *Scarlet* romances, every month for six months.

So don't delay – return your form straight away!*

Looking forward to hearing from you,

Sally Cooper

Editor-in-Chief, *Scarlet*

QUESTIONNAIRE

Please tick the appropriate boxes to indicate your answers

1 Where did you get this Scarlet title?
Bought in supermarket ☐
Bought at my local bookstore ☐ Bought at chain bookstore ☐
Bought at book exchange or used bookstore ☐
Borrowed from a friend ☐
Other (please indicate) _____

2 Did you enjoy reading it?
A lot ☐   A little ☐   Not at all ☐

3 What did you particularly like about this book?
Believable characters ☐   Easy to read ☐
Good value for money ☐   Enjoyable locations ☐
Interesting story ☐   Modern setting ☐
Other _____

4 What did you particularly dislike about this book?
_____

5 Would you buy another Scarlet book?
Yes ☐   No ☐

6 What other kinds of book do you enjoy reading?
Horror ☐   Puzzle books ☐   Historical fiction ☐
General fiction ☐ Crime/Detective ☐ Cookery ☐
Other (please indicate) _____

7 Which magazines do you enjoy reading?
1. _____
2. _____
3. _____

And now a little about you –
8 How old are you?
Under 25 ☐   25–34 ☐   35–44 ☐
45–54 ☐   55–64 ☐   over 65 ☐

cont.

9 What is your marital status?
   Single ☐   Married/living with partner ☐
   Widowed ☐   Separated/divorced ☐

10 What is your current occupation?
   Employed full-time ☐   Employed part-time ☐
   Student ☐   Housewife full-time ☐
   Unemployed ☐   Retired ☐

11 Do you have children? If so, how many and how old are they?
   _____
   _____

12 What is your annual household income?
   under $15,000   ☐   or   £10,000   ☐
   $15–25,000   ☐   or   £10–20,000 ☐
   $25–35,000   ☐   or   £20–30,000 ☐
   $35–50,000   ☐   or   £30–40,000 ☐
   over $50,000   ☐   or   £40,000   ☐

Miss/Mrs/Ms _____
Address _____
_____
_____

Thank you for completing this questionnaire. Now tear it out – put
it in an envelope and send it, before 31 January 1998, to:

Sally Cooper, Editor-in-Chief

USA/Can. address	*UK address/No stamp required*
SCARLET c/o London Bridge	SCARLET
85 River Rock Drive	FREEPOST LON 3335
Suite 202	LONDON W8 4BR
Buffalo	*Please use block capitals for*
NY 14207	*address*
USA	

WIFIR/9/97

Scarlet **titles coming next month:**

KEEPSAKES Jan McDaniel
They're enemies – but can they ever be *loving* enemies? Simon Blye and Yardley Kittridge are business rivals. But more than that, Yardley is certain Simon has stolen something precious from her. So how *can* she want a man she should detest?

IN SEARCH OF A HUSBAND Tegan James
Rue Trevallyn appears to have it all, but her life is thrown into confusion when her fiancé disappears just two days before their wedding. Going in search of John, Rue has no choice but to accept help from the mysterious Marcus Graham, who tells her: 'I want you . . . in bed and out of it!'

SHADOWED PROMISES Vickie Moore
Psychic Lark Delavan is trying to solve a crime that took place a hundred years ago, when she suddenly finds herself accused of murder – in the present day! Will attractive lawyer Thomas Blackwell be able to save her?

DEAR ENEMY Maxine Barry
Keira Westcombe knew gossip would be rife when she married a man old enough to be her father. But she doesn't care! She certainly has no intention of explaining herself to Fane Harwood, her stepson. Let him think what he likes!